New York Times and *U~~SA~~* ~~Today bestselling author~~
Jane Porter has written ~~over sixty romances and~~
women's fiction novel~~s. Her first book was published by~~
Mills & Boon in 2000. A five-time RITA® Award
finalist, Jane is known for her passionate, emotional
and sensual novels, and loves nothing more than
alpha heroes, exotic locations and happy-ever-afters.
Today Jane lives in sunny San Clemente, California,
with her surfer husband and three sons. Visit
janeporter.com.

Tara Pammi can't remember a moment when she
wasn't lost in a book—especially a romance, which
was much more exciting than a mathematics textbook
at school. Years later, Tara's wild imagination and
love for the written word revealed what she really
wanted to do. Now she pairs alpha males who think
they know everything with strong women who knock
that theory *and* them off their feet!

HIS SHOCK MARRIAGE IN GREECE

JANE PORTER

AN INNOCENT TO TAME THE ITALIAN

TARA PAMMI

MILLS & BOON

First Published in Great Britain 2019
by Mills & Boon, an imprint of HarperCollins*Publishers*
1 London Bridge Street, London, SE1 9GF

His Shock Marriage in Greece © 2019 by Jane Porter

An Innocent to Tame the Italian © 2019 by Tara Pammi

ISBN: 978-0-263-27348-9

MIX
Paper from
responsible sources
FSC® C007454

This book is produced from independently certified FSC™ paper
to ensure responsible forest management.
For more information visit www.harpercollins.co.uk/green.

Printed and bound in Spain
by CPI, Barcelona

HIS SHOCK MARRIAGE IN GREECE

JANE PORTER

PROLOGUE

KASSIANI DUKAS TRIED to sit very still on the white slip-covered upholstered sofa in the corner of the expansive villa's living room, not wanting to draw attention to herself as it would only lead to trouble.

She'd done nothing wrong but her father was furious and the last thing she wanted was him to turn on her.

Things were bad, though. Elexis was gone. Kassiani's older sister was to marry Damen Alexopoulos tomorrow but Elexis had mysteriously disappeared in the night, managing to sneak away from the estate on the Athenian Riviera before flying out of Athens with friends more than willing to whisk her away from a wedding—and marriage—she'd never wanted.

And now her father was about to break the news to her groom, powerful Greek shipping tycoon Damen Alexopoulos, a man everyone knew to be brilliant, ambitious and dangerous if crossed.

He'd just been crossed.

She shuddered as her father, Kristopher, paced the gleaming marble floor, hands knotted behind his back, his complexion ashen. Nothing good would come of Elexis's disappearance.

Footsteps rang in the hall. Kassiani sat taller on the corner sofa. Kristopher stopped his frenetic pacing.

Damen Alexopoulos entered the villa's living room, stealing Kassiani's breath. She'd seen him before, on the night of Elexis's engagement, but she hadn't actually talked to him. It had been a party for others—very public, very extravagant with Elexis and Damen spending maybe just thirty minutes together—before he'd flown out, returning to Greece. He wasn't classically handsome, but he had piercing hazel eyes, strong, arresting features and a full, firm mouth that fascinated her. He was also taller than she remembered, and broader through the shoulders, with a muscular chest and narrow waist and long lean legs.

Kass had never understood why Elexis hadn't found him attractive, because as Greek men went, he was truly a remarkable specimen, but then her sister tended to prefer the up-and-coming models and actors who fawned all over her, each of those young, pretty males hoping to benefit from her wealth and fame.

"I was told you wanted to see me," Damen said, his voice deep with a hint of a rasp that made the fine hair on Kassiani's nape rise while her insides did a peculiar quiver.

"Good morning, Damen," her father said with forced cheer. "It's a beautiful morning here in Sousin."

A small muscle pulled in Damen's hard jaw. Kassiani could tell he found her father annoying. That didn't bode well for what was to come.

"It is always beautiful here," Damen answered. "But I ended an important meeting to see you, having been told there was an emergency."

Irritation and impatience made the rasp in his voice more pronounced, and his English more accented. It was clear he hadn't learned English as a boy. Or at least, he hadn't become fluent as a boy.

"An emergency? No," Kristopher replied, smiling. "I wouldn't call it that. I'm sorry you had to rush here, worrying."

The muscle in Damen's jaw worked again. It was clear he

was fighting to hang on to his temper. "I don't worry, and I don't rush. But I am now here. Why was I summoned?"

Kassiani drew back in the corner of the sofa, as if she could make herself smaller. Not easy as she was a big girl... not tall like her sister, but rather, big boned, with even bigger curves—hips, breasts and the sort of generous backside that was fashionable if paired with a tiny waist. But Kassiani's waist wasn't spectacularly tiny. Her stomach wasn't flat. Her thighs touched. Unlike her older sister, Kassiani didn't have an Instagram account. She didn't take selfies. She avoided photos at all cost.

Unlike stunning, photogenic Elexis, Kass didn't photograph well. Nor was she part of high society's inner circle. She didn't travel on private jet planes, or party in Las Vegas, the Caribbean or Mediterranean.

If her last name hadn't been Dukas, she would have been incredibly ordinary. If her father wasn't one of the richest Greeks in America, she would have been forgotten. Invisible.

Over the years Kass had come to wish she really was invisible as invisible was far better than being visible and pitied. Visible and scorned. Visible and rejected. And not just rejected by superficial socialites and quasi-celebrities, but rejected by your own family.

Her father had never shown the least bit of interest in her, and why should he when he had everything he needed in his son and heir, Barnabas, and beautiful Elexis, who'd charmed him from birth with her big dark eyes and winsome pout?

Kass had never been a charming child. Family lore depicted her as silent and sullen, and impossibly stubborn. She reportedly scowled at guests, refusing to make small talk with her father's important guests. She wouldn't play the piano or sing, or bat her eyelashes at the visiting Greek dignitaries. Instead, Kass wanted to discuss politics with her father's friends. Even at four and five she was fascinated by economics. She'd make predictions about the future of the shipping industry, and her audacity horrified her father. It didn't matter that she read beyond her years. It didn't matter that she excelled in math. Good Greek girls didn't weigh in on national matters, or international policies and economics. Good Greek girls grew up and made good marriages with suitable Greek men and produced the next generation. That was their responsibility. That was their value. Nothing else.

It wasn't long before Kassiani wasn't included in the family parties. She wasn't asked to dress up and come downstairs. She wasn't invited to the dinners and weddings and reunions. She became the forgotten Dukas.

"I appreciate you coming straightaway," Kristopher said, still smiling, but less broadly. "I hate disturbing you but we have a problem."

Kassiani's father was a shipping tycoon like Damen, but Greek American, having been born and raised in San Francisco. She knew he was nervous, but his voice didn't betray it. If anything, he sounded positive and optimistic. She was glad. One couldn't ever betray fear in contract negotiations, and the merger of Dukas Shipping with the Alexopoulos empire through marriage of Damen and Elexis was the ultimate business transaction. A transaction that was now in jeopardy.

Her stomach knotted and cramped. There was no way her father could ever pay Damen back for the money he'd invested in the Dukas ships and ports. Her father lacked the means. The business and family were perpetually cash-strapped. It was why her father had sought out the merger five years ago. Dukas Shipping would fold without an investor. Damen had been the investor. He'd upheld his end of the deal, but now Kristopher had to inform Damen that the Dukases hadn't kept their side of the bargain.

Nauseous, Kassiani looked out the villa window, seeking the view beyond. The sun reflected brilliantly off the villa's whitewashed walls and bounced in cheerful rays off the water, the Aegean Sea so much brighter—a vibrant liquid turquoise—than the murky blue of the Pacific Ocean near her home in San Francisco.

"I'm not certain I understand," Damen answered just as pleasantly, both men employing the same friendly tone, but Kassiani knew this was just a prelude to battle.

Boxers touched gloves before a bout. Wrestlers bowed before a match. Soccer players shook hands.

Her father and Damen were already fencing.

She glanced from her father to Damen. No, he didn't look like a tycoon. He was too fit, too physically imposing. His skin was bronzed, and he had the toned, taut look of a man who worked in the shipyards, not at a desk. But it was his profile that held her attention, his features as chiseled and hard as the rest of him, the forehead high, cheekbones prominent, nose decidedly thick at the bridge, as if broken more than once.

He was a fighter, she thought, and he wouldn't take her father's news sitting down, which only made Kassiani even more grateful she was seated, tucked into a corner sofa.

"Elexis is gone." Kristopher delivered the news bluntly, before adding, "I'm hoping to have her back soon, we just need—"

"I'm sorry. I must stop you there, Dukas." Damen's voice dropped, the rasp softening into almost a caress. "We don't have a problem. *You* have a problem."

Kristopher held his position but his ashen complexion seemed to pale yet again. "I'm aware of that, but I thought we should notify guests while there is time."

"There is no canceling the wedding. There will be no broken promises. There will be no public humiliation. Is that understood?"

"But—"

"You promised me the best daughter five years ago. I expect you to deliver."

The best daughter. Kassiani's eyes stung and she bit into her lower lip to hold back the hurt and shame.

She hadn't thought she'd made a sound but suddenly Damen looked at her. His expression was shuttered, his black lashes framing intense, dark eyes. She could read nothing in his face and yet somehow that brief glance skewered her, intensifying her pain.

She was not the best daughter. She would never be the best daughter, not as long as she remained a Dukas.

Damen turned back to her father and his firm full lips curved ever so slightly at the corner, a contemptuous light in his gray eyes. "I will see you tomorrow at the church," he said. "With my bride."

And then he walked out.

CHAPTER ONE

IT WAS A perfect day for a May wedding on the Greek Riviera.

The sky was an endless, azure blue with just a smattering of puffy white clouds. The sun reflected brightly off the thick walls of the villa's tiny whitewashed chapel, glazing the tiled roof, while the Aegean Sea and the Temple of Poseidon shimmered in the background. The temperature was perfect as well, comfortable and warm, without being hot, or humid.

Ordinarily, a bride would be ecstatic at such perfect conditions, but Kassiani was no ordinary bride. She was not even supposed to *be* the bride.

Today was her sister's wedding, with the ceremony and reception to take place at Damen's historic seaside villa in Sounio, but early this morning Kristopher Dukas made the drastic decision to swap brides on the unsuspecting bridegroom, thus Kassiani now stood outside the villa chapel's wooden door, waiting her cue to enter, while knots in her stomach exploded, turning into frantic butterflies.

There was a huge possibility this would not end well. She fully expected the groom to walk out on her in the middle of the service, abandoning her in the tiny church.

The bridegroom was not a fool.

The bridegroom was one of the most powerful men in the world, and he would not like being duped.

Kassiani was not in the habit of duping men, either.

She was the youngest Dukas. The least remarkable in

every way. But when cornered by her father this morning, she'd agreed to his plan and would marry Damen Alexopoulos not because it would save her father's hide, but it'd save hers, as well.

Marriage to Damen would be her way out. She'd escape her father's house. She'd escape her father's control. *And* she'd come into the trust her late aunt had established for her, a trust that would give her some measure of freedom and financial control.

It was worth noting, too, that the wedding today would mean she had actually accomplished something significant in her father's eyes. Even if it meant she was giving up one controlling male for another, because at twenty-three, she was ready to do something, and be someone other than plain, dumpy, uninspiring Kassiani Dukas.

Marrying the fabulously wealthy shipping tycoon Damen Alexopoulos wouldn't change the way she looked, but it would change the way people thought of her, and spoke of her. It would force them to recognize her as someone of consequence, pathetic as that was.

The harpist played within the church, and her father—short, stout, with thick salt-and-pepper hair—gestured impatiently for her. Kassiani suppressed a sigh. Her father really didn't like her. As a little girl she'd never understood his coldness, because he absolutely doted on Elexis, but as she grew up and came to understand the world, she was able to put the pieces together.

Kristopher was not a handsome man, and he wanted to be liked. Respected. Having money was just one way to be respected. Having beautiful children was another. And while Elexis was their late mother's clone—their mother, having been a successful model before she'd given up her career to marry the Greek American shipping magnate—Kassiani unfortunately favored her father, inheriting both his build and his strong jaw. Not what a woman wanted when her mother had been a famous model.

Kassiani exhaled in a depressing whoosh. These thoughts were not helping. Her self-esteem—never strong—was plummeting by the moment. And then her father snapped his fingers.

It seemed it was time.

The butterflies returned and her hand trembled as she took her father's arm. He paused to adjust her heavy lace veil, better cloaking her face.

Kassiani felt utterly terrified, and yet also strangely calm. Once they stepped into the chapel, there would be no turning back. Elexis had let her father down. Elexis had let the entire family down. Kass would do no such thing.

For once she could do something to benefit her father's vast shipping business. She'd wanted to work for Dukas Shipping since she was in second grade. She'd even studied business and international law at Stanford so she'd be of value, but her father had rebuffed her, refusing to hire her, or even listen to her ideas. He was painfully old-fashioned, believing a woman's value was at home, producing heirs, and preferably male heirs.

After twenty-three years of being useless, after twenty-three years of being an embarrassment, she was aiding her father, significantly aiding him by saving him from bankruptcy and all the ensuing humiliation and shame.

Empowered, Kassiani drew a breath, lifted her chin and took her first step into the four-hundred-year-old Greek Orthodox church. It took her eyes a moment to adjust to the cool, dark interior, and then she spotted the groom before her. It really was a tiny chapel, with just five rows of pews on either side of the narrow aisle.

Damen Michael Alexopoulos stood at the front, just before the altar and priest. Once Kassiani spotted her future husband, she couldn't look away. Dressed in a severe black suit, he looked even more intimidating than he had yesterday in the villa suite. She didn't know if it was his height, or the width of his shoulders, but there was a dangerous stillness about him now that made the air catch in her throat.

Was he suspicious?

Had he already figured out she wasn't the right bride?

Kass was so heavily veiled that she could barely see through the thick white lace, but he was no fool and it wouldn't take much to assess her size and shape and realize that there was no way she was Elexis, of Instagram fame. Elexis was opposite Kass in every way imaginable. Even wearing treacherously high heels, Kassiani remained short, her plump figure wrapped in the tightest of undergarments, including the old-fashioned corset necessary to make Elexis's dress fit, and that was *after* the dress had been altered to include additional panels and a dramatically shortened hem.

"He knows," she said under her breath.

"He doesn't," her father gritted. "And it's too late for second thoughts. You cannot fail me."

A lump filled her throat. She wouldn't. She couldn't.

She clenched his arm and kept her chin high. The only way through challenging times was to go through them. There would be no retreat. There would be no panicking. She would make this work. She would find a way to please her husband. She would bring the two families together. And it would be her, Petra Kassiani, who did it, not Elexis, and not her playboy brother, Barnabas, who had so little familial love that he hadn't even bothered to show up for the wedding.

She could do this. She could.

The real question was, would he?

* * *

Damen knew the moment Kristopher Dukas entered the chapel with his daughter that it was the wrong daughter.

He watched them process—portly Kristopher with his heavily veiled daughter teetering in her heels—unable to believe the American's audacity.

It seemed that once again Kristopher took the easy way out. Instead of retrieving the wayward Elexis, Kristopher had simply swapped daughters, substituting the youngest for the eldest.

Who did that?

What kind of man treated his daughters like cattle?

Damen felt a jolt—shock, disbelief—as Kristopher placed his younger daughter's hand in his, handing her over at the altar, clearly the sacrificial lamb. Even Damen, who was ruthless in business, knew the difference between dishonesty and betrayal. And this was a betrayal.

It's not that he needed a beauty queen for a bride, but this younger daughter wasn't Elexis and he'd chosen Elexis for a reason.

Gleaming, polished, ambitious Elexis Dukas suited him in looks and temperament. She'd hold her own socially, and she'd be an accomplished hostess, things he knew he needed in a wife because he detested social engagements and refused to be part of any dog and pony show. Elexis loved the spotlight. She loved attention. She could easily represent them at important functions and no one would miss him. Why would they, when they had her?

He felt no affection for Elexis, but she was the one he wanted, and he hadn't proposed to her without knowing exactly what he was getting in a wife—both strengths and weaknesses. Elexis led an enviable lifestyle. She traveled with the jet set. She partied at all the best clubs. She wore the best clothes, sitting in the front rows of the biggest fashion shows. Her life was one photo opportunity after another, but he'd let her carry on as she always had during their engagement, aware that once she became his wife, she'd settle down and become a proper wife.

He needed a proper wife, one who understood her place in his world, and wouldn't make emotional demands. He didn't do emotions. And he didn't tolerate demands.

But now Elexis was gone and there was a very different Dukas at his side and it suddenly crossed Damen's mind that perhaps this had been Kristopher's plan from the beginning. Perhaps Elexis had never intended to marry him? Perhaps Kristopher had never planned on giving his beloved Elexis to Damen?

Perhaps Kristopher had always intended on dumping his youngest, the one he casually referred to as the Dukas Ugly Duckling, on him.

He should walk out now.

And just when he was about to drop the Ugly Duckling's hand, she lifted her face, her dark gaze finding his through her veil, and whispered, "I'm sorry."

They signed the registry in the chapel's antechamber. Damen gritted his teeth, angry beyond measure as it struck him that the worst part of this—no, not the worst but yet another negative among negatives—was that he didn't even know his new wife's name. "So who have I married, if not Elexis?" he ground out as the priest handed him a pen.

Her long lace veil had been folded back on the top of her head and she glanced at him but looked away, unable to hold his furious gaze. He felt a tightness in his chest as her ridiculously long black lashes dropped, concealing her eyes.

"Kassiani," she said huskily.

He felt angrier by the moment. His fingers itched to

smash something hard—like the narrow table, or the nearest stone wall. "That wasn't the name in the ceremony."

"No, the priest used my legal first name, Petra, but no one calls me Petra. I'm either Kass or Kassiani."

He ground his teeth together, not just upset with her, but with himself for not having walked out of the service when he could. Why had he let her apology sway him? Why had her whispered words kept him from leaving her there at the altar?

He didn't know the answers to any of those questions, and he wasn't in the frame of mind to sort it out. "Do not think this is over," he said curtly after signing his name and handing the pen to her.

She looked up at him as she accepted the pen, a faint line between her arched eyebrows, expression troubled. "I don't."

"Was this always the plan, to swap sisters on the unsuspecting groom?"

Color suffused her pale cheeks. "No."

"Don't take this the wrong way, but I didn't want you."

The pink color swiftly faded from her face. Her full lips compressed as she drew a slow breath and then she managed an unsteady laugh. "Understood."

"I'm not trying to be offensive."

She lifted her chin and met his gaze then, her eyes locking with his. "No offense taken."

In any other circumstances, he thought he would have liked her. She was direct and smart and articulate. But this wasn't a casual conversation. He'd just been played and he wasn't in the most charitable frame of mind. "I'm not one to forgive and forget."

He saw a shadow pass across her face, and he almost felt sorry for her, but then the shadow disappeared, leaving her expression calm and composed. "And as you can see, I'm not one to pass up a slice of cake, or a bit of a chocolate." Then she leaned over the registry and added her name, her long lace veil spilling across her shoulder in a waterfall of white. When she'd finished, she straightened and squared her shoulders and handed back the pen. "It seems we all have our crosses to bear."

He didn't know if it was her words, or her ridiculous bravado, but he felt a rush of intense emotion—emotion he didn't welcome—and drew her hard against him, tilting her chin back with one hand before covering her mouth, capturing it with his. She was petite, barely reaching his shoulder, and impossibly warm and soft, which made his kiss harder, and fiercer. It wasn't the kiss a man should give his young bride, but nothing about this wedding was right.

Upstairs in the luxurious villa bedroom Kassiani had dressed in earlier, she walked back and forth, chewing on a knuckle, trying to calm herself.

He didn't want her, and he didn't like her, and she had a feeling this could all still fall apart any moment.

The vows wouldn't hold, not unless the marriage was consummated, and she couldn't imagine him taking her to his bed right now. Quite frankly, she didn't want to be in his bed, either, and she shuddered remembering his coldness as he'd told her he didn't forgive and forget.

She didn't doubt him.

Which was why she was here in the bedroom, hiding. She'd lost her nerve. Somehow she'd found the necessary courage this morning to take Elexis's place for the ceremony, but that courage was gone.

Thank God the ceremony had been small and private. No one but the immediate family attended. However, the reception was large, with hundreds of guests flying in from all over the world to witness the marriage of Elexis Dukas and Damen Alexopoulos.

Kassiani stopped pacing to double over, wanting to throw up as she imagined appearing at the reception. The guests would laugh when they saw her. It was one thing to be Elexis in private, hidden beneath layers of thick lace. It was another to be Elexis in front of those who knew her sister best.

Kass couldn't imagine joining Damen on the terrace for dinner, or dancing, or cutting of the cake. She'd convinced herself she could do this—but she'd thought only about the ceremony and vows. She hadn't taken in the terror of appearing in public as his new wife.

His wife.

Kassiani's legs buckled and she dropped onto the edge of the bed, her full skirts billowing up around her, her feet aching from her stupid shoes.

What had she done?

She was wiping away tears when her bedroom door suddenly opened and Damen entered her room.

He hadn't even knocked. He'd simply barged in.

Her head jerked up, her lips parting in surprise, but she uttered no protest. His fierce expression silenced anything she might have said.

She waited for him to speak.

He didn't.

He simply stared at her, and the silence was unbearable. A tremor coursed through her.

Time slowed to a crawl. The seconds felt like minutes. She tried to meet his gaze but his scathing look of contempt was more than she could endure in that moment. "Please say something," she finally murmured.

"Our guests have been waiting."

Again she pictured the stone terrace filled with linen-draped tables and gleaming candelabras. The reception was a sophisticated palette of cream, bisque and white and Kassiani did not belong there. It wasn't her wedding. They weren't her guests. This wasn't her party. "I couldn't go down."

"Am I to bring the guests up to you?"

"No. Please don't."

"Do you want to be carried down?"

"No." She couldn't look at him. Her eyes burned. What had seemed so brave and necessary this morning now seemed like the worst idea imaginable.

"It's a little late to turn coward."

She hung her head. "I agree."

Silence stretched. The room was so quiet she could hear his low, irritated exhale. "If you're expecting sympathy—"

"I'm not."

"Good. This is your own fault."

She started to speak, but then closed her mouth, pressing her lips together. He was right, of course. How could she argue the point?

"You can't just sit up here all night," he added after a moment.

She plucked at a pearl embroidered into the skirt of her gown. "I'm not much of a party person. I never have been."

"Even if it's your own wedding?"

"As we both know, it wasn't supposed to be."

"Therein lies the problem."

She briefly met his gaze, her breath catching in her throat before she swiftly averted her head, blood rushing to her cheeks.

He made her so nervous. He was nothing like her father or brother. He was nothing like anyone she'd ever known before.

"How did you think this would go?" he asked, his tone shifting, less harsh, almost mild.

The change in tone surprised her, but still she couldn't speak.

Kassiani bit her lip, unable to answer.

"Truthfully," he prompted.

Her shoulders twisted. She hated this helpless, pathetic feeling. She hated feeling like a failure. She hadn't married him to be a failure. "I didn't think about the reception and the guests. To be honest, this part didn't even cross my mind. It was just the ceremony...and then..." She drew a quick breath and lifted her head, her eyes meeting his. "...the rest."

"And what was the rest?"

"Being a proper wife." She could see from the cynical glint in his eyes that he didn't believe her. "I understand what wives do. Your comfort is my responsibility—"

"Your father told you this?"

"I'm a Greek woman. I know what Greek men expect."

There was something in his dark, speculative gaze that made her skin prickle and her pulse lurch, and she didn't know how to manage so many new and strange feelings at the same time.

"Go on, then."

She swallowed hard, trying not to betray just how nervous she felt. "Besides taking care of you, I'm to manage your home...or homes. I'm to provide you with children. And I understand and accept those responsibilities."

"It seems one of the Dukas daughters is dutiful, then."

"Elexis and I have different strengths."

"She likes parties."

"She would have enjoyed the reception, yes."

"And the photographers."

"The camera loves her."

"What did your father do to convince you to take your sister's place?"

Her brow creased. "Excuse me?"

"Did he threaten you? Or was there a bribe involved? How did he get you to walk down the aisle and go through this whole...charade?"

"It's not a charade. I married you." She paused, gathering herself. "Of my own volition."

"So you volunteered?"

"No. I didn't volunteer. This isn't exactly a volunteer position."

He made a rough sound in the back of his throat and Kassiani calmly added, "But when my father presented me the...situation... I agreed that it was a problem and my family was indebted to you. It wouldn't be right for the Dukases to humiliate you. So I agreed to take Elexis's place so that the merger of businesses and families could still take place."

"Wasn't there a saint named Kassiani?"

"She was a hymnographer, not a virgin bride."

He gave her another long look. "I'm to be grateful the Dukas virgin has been forced onto me?"

She winced but refused to dwell on his sarcasm. "You're not being forced into anything. You can annul this afternoon's ceremony. Tomorrow. The next day. The day after." Her chin lifted. "As long as we don't consummate the marriage, you're free to annul this marriage at any time."

"Is that what you're hoping I'll do?"

"No. I said vows today and I intend to keep them. It is my expectation that we'll consummate the marriage tonight."

"And if I don't feel like falling into bed with...you?"

A lump filled her throat. She was aware of how disappointing she was as a woman. She could never compare, or compete, with Elexis. But she was still a woman and she had feelings. And hopes. And dreams. "I will do my best to make you want me."

The glance he shot her seemed laced with scorn and then he walked away from her, crossing the room to stand at the window, which faced the sea and the ancient Temple of Poseidon, which glowed golden in the setting sun. Tonight promised to be yet another spectacular sunset. Sunsets on Cape Sounio were the stuff of legends.

"Perhaps we should just dispense with this farce now," Damen said, his back still to her, his gaze fixed on the sea.

"Perhaps," she agreed serenely, grateful he couldn't see her hard jaw and how hurt and frustration welled. "I won't call you a coward if you do."

He turned suddenly, facing her. Temper blazed in his eyes. "I have done my part," he gritted. "I invested in Dukas Shipping. I sorted out your father's legal entanglements. I put aside my mistresses and waited patiently, celibately for your sister—"

"That was obviously a mistake."

"You're not helping your case, kitten."

"I don't think anything can. Because surely you don't want my sympathy, do you?" He didn't answer and her firm chin rose higher. "Maybe you should've spent more time with your future bride to make sure she was the right bride."

"Your father assured me Elexis was the right bride."

"And there is the root of all our problems. You trusted my father." Her full lips curved, but the smile didn't reach her eyes. "The world thinks you're smarter than that."

He stiffened, his eyes narrowing. "That does not sound very complimentary for a daughter to say of the father."

"Or for a bride to say of her new husband—"

"I wasn't going to say it."

She shrugged, and plucked at yet another pearl on her gown. "I'm a realist, I always have been." Kassiani drew a breath before continuing, her words cool and measured. "And I know who my family are. I know their strengths. I know their weaknesses." Her eyebrows flattened, her expression turning pensive. "Personally, I would not have gone into business with them. And I certainly wouldn't have climbed into bed with them. But you wanted the West Coast of North America. You wanted the ships and the ports and the agreements, and now you have them."

He walked back toward her, closing the distance with quiet, measured strides. Kassiani tried not to shrink as he stood directly before her, so tall that she had to tip her head back to see his face.

"You do not think highly of me," he said quietly.

Her heart did a painful double beat even as something like desire curled in her belly. The butterflies were back, but they weren't from fear. "I think you have underestimated the Dukas family."

"You didn't answer my question."

She hesitated for a long moment before looking up into his eyes. "I wouldn't marry a man I didn't hold in high esteem."

He stared down at her for even longer. "I'm not much for parties, either. We'll skip the reception and leave now."

CHAPTER TWO

DAMEN LED HER down stairs at the back of the villa, the hidden nature of the staircase indicating they were for the staff, before exiting the villa through a plain door, arriving into the villa's kitchen garden. They passed through herbs and fruit trees, and then turned left at an impressive beehive where they headed away from the orchard to a narrow path leading toward the water.

The path led to steep narrow stairs, and once down the wooden staircase they reached a simple dock, where a speedboat waited.

The driver of the boat offered her a hand in order to assist her into the boat, but Damen swept her into his arms and lifted her over the side, placing her inside on her feet.

She swayed in her heels, and immediately found the nearest seat.

Damen sat down opposite her and they were off, slowly at first and then picking up speed as they put distance between them and land.

The wind grabbed at her veil and Kassiani gripped the edge of her seat with one hand and tried to control her heavy veil with the other. From the water she could see the estate and villa. The estate was large, and one of the oldest on this part of the Athenian coast. The villa had been built facing the water, ensuring every room a sweeping view of the turquoise sea and the Temple of Poseidon on the hill across the water.

From their vantage point in the water, the garden glowed

with soft golden white light, with fairy lights strung in trees, and candelabras glimmering on the two dozen tables, while chandeliers inside the house emphasized the high ceilings and striking architecture. From here, the wedding reception looked downright magical, and Kassiani felt a pang of regret—this wasn't the wedding the guests had come for.

She tried to imagine their reaction when they discovered that the bride and groom were gone. She wondered how the evening would even go. Would anyone stay for the dinner once they realized there was no bride and groom? Or would others linger and dine and drink and take advantage of the splendid setting? She couldn't help thinking that there would be some who were grateful there would be no toasts, no speeches, no protracted dinner courses. And she was certain there were others, those who truly loved Damen, who would be confused, and worried.

The wedding really turned out to be a shambles.

What had Damen called it? A farce? A charade?

She felt a twinge of guilt followed by fresh anxiety. This was all so crazy, she hadn't really wrapped her head around anything that had taken place today. And now they were jetting off, but she had no idea where they were going. But as the cape fell farther behind, the boat suddenly slowed, drawing close to an enormous yacht in the bay, and then the engine turned off as they reached the yacht ladder at the back. Crew stood on a small platform awaiting them.

"Let's get your shoes off," Damen said. "I'd rather you not try to climb the stairs in those ridiculous shoes. How high are those heels anyway?"

"Too high," she admitted, grateful to remove the shoes that had pinched her feet all afternoon.

Once they were off, Damen swung Kassiani into his

arms and lifted her out, placing her on the platform. "Can you manage the stairs in that dress?" he asked.

"What are my options? Removing the dress here?" she answered.

He growled. *"No."*

She almost laughed. "Then yes, I can manage the stairs in this dress."

Her father's yacht had been built for her mother. And her father had never understood her mother's taste, and so the yacht had been over-the-top feminine with cream walls and gilded surfaces, floral tapestries and upholstery with horrendous columns everywhere to make the interior look like a Greek temple. Kassiani had found the superyacht garish and unappealing and she'd hated the few times her parents—she never knew which—decided they must all do a Mediterranean cruise together, trapping them on the yacht. She'd hated yachts and boats ever since, and held her breath as she was led up and down staircases and then down a narrow paneled hall toward bedrooms.

She wasn't sure if she was being taken to a master bedroom or just any bedroom, but when the uniformed staff opened a door and stepped back for her to enter, she was fairly certain it was the master bedroom by the fact that half the room was all floor-to-ceiling walls and glass doors with a private deck and a jaw-dropping view of the Temple of Poseidon, which had now been lit for the night and the dozens of majestic columns glowed yellow. The ancient ruins were beyond beautiful and she was drawn to the view, opening one set of the French doors to step out onto the deck.

And then on the opposite side of the bay, a villa and its grand gardens glimmered with light, competing for attention. Damen's villa.

For the first time since arriving in Greece, she felt the pull of Greece. Or maybe it was the stirring of her own Greek blood, recognizing that she'd come home. Her chest suddenly ached and she put a hand to her breast, pressing against the pain, overwhelmed by emotion.

What had she done?

"Second thoughts?" Damen's deep voice sounded behind her.

She turned suddenly, and struggled to smile but failed. "I don't know that I'd call them second thoughts, but certainly, this view gives me pause." Her head tipped as she studied him. "And you? Buyer's remorse?"

"You're a woman, not livestock. I haven't bought you."

"But I'm not the woman you wanted."

He didn't even hesitate. "No."

"I don't blame you for being disappointed. Elexis is stunning."

"She looks like your mother."

Kassiani stifled the pain. "And I take after Dad." She was grateful her voice sounded light, and breezy. She'd never want him to know how much it hurt being the Dukas her father called "pitiful."

"I didn't choose Elexis for her beauty."

Kassiani smiled politely. She didn't believe him for a moment. "Either way, I suppose it's a moot point now, isn't it?"

He looked from her to the Cape of Sounio, glowing gold with its famous marble temple built in 440 BC. It was remarkable that so much of the ancient temple remained.

"Did she ever intend to marry me?" he asked quietly.

Yes. No. Kass drew a deep breath. "I don't know," she answered honestly. "Elexis is a bit of an enigma."

"So there is more than what the eye sees?"

"No. The enigma is that she is just what you see. Beautiful."

His gaze narrowed and then he gave a half shrug. "It's been hours since breakfast. You must be starving—"

"Do I look as if I'm starving?" she interrupted with a faint smile.

He gave her another assessing glance. "I'll have a tray sent to you."

"Are you not eating?"

"I have things to take care of."

He didn't want to dine with her. Even though it was their wedding night. It shouldn't bother her. She shouldn't be attached to the outcome. She was here, the substitute bride, out of obligation, not affection. He was the humiliated groom. She shouldn't be surprised that he wanted to keep his distance. "A tray would be lovely." She nodded toward the glowing point. "Could I eat out here?"

"I'll have my steward set up a table."

She started to thank him but he was already walking out, and she watched him go, a lump filling her throat. This was not going to be easy.

Damen's office on the second deck was similar to his bedroom—a wall of windows, another wall of bookshelves and then large art pieces here and there. His oversize desk faced out, because he always preferred working with a view of the water. His parents might have preferred the land, and the olive groves they considered home, but he needed the sea. He craved the sea. It was when he faced out, toward the horizon of blue sky and blue sea, he could relax and breathe.

He ate only a few bites of his dinner before pushing it aside to concentrate on the agreements he'd pulled up on his laptop.

Agreements and contracts dating back three years, even though the discussion regarding merging Dukas and Alexopoulos began five years ago when Elexis was just graduating from college. Kristopher had been the one to approach Damen, suggesting that while each family was successful, they'd be even more powerful together, marrying the two families, and merging the two shipping empires, creating a truly remarkable empire. They'd be a world power together, controlling shipping lanes across the globe.

Damen had been intrigued but not sufficiently tempted because he knew Dukas's reputation. Dukas's deals could be shady as he tended to play a little too fast and loose. Damen might be ruthless, but he also knew that one's word mattered and he ran his business with integrity.

But two years later when Damen heard that Kristopher was dangling his daughter again, trying to find another Greek shipping company as a potential partner, he acted, flying out to San Francisco to discuss mutually beneficial scenarios. All of which included marriage to Dukas's daughter Elexis.

Damen wasn't emotionally attached to Elexis. She was simply a means to an end. And yet when he finally met Elexis, and saw how people responded to her, he was reassured, realizing she wouldn't just be a wife and mother to his heirs, but a valuable asset. The fact that people were drawn to her would be useful when entertaining clients. She could concentrate on the social niceties, leaving him free to focus on business.

Love never entered the equation because Damen didn't love people. He needed certain people in his life to get things done. He respected some of those he worked with, but tended to ignore most, having very little tolerance for people's weaknesses and idiosyncrasies. The more someone could prove beneficial, the more value he placed on them. It was cold, and unfeeling, but that was who he was and he wouldn't ever apologize for being pragmatic and strategic.

It was what had taken him from the olive groves on

Chios, to the helm of Aegean Shipping, which he renamed Alexopoulos Shipping of the Aegean after the elder Mr. Koumantaras died. The Koumantaras family wasn't happy that Mr. Koumantaras Sr. had left control of his business to the outsider, upstart Damen Alexopoulos, but Damen felt no remorse. Koumantaras's children had no desire to work for the family business. All they wanted was to live off the profits. So why should they care if the company changed its name?

One day Dukas Shipping would go the way of Aegean Shipping—the name would drop and the company itself would fold into the more powerful Alexopoulos Shipping.

Damen closed his laptop to look out the window at the now dark sky. At midnight the lights on the Temple of Poseidon would go out, but as it was only ten, the temple still glowed from the spotlights.

Damen tapped a finger on the arm of his chair, trying to ease the tension bottled within him. He hated how Kristopher Dukas had played him. He hated the feelings flooding him. He didn't like it when his temper flared. He had a hot temper. He used to have a horrendous temper. It had taken years to learn how to manage his anger, but today was testing him. Today made him want to let loose, and level something.

He thought of Kassiani in the master bedroom and closed his eyes and shook his head.

He didn't know why he'd allowed the steward to take her there. Kassiani should have been taken to a guest room. Somewhere out of his way. Somewhere he could forget her.

Instead she was in his room, waiting for his return.

His gut cramped.

He didn't want her. He didn't want to hurt her feelings, but he didn't want her. She wasn't the bride he'd been promised. Kristopher had promised the best daughter, and

Damen had believed him, investing heavily in Dukas Shipping's West Coast ports, building them up, buying new ships, aware that the heavy cash investment now would stabilize both of their businesses in the future. But the deal was off.

The marriage would be annulled.

And the contracts would soon be voided.

He'd already emailed his attorney to start the process of dissolution. Now it was just a matter of returning the Dukas girl to her father and moving forward the necessary legal action.

Her meal finished, Kassiani left the table and retreated inside to study the luxurious master bedroom. At least, she assumed it was the master bedroom, which meant Damen would be returning at some point, and they would be alone. Here. In the bedroom.

She, who had only pecked Damen on the lips at the chapel, needed to find the confidence to sleep with him. Correction, *not sleep*, but have sex with him, because if the marriage wasn't fully consummated, Damen could annul it and then the Dukases would lose everything.

Kassiani might not be the favored daughter, but she was loyal to her family and protective of the company. She'd agreed to marry Damen so that Dukas Shipping wouldn't be destroyed by legal actions. Damen could destroy them. His demands for restitution would bankrupt the company.

As her father baldly put it this morning—he couldn't afford to pay Damen back. The wedding had to happen, and the marriage consummated.

Which meant Kassiani had to seduce Damen tonight. It wouldn't be easy. She wasn't just a virgin, but a virgin with zero experience. Before the peck in the chapel, she'd only ever been kissed once before, a bumbling fumbling kiss that had been so wet and distasteful that she'd never wanted to kiss again.

Compared to that wet, violent assault on her mouth, today's chapel kiss had been rather exhilarating. When he'd tilted her chin up to kiss her, she'd felt a little shiver of anticipation, and he'd smelled lovely as his head dropped, his mouth brushing hers. His lips had felt firm and cool, and yet they'd somehow made her feel warm, and tingly. Her lips continued to tingle even after he'd lifted his head. She'd found herself wishing the kiss had lasted longer. She was curious as to what more would feel like, and with a longer kiss, perhaps she could process her thoughts and all the different sensations. Kass liked data and analysis. Information was immensely helpful.

More information was needed now.

How was she to seduce Damen when she had no knowledge of such things? Of course she knew what men's bodies looked like. She didn't live in the Dark Ages. She had a brother. She had a father. The internet was full of photographs, and movies, and she'd just have to piece together from movies what men would like.

From what she recalled, men seemed to like stripteases. They liked lap dances. They liked titillation, including women on their knees, obedient and eager to please.

Kassiani tried to imagine kneeling before Damen, her hands on his thighs, fingers moving toward the zipper of his trousers.

The image made her feel peculiar. Heat washed through her, making her skin prickle, and her breasts peak. The hot ball of tension seemed to center low in her belly, pulsing a little between her thighs. She was nervous and excited at the same time. Her entire world had been turned upside down. She'd come to Athens five days ago expecting to attend her sister's wedding. Instead she'd been woken by her father early this morning with the news that he expected her to marry Elexis's groom. And Kassiani, so desperate to earn her father's favor, had. Now instead of returning to San Francisco, she was to remain in Greece, and make a new life for herself as Damen's wife.

Kassiani shot a glance into the wood-framed mirror on the wall. She was still wearing Elexis's wedding dress, and the lace panels that had been added were pulling at the seams. Even in a corset, even with the additional panels added to the dress, the gown was too tight. The fabric pulled in all the wrong places.

Kass had never let herself dream about her wedding day, but if she was being honest, she'd say it certainly wasn't the wedding that took place today, and she certainly wouldn't have chosen this dress...a dress that made her look even curvier and stockier with all the lace panels.

No, she would have chosen something simple—an off-the-shoulder white satin gown that minimized her bust and skimmed her hips, before falling into a long graceful skirt in the same clean white satin. There would have been no plunging necklines and no bustle and no ornate beading adding thickness and weight to the lace panels worked into the bodice and skirt.

Kassiani placed a hand to the plunging neckline, running her fingertips lightly over her curves. Her breasts were beyond voluptuous. She'd always hated the thickness of her hips and thighs, as well as the shape of her belly, somewhat round as if she practiced belly dancing regularly, instead of the hours she spent on a treadmill walking, walking, walking, forever trying to reduce her form, wanting to be lean like her mother and sister. She would never be lean.

Her exterior was what it was—it couldn't be changed—and she was certain her new husband was disappointed, which was why she had to prove herself. She had to prove to him tonight that she fully intended to be a good wife. She'd find a way to satisfy him.

But how?

And what if she couldn't get him to respond?

Kass grabbed her phone and, while struggling out of her gown and layers of girdles and undergarments, researched men and arousal. Peeling her stockings off, she found quite a few sites offering numerous tips on how to please your man in bed, ranging from "Twelve Erogenous Zones That Shouldn't Be Ignored" to a very useful and practical article on "How to Give Unforgettable Oral Sex."

Naked, she headed into the adjoining white marble bathroom and, careful not to get her hair wet—it was still coiled up in an elaborate updo—she used the body wash in the shower to try to rub some of the marks out of her skin, but the angry red marks created by the corset weren't ready to fade. Leaving the shower, she wrapped herself in the white robe hanging on the back of the door, and then sat down on the edge of the bathtub and began reading everything she could about pleasing a man.

She was still reading when she heard a firm knock on the bathroom door. "Are you hiding, *mikrí sou gynaíka*?"

Her Greek was a little rusty, but not so rusty she didn't understand his words. *Are you hiding, my little wife?*

She jumped up and turned her phone off. "No." Kassiani opened the door and faced him, tugging the lapels of the robe so that they better covered her chest. "I'm using your robe. I hope that is okay. I'm sorry. I didn't think to bring any clothes with me."

"I don't think either of us was thinking clearly." He hesitated, and then shrugged. "This isn't going to work. I'll ask the crew to find something for you to wear and then my security will get you back to the villa at Sounio."

"Am I that much of a disappointment?"

"You're not a disappointment."

"Then why send me away without giving me a chance?"

"Because I was engaged to Elexis, not you."

"But Elexis left and I was there."

"The Dukas sisters are not interchangeable!"

"Because I'm not beautiful like her?"

"Because you're not hard like her." He didn't quite yell, but he flung the words at her with enough ferocity to make her flinch. He must have seen her reaction because he dropped his voice. "I wanted a wife who wouldn't feel. A woman I couldn't bruise. I don't know you very well, Petra Kassiani, but my gut says you feel, and feel deeply."

Heat rushed through her, and shame, because he was right. She did feel deeply but she hated that aspect of her personality, far preferring her intellect over her emotions. "I understand the kind of marriage you want. I won't ask you to romance me. I won't expect flowers and poetry—"

"Or tenderness? Or kindness? Or patience?"

"I can't believe you're capable of all of the above."

"Well, I am. Trust me."

"You were marrying Elexis to help save Dukas Shipping."

"I was marrying Elexis to dismantle Dukas Shipping."

Her eyes widened and her heart skipped a beat. "I don't believe you," she whispered.

"If you stay here, if you remain my wife and the agreements and contracts hold, there will be no Dukas Shipping in five years. It will all be Alexopoulos Shipping of the Aegean."

She stared at him, skeptical, but also wary. "Is this your way of making me throw up my arms and run back to my father? Am I to choose him and his business over you?"

"I am nothing to you. You are nothing to me—"

"I married you. You are my husband."

"But you do not know me. You should have no loyalty to me."

"I pledged to care for you and be a good wife. I intend to keep my vow."

"Even though I want to destroy what's left of your father's business?"

She didn't immediately answer, taking needed time to form an answer. "From the beginning this was to be a merger of families and businesses. The stronger business always wins in mergers. You are the stronger partner and change was inevitable."

He turned away and walked through the French doors to the deck. She could see him run his hand across his jaw, once, and then again. He was battling himself, she thought. He was battling and she didn't even know his fight, but whatever it was, she was firmly on his side. She had to be. She had chosen him, and she'd wanted a new life. A different life. She'd wanted to be an Alexopoulos, and not a Dukas, and if she wasn't careful he'd cart her back to the mainland and she'd be back with her father, which was the last place she wanted to be.

Kassiani followed him outside. Clouds half covered the moon, casting shadows on the deck. She couldn't see Damen's face clearly. But his shoulders were rigid, and even from this angle, he looked utterly unapproachable.

"Damen."

"Go back inside. I can't think clearly with you near me."

"Maybe that's good."

"It's not."

The night had cooled and a wind blew, tugging at her hair, and the label of her thick white robe. "Please, just give me a chance—"

"For God's sake, do not beg, Kassiani."

"Just give me a chance. *One* chance. That's all I ask."

"Why?"

"I want out. I want a life away from my family—"

"You're not going to get a happy family with me."

"I'm not asking for a fairy tale. I'm not pretty and popular. I find dating a nightmare. I'm so awkward but at the same time, I'm practical. I know you were marrying my sister because you wanted heirs. Obviously she's not ready to marry and be a mother, but I am. I want children. I'll be a good mother, too. So give me a chance to show you I could be a good wife, and…please…you. If I can't, and you have no…interest…despite my best efforts, then I will go home, and I'll accept your decision. But I can't accept rejection before I've had a chance to prove myself—"

"This isn't about you," he gritted, spinning around, features twisted. "This is about your father manipulating me—"

"But you got everything you wanted…the deals, the ports, the ships, the agreements, everything but Elexis. And you said you didn't love her, so why can't I be a substitute bride? Why can't I be the woman to give you your children? Is it because I'm so much plainer?"

"No."

"You protested too quickly." She struggled to smile. "I don't believe you. But that's okay. I know what I look like—"

"Stop it, Kass!" He grabbed her by the upper arms and gave her a shake. "Stop this madness. Because it is madness. I may not have been born with much, but I would never take a woman against her will, and you were forced into this marriage by your father to save his hide, not yours."

"But that's not true. This marriage saves mine. This marriage gets me out." Her voice broke. Tears fell. "I hated living in that house on Nob Hill. I have never fit in, never belonged, and I'm fully aware of who I am in that family. I'm the ugly one. The embarrassing one. The one they choose to leave behind. Marrying you lets me escape that legacy. You give me a new life, and a future."

"You'll be no happier with me."

She hesitated, a lump welling in her throat, a lump so big it made swallowing hurt. "I know it's not easy to look at me—"

"Good God!" He gave her another shake. "Do not say such things. You are not your sister, but you are not ugly, not even remotely ugly." His grip eased, his hands half sliding down her arms. "Don't ever say such a thing again because it's a lie and you seem far too intelligent to believe lies and mistruths."

Her head jerked up and she searched his face. "Could you make love to me?"

"Kassiani."

"You can't imagine it?"

"That's not the point."

"But it is. If I can please you, and prove to you I'm a good wife, you might realize this is the right marriage." Her chin lifted, her expression provocative, despite the trace of tears. "So do we have a deal, Damen Alexopoulos? I know you like making deals, so make one with me."

"This is a terrible deal."

"Because if you lose, you're stuck with me?"

"No, because if you lose, you'll apparently be weeping all over my villa and I'll feel like a—oh, what is the word in English? A *beast*? An *ogre*?"

"A schmuck."

"A schmuck," he echoed.

"But I won't be weeping and you won't have to feel like a schmuck if you give me a fair chance. I understand your objections. I know you don't want me. I know you have no feelings for me. But history is filled with arranged marriages and many of them turned out to be good partnerships. Beneficial relationships. Why can't we be one of those?"

"So how do we know who wins?"

"You give me to dawn. If we consummate our marriage tonight, I win. If we don't, you win, and you can have your security return me to the villa first thing in the morning."

He sighed and dragged a hand through his thick dark hair, rifling it on end. "Do you have a plan, kitten?"

"I do. I'm going to seduce you."

CHAPTER THREE

HE HADN'T COME to the bedroom to make love to his new wife. He'd come to send her home, and yet she was fierce and stubborn, determined to fight for this marriage.

So different from Elexis, who hadn't even bothered to show up for the ceremony. So different from Elexis, who couldn't even hold a conversation with him. Kassiani could hold a conversation and more. She was fierce, smart, *eloquent*. She would have been an incredible trial attorney. She'd be amazing in the boardroom.

Maybe that's why he was here, sitting in one of the leather chairs in the master bedroom, telling Kassiani to unpin her hair and then shake it out, before letting her try to entertain him.

He was intrigued by her, curious as to her next move.

Her next move proved to be a rather awkward, but earnest, dance in front of him.

She was still wearing his robe but every now and then a lapel slipped open, revealing the pale slope of a full breast, or a knee and thigh.

He hadn't allowed himself to think of her as a woman before this, because she hadn't been his woman, but as she danced, her hips slowly, sensually gyrating, her arms lifted over her head, eyes half-closed as she swayed, he couldn't look away. He was fairly certain she'd never done this before, which was maybe what made her efforts so appealing. He hadn't thought he'd find her arousing, and yet he was hard, and growing harder as she danced and swayed, using her body to entice him.

He watched her from beneath heavy lids, body heating, blood humming in his veins. He'd wanted to be done with her. He'd come to his room to dispense with her, and yet here she was, dancing as if her life depended on it. As though he were a sultan, and she a disgraced member of his harem.

And perverse as the thought was, that, too, aroused him. The only way he felt anything, anymore, was through sex. Hard, carnal sex. Sex threaded with power. Sex laced with pain. He hadn't always been this way. He'd been...normal... once.

He'd had feelings, and tenderness. But that had been stripped from him in his teenage years, along with his pride, leaving only failure and shame.

It's why he wanted to marry Elexis. She was hard. He wouldn't break her. But Kassiani...she was entirely something else.

And she was entirely something else right now, as she slowly sank down, going to her knees before him. Her hands rested lightly on his knees and her head tipped back to look up into his face.

He didn't know what he saw in his face, but whatever she did see, it emboldened her. She ran her hands lightly up his quadriceps, her palms warm against his thighs. Reaching his hips, she lightly stroked down, brushing the inside of his thighs. His shaft throbbed. He felt as if he would burst out of his skin in a moment. His virginal little bride was not acting so very virginal in that moment.

It had been a long time since he'd been so turned on. A long time since his chest felt heat and warmth along with his groin. Normally only his erection worked, but tonight his entire body heated and thrummed as her hands stroked back up his thighs, moving toward his zipper.

Damen had to steel himself to keep from making a sound.

He watched, fascinated, as she unzipped him and reached into his cotton briefs to draw him out. He was long and thick and he pulsed in her soft, warm hand.

He wanted to tell her to wrap her fingers around him. He wanted to tell her how to stroke him—firmly, from the base of his shaft to the tip of his rounded head. He wanted what he wanted, and yet, he was also curious to see what she'd do next, and how she intended to satisfy him.

Her fingers slowly curved around him and she lowered her head to touch the tip of her tongue to the head of his shaft.

He stifled his growl of appreciation as her tongue lapped at him, licking the throbbing tip as if he were a lollipop or ice-cream cone.

It was all he could do not to rock his hips. He wanted to be in her mouth. He wanted the pressure of her hand and the wet heat of her mouth, and she wasn't quite getting the hang of it yet, but just watching her lick him, and suck him, made him hungrier, and fiercer.

She was trying so hard to please him, and she was applying herself so passionately to the task, that every flick of her tongue across his swollen head made him groan inwardly. She was either a splendid actress, or she genuinely enjoyed sucking him. The fact that she might just enjoy this…night…had never once crossed his mind. He hadn't ever thought of her wanting him, or desiring him, and watching her lavish him with attention made him want to explode.

He stopped there, aware that these weren't the thoughts of a considerate husband.

Not that he'd ever be a truly good, considerate husband, because he wasn't a good or considerate man. He was too bitter and broken. Too ambitious. Too driven. He'd come from nowhere, having risen up from nothing—literally olive trees and a stone hut in the middle of a hilltop orchard—and then even that had been taken from him, taken by those who believed money made them better than others, that money gave them the right to use and abuse.

It's why he'd worked so hard his entire life—to distance himself from the victim he'd been.

Having hit the absolute bottom, he knew he'd never be weak again.

His world was strength, power, domination. It was his one and only goal.

He wanted a family to prove that he'd overcome a dark past, and he had the means to ensure they'd be safe. They'd be comfortable, guarded, protected. His children would be able to go to the best schools. They'd have the best security. They'd never be exploited. But he needed a wife who would love them, because he didn't love. He didn't have normal emotions and feelings, and there was no room for feelings, just as there would be no romance.

Should he take Kassiani to his bed, it would be strictly business. Just like consummating the marriage was serious business. The moment he took her virginity, there would be no going back. The moment he claimed her, there would be no annulment.

Did he *want* to claim her?

He studied her from beneath heavy lids, his erection aching in her hands, the thick tip damp from her mouth.

Even though she was the wrong bride, she was still a Dukas and the marriage still gave him what he wanted—all of North America's West Coast ports. All the Dukas ships. All the trade agreements.

Part of him wanted to punish the Dukas family for playing him, but that would be cutting off his nose to spite his face. Kassiani would meet his needs just as well as Elexis. Maybe even better because his children did need a mother who would feel and care and fight for them. They'd need one parent with a heart.

He should just take her to bed, and claim her. He wouldn't be rough with her, even though he liked hot, hard sex. Sex without apology. He'd never made love to a woman and felt love. Sex—intercourse—was a release, and it felt good after he climaxed, but there wasn't much else he felt in the bedroom, other than loathing. He'd never tell anyone but he could barely tolerate being touched. He could barely endure being inside his skin. It was always a fight, a battle, to not remember the past. To not let memories resurface.

It's why he'd kept mistresses over the years, not girl-friends. It's why he'd wanted an arranged marriage. It was clean, clear, undemanding. There would be no affection, no emotion, no demands.

He avoided drama at all costs. He avoided feelings, and he certainly avoided feeling anything that hurt. Damen couldn't even remember the last time he felt tenderness. And yet, glancing down to his lap where Kassiani's dark head bobbed over his thick shaft, he felt strangely undone. It crossed his mind that he didn't deserve her. It crossed his mind that she shouldn't have been the sacrificial lamb.

Elexis was so much better suited to him. Consummating the marriage with her would have been far easier because he could take her and leave her and there would be no guilt. No remorse.

Tonight, even if he managed not to physically hurt Kassiani by taking her virginity, he suspected she'd still be bruised by this new life. She'd be bruised by him. He knew she hadn't been treated well by her family, and now she'd married a man who wouldn't treat her much better. Worse, she'd be grateful for the crumbs thrown her way.

The thought made his skin crawl.

She deserved so much more. She might be a Dukas but she wasn't shallow and hollow like the rest of them—

Kassiani's head suddenly lifted and her eyes met his. Something in her expression made his body tighten all over again, his shaft pulsing against her full lips.

He couldn't tear his gaze away from his head pressed to her mouth. It was hot and dirty and sexy all at the same time.

He shouldn't have allowed his virginal bride to go down on her knees in his white robe with nothing else on. He shouldn't have let her take him in her sweet, hot mouth, not when he was still trying to decide if he wanted to keep her. He was an ass. Selfish, ruthless, uncaring.

And desperately aroused.

So unusual for him and his numb body.

"You don't have to do that," he rasped, involuntarily reaching out to run the pad of his thumb across the sweep of her cheekbone. Her skin was soft, and warm. He wondered if she was as warm between her thighs. He wondered if she was wet.

"Why not?" she answered unsteadily. "Am I doing it wrong?"

Her question, in her low, throaty voice, made his body shudder. It didn't help that she followed her question with a light lick up the side of his shaft. He felt her lick all the way to the base of his penis, his balls tightening with pleasure. "You are doing quite well," he gritted.

The corner of her lips turned up, her long black lashes lowering over eyes that seemed to gleam with satisfaction. He'd never seen anything so erotic, this curvaceous little siren, his unexpected, swapped bride.

"I want to make you come," she whispered, "but obviously I'm not doing something right because it hasn't happened."

"It hasn't *happened* because I'm holding myself back."

For a moment there was just silence as her eyes widened as she processed what he'd said.

And then she rose slightly on her knees, her face lifting, expression surprised. "You can do that?"

"I can do many things."

Her expression shifted, increasingly curious and mind-blowingly sensual, reminding him of a courtesan rather than an untutored virgin. "Show me," she said, her hands on his inner thighs, her fingertips against the base of his shaft.

He clamped his jaw tight, fighting to steady his breathing. He had no idea why she tested his control. At twenty-three she was thirteen years younger than he, but in that moment he felt as if she had all the power and experience. "Show you what, *gataki*?"

"How to do it. How to make you feel so good that you can't...hold back."

"I think you're doing fine for a beginner."

"*Fine* is my least favorite word in the English language. *Fine* indicates mediocrity. I hate mediocrity."

He found himself almost smiling and then he clasped her face and kissed her deeply, claiming her mouth the way he should have in the beginning. She froze and stiffened, and then after a moment her lips softened, parting for him.

It was in that moment he stopped vacillating.

It was in that moment when she opened her mouth, giving herself to him, that he knew he would take her, claim her and make her his.

There would be no turning back. Not now, not anymore.

He took her mouth the way he intended to take her—with single-minded focus, his tongue sweeping the seam of her lips before thrusting into the warmth of her mouth and finding the hollows of her cheeks, the inside of her lips, the pressure and release so similar to what his body would do to hers, and how he'd find a rhythm and make her feel.

She whimpered softly, her hands reaching up to cover his, her fingers wrapping around his wrists. But she wasn't pulling his hands away. No, she was pressing his hands against her jaw, pressing him to her for more sensation even as her fingertips stroked the inside of his wrists and the sensitive mound of his palms.

Blood roared through his ears, pulsing in his veins. He felt his shaft bob, thick and heavy with need.

Sweeping her into his arms, Damen carried Kassiani to the bed. She lay on her back, looking up at him, the white robe parting to reveal pale skin. Her curves were ripe, the fabric clinging to the blatant fullness of her breasts and swell of her tummy. He tugged on the sash of the robe, untying it before pushing the robe back, exposing her.

She was an hourglass—full breasts with dark pink nipples, narrow waist and generous hips perfect to cradle him. He'd expected her to have a patch of trimmed dark curls, but instead she was bare, and the sight of her so smooth tested his control.

He needed to take it slowly, though. She wasn't experienced. He didn't want to hurt her. It was important she was ready for him.

"Eísai axiagápitos," he murmured, telling her she was lovely, because she was. The dark pink of her nipples were in stark contrast to her alabaster skin, and the tight tips called to him, as did the bareness between her thighs.

He leaned over her to lightly trace one puckered areola with his tongue, before turning to the other. Each swirl of his tongue was awesome. He leaned over her, his mouth closing over one taut nipple and sucking it the way she'd sucked his cock.

She whimpered, one hand pressed to the mattress, fingers flexed as he worked the sensitive peak. He cupped her other breast as he teased and nipped at her nipple, enjoying her soft, hoarse cries of pleasure. Her skin was warm and satiny smooth as he pressed a kiss between her breasts, and then lower to her trembling belly.

Every kiss he placed was rewarded with another throaty pant of pleasure. He continued kissing lower, even as he caressed up, shaping her, discovering how very sensitive she was.

He pressed one of her knees down, creating space for him, and he found himself just wanting to look at her, and drink in her feminine shape—soft curves and secret shadows. His shaft ached.

Damen dipped his head, his lips brushing the inside of her creamy thigh. She sighed at the feel of his lips. She sighed and stirred restlessly as he continued kissing his way up the inside of her thigh, his tongue drawing lazy circles on the tender skin where her thigh joined her hip.

Her skin burned and she smelled sweet, like honey in the sun. He wanted to drink her, but he was determined to make her wait, wanting her fully aroused, and wet, before he entered her.

She squirmed and exhaled hard as he placed a kiss at the top of her mound, just above her lips.

She exhaled again, another devastatingly sexy gasp of pleasure and wonder, as he breathed on her, letting his breath warm her, and tease her.

"You are bare," he said, stroking her mound with a fingertip, lightly caressing the plump outer lip that was perfectly smooth. "You've been waxed."

She shuddered and closed her eyes. "I was told you would prefer me this way."

"Who told you?"

She shook her head, her teeth catching on her lower lip.

He continued stroking her, lightly down the one side and then up over the other until he reached the top again.

Her thighs were trembling. Her body quivered and she was breathing more quickly, her breasts rising and falling, her nipples even tighter than they'd been a moment ago.

"Have you ever been waxed before?" he asked, his tongue dipping between those plump bare lips to flick across her.

She jumped at the touch, reaching for him with one hand, her fingers brushing his shoulder before tangling in his hair.

"Hmm?" he persisted, tongue tracing her folds, discovering she wasn't just damp, but wet. Soaked. Her hips rotated beneath him and he licked the silken inner lips, tasting her. She tasted like sun-kissed honey, too, hot and sweet.

"Never waxed before," she panted, as he used two fingers to trace her, and shape her, her outer lips, then her inner lips, skirting her damp core.

"Do you like it like this?" he asked, his mouth following his fingers, teasing, tasting, turning her into a mass of quivering nerve endings. "So smooth and bare?"

"It's different—" And she broke off in a gasp as he drew her clit into his mouth, sucking on the nub, even as he slipped his fingers inside her, stroking her on the inside.

Her hips rose and fell as he played her, and when she cried out as she climaxed, he gave her a moment to settle before spreading her knees and sinking into her, claiming her as his, forevermore.

It was more than a pinch when he thrust into her. It hurt, and part of her objected to the intense fullness and pressure, but then as the sting eased and her body relaxed, the sense of fullness gave way to new and interesting sensations, with the uppermost sensation being that of wonder.

She loved the feeling of him on her. She loved the slow hard strokes of him in her. Her lips parted as she struggled to catch her breath, but it was virtually impossible to contain the tension and pleasure.

She positively buzzed from head to toe. Closing her eyes, she gave herself over to feelings, and they were such good feelings. She could still remember how his mouth had felt on her. It was unlike anything she'd ever felt before. His mouth and tongue and breath had created so many different impressions—each of them thrilling and arousing.

Tonight had to be the most incredible night of her life.

She knew she'd never forget it. How could she when Damen was making her body hum and sing, lighting her up as if she was a living Christmas tree? Each of his deep thrusts hit a sensitive spot inside her, and as he moved faster, and harder, she arched to receive him, glowing, burning, feeling incredibly alive.

She was going to come again, she thought, as the sensation continued to build and center, intensifying, the pleasure so intense it was almost painful, and just when she thought she couldn't hold on to the exquisite sensations a moment longer, she shattered all over again, her body climaxing, rippling with one delicious wave of bliss after another.

Two orgasms on her wedding night. Amazing.

And then he groaned and stiffened, plunging deep within her, and she realized he'd just climaxed, too.

After a bit he shifted his weight, stretching out next to her, leaving his arm around her waist, holding her to his side.

Peace flooded her. She hadn't been sure about tonight,

but everything was beautiful, and for once in her life, she felt perfect.

Kassiani tried to keep her eyes open but she was exhausted, and she fell asleep nestled to Damen's chest, her legs tangled with his.

Later in the night, Kass felt the bed shift. Damen was moving away, rolling toward the edge. The mattress dipped and then he eased himself out of the bed.

She didn't know why she feigned sleep and yet she listened to the bedroom door open and close.

It was only when the door clicked shut that she opened her eyes. Moonlight spilled into the room. The Sounio Cape was almost dark, everyone in bed for the night.

Kassiani didn't know if Damen was permanently gone or if he'd be coming back. She didn't know where he'd gone, or why.

Sleepily, she struggled to sort through her feelings. So much had happened in one day. Her father's announcement that she needed to take Elexis's place. Her shock and initial resistance until she realized that marrying Damen would be good for her. It'd give her opportunities she'd never have trapped in the Dukas mansion on Nob Hill.

And once she said yes to her father's idea, the wedding gown alteration and the rigorous wedding prep—the salt scrub, the waxing, the hair mask, the application of lotions and polish—before the wedding itself.

Damen's fury as he discovered the truth about his bride.

The reception they didn't attend.

The early departure in the speedboat.

The arrival on the yacht.

And then Damen, finally claiming her.

Her body was sore, but not unbearably so. She also felt warm and languid in a way she never felt before. Their coming together was nothing like she had imagined it would be. It wasn't sex but something bigger, something more, something…significant.

And she couldn't explain how or why, but she sensed that Damen felt it, too.

CHAPTER FOUR

DAMEN LEFT THE mahogany-paneled bedroom to tackle the details needing attention, details like sending staff to retrieve Kassiani's belongings from his villa, and changing the travel plan because he couldn't stomach the idea of taking Kassiani on the same honeymoon that had been planned for Elexis. Elexis needed people and activity and so they were to spend a few days anchored off the island of Mykonos so Elexis could have her fill of the cafés and restaurants, nightclubs and high-end shops, before continuing to Santorini for more of the same.

Damen didn't know his new wife well yet, but he could safely say that Kassiani would prefer not to shop and cared little about hip nightclubs and trendy bars.

While staff went to collect Kassiani's luggage, he discussed the change in itinerary with his captain, and then retreated to the far end of the top deck so he could be alone, needing the night air to clear his head and cool his body.

It was rather shocking to discover that his body still hummed with desire and hunger. Usually after sex he was done. Sated. After a long night of sexual play, he wanted nothing more to do with his mistress for a length of time, but right now he still craved his shy, innocent bride who seemed to be anything but shy in bed.

He shouldn't want Kassiani this much. He shouldn't already want to return to her. And yet right now all he wanted was to be with her again, to push her back onto the bed and feel her softness beneath him. He wanted her heat and shape, and he was impatient to discover all the mysteries she had yet to share.

Frustrated, Damen left the deck, retreating to a guest bedroom on a different level from the master, stripping off his clothes to take a cold shower before stretching out on the bed.

He refused to think about her anymore tonight. This wasn't normal. He didn't like feeling his control slip. She was just a small part of his world, and he needed to remember that.

Sometime before dawn they pulled anchor and set off. It was still dark out when Kassiani woke to the hum of the engine, and opening her eyes, she glanced over to the space next to her and discovered it was empty. She reached out and touched the place Damen had been earlier and his spot was cool.

Had Damen never come back?

She looked past his side of the bed to the tall windows with their view of the deck and sea. The sky was still purple, and stars glittered overhead, and yet they were no longer anchored in the bay, but powering through the Greek islands.

Kassiani reached for her phone to check the time but she hadn't brought a charger and it had died during the night.

For several minutes she lay there, thinking of Damen, and what had happened between them, and she wondered if she should go find him, but knew it would look silly to search for him on his own ship.

And then she felt the yacht surge forward, and realized that the engines had started because they were leaving the bay. She lay on the bed and gave herself over to the lovely motion of the yacht traveling through the water. The gentle rocking motion lulled her back to sleep.

When she woke again, it was morning, the sun high in the sky, and a breakfast tray waited for her on the table next to the bed, with a pale pink robe draped across the foot of the bed and her set of luggage from the villa standing sentry next to the door.

Kassiani slid from the bed and picked up the robe, slipping her arms into the silk sleeves. The robe was soft and incredibly light, hugging her curves as she tied the sash at her waist. Glancing into the mirror, she loved the color of the kimono. It was a pale pink that deepened to a rose at the thigh and by the hem had become a gorgeous burgundy. Burnt-orange peonies and delicate little birds had been hand-painted on the watercolor background and yet the cinched sash made her waist look wide and her body overly lush.

She really, truly hated her shape.

Damen hadn't seemed to mind when they were together, but then, he'd left in the night and hadn't returned. What did that mean?

She set the breakfast tray on the bed before climbing back in, and pulling the covers up. As she sat back down, she felt a little sore.

Suddenly she felt nervous and shy.

What did Damen think of last night? Was he disappointed? Or had she been able to satisfy him?

She reached for the pot of coffee, and filled a cup. Steam rose from her cup so it was still quite hot. The tray had only recently been delivered, then. She wondered if Damen had brought the tray to her and then grimaced. Unlikely.

She took a sip from her cup, savoring the coffee. She loved her coffee black, and strong, and this coffee was perfect. Everything was fine. Damen was fine. Last night had been fine…more than fine… There was no reason to worry. Things were just new and different.

She took deep calming breaths as she sipped her coffee, practicing the yoga breathing she'd learned, the breathing more helpful than the yoga poses that had just made her feel clumsy. Just like that, Kassiani felt a wave of insecurity, and she deliberately smashed her fears. Worrying wouldn't accomplish anything. Instead, she reached for one of the pastries, selecting a flaky *bougatsa* filled with custard, and tried to decide how she was going to spend her first day as Mrs. Damen Michael Alexopoulos.

Damen had more than enough work to do to spend the day, and evening, at his desk.

He told himself he didn't need to worry about his new bride, that it wasn't a good use of his time and energy to obsess about her.

They'd survived the wedding. They'd consummated the marriage. They would be together for the next week or so as they sailed the Aegean Sea. Why should he worry? Kassiani had an entire yacht of entertainment at her disposal. She'd be content, and for his part, he was far more content away from her. She wasn't what he'd expected. He hadn't been able to sleep even in the guest bedroom. His body didn't feel like his body. His senses remained stirred. Everything in him was still alert, aroused.

It boggled his mind that he'd responded to her the way he had. He didn't normally feel so much in bed. Sex was exercise, a release. It didn't move him. It didn't confound him. But Kassiani had made sex new somehow. New and fascinating and unbelievably good. Better than some of the best sex with his most experienced mistresses.

Great sex, hot sex, hard, carnal sex, wasn't normally an issue for him, but he had rules, and walls, and boundaries and hot, hard carnal sex stayed in the bedroom, and didn't intrude on the rest of his life, and yet last night, even after leaving the bedroom, he felt her.

He thought of her.

He wanted her.

Even now he wasn't relaxed. Instead, he'd wanted to return to the bedroom and wake her with his mouth and fingers and cock. He wanted to hear her make those whimpering sounds as she came. He wanted to feel her body arch, her full breasts crushed to his chest, her moisture creating the perfect silken slickness for each of his hard thrusts.

Damen jerked off twice in that damn guest bedroom, his mind and body too aroused and refusing to be soothed.

Feeling so much was disorienting, and distracting. He kept having washes of memory. Memory of home. Memory of olive groves. Memory of a lean tan boy who'd once loved deeply, before becoming a monster.

Damen slammed his hand against the door, slamming away memories, suppressing sensation and emotion. He refused to go there. He refused to get caught up in the past. And if Kassiani was wakening the past, then far better he take control of their relationship now before she let the monster loose.

In the end, it was a disappointing day for a newly married woman.

Kassiani had tried to keep busy. She'd tried to remain upbeat. She'd tried to fill her hours, which was why she swam in the fitness pool, sunbathed on the sundeck, napped for an hour in the shade, found two books in the library and watched a movie in the theater, with meals and snacks and cold beverages served in between by attentive staff.

Kassiani had successfully kept herself occupied, but as she finished her after-dinner liqueur, and changed for bed without a single appearance by her new husband, she couldn't help feeling let down. Maybe even betrayed.

Yes, it was a superyacht, but theoretically, it wasn't *that* big. He knew she was there. And he hadn't once sought her out.

Turning out the light, she sat on the foot of the bed in the dark. Her emotions swirled within her, cloudy and confusing. Last night when she had fallen asleep next to him, she felt safe. Secure. There had been no regrets, just relief and surprise...maybe even joy. The lovemaking *had* been a joy.

She hadn't expected that. She hadn't expected to feel so good in his arms. She hadn't expected to relish the sensation of him, in her, filling her.

But now, in the fading light of day, she didn't feel as calm and content. In fact, she didn't feel calm at all. She was unsettled, and bewildered.

The lovemaking had been so intimate. They'd explored each other's bodies and given each other so much pleasure, and yet now Damen had retreated, and she didn't know if it was intentional or not, but today he'd shut her out, completely.

She drew her knees up to her chest, and sighed, because on second thought, she was sure it was intentional.

Damen Alexopoulos was a man who left nothing to chance. If she hadn't seen him, it was because he'd avoided her today, not easy on a yacht because they were confined. At sea.

If he hadn't bothered to find her, and speak to her, and check on her well-being, then it was because he wanted her to understand that he was the boss. Not her. He was teaching her her place. And her place wasn't with him.

It was deflating, especially after what had taken place last night.

But in a strange way she understood. They had been so

intimate, and so open, that it was understandable that today he wanted to take back some of that power, because Greek men were all about power. Her father had been the same. Damen was letting her know that she might be his wife, but she wasn't an equal, and she most definitely wasn't his partner.

He wasn't going to go to her tonight. He would lay down the routine now, the pattern that they'd live by. The sooner she understood that he had control, and he valued control, the better.

But lying in the guest bedroom he'd taken since his room had become Kassiani's, he couldn't relax, instantly hard every time he thought of her. Last night she'd felt so good. Just remembering her soft skin and her soft pants and husky little breaths turned him on even now. He needed relief and he wanted to return to the master bedroom, and take her again, and he was certain she wouldn't refuse him. No, his little kitten would welcome him, and she'd be ready for him, and he ached, imagining how good it would feel to sink into her creamy satin heat.

But he wasn't going to just go to her every time he wanted release. She would assume his visits meant that he wanted her—not sex with her. She would imagine, as women did, that there was more to their relationship than a contractual marriage. She would then try to share things with him—thoughts and feelings—and expect him to reciprocate, and that wasn't going to happen. Ever. Better to disappoint her a little now than to risk greater drama later.

Kassiani had just finished dressing when a light knock sounded on the bedroom door. She opened it to discover one of the ship's stewards in the hall. "We have just anchored and Mr. Alexopoulos is waiting for you on the deck. He suggests you bring a sweater." The steward glanced down at her feet. "He also suggested comfortable shoes but I think you'll be fine in those sandals. I'll wait for you here to show you the way."

"I'm ready now," she answered. "Let me just grab a sweater."

Kassiani was excited and also curious. She'd thought the yacht had slowed, and maybe stopped, but she hadn't realized they'd actually dropped anchor. "Where are we?" she asked as she followed the staff member down several flights of stairs to the level where they'd board a smaller boat.

"Paros," he answered simply.

"I've never heard of it," she answered truthfully.

As they stepped into the sunlight, Kassiani spotted her husband by the railing, and her stomach dropped amid a sudden flurry of nerves. He was tall and lean and quite devastatingly attractive this morning in a black knit shirt and khaki shorts that hit just above his knee. The shirt wasn't overly tight and yet even then it clung to his muscular shoulders and outlined the hard planes of his chest, while wrapping firm biceps, biceps that drew her attention.

He was far too handsome for her. She felt even dumpier as she joined him, only then noticing the sleek, white speedboat tethered to the side of the yacht. He extended a hand to her, to assist her into the boat. "We're having breakfast on shore."

"Good. I'm desperate for coffee," she answered, painfully self-conscious as she put her hand in his. In bed with him she'd felt confident, but yesterday had made her insecure again, and yet when his fingers closed around hers, she felt an electric shock and her shyness turned to heat, with disconcerting warmth flooding her limbs.

She wasn't sure if it was a good or bad thing that the racing boat made it virtually impossible to talk as they zipped across the water toward a whitewashed town flanking a gorgeous little bay. The shimmering buildings rose up on the hill and lined the small bay. "Tell me where we're going," she said as the boat slowed, approaching the wharf.

"We're going to spend the morning on Paros, one of my favorite Greek islands. Most tourists don't know about it, and yet it's only several hours by ferry from Athens. First we'll have breakfast in Naousa, the fishing village in front of us, and then we'll go explore for a bit before having a glass of ouzo and returning to the yacht."

She listened to this without comment, butterflies flitting madly in her middle as her gaze settled on his strong, muscular legs, his skin a warm burnished bronze. She'd thought he looked powerful and handsome in his wedding tuxedo, but this casual dress made her think wicked, carnal thoughts, thoughts where he had her naked on the bed, and he was doing the most wonderful things to her.

He took her hand again as they docked, his fingers interlacing with hers, and kept it as they entered town, traveling through narrow whitewashed alleyways with shutter-framed windows. Flowers spilled from huge glazed terra-cotta pots, and purple bougainvillea bloomed over doorways.

She didn't know where they were going, but he did, and they traveled through town, up a narrow cobblestone road to a building partway up the hill. It was a café, she discovered as they crossed the threshold, and a waiter came forward to greet them, escorting them to a table on the terrace with a view of the port.

"That was a hike," she said with a small laugh as they were seated. "Now I know why I needed appropriate shoes."

"Are your feet sore?"

"No. I'm good."

"It's a bit of a climb, but the view, and the food, is worth it."

Coffee and slender glasses of bright orange juice arrived, and then the waiter rattled off the menu options to them in Greek. Kassiani understood most of what the waiter said, and so when Damen turned to her to translate, she said she'd have the option of omelets.

After ordering, she glanced around, soaking in the scenery. The terrace wall was stone, and more pots of flowers and small trees dotted the patio. A half-dozen small wooden tables and chairs were scattered across the terrace, the chairs a lovely blue, and a perfect reflection of the turquoise water below.

Inside the café she could hear voices, but for the most part, it seemed as if they were the only customers.

"Why is no one else here?"

"I called ahead and reserved the terrace."

She laughed. "Why?"

He shrugged. "The tables are too close. I didn't want to risk others listening to us."

"Are you afraid we're going to fight?"

He gave her a puzzled look. "Why would we fight?"

She took a sip of her juice. "I suspected from your distance yesterday that you were upset with me."

He looked at her a long moment, and then glanced away. "Not upset, but I'm accustomed to space. I thought we could both use some space."

She returned her glass to the table. "This is off topic, but this is some of the best orange juice I've ever had."

"It's probably from Laconia or Argos."

"Well, it's delicious." She dabbed her mouth with her linen napkin and set it back on the table beside her plate before rising. "And with regards to space and independence, I'm very independent, but to be honest, I was concerned yesterday that I'd done something wrong on our wedding night, and that my inexperience left you disappointed."

"It didn't. You didn't."

That wasn't a good enough answer in her book. He'd been rude yesterday. He'd hurt her. And she didn't expect him to slather over her, but this was their honeymoon and a chance for them to get to know each other. "Because when I didn't see you yesterday, or hear from you in any way, it was logical to assume that I'd failed in my wifely duties."

He shrugged carelessly. "I don't know how else to reassure you that you did not disappoint me. I enjoyed our wedding night, and I hope you did, too."

Any pleasure she might have felt in his words was diminished by his cold, measured delivery. There was no warmth in him, and none of the passion of their wedding night.

Damen lifted a finger, signaling the waiter, indicating she wanted more juice since her glass was now half-empty.

She found it interesting that he couldn't give her any emotional warmth, but he'd make sure she had plenty to eat and drink. Did he imagine this was how good husbands behaved?

Apparently he did, because as soon as the waiter retreated, Damen said bluntly, "I've been a bachelor for thirty-six years. I'm accustomed to my routine and doing things my way."

"Of course."

"Which means, we're not always going to see each other every day, and we won't be sleeping with each other every night."

"When you say *sleeping*, is that your euphemism for sex?"

"Yes."

"Interesting."

"I warned you I wouldn't be a tender husband. I tried to protect you from who I am. You didn't listen. You insisted you wanted this marriage. This is who I am."

"And who are you?"

"Hard. Cold. Indifferent to the needs of others."

She swallowed with difficulty, refusing to let herself be intimidated. "You weren't indifferent in bed."

Silence followed, so thick and heavy that Kassiani could barely breathe, and then he leaned forward, leaning so close that she could see the silver flecks in his gray eyes. "Sex is the only time I feel anything, and I prefer sex rough. I like to dominate. I enjoy the power. It turns me on."

No wonder he didn't want anyone around them.

Kass swallowed again, her face flushing, her body tingling, wondering why she wasn't scared as much as... aroused. "Fascinating. This is a new world to me. Do you like toys? Whips? Nipple clamps? Handcuffs?"

Damen pushed his coffee cup back, incredulous.

Kassiani might gaze innocently at him, all big brown eyes and sweet smiling lips, but he was beginning to discover that her placid cheerfulness hid a very sharp mind and an extraordinarily steely spine.

"No nipple clamps or whips yet," he answered, checking his testy tone, not wanting her to know just how much she tried his temper. "But there's a place for handcuffs, and the right toy."

Her cheeks turned an even darker pink but she held his gaze. "So since we're on our honeymoon, why wouldn't you want to have sex every night, with or without toys? Unless, you don't really want...me."

"I do want you." In fact, he'd like to bend her over the breakfast table and lift her pretty navy sundress and show her how good it felt when he took her from behind. He was certain he'd get more than a few pants and hoarse cries of pleasure. "But I don't need to have sex every night," he added, grateful the table with its blue-and-white linen cloth hid his lap and his thick, heavy erection.

"But do you want it?" she asked. "Every night?"

His jaw nearly dropped. Her questions astounded him. "I don't find it necessary to impose on my wife every night."

"Even if your wife wants your company in her bed?"

She might have been a virgin when he married her, but she wasn't an innocent. The woman was provocative as hell. "I don't spend the night with anyone. After sex, I always leave."

"Why?"

"Because that is how I prefer it." He ground down, jaw tightening. "It's not necessary for me to explain myself to you, and I'm not sure why I'm even trying."

"Maybe because your wife wants to get to know you, and seeks to understand you."

"There is nothing to understand. Some weeks we might have sex nightly. Other weeks we might have sex a couple times a week. It depends on my work schedule and my mood."

"So I'm not to initiate?"

A picture of her taking him in her mouth flashed through his head and burned all over, so hot he felt as if he might pop out of his skin. "I didn't say that."

"So if I want to sleep with you each night, I can approach you?"

And just like that, he hardened all over again, his shaft throbbing, aching to be freed. "You can't want it every night. In fact, I'm sure you don't want it every night. You've only just lost your virginity."

"The point is, what if *I* want you to come to see me at night? What if *I* want your company in my bed?"

"This isn't a love marriage. I'm not going to romance you."

"I don't believe I asked for romance."

Damen wasn't accustomed to being questioned, or challenged. No one questioned him and he couldn't quite believe she was now. What did she hope to gain? Was this some kind of ill-conceived marital test? "Are you some kind of sex fiend?" he drawled, deliberately using words he was sure would offend her. It was best to check her now, let her know that he wasn't her father, he didn't invite arguments or challenges. He was a traditional male, and he was expecting a traditional wife. Those were the terms of their marriage and she had agreed just the other night, promising to put his comfort before all else.

If he'd thought his offensive words would check her, he was wrong. Her eyes didn't well with tears. There was no quiver of her lower lip. Instead she held her place, lips curved, chin tilted, expression cheerfully defiant. "Would you be unhappy if I *was* a sex fiend?"

"You're not," he answered shortly, impatiently. "You were a virgin just the other night. The sheets bore witness to your lack of experience."

"But maybe I have tapped into long-suppressed desires. Or—" she paused, head tilted, expression thoughtful "—or, I have discovered how much I enjoyed being with you." She paused again, a dark winged eyebrow arching. "Or is that not allowed? Am I not to have any desire of my own? Am I to only serve you but not feel pleasure in our coupling?"

Damen ground his teeth together, beyond exasperated. She was pushing him, and hard, and this was only day three of their marriage. "You're not playing by the rules," he gritted.

Her winged eyebrow rose higher. "I should have realized you had rules. Because, of course, a man like you has *dozens* of rules, rules that can't be challenged. So list them now and we can be on the same page."

"You are not the meek, compliant woman you pretended to be."

"I never pretended to be meek, or compliant. If you recall, I fought for you, and I fought for our marriage."

The fact that she was right didn't improve his mood. "Are you goading me?"

"I just think it's time I heard your expectations."

Damen was holding on to his temper by a thread. "I expect my wife not to harass me."

She laughed. Out loud. And then she reached up and covered her mouth, her lush, ripe mouth that made him think of all the sinful things he wanted to do to her mouth. "I'm sorry," she apologized, and yet her dark eyes glinted, glimmering with fresh amusement. "I'll try not to laugh—"

"Not try. Do it."

"Right. I'm not to laugh, and I'm not to talk, and I'm just supposed to listen."

"About time," he muttered.

She crossed one leg over the other and smoothed the navy fabric of her skirt. Her gaze met his and her expression was more sober but a hint of amusement still lurked in the warm brown depths. "I'm ready."

He would ignore the bright light in her eyes, just as he'd ignore the flecks of gold that made her eyes so warm and beautiful. Her dark brown hair had the same bits of copper here and there. She reminded him of fire and veins of copper amid granite rock, and her strength coupled with her lush shape made him question everything he knew about women.

"I am not looking for a best friend, or even a friend," he said tersely, sounding to his own ears like an unlikable ogre, but it was the truth and he wasn't ashamed of it. "I am not looking for a partner. I live for my work, and when I need something personally, I reach out to have that need met, but once I have what I need, I am again content being left alone."

And then he stopped talking and silence stretched. Kassiani finally gave a short nod, her expression perfectly neutral. How she didn't look offended by his brusque delivery, he didn't know.

Their hot breakfast arrived, eggs with cheese and tomatoes and olives, along with some pan-fried potatoes. They ate in silence and drank their coffee in silence and only when they were finished and Damen was paying the bill did Kassiani speak again.

"How will I know when you want me?" she asked quietly, her smile tight. "I want to be sure I understand the signal. I would hate to impose when I'm supposed to be hidden, and out of your way."

He slipped the folded bills beneath the small plate, and then rose. "That's not what I said."

She rose, too. "No? Because from what I heard, my job description reads obedient, self-sufficient and, above all, convenient."

CHAPTER FIVE

SHE WAS SO glad to be out of the restaurant and moving, even if she didn't know where they were going. She let Damen walk in front of her, and she followed, not wanting to talk to him, wishing she could escape him, but that was unlikely since she didn't know where they were and hadn't brought any money with her, either.

A car was waiting at the foot of the cobblestone street, and it turned out the car was waiting for them. Damen opened the door for her and climbed in next to her.

As the car traveled away from town, she stared out the window, eyes prickling and burning. Despite the fact that it wasn't an overly warm day, she felt hot and flustered... *furious*, actually. She'd always thought her father was unkind and self-centered, but at the moment Damen made her father look like a jovial Santa Claus.

She was still seething when Damen pointed out a glimmering path in the distance. "The Byzantine Road," he said. "If we had more time, we could walk it. It's a marble path that connects the villages of Prodromos and Lefkes."

"What are we doing instead?" she asked.

"We're heading to Parikia, the island's capital. There are several really interesting places I thought you might enjoy, including a cathedral, a thirteenth-century Venetian castle, the Archaeological Museum Parou and an ancient cemetery, which has always drawn me. Not sure why."

It all sounded fascinating and Kassiani focused on the adventures ahead, and it was only later when they were ending their day with the glass of ouzo in a beachfront *taverna*, she realized that the way he'd described the attractions—a cathedral, a castle and cemetery—all sounded rather grand, but nothing in Parikia was grand at all. Even the museum was quite small. But the sites were interesting and she enjoyed visiting places that weren't teeming with tourists. The cemetery grounds were a bit overgrown, but the tombs and marble headstones were a testament to the antiquity of the cemetery.

As they sat with their glass of ouzo in the *taverna*, her gaze swept the little town with the cobblestone streets and gleaming white buildings with colorful blue painted doors and shutters. "It's a charming little town, but I think I'd go mad here," she said, turning back to Damen. "I'm afraid I've lived in a city too long. I wouldn't know what to do here."

"What did you do at home?"

"Visit museums. Go to the library. Walk along the waterfront. Read in Golden Gate Park."

"Who did you do those things with?"

"Myself."

"I'm sure you had friends."

"Not really."

"Why not?"

"Like you, I enjoy my own company. I don't need constant attention."

"But you were upset that I gave you space yesterday."

"A little reassurance after our wedding night would have been nice, but there's no point in rehashing that, is there?"

"I didn't mean to hurt you," he said tersely. "But I do think—" He broke off, shook his head. "I don't want to argue."

She didn't want to argue, either, and yet she did wish

to understand him. "Is it arguing if we are trying to clarify things?"

He reached out and captured her chin, turning her face to his. "Arguing is conflict. I don't do conflict."

She could feel the heat of each of his fingers against her jaw, and his voice had dropped, and his deep, husky tone sent a strangely delicious shiver up and down her back. "Because you're a traditional Greek man, or you just have an overwhelming need to dominate?"

"Just an FYI, kitten, you are neither obedient nor convenient."

His voice had grown even huskier, which sent a frisson of pleasure through her. "I'm sorry I can't please you."

His silver gaze warmed. "Perhaps you need to try a little harder."

"Perhaps you need to work with me a little more," she flashed. "Perhaps training a new wife takes more time than you anticipated."

"Is that where this has gone all wrong? I've failed to train you?"

There was a smoky promise in his words that made her heart thump and her insides melt. She pressed her knees together, excited. "You have deck crew, and a captain and an engineer. You have a chief officer, and a second officer and a third officer. A chase boat captain. An officer on watch. Bosun, security officers, purser, chief steward, a second steward, housekeeper, chefs, cooks, laundry and spa therapists—"

"I'm fully aware of all the staff I employ," he interrupted drily.

"But you haven't hired anyone to train me," she concluded. "Which means you either need to bring someone on board to teach me how to be a proper wife, or you'll have to do it yourself—"

He dropped his head, his mouth covering hers, silencing the stream of words, and when he lifted his head again, his gray eyes glittered and dark color stained his cheekbones. "It seems it's time to continue your training. We'll return to the ship now."

The speedboat was there in pretty Parikia Harbor as was the yacht, as they'd both traveled around the island to pick them up.

Kassiani tried to ignore her rapidly thudding pulse as they approached the yacht but Damen's words echoed in her head.

Time to continue your training.

"Am I in trouble?" she asked breathlessly as they boarded the yacht and Damen took her hand and led her up the flights of stairs to the master bedroom.

"Do you want to be in trouble?"

"I am a little nervous," she confessed.

He pinned her against the bedroom door. "Good." And then he kissed her again, a hot, demanding kiss that made her legs tremble and her heart race. He was, without a doubt, the most exciting thing that had ever happened in her life. By the time he lifted his head, hers was spinning and her heart was racing and it felt like she had honey wine in her veins.

"When we go inside, you're going to listen to me," he said. "You're not going to argue. You're going to do exactly what I tell you."

"Because it turns you on?"

"Yes." His lips brushed her cheekbone, and then near her ear. "And I think it turns you on, too." And then he reached down and twisted the doorknob, the bedroom door opening so abruptly she nearly fell into the room. He caught her by the elbow, righting her and steering her into the bedroom before closing the door hard behind them, and then locking it.

Her pulse hammered as he locked the door, and then the air left her lungs when he quietly commanded, "Take off your dress. I want to look at you."

Heat flooded her, and she could feel herself turning pink, the blood rushing from her chest, up her neck to burn her cheeks, but she headed to the windows to draw the curtains.

"What are you doing?" he ground out.

"Closing the curtains."

"Why?"

"Because someone might see."

He barked a laugh, the sound low and so husky that it sent a thrilling ripple through her. "Like me?"

"Perhaps," she answered, her voice quavering. Her voice wasn't the only thing shaking. She was trembling, but she wasn't afraid. No, she was aroused and she felt hot and wet and completely needy, but this was all still new to her and she couldn't help feeling timid and uncertain.

"You weren't shy the other night. Why be shy now?"

"It was night. The room was dark."

"All the better to see you clearly now."

Some of the warmth inside her faded. Air bottled in her chest. She struggled to keep her emotions in check. "I'm not Elexis."

"No? What a surprise."

"I'm serious."

"So am I. Take your dress off, Petra Kassiani. Your husband grows impatient."

Her eyes burned. Her throat threatened to seal closed. He would see just how plump she was. He'd be impossibly turned off. But collapsing into tears wouldn't help, nor would they protect her from his scorn. Maybe it was better to get this over with. Let him see just who and what he'd married. Summoning her courage, she reached down, gathered the skirt of her sundress in her hands and lifted it up, drawing the dress up over her head before dropping it on the floor next to her.

She stood in her navy lace bra and panties, the bra straps not dainty, because her breasts weren't dainty. At least the matching navy lace panties weren't large. They were cut low on the hip with high legs that tried to make the most of the figure she had.

She kept her head up as he studied her pale form in the sunlight. It was all she could do not to cover herself. Kassiani knew she had too many curves and not enough flat-toned places. Exercise did little to change her shape, too. But she wouldn't cower, and she wouldn't let him know how painful this was for her.

She needed their relationship to be successful. Yes, she'd come into an inheritance when she married Damen, her father's late sister having set up a trust fund for Kassiani when she was a young girl because Kassiani had reminded her aunt Calista so much of herself as a girl. And Aunt Calista had not had a happy life.

Aunt Calista had never married, and had lived trapped with her own family as a single woman, and she hadn't wanted that future for Kassiani, and so she'd created a trust for Kass, ensuring she'd inherit money at twenty-five, or when she married, so that she'd always have options and not be dependent on her family.

But her aunt Calista didn't understand that Kass wanted to be married, because she wanted children. She hadn't married Damen so that she could leave him and live off her trust fund. She'd married Damen to be a wife and mother, and maybe she didn't know how to be a traditional Greek wife, but she could be a good wife. She was determined to be what Damen needed. After twenty-three years of being shunned and invisible, she was ready to be seen.

"You are beautiful," Damen said abruptly, his deep, rough voice breaking the silence.

"I'm not—"

"You are. If you weren't, I wouldn't say it." He dropped onto the bed, and leaned back, watching her from beneath heavy lids. "Take off your bra."

Heat rushed through her, making her skin prickle, and her breasts tighten and peak. She reached behind her and unhooked the bra, peeling it off before discarding it on the floor on top of her dress.

"Now your panties," he directed.

"You're not making this very comfortable," she flashed.

"Good. That makes it even more stimulating."

"Why do you like dominating?" she asked, stepping out of her panties.

"Why do you like being dominated?"

"I don't."

"I think you do, and here is why. You're smart. You're smarter than anyone else in your family. They are all predictable. Your life has been predictable. It's unpredictable now, and you and your interesting brain like that."

She couldn't argue with that, and his insight astounded her. "Do you say this to all your women?"

"No. You're nothing like the women I've had in my life. You're like nothing I've ever known."

"Is that bad?"

"No. It's good. Now touch yourself," he interrupted. "Play with your nipples."

She stiffened, flushing. Her hands wrapped around her middle. "I can't do that."

"Why not?"

"That's just…weird. Awkward."

"But doesn't it feel good?"

"My breasts are awful. They are so big—"

"They're perfect. But as it makes you nervous being the only one naked, I'll disrobe, too, which should level the playing field slightly." He rose and removed his clothing.

Shirt, pants, snug briefs off, one after the other.

She gulped as his thick erection sprang free. He was big, and the head of his shaft was equally thick and round. He reached down and stroked the length of him, his palm giving extra attention to the smooth head.

She remembered him in her mouth, and remembered how he'd filled her, and how incredibly good it had felt when he'd thrust in and out, finding sensitive spots within her that she hadn't even known about.

"Now touch yourself," he said, sitting back down on the bed, his powerful thighs parted, his hand still on his erection.

He was bronze all over. He had no tan lines. Her mouth dried and she felt a wobble in her legs.

"Surely you, brilliant young thing, can follow a few basic instructions," he said, and yet his tone wasn't harsh, more amused than anything.

Her cheeks heated. She exhaled hard, her nipples tightening into aching points even as she began to throb between her thighs. "I have. I'm here, and naked."

"But you're not touching yourself."

"I can't."

"You could if you knew there were consequences for disobeying me."

"Like?"

"Tie you up, and leave you there all day, naked—"

"You wouldn't."

"Or tie you up and lick you but not let you come." He paused considering other punishments. "Would you prefer me to spank you? A sharp slap on your pretty ass and then a lovely warm rub?"

She pressed her knees together, growing wetter, feeling positively drenched. "If I touch myself now, will you do what we did the other night? I loved that. I loved being close to you. I'm too far away right now."

"You should be proud of your body. It's beautiful."

"It's thick—"

"Why do women assume men want to take scrawny bony sticks to bed? I think you have an astonishing figure."

"You really do?"

"I've been hard all day. I find everything about you incredibly appealing. Maybe too appealing."

"Is that possible?"

"Yes. I can't get work done if I'm thinking about you and being in you and making you come."

She dropped her head, shy, and yet also rather victorious. He'd been thinking about her? It was heady and empowering. "It's all I thought about yesterday."

"So my little kitten is a sex fiend."

Her head shot up and she looked at him, but he was smiling and his expression was warm. Far warmer than she'd ever seen from him.

"Maybe," she murmured, voice husky. "Because I do want you."

"Enough talking, then." He rose and crossed to where she stood, and carried her to the bed, where he half dropped her into the middle of the mattress. He moved over her, his knees parting her thighs, and then spreading them wider so that he could look down at her, and see all of her. "I do like you bare," he growled.

Her thighs trembled as his fingertip traced her cleft and then between her soft swollen folds.

"So wet," he said, voice dropping lower.

She closed her eyes as he dipped a finger into her and spread the moisture up over her, teasing the hooded nub. She felt her hips lift, and arch as he did it again. And then he was there at her entrance, and pushing into her, his shaft so warm, instantly making her feel hot, and impossibly connected to him.

Something happened when he was buried in her that made her want to hold on to him, and keep holding on, keeping him with her.

She wrapped her arms around his neck and drew him down, wanting to feel him against her breasts, wanting to inhale his scent, wanting his warmth all around her.

He said he was awful and didn't feel, but that wasn't true. He wasn't as hard as he said he was, and clearly, he did have feelings. Damen might say he didn't care, but actions spoke louder than words, and when he kissed her, a deep scorching kiss where his tongue took her mouth just as he took her body, he was warm and protective. All day he'd been attentive and protective, making her feel as if she truly was his.

In a strange way, she felt as if she was the one who was supposed to be here, not Elexis. Elexis would never understand him, but she could. She would. She liked puzzles and challenges, and she was good at reading not just text, but subtext. And when she and Damen were together like this, it felt rather like perfection in an imperfect world.

Together like this, she felt as if she belonged. She belonged with him. She belonged to him. For the first time in her life, she belonged somewhere.

Kassiani shattered just as Damen began to come, their bodies climaxing together, and she welcomed his last hard, driving thrust, accepting everything he had, and everything he could give her. He was home.

Moments passed, and Kassiani struggled to catch her breath, her thoughts cloudy, her body still floating.

Their wedding night had been incredibly satisfying, but the lovemaking just now, and the orgasm she'd had, was, well, life changing. She liked being with him, even when he was edgy and dangerous. No one had ever challenged her in her life. Until now.

She felt Damen shift, rolling onto his back, and he drew her against his chest. His skin was warm and slightly damp, and as she rested her cheek on his chest, she breathed him in. He smelled delicious. She inhaled the scent—man, sex and a spicy fragrance—and it crossed her mind that she needed to be careful. He was potent. She would need to guard her heart.

"How do you feel?" he asked, lightly stroking her back.

How did she feel? Amazing. Surely he knew that. She glanced up into his face, feeling rather lucky in that moment to have a husband who was famous for his shrewd business acumen and a threat in the boardroom, as well as gifted in the bedroom. "Good."

His hand continued the slow caressing of her back. His touch made her want to purr. "I hate that your family has treated you so shabbily. It makes me want to take your father apart, limb by limb."

She smiled crookedly, and stretched up to kiss him. "Please don't do that, but thank you for being my protector. I've never had one before."

"I'm not a hero."

"No, you're definitely more of a thug, but you're handsome as heck, so it works for you."

He laughed, softly. "You're one surprise after another."

"I hope that's a good thing."

"It is." He kissed her back, a hand threading into her

hair, and the kiss flared into something hot and bright. "I hate to go, but I need to."

"Why do you need to go?"

"I've been out of touch with the office all day. I'm sure there are dozens of emails and phone calls and matters awaiting my attention."

"Just stay a little longer. Stay and talk to me. Please?"

She could feel him tense and she stroked his chest. "There is so much I want to know about you. Tell me about your work and family, tell me about your first girlfriend, tell me—"

"That's an awful lot to cover in five minutes."

"Okay, then forget all that. Just answer this. Have you ever been in love?"

He hesitated. "No."

"That wasn't very convincing."

He didn't reply.

"So you have been in love," she persisted.

Damen sat up and rolled to the side of the bed. "The less you know about me, the better. Knowing more about me would just lead to disappointment. I'm good at what I do because I'm focused and ruthless. I've perfected the art of not caring about others, or what they think."

"That can be a good thing in business."

"It's who I am all the time. I don't have different sides. Whether at work, or home, I'm the same. Unfeeling. Driven. Relentless."

She considered this a moment. "I don't think you are all that. If you were, you wouldn't care about what I want or need, and you wouldn't take such good care of me in bed."

"That's bed."

"Or on the island today."

"Don't make too much of it."

"It's more kindness and attention than I've had from anyone, ever."

Damen reached for her and rolled her onto her back, his big body angling over hers. "Don't say such things. It makes me hate your family even more."

She reached up to brush his thick black hair back from his brow. "Don't hate them. Hate is such a useless emotion."

"Hate can be powerful."

"You don't need hate, and you don't need more power."

His light gaze locked with hers and he stared intently into her eyes. "So what do I need, then, Little Miss Know-It-All?"

"Maybe just how to be happy?"

"Because you're so happy?"

"I'm happier than I have been in a very long time."

"Because you're away from your family."

"Because I'm with you."

He made an incredulous sound and climbed off the bed. "Now you're playing me for a fool."

She sat up, drawing the light crisp sheet with her to cover herself. "Why can't I like you?"

"Because we don't have that kind of marriage. This is not a love marriage—"

"I know. And I said like, not love," she flashed irritably as he yanked on his clothes, first his shorts and then his shirt. "And right now, you're being ridiculous but that doesn't mean I don't still find you likable."

"That is not part of our agreement."

"I'm sorry."

"If you're sorry, why are you smiling?"

"Maybe because you look really handsome right now."

He growled his frustration. "I'm not handsome right now, and I'm not likable, and we don't have that kind of marriage, either."

"What kind is that?"

"The kind where everybody is happy and dreams come true." He turned and gave her a dark, tortured look. "You're a smart woman. You of all people should know that happiness is a myth and dreams are just that. Dreams."

CHAPTER SIX

HE'D SPENT ALL day with Kassiani today. Damen couldn't remember when he'd last spent four hours with anyone, never mind a woman.

And he'd enjoyed almost every minute. The only minutes he hadn't enjoyed were the minutes where she'd tried to convince him he was a good person, when he knew the truth about himself.

Kassiani. She was something of a revelation.

He'd known very little about her before their wedding, other than she was the youngest daughter, and a rather mysterious figure in her family, one her father had portrayed as eccentric, which was apparently why she didn't travel with them, and wasn't paraded about like Barnabas and Elexis. But now Damen could see that Kassiani had been forgotten and ignored by her family because she wasn't like them—she wasn't shallow and superficial. She didn't take advantage of people. She didn't use others. She actually thought of others.

Thank God her family hadn't corrupted her, but at the same time, she'd deserved so much better from her family. A great disservice had been done to Kassiani all these years. She actually believed she was fat and unattractive. Unworthy.

It was wrong.

And now he was handling her wrong, too, but Damen didn't know how to be a better husband. He wasn't accustomed to being patient or kind. So maybe that was the first step. Practicing patience. And maybe a little bit of kindness.

If Kass was surprised to see him on deck before dinner, she gave no indication. She was standing at one of the railings on the upper deck, and she turned her head to smile at him. "Good evening."

"Good evening to you. Have you been up here long?"

"Fifteen or twenty minutes. It's such a gorgeous night. The view is spectacular. The island ahead of us sparkles with light."

"That's Mykonos."

Her brow creased. "Weren't you and Elexis supposed to visit Mykonos?"

"We were, yes."

"Are we?"

"No." He saw the searching look she gave him. He shrugged. "I don't want to take you where I was going to take Elexis. It seems wrong somehow."

"It's okay. I've been there. It's fine, but it's not my favorite island."

"Which is your favorite island? Wait, let me guess. Santorini."

She grinned. "It's everyone's favorite, isn't it?"

"It's certainly picturesque." He turned from the view of Mykonos to face her. "How did you know about the honeymoon plans?"

"Elexis asked me to read through the itinerary and make sure she would like it."

His jaw dropped slightly. "And did you?"

Her shoulders twisted. "It gave me something to do."

"And you like to be helpful."

"I like having a sense of purpose, yes. It's frustrating to me that I've gone to school and have a degree and yet my father refuses to allow me to work outside the home."

"So you've never held a job?"

"Charity work. That's about it."

"And your brother and sister?"

"The same. Although Barnabas was supposed to work with Dad once he finished university, only he never finished university because his grades were so bad."

"How does he get his money?"

"Dad transfers money each month into Barnabas's bank account."

"Why?"

"I guess it's like an allowance."

"Your brother is twenty-eight years old. Isn't that a little old to be getting an allowance?"

"Dad is afraid that if he cuts Barnabas and Elexis off financially, they'll cut him out of their lives. And he couldn't bear that, so he gives them whatever they want."

"So you get an allowance, too?"

"No." Her voice was sharp and her smile brief. "I get nothing other than a roof over my head and the food I eat."

"Why the double standard?"

"Barnabas and Elexis tell Dad what he wants to hear. I don't."

"What do you tell him instead?"

"That the company needs more leadership, and the family shouldn't be sponging off the company. Dukas Shipping isn't there to be the personal bank account for lazy family members that don't want to work."

Damen's eyebrows shot up. "You've said all this?"

"And more."

His lips twitched. "I can't imagine he valued the input."

"Not at all, but he values his business, and I'd be wrong to remain silent when so much is at stake. It could be such an incredible company—"

"It will be, once I'm completely in charge."

"Are you removing my father as president and CEO?"

"He hasn't actively managed the company in years. He knows I'll be taking over after the honeymoon." He shot her a swift side-glance. "Does that upset you?"

"I'm relieved, actually. Something has to be done. I just…" She sighed, shrugged. "Never mind."

She turned away from him to stare out over the water and he used the moment to study her elegant profile. She truly was beautiful, with the regal features of a Greek goddess. "Tell me," he said quietly. "Finish the thought. I want to hear it."

She glanced at him, eyes bright, lips compressed. "If I was a son, he would have made room for me. I would have been an asset. Instead I was a daughter and nothing but a disappointment."

Before he could reply, one of his stewards appeared with the champagne he'd requested twenty minutes ago and made a big production about opening the bottle and filling their flutes.

Damen checked his temper as the steward settled the champagne bottle into the ice bucket, rattling the ice as if he was doing the most important job in the world. Finally the steward was gone and Damen handed Kassiani a flute.

"We didn't have a toast on our wedding night. So, *stin yeia sou*," he said, lifting his glass. *To your health.*

"Yamas," she answered, to *our* health, before clinking the rim of her goblet to his and lifting her flute to her lips.

Just watching her bring her glass to her full lips made him hard. He didn't understand this fascination with her, or why he found it so hard to stay away from her. She was so naturally sensual that she had him in a constant state of arousal.

"What else have you told your father that he doesn't want to hear?" Damen asked, determined to shift his attention from her luscious mouth to the topic they'd been discussing before the champagne had arrived.

"Dukas Shipping was worth so much more five years ago, when my father first approached you. He's been cutting away into the principal. You've gotten a rotten deal. Instead of the Dukas beauty, you got the Ugly Duckling *and* a company teetering on bankruptcy."

"You wanted to work for him."

"Desperately." She swallowed hard. "I have tried for years to get him to bring me on board. I even told him he didn't have to pay me. I'd be an intern. Just let me go to the office and give me a chance to learn the ropes."

"Is it true you studied business and international relations at Stanford?"

"It is true."

"That couldn't have been an easy course of study."

"It was actually not that difficult. I read quickly, and have one of those memories that forget nothing." Her lips quirked. "It's a blessing and a curse."

"So you've been out of school a couple years."

"Four years end of this month. I started Stanford at sixteen and finished the dual major in three years."

Very little surprised Damen, but she'd just caught him completely off guard. "Most Americans don't start university until they're what…eighteen?"

"I tend to do accelerated studies. I can take more classes than most students. The workload isn't a problem for me." She grimaced. "More of that blessing and a curse."

"Have you ever been tested? Are you considered gifted?"

"I have, and I am. But I wish I wasn't. My mother wasn't particularly intellectual and she used to say that brainy women were objectionable as they tended to challenge the status quo, competing with men rather than allowing the man to feel like the man."

"She wasn't a feminist."

"No."

"Little wonder your father adored her. Greek men expect to be the center of the world."

"Yes, I know." She hesitated. "It's why my aunt never married. She was brilliant, and smart, and strong, and her parents were traditional Greeks, and they didn't know what to do with her." She tapped the rim of her flute. "I think it's why she created the trust for me. She recognized a kindred spirit and wanted to be sure I had...options."

Her tone, and the bittersweet twist of her lips, made his chest tighten. Kassiani was a constant source of surprise. "What else did your mother teach you?"

"That beauty is a woman's greatest strength and virtue, and a socially inept woman was nothing short of a failure."

"Oh, dear."

"Mmm. In my parents' eyes, I've been a failure my entire life. Not attractive, and a social misfit. How could I be such a blight on the Dukas name?"

"Did you feel awkward at Stanford?"

"No. I loved being in school. I enjoy academia. I'm comfortable in certain environments, but hopeless in others. Like parties. I'm not comfortable at parties. I'm not good with chitchat. I'm the least fashionable woman you'll ever meet—"

"Oh, now, I'm not sure you can claim that honor. My mother only wears smocks, and these slipper-like shoes, with socks. It's terrible. Really. So, I think she has you beat."

Kassiani gurgled with laughter and Damen was pleased. He'd meant to make her laugh, and was glad he'd succeeded. He'd hated the pain in her voice, her pain making his chest tighten, and his temper stir. How dare her father treat her so shabbily all these years? How dare her parents make her feel less than something when she was the greatest Dukas of them all?

"Besides," he added after a moment, "fashion and parties are overrated. I would much rather have a brilliant wife than one who merely looked good in clothes."

For a moment there was just silence and Kassiani stared out over the water, toward the island glittering with light. Damen congratulated himself for soothing Kassiani's fears, and then she turned her head and looked him square in the eye. "Then why did you want Elexis in the first place? Why didn't you want...*me*?"

Her voice was calm, her tone thoughtful. It took him a second to realize she wasn't accusing him of anything, or trying to guilt him. She genuinely wanted to know.

Again his chest tightened and he felt a wave of remorse, and pain. She deserved so much better from all of them.

"You were never presented as an option," he said at length. "I didn't know enough about you to think to ask for you."

"You didn't realize there were two Dukas daughters?"

"Vaguely. You were, how shall I say? Mysterious."

"Kassiani, overly fond of math, burdened by a photographic memory." Her lips lifted in a wide, self-mocking smile. "Most mysterious indeed."

The moonlight bathed her in a lovely glow, illuminating her profile with her strong, elegant features. She was wearing a white dress with ruffles and flounces and it crossed his mind that while the white paired well with her dark hair and complexion, the flounces and frills were too much for her petite build, overwhelming her curves, adding to them, making her look bigger than she was. Kassiani was actually quite small physically. She just had exceptional curves, amazing curves, like Hollywood stars of old.

"You should be proud of your exceptional abilities and talent, not ashamed," he said.

"Do you think my father should have hired me?"

"I do."

Her gaze found his again, her expression somber. "Would you hire me?"

Damen straightened, feeling sucker punched. What a question. How could he answer that without becoming a villain, like her father? "I've hired a number of women for management positions. There is also a woman on my board."

"Out of what? Twelve?"

He didn't answer since they both knew the answer. Kassiani didn't pull punches, did she? Damen was beginning to understand why Kristopher preferred not to deal with his youngest. "The Greek shipping business is dominated by men, and in general, it isn't very receptive to women in key positions."

Kassiani sipped her champagne thoughtfully. Her silence felt like a condemnation and Damen didn't enjoy feeling judged.

"I didn't say I agreed with the attitude," he added somewhat defensively, and then felt angry about being made to feel defensive. "Men just want to get things done without all the emotional baggage women bring to the table."

She shot him a look of surprise that quickly morphed into one of disappointment and Damen gripped his flute so hard he was certain it would shatter.

"I had no idea you were one of those," she said calmly with just a hint of censure. "For some reason I thought you were more...progressive."

"Business is business," he said curtly. "I don't spend long hours at the office because I enjoy sitting at my desk. I'm there to get things done."

"And women don't get things done at the office?"

"You're twisting this, you know. You are deliberately twisting my words. But to answer your last question, this is exactly what I don't want in my office. I don't want to spar with a woman over real or perceived slights. I want to execute contracts. I want financial growth. I want to develop markets. What I don't want is to be challenged on my domain. It's not conducive to company morale—"

"Or yours," she interjected softly.

He broke off, frustrated, and rather furious, because this entire conversation had flipped. A couple of minutes ago they were having a really good and open conversation and now it was antagonistic. Why? What had happened?

And before he could answer that question, he had a sudden insight into why Kristopher had chosen to leave Kassiani at home, behind.

It wasn't because she was dumpy and dull. It wasn't because she was the proverbial Ugly Duckling. It was because Kristopher didn't know how to manage his youngest daughter. Kassiani was too smart for him, and probably talked circles around him, and Kristopher—not the brightest of men—couldn't cope. The only way he knew how to handle her was by shaming her.

Marginalizing her.

Making her feel small and less than.

Damen didn't agree with Kristopher's behavior, but he felt an unexpected surge of sympathy for the older man. Kristopher knew exactly what to do with Elexis and Barnabas—indulge them, give them money and toys. But Kassiani couldn't be bought off so easily. She was young, smart and fierce, honest and real.

"You know, kitten," he said quietly, "if you want to be part of the game, you have to play the game."

"Is there a game, then?"

Damen flashed back to Adras, and the horrors of being a young male trapped in a situation beyond his control, forced to do and say things that still made him physically ill. He knew then, at fourteen and fifteen, he'd never forgive himself, and he hadn't, even though twenty-two years had passed. "If you feel like you're always on the losing side, I'd say there is a game in play."

"And if I'm tired of losing?"

"Then figure out the game."

Dinner was strained that evening and Kassiani knew she was to blame—not because she was wrong, but because she couldn't remain silent on issues. Growing up, she'd never been able to accept the status quo, and she realized early on that what was acceptable in one family wasn't going to be acceptable in hers. Her family was old-world. Traditional. And if her feminist opinions weren't welcome at home in San Francisco, she should know they'd be a problem here in Greece.

Back in her bedroom, she kicked herself for not being able to hold her tongue. It had changed their evening. Damen had been in a good mood when he had joined her on the deck and had champagne delivered, and then she had to ruin the lovely champagne toast by being too pointed, and too direct, creating conflict, which was so typical of her.

Kass didn't know why she couldn't stop when she was ahead. If only she could harness the frustration she felt at not being given more opportunity.

The narrowness of her life wore on her.

The lack of challenges made her feel somewhat desperate and crazy.

She read half a dozen international newspapers a day, and tried to stay busy by digging in deeper into current events, researching current topics in world economics, international politics and international law. She subscribed to various university magazines, wanting to know what was happening in the academic world, as well as the corporate world. But all the research in the world did little to alleviate her sense of isolation.

But Kass didn't feel isolated when Damen claimed her, and made love to her. Kass didn't feel like a failure when he responded to her in bed. She wasn't a radical feminist. She didn't think of herself as a rabble-rouser. But Kass had always struggled with remaining silent when confronted by injustices. Women really were capable of so much.

And she, personally, was capable of so much more.

Maybe her need to be heard and seen…to contribute… was based on the fact that she didn't feel valuable as a decorative object. How could she? She wasn't very decorative. She added little value in terms of physical beauty. The only time she truly felt attractive was when she was using her brain.

Or using her body to seduce Damen.

She smiled weakly, ruefully. At least she still had her sense of humor. It wasn't appreciated in her family but Kassiani had always been grateful she could laugh at herself. Far better than always crying over one's faults and failings.

The door to the master bedroom opened. Kass jerked her head up, and her heart fluttered as Damen stepped into the room and closed the door behind him.

Suddenly the tears she'd been holding back fell and she reached up to swipe them away, one after the other before he could see.

"Why the tears?" he asked, standing at the foot of the bed.

So she hadn't successfully hid them. She sat taller and swiftly swiped away another, scrubbing at her cheeks to make sure they were now dry. "I didn't think you were going to come tonight. I thought I'd chased you away."

"So you don't believe what you were saying?"

"No, I do."

"Then don't apologize. Your problem is that you're smarter than everyone else."

She sniffed and swiped away a last tear. "Not smarter than you."

"I wouldn't say that. You are certainly book smarter. To be fair, I probably have you beat when it comes to street smarts."

She settled her nightgown over her knees, and exhaled slowly, trying very hard to bridge whom she was with what a wife was supposed to be. It was a tricky balancing act. "All right, so I don't apologize for having opinions, but I am sorry if I upset you at dinner. Trying to be a good wife is more complicated than I imagined."

"Why shouldn't you speak freely? I do."

She exhaled in a painful rush, her cheeks heating. "We both know the answer to that."

"Because men can, and women can't?"

"You've told me that my value lies in me being a supportive wife, not a critical, oppositional one."

"I actually don't think I ever told you that," he said mildly.

"A traditional Greek wife—"

"Isn't what I asked for. It's what you said I needed, because apparently I need a meek, submissive wife." He arched a black brow. "Now, there are things I would enjoy from a submissive wife, but it would probably not be what you're thinking."

Or would it? She silently countered, as unbidden images came to mind, images of her kneeling before him, worshipping his body, drawing his thick shaft into her mouth, sucking, licking, making him groan and slide a hand into her hair, his fingers wrapping around the strands, holding her head so that he could take his pleasure.

Kassiani exhaled again, her body hot, her senses stirred. Flustered, she pushed back a heavy wave of hair from her face, feeling overly warm, and more than a little claustrophobic, because suddenly the atmosphere felt charged, the air heavy, crackling with awareness, and desire.

She could tell that Damen felt the tension, too, as the look he gave her was blatantly sexual, as was his slow, possessive perusal, his gaze resting on the jut of her breasts and then lower to the swell of her hips and then finally to the hem of her nightgown where it clung to her thigh.

"Let me see you," he said slowly, arms folding over his chest.

"What do you want to see?"

"Everything."

"Then let me see you."

"What do you want to see?"

"Everything."

He laughed softly and gave his dark head a shake. "You are a fearless negotiator. I admire that." The corner of his mouth lifted. "Now let's see how good you are at asking for something. What do you want, Petra Kassiani? What would be your pleasure?"

She hesitated, thinking. "Something new. Something we haven't done. But something *I* would like," she added quickly, fighting her blush.

"Oh, that's easy, then. I haven't even taken you from behind yet. I think you'll like that position very much."

CHAPTER SEVEN

HE WAS RIGHT. She did like that position very, very much.

She was still trying to catch her breath after the most intense orgasm of her life, and Damen was stretched out next to her, his hand lightly running over her back, caressing from her back to her butt, and then up again.

Part of her was so relaxed but another part of her was already being stirred.

"Tell me something about your boyhood," she murmured, trying to distract herself. "Do you have brothers and sisters?"

"None. I was an only child."

"Why?"

"There were complications during my birth. My mother was lucky she and I both survived the pregnancy."

"That's scary."

"I am sure if we lived someplace else, and had easier access to doctors, it might have been less dangerous."

"You were poor."

"Very."

She curled closer to him, her arm wrapping around his waist. "And yet you have so much now."

"I made a vow when I was fifteen that I would never be poor again, and it's driven every decision I've made since then."

"What did your father do?"

"He worked in an olive orchard. My mother did, too. They earned so little that they couldn't afford child care for me, so from the very beginning I went to work with them, first strapped to my mother's back as an infant, and then later I ran about, trying to help. I didn't actually get paid until the year I turned ten. That was a big deal for me, and my family. It wasn't much compared to what my father earned, but it helped."

She pressed her hand to his chest, just above his heart. They'd had such different backgrounds, such different lives, and yet here they were together. "When did you find time to go to school?"

"I went seasonally. When I wasn't needed in the groves or the olive press."

"It doesn't sound like you had a lot of formal education, then."

"I attended off and on until I was fourteen—" He broke off, jaw hardening, brow darkening. "And that was the end of my boyhood. I never went back to school, and within eighteen months, I left our island, Adras, for good."

"Where did you go?"

"Athens. I got a job in the dockyards and worked hard, and here I am."

"How does a relatively uneducated boy become...you?"

"Relentless ambition." He smiled grimly. "And the desire for revenge."

She pushed up on her elbow to get a better look at his face. "Revenge? Why?"

"When you are poor, you are dependent on others." His jaw flexed. "There is a terrible imbalance of power."

She frowned. "What happened?"

"It's nothing I discuss. It's just...fuel. Anger and desperation are remarkable motivators."

"Why won't you tell me?"

"It doesn't matter anymore," he answered carelessly, his voice hardening. He sat up and kissed her forehead. "And now I just like working hard. Work gives me a reason to wake up every day. It gives satisfaction at the end of the day." He glanced at the bedside clock. "I'm actually hungry. Are you?"

"Hasn't your chef gone to bed?"

"No one sleeps if I want something," he said so matter-of-factly that she smiled.

And then he smiled, too, as if amused by his own arrogance. "All I want is a snack," he added, "and half the fun of a snack is going through the refrigerator and pantry to see what you can find."

The kitchen was surprisingly large with an enormous center island dominating the middle of the room. The backsplash, refrigerators, stove, ovens, even the four portholes above the prep area, all gleamed silver, while the cabinets were a rich espresso and the counters a creamy ivory marble shot with veins of pale caramel.

It was a beautiful space, and welcoming. Kassiani ran her hand over one of the lovely marble work surfaces. "This is a gorgeous kitchen. I wouldn't mind cooking in here. The kitchen on our family yacht isn't half as nice. For one, there are no windows or portholes, and for another, it's a rather hideous vanilla-and-stainless mix, and not pretty stainless like this, but restaurant grade and very commercial looking. This is like something you'd see in a stunning house."

"My chef is picky. He wouldn't come on board if he didn't have the right appliances and utensils and work space."

"You must like your chef quite a bit, then. My father fired staff right and left. He had no qualms replacing them."

"Most of my staff have been with me for a while now. There are a few new faces on this sailing, but the majority have been on my payroll for years. I'm happier surrounded by familiar staff, people I know I can count on."

Kassiani was surprised. She'd gotten the impression that

Damen wasn't attached to anyone, or anything. "Do you spend that much time on your yacht to keep everyone fully employed, then?"

"Half of the crew only work here on the yacht, while the other half work for me in another capacity. My chef here is also my chef in Athens. I just steal him from the house and bring him on board. Some of the housekeeping staff are also from Athens. Three of the hands work on my Adras estate, while others are from my Sounio villa."

"So are those your main homes?" she asked as he opened the refrigerator and began pulling out cheese after cheese, as well as a plastic container filled with washed fruit. "Athens, Sounio and Adras?"

He moved to a cabinet and found plates and silverware. "I have an apartment in London, but I haven't been in years. Too busy working to travel." Damen deftly arranged place settings in front of them before going to the tall narrow pantry and retrieving a set of pottery jars she suspected were filled with olives.

The jars of olives joined the cheese and fruit. Damen lifted the lid on one jar and, using a tiny wooden fork, reached in to pluck out a tiny, dark green olive. He held the olive to her mouth in an offering, and she took it, licking her lower lip to capture the droplet of olive oil. "Delicious," she said.

"Some people call these Cretan olives, but we also grow them on Adras."

He reached into another jar, and stabbed a small light green olive. "These are *nafplion*. One of my favorites. The texture is firm and a little crunchy, and the flavor is even better. Slightly nutty, slightly smoky. These are a true table olive and perfect with a sprinkle of lemon juice and bit of dill."

She plucked the offered olive from the wooden fork and

popped it into her mouth. He was right. It was a little bit crunchy and deliciously salty and somewhat nutty. "That is amazing," she said.

"There is nothing better than olives and bread. Now we just need bread." He turned around, his gaze narrowing as it swept the kitchen. Everything was so tidy. There was no food out anywhere on the counters. "Chef used to have a bread box where he kept the loaves, and the leftovers, but I don't see it."

"I'll have a look," she offered.

And as she moved past him to search the pantry, he caught her by the neck, his hand wrapping around her nape, and drew her to him.

Kassiani felt a jolt of electricity as his head dropped and his lips covered hers. She felt another sharp surge of sensation as his mouth moved across hers. He was hungry and he parted her lips, claiming her mouth, making her weak in the knees.

She always responded to him, and desire washed through her, hot and needy, her body softening against him, her arms reaching up to wrap his neck and bring him even closer. Damen held her firmly and she relished the feel of his hard, warm, muscular body pressed to hers as well as the seductive promise of his shaft urgent against her belly.

Nothing in her life had prepared her for this heat and desire. This physical need matched her emotional need, creating a vast yearning for more. Being in Damen's arms made her feel powerful and vulnerable at the same time, and she wanted to be completely herself, and completely real. Was this love? Or was this lust? She didn't know. She wished she knew. She wished she'd had more experience because what she felt with Damen was incredible and consuming and she couldn't imagine ever feeling this way with anyone else. It was as if he had been made for her. His body was extraordinary, and the way he used his body was extraordinary. She loved his scent, his skin and the very shape of him.

Kassiani hated it when she disappointed him. She hated it even more when he hurt her, but she'd come to crave time with him. Truthfully, her day only really began once she saw him. The only hours that were important were the hours with him, and the only hours she felt truly alive were the hours in his company. Was that normal?

What was this terrible need she felt for him?

Kassiani slid her hands under his shirt, relishing the texture of his hot skin. She wanted her mouth on him. All of him. She wanted to wrap herself around him and never let go. Damen leaned her back against the marble counter, exposing her neck and throat. His lips traveled the length of her jaw, lighting fire beneath her skin. She whimpered, and whimpered again as his teeth scraped a sensitive place on her neck that made her desperate for more. Her whimpers always stirred him, and he growled against her throat, his hips pressing against hers, and then his knee was between her thighs, his knee grinding against her, driving her wild.

She felt wild now.

"Security cameras," he panted, peeling away from her to go punch buttons into a box on the wall. "Don't need to give everyone a show."

She smiled, answering breathlessly, "It would be a good show."

"You are shocking."

"But you like it," she flashed, as he closed the kitchen door, locking it before returning to her side. "You like that I can't get enough of you."

They made love on the marble island counter. Damen

took her in so many different ways. Kass prayed the kitchen was soundproof because tonight he took advantage of those jars of olives and the accompanying olive oil to feast off her, dribbling the oil across her breasts and down her tummy to her thighs. After he made her come with his mouth, the oil became a massage, and then a lubricant and used for an exploration of her most sensitive, private places. Each orgasm was more intense than the last, and the pleasure so overwhelming that there were moments where she thought she would break down and cry, and she did end up crying after the last orgasm, the intensity of the intimacy making tears fall. She didn't even know why she was crying, only that she felt spent, and turned inside out. Her body didn't hurt, but she felt him everywhere even now when he wasn't in her. She felt his imprint and felt his possession and so the tears came and she tried to hide them from him, but he gathered her to him and held her, her body slippery and shuddering against his.

"I'll get oil all over you," she choked.

"I already have oil all over me."

"We're a mess."

"Chef is going to have to sanitize this center island to-morrow."

She laughed unsteadily and Damen used the pads of his thumbs to wipe beneath her eyes.

"I think I push you too far," he said, drawing her back against him so that her head rested against his chest. "I fear I am too much for you sometimes."

"You haven't broken me."

"I'm not trying to hurt you," he said hoarsely. "That's the last thing I would ever want to do to you."

She lifted her head to look up at him. "But you like the forbidden."

"This is true."

"So how far is too far?"

"That is up to you. I suppose I push you to see where you will draw the line."

"I don't want to draw lines between us. I don't want walls and boundaries. I want to trust you," she said softly, breathing in the scent of his skin, nearly always comforted by his nearness and the warmth of his skin. It was in these moments where she could hear his heart, and feel him relax, that she felt most comfortable, and safe.

Despite the unpredictable quality of the lovemaking, Damen felt like hers, and he still felt like home, and she couldn't remember a time, or place, or person who had felt like home...until now.

She kissed the side of his neck, and then the upper plane of his chest. "My goal is to trust you," she whispered, "so *you* can also trust *me*."

She felt him stiffen and she loosened her arms, but didn't let him go.

His hands smoothed over her arms, a caress to her upper arm, before carefully, deliberately peeling her hands away from his shoulders. "Do not take this the wrong way, but it will be years before I trust you. I find trust a very difficult thing. It's why when I find the right staff, I keep them. I pay them well and reward their loyalty because it's vital I retain them. Turnover makes me uneasy. I like to know who is true."

"Then I hope you will discover that I can be trusted, and not because I am your wife but because I care about you."

He let her hands fall and he pulled away, taking several steps back, putting distance between them. His features hardened, his expression had shuttered. "I don't need those words. I don't respond to those words. I would prefer not to say things like that in the future. If you don't mind."

Kassiani blinked, confused. "I don't understand."

His broad shoulders twisted carelessly. "I don't trust strangers. I don't trust people in general. And I most of all do not trust words. Your actions will matter to me more than anything you can say. So please do not use words of affection here. Don't say I care for you. I don't believe it. I will never believe it. Just show me with your actions that you are a loyal wife, and with time your actions will reveal the truth."

A knot formed in her throat, matching the knot in her chest. His voice had become brittle and icy cold. His features looked as if they'd been carved from stone. This harsh, unfeeling man frightened her a hundred times more than their edgy sex games.

When he spoke so disparagingly about love and affection, it made the fine hair on her nape rise, and her stomach cramp, and her survival instinct scream at her to run. But run where? Go where? He wasn't a date. He wasn't a boyfriend. He was her husband. She had to make this work. She had to find a middle ground. "We have been spending a lot of time together," she said quietly, calmly, trying to keep her voice even and reasonable. "It's only natural that I will develop feelings—"

"No," he interrupted sharply. His jaw flexed, his body tensed. "No," he repeated more quietly. "Feelings are not natural to me. I find 'feelings' suspect, particularly any that you might have for me. Why would you have feelings for me? I don't give you affection. I am not tender in bed. I use you as I use my mistresses. I'm hard, and demanding, and when I take you I…"

She flinched at his words, but refused to look away.

"I warned you that first night. I said I was hard. I am hard. And it gives me pleasure to be ruthless. It turns me on—"

"Yes, I know. You've made that abundantly clear," she

said coolly, impatiently, masking her frustration and hurt. "But just because you like sex a certain way doesn't make you a bad person."

"But I am a bad person."

"I'm sorry, but I see no evidence of that, anywhere."

"Oh, no?" he retorted, in that deep, rough, unapologetic voice, before running his hand across the firm, carved plane of his chest, sweeping the sheen of oil lower, over his chiseled abdomen, and then down to his cock, which was thick and hard and fully erect. "Would a tender groom do this? Would he enjoy shocking his bride? Wouldn't a good man try to be a gentleman in front of his bride?"

She shrugged. "I don't know. I don't really care. What I care about is you, and me, and you don't intimidate me, and you don't threaten me. You're my husband."

"Then you're not as smart as I thought you were, because I'm dangerous, kitten, I am destructive. You should be careful around me. And you should be careful about what you feel, because if I were you, I wouldn't trust me. I know who I am, and I know what I am, and I'm not safe."

His words made her go hot, and then cold. She didn't understand how he could go from sensual and passionate to volatile and destructive, but she knew this—she wouldn't stand here and listen to this. For one, she didn't believe it, and she wasn't going to buy into the fact that he was some treacherous monster.

Kass turned, searching for her clothes, and then remembered she'd come to the kitchen with him just wearing her nightgown. She couldn't imagine putting the silk gown on now, not over the oil covering her body. It would ruin it, stain it. She liked this pretty nightgown too much to ruin it. She wasn't the type to be careless with her things.

Or her people.

She clamped her jaw tight, grinding her teeth together

to keep her emotion in check, as she grabbed his shirt from the ground, and stuffed her arms into the long sleeves. He was tall and his shirt had plenty of fabric and it covered her better than most of her sundresses. Once dressed, she scooped up her nightgown, pushed her hair back from her face and faced him, her expression smiling but fierce.

"Thank you for your attention, and your helpful advice," she said. "I've made a mental note of your wishes, but just as I can't control you, you can't control me, and I shall care for whomever I want—"

"I don't want feelings in our relationship."

"Desire noted. I shall do my best to refrain from expressing emotion so that our sexual encounters be more like the ones you enjoyed with your mistresses. Now please unlock the door and let me return to my room."

Kass tossed and turned all night, too upset to sleep well. She was so angry with Damen. And if he thought he could bully her into submission, he was wrong.

He had no idea who she really was, or what she was made of, and she hadn't survived life in the Dukas household to come to Greece and become a doormat. Maybe being a traditional Greek wife was off the table. Maybe she couldn't be what he wanted, but my God, she'd be what he needed.

She turned her pillow and punched it and then snorted as she remembered how he'd thrown his mistresses in her face.

Did he think she'd be jealous? Did he think that would hurt her, or offend her?

Of course he had mistresses. He was one of the wealthiest men in the world. Men like Damen preferred mistresses to girlfriends because they liked the power, and control, and they liked having a relationship on their terms.

In fact, it was one of Damen's past mistresses who had

told her father to make sure Elexis was beautifully waxed because Damen wasn't a fan of body hair. The former mistress had been happy to share a few helpful tips...since her father was happy to do something for her in exchange.

Kassiani was up so late that she ended up sleeping in the next morning, and the first thing she noticed when climbing from bed was that they weren't moving, and then as she pulled open the heavy blackout curtains she discovered they'd anchored in another harbor, and she'd been to this one before. Mykonos.

She was surprised they were here, because Damen had said he didn't want to take her to the same spots he was going to take Elexis, but at the same time, she'd really enjoyed playing tourist yesterday and she'd welcome the opportunity to explore Mykonos today...if that's what Damen had in mind.

She dressed quickly and left her room, going in search of her husband, but it seemed he'd already gone ashore. The captain informed her they were to take her to him in Chora, Mykonos, if she wanted.

And since she wanted to go to Chora, they set off immediately.

Damen was waiting for her on shore, and he arched an eyebrow when she stood on tiptoe and kissed his cheek. "Good morning, husband," she said sunnily, determined to at least start the day off on the right foot. "So what is the plan for today?"

"Chora is a traditional Cycladic village, and I thought we should wander the streets, visit my favorite bakery, stop in at some of the beautiful churches and chapels and then we talk business."

She felt a rush of excitement. "Business? As in Greek shipping business?"

"No, business, as in between you and me."

The excitement faded, but she tried to hide her disappointment, struggling for a nonchalance she didn't feel. "Then I'm going to need some serious coffee for that."

They made their way through the narrow streets, turning this way and that, until they reached the bakery, which wasn't up, but down, below street level. The medieval bakery's thick arched doorways, creamy white walls and flagstone floor attested to its age, and there were tables in the back for cozy seating and a delectable display of baked goods at the entrance.

"Best baklava anywhere," Damen said, "but for breakfast, I highly recommend the ham and cheese croissants, or the feta spinach pie. I never come to Chora without stopping here."

They squeezed past other customers to sit down with their coffee and feta and spinach pie at one of the little white-painted wooden tables in the back.

Kassiani concentrated first on her coffee, and then started on the warm, fragrant, savory pie. It was delicious, and the owner came out briefly from beyond the counter to welcome Damen back. The bakery was family owned and had been in business in this spot for two hundred years, with the bakery passing from one generation to the next. After George left them, Kassiani looked at Damen. "So are we here to sightsee, or talk business?"

Damen could hear that Kassiani was guarded, and her voice revealed wariness, too. He hated that he'd taken much of the joy out of her morning, but at the same time, he had to manage their relationship before it imploded.

Last night had turned into a proper mess, and he blamed himself for letting Kassiani get too close to him. She was wanting more from him, not less, and he didn't have more to give her. He'd reached his limits, and she needed to accept the reality of their marriage. Both good and bad.

This marriage was good for her. This marriage gave her advantages she'd never have as a single woman, living in her father's house.

But the marriage wasn't without cost. She didn't have a love marriage. This wasn't a relationship where the husband and wife became close…became best friends.

He didn't want or need a best friend. And he wasn't going to ever be a doting husband.

She needed to accept that this was a businesslike arrangement, a relationship based on clearly delineated jobs and responsibilities.

In the past, he had a contract with his mistresses. The contract spelled out how the relationship would work, and what his mistress could expect of him, and what he expected of her, and how she'd be compensated, as well. It was very black-and-white, and had nothing to do with feelings and emotions. It was a mutually beneficial arrangement that could be ended by either party at any time.

That was what he needed now—minus the clause about terminating the relationship. He and Kass were married. There was no divorce for them. But they could use a contract, something that would spell out needs and expectations. Kassiani might initially object to an agreement, but ultimately it would help her, giving her a better idea of Damen's wants and needs.

In hindsight, he should have had an agreement, or contract, for her on day one. He should have been more organized and logical. If he had been better prepared, last night's uncomfortable scene might not have taken place.

Although, he wasn't entirely sure that a contract would have saved them from all drama because Kassiani didn't play by the rules, but if it would help save them from a great deal of drama, that was a start. Because he didn't like surprises. He hated being caught off guard, and he hated feeling whatever it was he was feeling right now.

What he was feeling made his head ache and his chest feel heavy and tight as if he couldn't get enough air.

He wouldn't say he was panicking, because he didn't panic anymore, but the sensation was enough to make him remember who he had been as a young teenage boy, and how as a fourteen-year-old boy he'd been rendered helpless, and Damen despised the boy he'd been.

Damen despised weakness in himself.

Weakness was pathetic and memories of the past still managed to make him feel worthless and pathetic, which was why Damen didn't just allow things to happen. It's why he didn't welcome emotion. It's why he kept control of situations. And he needed that control back.

He needed Kassiani to follow his rules so Damen could close the door to the past, and keep it closed, and locked. Always.

Kassiani's breath caught as she watched Damen draw a folded envelope from his pocket.

She frowned as he pulled papers from the envelope, unfolding them and laying them in the center of the bakery table.

She forced a smile as she nodded at the paperwork. "So what do you have there? Honeymoon itinerary? A postnuptial? Something else even more intriguing?"

"It's just an agreement," he said, tapping the paperwork lightly, carelessly. "I thought it'd be useful for us."

She held her breath, containing her worry.

"I've always had one with previous relationships," he added. "The agreement is designed to streamline communication and reduce, if not eliminate, misunderstandings."

"How practical," she said brightly, suppressing the urge

to laugh, hysterically. What on earth was he talking about? And he couldn't seriously be referencing his mistresses again, or had there been some significant relationship she hadn't known about? "I'd love to have a look at this useful agreement."

"It's probably best if I go through it with you. I'm happy to read it aloud and then I can explain various points."

"That's not necessary," she answered, reaching for the creased paperwork. "Reading is one of my underutilized strengths." She wasn't just a good reader, but a speed reader, and it didn't take her more than a few seconds to understand what he'd given her.

It was a contract stipulating what he expected from her in terms of *behavior*.

Kassiani snorted as she turned the page, scanning the second sheet, and then the third, and finally the fourth. Finished reading, she dropped the paperwork on the table and leaned back in her chair to give Damen a long, level, concerned look. "I'd love to understand your rationale. What do you think this paperwork is going to accomplish?"

"It will simplify things between us."

"How?"

"You won't be confused about what I need from you, and you won't be surprised by my expectations, either."

She tipped her head, considering him. He was so ruggedly good-looking, and had the most amazing skills in bed, but goodness, he was also incredibly out of touch with reality. "My gut tells me this…document…was something you used to give your mistresses. And I am sure it was *useful* for them. But it's not at all beneficial for us, and I'm not going to sign it because there is no way it would work—"

"Why not?"

"Because you can't tell me what to feel, or if I'm allowed

to have feelings, including feelings of attachment. I'm not a hooker, I'm not a mistress, I'm your *wife*."

"This was not a love marriage. I do not love you, I will not love you, and I will not discuss love every single day."

Kassiani laughed, tucking a flyaway tendril behind her ear. "I only asked you once if you'd ever been in love. Once. And I never said I loved you. I never said I wanted to love you. I merely said I *cared* for you. Frankly, I don't expect you to love me after everything you said. I've accepted you have rocks in your chest instead of a heart. But your determination to control who I am, and how I feel, makes me think you don't just have rocks in your chest, but rocks in your head."

She stood up, leaving the paperwork on the table between them. "I'm not one of your silly mistresses," she said, voice dropping to little more than a whisper. "I don't need your money, either, but thank you for offering me a very generous allowance in exchange for keeping my unnecessary and unwanted feelings to myself. Thank you for thinking of me, and trying to be a good provider. I can respect that you're trying to give me something."

And then she squeezed between the small tables, and climbed the stairs to reach the street, the white skirt of her sundress swirling around her legs, her temper seething, her vision blurred because all she could see was red.

She didn't know how he did it, time and time again, but he had the ability to take a perfectly lovely morning and ruin it. Honestly, all he needed was sixty seconds and he smashed life's gorgeous possibilities in no time flat.

Damen caught up with her before she'd walked too far. "Where are you going?" he demanded.

"Back to the ship. I don't feel like dealing with tourists, or you, at the moment."

He blocked her progress down the street. "You can't just walk away from me every time you don't like what I have to say."

"You wanted a wife, and I wanted to be a good wife, but I realize I will never be a traditional Greek wife. I'm Greek American, and obviously more American than Greek because I wanted to laugh in your face when you presented your contract. It was ridiculous. Damen, you have a problem with control, and I'm not good with that. That was not part of the marriage deal. I never agreed to relinquish all control—"

"You said you'd make my comfort your chief goal."

"Yes, I did."

"Then understand that your emotions are making me uncomfortable."

"You make it sound as if I'm a hysterical female, crying and screaming and having tantrums from one end of your ship to the other. Have I cried on this trip? Yes. But I have only cried in the privacy of my bedroom—"

"It's actually my bedroom."

She threw up her hands in dismay. "Do you want your bedroom back? Would you like to move your wife to a guest bedroom? Is that where your mistresses usually sleep?"

His silence told her all she needed to know.

Kassiani laughed, because it was that, or scream, and she couldn't allow herself to lose control now, not after everything he'd said. "What were these other women like, the ones you love throwing in my face? I'd love to know more about your mistresses, and how they were such paragons of virtue."

"They weren't paragons of virtue," he said tightly. "But they understood the limitations of our relationship and didn't make excessive demands."

"Because they were grateful you paid their bills. I'm sure

you spoiled them with jewelry and trips and clothes, and they probably loved every little trinket and special treat, but I don't care about things, Damen. I don't care about the yacht, or your villas, or your numerous expensive cars. I've grown up surrounded by nice things, expensive things. What I want from you isn't trinkets and treats. I want honesty, kindness, happiness, respect. I want a marriage that is a partnership—"

"I don't do partnerships."

"My father thinks he and you are partners."

Damen's jaw tightened, and his expression hardened.

She lifted a shoulder. "You allowed Elexis to think she'd be your partner."

"Because she would have been happy with trinkets and treats and trips to London and New York and Milan for Fashion Week."

"Because she would have accepted your idea of a partnership." Her chin jerked up. "And she would have been happy with the lies and deceit because she would have been just as deceitful. She wouldn't have been faithful to you, and maybe you don't care. You wouldn't be absolutely sure, short of a DNA test, that your children were your children. And you probably would have been happier with a woman who pretends to care for you, but doesn't. You would be able to sleep at night knowing you got what you wanted— money, power and the illusion of control—while she got what she wanted—money, prestige and tremendous freedom away from you."

"You make me sound like a horrible human being."

"You don't have to be horrible," she said softly. "It's a choice you make." And then she shrugged and stepped around him, her shoulder bumping his chest as she pushed by, before continuing down the street, grateful she'd been to Chora before because it meant she knew how to get back to the harbor and out of these narrow, twisting streets.

The speedboat was waiting for her, as if it had never left, and it ferried her back to the yacht anchored in the harbor.

She kept her jaw set during the short trip, and as she climbed the stairs to the master bedroom. Once there she rang for staff and asked them to pack her things and move her to a different room, one that Mr. Alexopoulos's female guests usually enjoyed.

If he wanted his room, he could have his room.

And if he wanted a marriage, it was going to be a partnership.

She could appreciate the erotic sex, and she could handle his being dominant in the bedroom, but she wasn't going to be a doormat out of the bedroom.

She might not be beautiful, and she might not ever command admiration and respect from the rest of the world, but she refused to feel less than worthy in her new home.

Damen wandered around the charming old town with the whitewashed buildings and brightly painted doors in a temper. He didn't know which upset him more: the fact that Kassiani had moved out of the master bedroom, or the brazen announcement that she didn't need his money because she had her own. He also knew why she'd left the master bedroom—his flippant remark about it being his room had annoyed her—but he didn't understand why she felt it necessary to brag about having her own money. Of course she had money. She was an heiress. The Dukases owned large chunks of San Francisco's waterfront, a historic mansion in the most coveted neighborhood of the city, plus more valuable real estate all over the West Coast. So what did she think she was accomplishing by mentioning her wealth?

What did she think she'd accomplish by throwing her weight around?

After an hour of walking, he returned to the yacht, going to the master bedroom, but she was no longer there. He was informed by one of his maids that she'd changed rooms, taking a smaller room on another floor.

Temper stirred all over again, he descended a flight of stairs, and knocked hard on the door of the guest room she'd claimed as her own.

It took Kassiani forever to open it.

She stood in the doorway in what looked like comfortable yoga pants and a soft T-shirt, her long thick hair loose and tumbling over her shoulder. She looked up at him, eyes wide, expression innocent. "Hello, Damen. How was your morning?"

He had to draw a careful breath to check his temper. He was not going to fight with her. There would be no scene. "How are your new accommodations?" he asked, because he could match her at her game. She wanted civilized. He could give her civilized. "I hope the guest room will be sufficiently comfortable. The bed is much smaller, and there is no private deck, or I believe a jetted tub, but I suppose if you are craving a really long soak, you could use the master bathroom."

"Or I can visit your spa here on the yacht. It's a very well-appointed spa."

"I spared no expense," he agreed.

"I've been able to take advantage of the spa on a daily basis, so thank you."

He gazed down into her upturned face, thinking the softness of her mouth, the pale pink flush in her cheeks and her firm chin belied her inner strength. Kassiani was nobody's fool. He felt grudging respect. "So are you going to invite me in, or do I carry you back to the master bedroom?"

Her nose wrinkled. She appeared to think, her head cocked, a finger tapping her chin. "Hmm. I wish I had remembered the details of that agreement better. Because there *was* something in that document about me being available for sex, on demand, and it was strange, because in the United States we have television like that. You can watch whatever you want when you want. Is that what you are thinking I would be? A wife on demand? With my very privates on demand?" Her brows pulled and she gave her head a faint, frustrated shake. "Maybe I should have paid better attention to that agreement."

"I knew I should have read it to you."

He enjoyed the flash of outrage in her dark eyes. Her eyes glowed hot, the little sparks of gold unusually bright right now. If he had an issue with her, it wasn't with her desirability. He found Kassiani incredibly seductive. There wasn't anything about her body he didn't like. But she was never more beautiful and appealing than when she was unhappy with him. He usually didn't like angry women, but Kassiani in a temper was absolutely arousing.

He was getting hard just looking at her now, and seeing the defiant shine in her eyes and the set of her full lips.

Maybe he shouldn't be turned on right now, but he was, and he wondered if it was because she was the first woman who had ever truly stood up to him. He couldn't even remember the last time anyone had stood up to him. It was interesting. Maybe a little refreshing.

"I feel as if I need to prepare a statement or tutorial for you, my husband, because I am happy to be in your bed, when you treat me as an equal. I am happy to be in your bed when you respect me. But I won't be happy if you treat me as if I am something you own. I am not real estate. I am not your property. I am not a possession."

"You are making too much of the agreement. And there were benefits to you signing the agreement."

"Yes, I would receive extra bonuses with my allowance when we have smooth, drama-free weeks. To receive those bonuses, all I have to do is be compliant, serene and undemanding." She smiled up at him and yet her smile was fierce. "You don't like women very much, do you?"

He shrugged. "I don't like anyone very much."

"What happened to you to make you so...you? There are selfish men in the world, and there are arrogant men, and there are detached men, but you are without a doubt—"

"I really am not interested in discussing my personality," he interrupted, leaning his shoulder against the door frame. "Or whatever you perceive to be my personality—"

"Disorder," she now interjected.

"Or disorder you want to assign me." He smiled, and he could see that his smile infuriated her and his shaft just grew harder. What was it about her that made him want— even be willing—to engage her in these conversations? Because he didn't allow criticism from others. He didn't tolerate dissension, either. But with Kassiani, he gave her so much freedom. He was shockingly patient, and tolerant. And lenient.

He smiled again, aware that his smile would provoke her. "I really don't care about labels. I am who I am. I am comfortable with who I am." He stopped talking and waited, curious to see what she'd do now. And Damen was never curious about anything. He wasn't curious about anyone. What kind of power did Kassiani have over him?

The silence was thick and crackling with energy. Kass lifted her chin, and looked him in the eye, her gaze locking with his. She was so mad at him, he could see it in the quiver of her lip, a lip she punished by biting into it.

"Invite me in," he said lazily, even though nothing in his

body felt lazy. His erection ached in his trousers. His body tensed. He wanted to bury himself in her soft wet heat and make her arch and whimper and shatter.

"Or what?" she flashed. "You'll reduce my allowance? Take away my privileges?"

When he didn't answer quickly enough, she added, "And just what are those privileges, my dear husband? What do I get from this marriage besides money? Because there has to be something else I get from this relationship, otherwise what is my incentive to remain? I have money. I don't need your money. What I need is something I can't give myself. Have you ever asked yourself that?"

Suddenly the heat in his groin faded, and the warmth he'd been feeling cooled. He no longer felt like smiling. "What are you saying?"

"I'm saying I married you for companionship and friendship. I married you so I'd have someone to share my life with. I didn't marry you so you could constantly control me and lecture me and make me feel worthless. My father did that quite nicely and I've had enough of being marginalized. I expect better of you. In fact I *demand* better."

Ice water seemed to wash through his veins. Damen stiffened. "This is not the way to entice me into your bed, kitten. I do not respond well to demands. Not from anyone."

"I want you to take me seriously. I want you to respect me the way I respect you."

"But you don't sound respectful. You sound like a spoiled, rich woman who thinks she is entitled to whatever she wants."

Kassiani flinched. "You are calling *me* entitled?"

He shrugged. "If the shoe fits?"

"It doesn't!"

"If you say so," he added with another careless shrug before turning around and walking away from her.

* * *

Kassiani refused to give in to tears. She wasn't going to cry, not again today or tonight. But her guest room, even though luxurious, felt like a cage and she couldn't bear feeling trapped so she went down a floor to the living room and dining room and its expansive deck so that she could walk outside on the deck and try to calm down.

Damen had called her *entitled*. Clearly he—captain of his universe—didn't know what the word *entitled* meant.

CHAPTER EIGHT

KASSIANI CHANGED INTO one of her swimsuits and headed upstairs to the pool deck with one of the books she'd brought to Greece with her. They were at sea again and the afternoon was warm, and as she stood at the railing she welcomed the breeze and the panoramic views of shimmering water dotted with distant islands. The Aegean was truly remarkable and she loved how the rich sapphire sea lightened to turquoise and aqua as the yacht approached islands with their shallow bays and inlets.

It was a shame they hadn't spent more time on Mykonos today.

It was a shame that she and Damen couldn't get along. She could almost understand why he wanted a contract... He wanted peace. He wanted undemanding companionship. She could respect that. But she didn't like how he went about it. She didn't want to be paid to be kind, and pleasant. She was his wife!

After swimming several laps in the pool, Kassiani climbed out and claimed one of the lounge chairs, and tried to read, but her thoughts kept circling back to Damen.

He was such a puzzle. Something had happened to him at some point that had made him mistrustful. Something rather terrible.

She didn't know what it was, and she wished she didn't care, but she did. When she and Damen weren't fighting about power and position, she really enjoyed his company. He was smart and driven and utterly gorgeous, which made him fascinating.

And then as if her thoughts had conjured him, he appeared on the pool deck.

"Is this lounger taken?" he asked, pointing at the chair next to hers.

"I was hoping my husband would claim it, but he's gone, working."

"Your husband is working on your honeymoon?"

"Tragic, I know," she answered lightly. "But he's brilliant, and really successful, so I try to be understanding."

"Is that so?"

"Yes, and please don't tell him, because it will only upset him, but I like him." She smiled wryly. "Do you still want the lounge chair?"

Damen smiled crookedly, and creases fanned from his gray eyes and he looked young and rather boyish. "That was a lot of information. I'm not sure your husband would appreciate you spilling intimate marital secrets to strangers."

"No, he'd want to tie me up and maybe put some nipple clamps—"

"Kassiani!" Damen choked on smothered laughter, before dropping onto the foot of the lounge chair. "That should not be mentioned outside the bedroom."

"You have so many rules," she answered. "It's hard to keep up. You might want to have one of your secretaries type them all up and put them in a binder or something. That way I'll have a marital reference manual."

He laughed again and gave his head a shake. "You are nothing like your sister."

"Oh, I know. My father couldn't manage me at all."

"No, I'm quite sure he couldn't. You are trouble."

"I take after his sister. The one that never married." She grimaced. "She was lovely but so misunderstood."

"Just like you."

"Oh, Aunt Calista was far prettier than I am, but I think

we both have the same brain. She was miserable. I don't want to be miserable."

"I don't want you miserable, either." He hesitated, his expression growing sober. "But we're struggling, aren't we?"

She nodded. "And I don't know how to change to be what you want me to be."

"I don't know how to change, either."

She nodded again, and looked out at the sea, still glimmering that stunning blue. Her heart felt suddenly too heavy for such a beautiful place. Damen baffled her, he did.

He could be truly awful at times, and yet she still somehow found him terribly appealing. She wished she wasn't so attracted to him. It would make dealing with him far easier. As it was, her pulse was a little too fast and her senses a little too stirred. He looked so fit and virile in his linen trousers and fine wool knit shirt, the soft fabric of the black shirt wrapping his biceps and muscular chest as if it had been made for him, that her heart raced, the same wildly distracting feeling she had when she drank too much black coffee.

"What do we do, then?" she asked at length, hating the helpless feeling.

"I don't have friends. But maybe we try to be friends. Or treat each other as if we'd like to become friends."

The corner of her mouth lifted. "Okay. Starting...now?"

"Yes, and in the spirit of friendship, would you like to have dinner with me tonight? We'll meet in the living room for a predinner cocktail and some light conversation before a nice meal."

She held out her hand, her smile impish. "You have a deal."

Kassiani dressed with care for dinner, choosing a long burgundy chiffon gown, with black beading on the neckline and delicate burgundy wispy sleeves. It was a dress she'd planned to wear to Elexis and Damen's rehearsal dinner, but with Elexis disappearing, the dinner hadn't happened and the gorgeous dress hadn't yet been worn.

She drew her long dark hair into a side ponytail and slipped on the pair of burgundy heels. She felt very glamorous even before she added some black pearl teardrop earrings.

Kassiani arrived early and, seeing the living room still empty, opened the sliding glass door to step out onto the deck. The sky was a dark purple and in the distance she could see lights twinkling on a small island, and there was another small island on the other side. Beautiful Greece with the sparkle of water and light everywhere.

She breathed in the cool night air, and shivered a little at the breeze. She probably should have brought a wrap. Deciding she'd be better off inside, she entered the living room just as a young housekeeper began to plump the living room pillows on the two low linen-covered sofas. The maid, who seemed to be close in age to Kassiani, then took a soft cloth from her apron pocket and wiped down the various tables, and along the glass-and-chrome coffee table.

The maid startled when she spotted Kassiani, and Kassiani apologized for frightening her.

The young woman answered in broken English that she didn't speak good English. Kassiani switched to Greek, apologizing for not being terribly fluent in Greek. The maid laughed and Kassiani smiled, too.

"Where are you from?" Kassiani asked, still speaking Greek.

"Adras. It is a small island near Chios."

"Isn't Mr. Alexopoulos from there?"

The woman nodded. "I come from his village. Many

of us on the ship come from the village. He is very good about helping us find jobs."

Kass was surprised. She'd gotten the impression that Damen had few ties to his childhood home. "Have you worked for Mr. Alexopoulos very long?"

"Two years. Ever since I finished high school. That is Mr. Alexopoulos's rule. He will help everyone on the island to find jobs, but they must first finish school. He says education is very important."

Kassiani was pleasantly surprised to hear this. She respected Damen even more for stressing the importance of education with the young people of his hometown. "Even the girls?"

"Especially the girls. He said it is vital that women have options." Her smile turned wistful. "But sometimes those options mean we must leave home. That is the difficult part."

"You're homesick?"

The woman adjusted a chair and then squared a large glossy book on the low coffee table. "It's easier now. It was difficult in the beginning. I've learned from the others that being homesick is natural. Some find it worse than others. Some girls, they just want to go home as soon as they can."

"Does Mr. Alexopoulos allow people to return home?"

"But of course. He is the best employer. Everyone wants to work for him, and he finds us jobs, good jobs with benefits and three weeks paid holiday every year. That is a lot for us in Greece. Some people use their holiday to go home, others like to travel. I went to Croatia for my last holiday. I enjoyed it very much."

"When do you go home next?"

"In October, for olive picking. Everyone goes then. It's our economy."

It was on the tip of Kass's tongue to ask if Damen returned home then, too, when Damen suddenly appeared in the living room door, dressed in black trousers and a black shirt, open at the neck, revealing his strong, bronzed throat. He looked devastatingly attractive.

The maid, spotting Damen, bobbed her head and murmured a shy greeting to her employer before swiftly exiting the room.

Kassiani watched her go and then turned to face Damen. Her husband. It was still so strange to realize this man, this gorgeous man, this dazzling man, was her husband.

Kassiani cleared her throat, trying to hide some of her butterflies. "That young woman in housekeeping said she was from Adras, and she was telling me you provide incentives for helping the young people stay in school. I find that most admirable." She hesitated. "I wish you would tell me things like this. I wish you would tell me things about you. I learned more about you from talking to her for five minutes than I learned after spending five days with you."

"I don't like to talk about myself."

Kass sat down on one of the couches, gently smoothing the delicate chiffon of her skirt. "But don't you think it would help *us* if I knew *you*?"

"Maybe." He walked to the sleek bar in the corner, and moved bottles and decanters around. "Can I pour you a drink?"

"Yes, that would be lovely. What do you recommend?"

"What do you like?"

Her nose wrinkled. "I don't actually drink very much. And I know it's Greek, but not ouzo tonight."

"Something a little fruity and fizzy, then?"

"Please."

"Your Greek is a little rusty," he said, uncorking a bottle of champagne and then adding a splash of a dark ruby liqueur. "But better than your father led me to believe."

"I grew up speaking Greek, and I understand it fairly well, but you're right, it's been years since I actually spoke it."

"Did you attend a Greek language school in California?"

"No, Dad's parents only spoke Greek to us."

"I think I remember Kristopher mentioning his parents lived with you for a number of years."

"Yia-yia did. She joined us when Pappous died. My dad wanted them to join us in San Francisco sooner, but Pappous preferred Greece. He said San Francisco was too cold and gray for him."

"Your grandfather was right. It's miserable in summer."

"Not always. It can be nice."

He carried a crystal flute to her, the golden champagne now a pretty pink hue. "Not my memory," he said, handing her the glass. "I was there once visiting friends. It was your Fourth of July. The fireworks in the marina had to be canceled due to fog."

"That does happen," she agreed. "But it's almost a joke to those of us who live there. Will we see the fireworks? Won't we? And if the fireworks are canceled, you just watch them on TV." She sipped from her flute. "Mmm, this is nice. What is it?"

"Champagne with a generous splash of Chambord."

"I like it."

"The cocktail was inspired by your dress. You look beautiful tonight."

The quiet sincerity in his deep voice made her heart jump and her stomach flip. "Thank you," she whispered, touched, flattered. "I feel pretty tonight. Not normal for me."

"I'd like to destroy the person that filled your head with lies. You are beautiful, Kassiani. You are beautiful inside and out."

She opened her mouth to argue and then thought better of it. She and Damen argued too much as it was. "Thank you," she said instead, aware that she was blushing. For a moment she was too flustered to concentrate and then she remembered the young woman from housekeeping. "The maid—"

"Neoma," he supplied.

"You know her name?"

"I know the names of all my staff. I hire them myself."

She was silent a moment, processing. "Neoma says she goes home every October when it's time to pick olives."

"The majority of my staff do. Olives are Adras's chief economy. Olives and honey."

"Do you go home—"

"Adras isn't home."

She suppressed a sigh. "Do you go back for harvest season?"

"I have."

"Do you have your own groves?"

He hesitated. "I own all the groves on Adras."

"All?"

"I essentially own Adras."

"What does *essentially own* mean?"

"I bought the island."

"Can you do that?"

He shrugged. "It was privately owned before, so it was a straightforward purchase, but over time, I've complicated things by encouraging the village to grow, and the people to assert themselves in terms of commerce. I thought it would be healthier for the people of Adras to have true economic independence. So while many on the island do work for me, they also have other options."

"But the main source of income comes from the olives?"

"Olives and olive oil, yes."

"Is there any tourism?"

"There has always been some during the summer, but once summer ends, tourists return home. So a few years ago, a half dozen of my more intrepid locals created a working holiday program, and it was so successful that this year, the accommodations are already fully booked for this fall."

"What is a working holiday?"

"It's where tourists come for our harvest season on Adras, and they stay in one of the small traditional Greek houses in the village, are served traditional Greek meals and exposed to our local culture, and in return, we put them to work in the groves, picking olives."

Kassiani was fascinated. "People *pay* to do this."

"Yes, and willing to pay a great deal for the privilege of working in our groves."

"Do they actually help, or do the tourists get in the way?"

"Probably a little of both, but these aren't the tourists that like being pampered on a cruise ship or luxury resort. They're adventurous and are looking for new experiences, and being part of Greek culture is exciting for them. They have a fair amount of time off, and they enjoy exploring the island in their free time. They ride bikes and visit the beaches, and want souvenirs to take home so they spend money in the village, buying the honey and olive oil soaps and various olive oil products. They also eat in the *taverna*. They drink. They bring life to the little town."

"You don't mind them roaming about on your island?"

He shrugged. "I'm hardly ever there. And I don't think of it as my island. I bought it so that I could give it back to the people of Adras."

"Have many Americans participated in the work holiday program?"

"No Americans yet. Most have been from Holland and

Scandinavia. Americans don't seem to like taking their vacation days, or at least working on their vacation."

"I think it's a fantastic idea. I'd love to do it."

"You're not going to pick olives."

"Why not? Haven't you worked in the groves?"

"That's different. I was born in the village. You're a Dukas—"

"What does that have to do with anything? I'm Greek. The olive harvest is sacred in Greece."

"Adras's work holiday program is for seasoned European travelers who want authentic experiences, not my wife, or the lady of the estate. Women like you do not belong in the groves, or in the olive press. Period."

"Even if I want to help?"

"It's not up to you."

"Why not? Maybe I can't be a traditional Greek wife, but can't I try to participate in Greek life? Locking me up in your villa will only create distance between me and the people who live on Adras."

"As it should be. The villagers aren't there to be your friends, or your playthings. They have their own lives and you're not part of it."

Kassiani's jaw dropped. "That is so incredibly offensive."

"Maybe. But it's better that we are clear on this point now, because I am quite serious about this, and if it's a problem for you, we simply won't ever go to Adras—"

"You have a ridiculous need for power." She jumped to her feet, and set her flute down on the table. "And this marriage is doomed if you think issuing me orders is going to help bring us closer!"

"I don't understand your obsession with closeness."

"It's not an obsession!"

"Maybe because you were inexperienced when we married you don't realize we have a really good physical relationship, one that is mutually satisfying—"

"It's sex, Damen."

"Yes. Good sex."

"But it's only sex. That is all we have. Any conversation out of bed is fraught with tension because you don't want me to think, or challenge you, or have a brain. In your mind a good Greek wife is little more than a blow-up doll—"

"So tell me, kitten, is this how friends talk to each other? I'm serious. I don't have many friends. Is this the way for us to be friends?"

She could see from his expression that he was serious. He really wanted to know.

Did he truly have no friends? No one close to him?

Sympathy flooded her. She sat back down on the low linen sofa. "It depends," she said carefully. "Friends—real friends—are honest with each other. Real friends want the best for each other. Friends understand you, and try to be supportive of you."

He said nothing and her brow furrowed. "Surely you had friends when you were younger, Damen? Surely there were people in your life that mattered?"

"Were, yes, but they're not…there…anymore."

"Why not? What happened?"

He shrugged, powerful shoulders rolling beneath the luxurious fabric of his shirt. "I became me," he said flatly, before stepping past her and exiting through the glass door to the deck.

CHAPTER NINE

DAMEN GRIPPED THE railing tightly, and leaned forward, his gaze fixed on the water, watching the slow churn of the wake and where the water foamed white.

He was tired, and frustrated.

He truly wanted to make things smoother, but he didn't know how to be this person she wanted him to be.

Kassiani didn't understand that his past wasn't a charming fairy tale. Yes, he was self-made, but the climb up had been horrendous. He'd accomplished huge things because he had no choice. If he didn't become someone powerful, someone significant, he would have cracked and shattered.

If he hadn't channeled his fury, if he hadn't been bent on revenge, he might have been swallowed by his rage and pain.

Instead he channeled it, over and over until it became a discipline—head down, mouth shut, work harder.

Head down, mouth shut, work miracles.

Head down, mouth shut, change the world.

Change the world, or at least those in his sphere who were like him—helpless, dependent—so that poor people without choices and options didn't have to be helpless and dependent. And his efforts were making a difference. His efforts had already changed the future for people on Adras, especially for young girls and women who aspired to be more. And his success meant they didn't have to ever be in his position—trapped, cornered, without options.

But knowing that he'd accomplished that didn't ease how unsettled he felt right now.

Damen thrived on challenge and success. He never accepted less than victory. But Kassiani's claim earlier today that she was little more than a blow-up doll rankled.

No, he wasn't comfortable with emotions, but that didn't mean he wasn't trying. Because he *was* trying. It's why he searched her out when she was at the pool, and why he'd invited her to dinner, and why he'd asked Chef to make a special meal. He wanted to try to smooth things over. He wanted to try to make things calmer, but if Kassiani truly wanted intimacy, then she needed to give him time. She wasn't going to get more from him by squeezing him. If she truly wanted more, she needed to push less.

Kassiani sat back down after Damen stepped outside, shoulders slumping, fear enveloping her.

She didn't know how to do this. She didn't know how to be the wife he wanted. She only knew how to be herself—a misfit.

Perhaps if she had more confidence she could trust that everything would be okay, but she had no experience to judge this relationship by. It was her only relationship and she was making such a mess of it.

It would be so much easier if she cared less.

It would be so much better if she didn't want to make him happy.

But she did. He was difficult and demanding but he was also gorgeous and fascinating and maddening and addictive. He entered the room and she felt something inside her light up. When she didn't see him she felt restless and incomplete until she was back together with him.

And maybe part of her anxiety was because she never had been in a relationship before. Maybe she didn't know

what relationships were like. Maybe she was the problem…
she with all her fears and insecurities, insecurity from never
being wanted, never being desirable, never being good
enough for even your own family.

"You didn't go." Damen's deep low voice came from
the glass door.

She straightened quickly, hoping she didn't look as woe-
begone as she felt. "That seemed too easy. Apparently I
enjoy conflict more than I should."

She was rewarded with a faint smile. Creases fanned
from his eyes. "I think you do like to poke the bear."

"I'm sorry."

"It takes two. I'm not one to back away from a good
fight."

"Have you ever been in a fight? A real fight?"

"Of course."

"Are you a good fighter?"

"I win more than I lose."

"I don't doubt it," she said softly, feeling a perverse
thrill that he could handle himself so adroitly in a fight.
"My brother, Barnabas, doesn't win many. I remember
my dad once telling him only fools start fights they can't
win."

"So your brother has given up fighting?"

"He has people now who manage those situations. He
calls them security, but honestly, they're more babysitters
than anything else." She looked up at Damen, feeling terribly uncertain about everything. "I don't mean to be difficult. Apparently I just am."

Damen smiled faintly. "You're not that difficult. You are
who you are, and I like you."

Some of the tension in her chest eased. "You do?"

"You're my wife." He must have seen her disappointment because he shook his head, his expression rueful. "I

don't have to like you. There was nothing in the agreement saying we had to like each other. I like you because I do." One of his dark eyebrows lifted. "Or do you want to argue about that, too?"

She shook her head swiftly. "No. Should we do something else?"

The air suddenly felt electric and he gave her a slow, scorching look. "I can think of a thing or two," he said lazily. "But before I make you dessert, I think we should have some dinner. Chef has set a table for us upstairs in the wine bar. Care to join me?"

"Yes." She rose, smiling. "Absolutely."

Their footsteps were muffled by the carpeted curving staircase in the yacht's stairwell.

The enormous venetian glass chandelier hung from the ceiling, and descended midway down the first flight of stairs, filling the stairwell with glorious gold-and-rose light. The rest of the yacht's interior was sleek with mahogany walls and gleaming wood and chrome railings, and for a moment Kassiani allowed herself to be distracted by the stunning glass artistry and how the golden base covered with countless rose, violet and red glass flowers reflected glittering light onto the adjacent walls and banister railings, before she caught a glimpse of her husband's even more striking profile.

Butterflies filled her tummy and her pulse did a jagged little dance. She was so attracted to him, and found him ridiculously compelling.

He caught her side-glance and gave her a faint smile. "What are you thinking?"

"Just that you are deliciously handsome."

"You flatter me."

"I don't. Women must fall all over themselves trying to get close to you."

Her words had the wrong reaction. His brow darkened and his features hardened. "Some women only want what they can't have," he said. "And I don't care about any other woman. Just you. You are my wife, and I will be loyal to you." They'd paused at the top of the stairs, and he lifted her chin, his gray gaze holding hers. "I don't have a mistress now. I won't take another mistress again. There won't be any affairs. You are my wife and I promise you my fidelity. Do you understand?"

She nodded.

"Good. Because I expect the same of you."

"Of course," she answered, somewhat perplexed by how serious he'd become. But then, Damen was serious. He was clearly scarred from a past she didn't yet understand.

Dinner was delicious, with course after course, from shrimp *saganaki* to scallops and pasta. Kassiani ate until she couldn't take another bite, and then coffee and dessert were served, a gorgeous Greek custard named *galaktoboureko* that melted in her mouth.

Finally she truly was finished and she glanced up to discover Damen watching her.

The dark intensity in his gaze made the air catch in her throat and the blood heat in her veins. Just a look from him and she went hot and molten. "What are you thinking?" she asked, her voice dropping, growing husky.

"I think you know."

"Tell me anyway."

"I'm sick of words," he said.

She flashed a provocative smile. "And I can't get enough."

He made a low rough sound that made her breasts tighten and her skin tingle. "If you're not careful I will have you on your knees worshipping me," he growled.

Her nipples hardened and heat rushed through her, making her prickle and ache. "I'd never say no to you."

The air thickened, heavy with desire. Damen pushed away from his seat at the table, and approached her. "Have I told you that you're not as demure as you look?"

"I do believe you've told me I'm not demure at all."

"Ah." He hit a button adjacent to the bar and the curtains across the wine bar closed. He pressed another button and she heard a soft click, as the door locked.

"No security cameras here?" she asked.

"I've already taken care of that." He took a step away from the bar, pointing to the marble floor. "Come here."

She rose from the couch and crossed the room, going to stand before him. Lifting her chin, she gazed up at him, her eyebrow arching.

"Closer," he murmured.

Her pulse raced and she took a step closer. They were now practically touching. Again she looked him in the eye, and his upper lip curled. And then he reached for her, and turned her around to unzip her delicate chiffon gown, slipping the sleeves from her shoulders to allow the gown to puddle at her feet, revealing her black lace bustier and garter belt. He hissed a breath.

"What is this?" he demanded.

"Something sexy for you."

His hands cupped her breasts and then shaped her waist. "Where did you get it?"

"I brought it with me from California. If you have a beautiful dress, you should wear beautiful undergarments, don't you think?"

"I do," he answered almost reverently, stroking her hips and then the curve of her buttocks. His fingers slipped between the garter belt, and her skin. "You are testing my control."

"And you do hate that," she teased, unbuttoning his shirt, before reaching for his belt, and then unfastening his trousers.

Naked, he swung her into his arms and carried her to the low dark leather couch in the corner, the leather soft and supple as he laid her on her back.

For a long moment he just looked at her, and then he caught her hands in one of his and raised them over her head, pinning them to the leather. With his other hand he explored her curves, and then under the black satin of her panty to the damp heat between her legs. "So wet," he murmured, finding her delicate nub and making her shudder with pleasure.

He straddled her hips, his shaft hard and heavy against her belly. "What do you want?"

"You."

He needed both hands to rip the panty in half, and then he moved down her body to kiss her where she was so warm and wet. He was so good with his hands and mouth that she climaxed far too quickly, and then he shifted his weight, and she welcomed him back into her body, where he seemed to be a perfect fit.

They made love on the wine room's leather couch, and then again later in the master bedroom. It was past midnight now, and Kassiani was trying to decide if she should return to her room, or stay put for the night.

"Stay here," he said gruffly. "I can't have my wife running out of the room after we make love."

"You run out of the room."

"I don't run. I never run."

"But you do leave."

"I can't spend the night with anyone. I don't sleep when in bed with someone else. It's not personal. I promise you."

"Even as a boy?"

"Kass," he growled.

She snuggled closer. "Okay, no more probing questions tonight." She closed her eyes, relishing the feel of his hand as he stroked her back and her hip. She wished he would stay with her all night. She so very much liked it when they were together, like this. After sex he was so calm and relaxed. It was almost as if he was a different man.

She was almost asleep when she heard him ask abruptly, "So how much money do you have?"

Kassiani frowned sleepily, trying to figure out what he meant. And then she recalled the conversation he was referring to and tried to shrug it away now. "Not enough to rule the world, but enough to have a little nest egg should I need to take care of myself."

"You won't ever need to do that. It's my job to take care of you," he said after a moment. "Just as it's my job to protect you. I am responsible for you and the family—"

"We don't have a family yet."

"But we will. And you'll be a good mother."

"And you'll be a good father, too," she said.

He stiffened. "Don't say that. Friends are supposed to be honest. We're supposed to be honest with each other, aren't we?"

"I think you will be a good father. I think you'll learn to open up more—"

"I wouldn't count on it."

"I'm an optimist." She pressed her fist to his chest. "And I'm not giving up on you. I'm determined to get to know you. You don't talk about your past. You don't talk about your family. You don't talk about anything personal, or important, with me. Why can't you let me in a little bit? How would it hurt?"

"I don't like the past. I like the future. It is the future that interests me."

"I respect that, I do, but can't you see that you're a mystery to me? I know virtually nothing about you, whereas you know everything about me and my family—" She broke off, grimacing. "Well, not me, per se, but the Dukas family."

"So what do you want? To tour my village? See the house where I was born?"

"Yes! Yes, please. Are you serious?"

He groaned. "No!"

"Why not? It would be fun. I'd love to see where you were born and raised. I'd love to visit the village and see the houses that you rent to the tourists and the olive press—"

"Slow down." He kissed her, to stop the stream of words. The kiss grew heated, and she was breathless by the time he lifted his head.

His black brows tugged into a line and, frowning, he pushed back her long hair from her face, tucking the strands behind one ear and then the other. "I wasn't being serious, kitten, no, but is that really what you want to do on our honeymoon? Visit Adras? Rather than Crete or Santorini?"

"Yes. It would be amazing."

"It's a very small island, and very rustic."

"All the better."

"You're going to be disappointed."

"I won't. I promise."

It took a day of sailing but by evening they would reach Adras.

Kassiani was excited, ready to see where Damen came from and ready to be part of his real world. She passed the afternoon peppering Damen with questions about his childhood on Adras. She noticed he was selective in which questions he answered. Sometimes he avoided saying anything at all and she'd let it slide at first but now they were within an hour of anchoring at Adras and she still knew virtually nothing about his family.

"Come on," she begged, turning over on her lounge chair on the sundeck, "tell me something about your parents. Are they going to be there when we get off the boat? Do they still live on Adras? Are they even alive?"

He sighed, and dragged his chair out of the bright hot sun and into the shade. "My father passed ten years ago, but my mother still lives in the village."

"What is the village name?"

"It's simply Town, or Adras Town."

"We won't be staying in the village, though?"

"No, we'll be at my villa. But I have a car and we can use that to drive around, so it's not as if you won't have a chance to go to town."

"Does everyone in the town know you're married?"

"Yes. Although some might still think I've married Elexis."

She fell silent, and tried to ignore the anxiety his words created.

"I can see the wheels turning," he said. "What are you thinking right now?"

Kassiani glanced down at the plain gold band he'd put on her finger during the ceremony nearly a week ago. It was far too large but at least it hadn't been worn by her sister. "Sometimes I forget you were ever supposed to marry Elexis."

He must have followed her gaze because he said, "As I said before, we'll get you a proper ring, with a big stone, when we return to Athens."

"I don't need a big stone. This is fine. This is mine."

"Your sister had—"

"Can we not discuss Elexis?" she interrupted tautly. "I realize it's natural to mention her but she's not my favorite person right now."

"Right now, or ever?"

She stared at Damen, her gaze searching. A lengthy silence followed. "We've never been close, no."

"Are you jealous of her?"

"We're four years apart and we have always had different interests, as well as different values. I admire her in many ways—she is the person I could never be—but it wasn't easy growing up in her shadow."

"I would think it's the other way around. It can't be easy being the big sister to a brilliant, precocious younger sister. I am sure she has had to struggle to find a way to be successful as herself."

"She's stunning. People love looking at her."

His broad shoulders twisted. "And I love looking at you."

Heat bloomed within her, heat and a whisper of hope that one day there would be more between them than just the physical. That there would be a relationship. Feelings. Love.

Kassiani abruptly stopped herself.

She couldn't let herself go there, not yet, because he certainly wasn't there. But would he ever be able to love her? Would he ever be able to give her what she needed?

She had things.

She needed love.

Heart aching, she forced her attention to other topics. "I remember hearing that some of your cousins would be attending the wedding, but not your mother. She didn't go to Athens, did she?"

"No. She doesn't like to travel."

"Then why not marry at the church in your village?"

"It wouldn't be proper or convenient. There are no hotels on Adras. There would be nowhere for the reception—"

"Your villa wouldn't be large enough?"

"The church wedding is important, but our family church in the village is humble. And the locals would be uncomfortable with the outsiders flooding the town. My mother, especially, would be uncomfortable with the attention. Far better to marry in Athens and keep that part of my life separate from my mother and those who know her."

"So she wasn't hurt by being excluded?"

"I offered to fly her in, she said no. I offered to send the boat for her. She said no. She doesn't like to be out of her element, and I can respect that. Why make her unhappy? She is a simple woman. There is no room in her life for wealthy or pretentious people."

"So you only see her when you return home?"

"Yes."

"And when was the last time you returned home?"

"To Adras?" He paused. "Christmas." Then he shook his head. "Actually, the Christmas year before last. It's been a while."

Almost sixteen months. Kass chose her words carefully. "You will introduce me to her?"

"Before we leave, yes."

"But not right away?"

"There is no rush. I would rather you settle in. Become familiar with the villa and the gardens and the estate."

"Are you worried that your mother won't like me?" she asked carefully, aware that most mothers did not like their daughters-in-law. Her paternal grandmother, Yia-yia, had certainly never thought Liliana—Kassiani's model mother—was good enough for her son. From the start there had been bad blood between her grandmother and mother, and it had never improved during the marriage, either. Yia-

yia had moved in only after Kassiani's mother and grandfather were both gone. "You do not have to worry about protecting my feelings," she added. "I will not be crushed if your mother doesn't like me."

"Are you truly so unlikable? Do you not expect anyone to enjoy your company?"

There was something in his tone that made her lips twist. He sounded almost affronted on her behalf.

"Would it surprise you to learn that I enjoy your company, kitten?" he added. "Or is that not allowed?"

The corners of her mouth curved, and she felt that whisper of hope return, even stronger than before. "It is allowed. I get fuzzy on the rules, but that is most definitely allowed."

The sun was still relatively high in the sky as Damen's yacht neared Adras. The weather remained almost unbearably perfect, and the colors of the Aegean were so clear and true it almost made Kassiani's heart hurt. The blue overhead teased the blue of the sea, and in the distance, she could see the dark green of the groves dotting the island. For a moment Kass was reminded of California's Napa Valley, and how the grapes rolled up and over the hills, but then the sun reflected brightly, blindly, off the water, and she was firmly back in Greece, with this intense brooding husband of hers who overwhelmed her in every possible way.

Feeling a prickle of awareness, she turned her head and discovered that Damen was watching her, and just like that, heat enveloped her, and an awareness of how he made her feel, and all the ways he pleasured her, and how easily he dissolved her defenses. Even without touching her, she felt breathless and weak. Or maybe that's because she remembered how he held her down on the couch and claimed her last night, taking her with slow, deep thrusts before withdrawing and slowly entering her again. It had been maddening and exciting and she'd begged for him to thrust faster, but he'd held off until she was panting and writhing and trembling and only then did he finally let her come. The orgasm had been intense, and he'd held her after, and in that dreamy place between pleasure and reality, she'd felt so close to him, so much a part of him, as if they were two halves of a whole, and whole only when together.

She knew it was an arranged marriage, but the love-making and sexual intimacy only served to make her feel more…more of everything, both good and bad.

"We're here," he said, breaking her reverie.

She blinked and focused on the island, and yes, they were close. The yacht was slowing down, too, carefully approaching a narrow dock that extended out into the water.

"It must be quite deep here," she said.

"It's not a good swimming beach, no," he answered. "But there is a fantastic view from the house." He gestured above, pointing to a mass of white buildings set among the green covering the slope. "My villa and pools are just there."

It took a little bit of time for the crew to moor the yacht, and while the crew was tying the ropes and dropping anchor, two open-air Jeeps came tearing down the mountain.

Damen offered his arm to Kassiani as they disembarked, and then thanked the staff before walking her to one of the lifted Jeeps with the large off-road tires. There was no step stool, or low sideboard to step on, and before she could even ask for help, Damen wrapped his hands around her waist, and lifted her into the vehicle.

Just the feel of him against her back, and his breath against her nape, made her breath catch and her skin sensitive.

"Could your mother please join us for dinner tonight?" Kassiani asked as he slid behind the steering wheel.

"No."

"Or at least, could she join us for drinks?"

"*No.* You'll meet her before we leave, but there is no need to introduce you right away."

"But there is! She's your mother, Damen. I'd like to have a good relationship with her, if possible, and it's disrespectful of me not to reach out to her early—"

"She's not going to be a big part of your life, Kassiani, and I'm becoming annoyed that you keep pressing the issue."

Kass balled her hands into fists. "So it doesn't matter what I want?" she said huskily. "It only matters what you want."

"Discussion closed."

She stared at him, hurt, and frustrated, and more than a little furious. What she felt didn't matter to him. She was not a real person, or a valuable person. In his mind she was just another thing he owned…another person to command. "I'm not your employee," she answered lowly, fiercely. "You cannot issue commands. Correction, you can, of course you can, but I don't have to listen, or respond to them. In fact, you'll discover I respond so much better when you treat me like an equal."

"I am not going to do this here," he ground out. "Not in front of my staff."

She averted her head, angry, and furious and hurt, so hurt, so impossibly hurt, and she didn't understand how in just a week he could make her feel so much when this was just an arranged marriage, and it was only a business deal.

Except that maybe she'd forgotten it was business.

Maybe the nights of intense lovemaking had done something to her head, and heart, because he was not a "business deal" to her. He was her husband. He was the man she wanted and needed. The man she craved. The man she…loved.

Her eyes burned and her throat ached. She'd been trying to fight the feelings, but they were just growing stronger.

"Buckle, please," he said as he started the engine.

She did as she was told, but her heart was somewhere in the pit of her stomach. Was it possibly true? Had she inadvertently fallen in love with her husband?

CHAPTER TEN

THE VILLA WAS EXQUISITE, and massive, sprawling in every direction, towers and squares, and courtyards with individual pools and fountains. It was also all new construction, elegant and contemporary without being cold. The white rooms had high ceilings and huge windows and every room seemed to have a sweeping view of the sea. The only color in the rooms were the touches of blue from the mosaic tiles in a pool, to the glazed pottery on an end table, or the woven textile pillows on chairs or the low linen sofas, while outside color came from the profusion of purple and pink bougainvillea blossoms.

Damen gave her an excruciatingly brief tour of the house before leaving her at a suite of rooms that he said were hers. "We're not sharing?" she asked as he headed out the door.

He paused in the doorway and glanced back at her. "I know where to find you every night."

She kept her tone light. "And where am I to find you? The villa is considerably larger than the yacht."

"Staff always know where to find me."

"I suppose that's preferable to your wife knowing."

"You're picking a fight."

She opened her mouth to protest, and then stopped herself. "You're right. I'm just…anxious."

"Why?"

"I want to make you happy—"

"Stop trying so hard. Just let things be."

"And I want to feel like we're family."

"That won't happen overnight. It will take time. When we have the children it will be more natural."

She knotted her hands at her sides, emotions running high. "What if it takes us years to have children? What if we can't—"

"We haven't even been married for a week yet. Why think the worst? It's just going to make you unhappy."

"You're right. I agree." She drew a breath to slow her racing heart. "It's just that I want us to *feel* married. I want us to be a real family."

"We're married. We are a family—even if it doesn't yet feel like it." His brow creased. "This is the danger of relying on feelings. They cloud facts."

"But I feel like you use facts to keep me at arm's length."

"Kitten, you're in my arms all night long."

Her eyes felt hot and gritty and her throat ached with all the emotion she was trying to hold in. "It might surprise you to learn that I hate conflict. I do. I don't argue with you to push you away. I'm not fighting with you to win some imaginary war, I'm fighting to get closer to you—"

"You're closer to me than anyone has been in years. Take that in. Let things be. Don't push so hard. It's not going to help us."

"I want to be your friend."

"Then listen to me. Listen to what I'm saying. I am comfortable with who I am. Pushing me for more will only result in animosity and increased distance, because this is what I am, and this is all I am, and you will not get more from me. Not now, not ever."

They didn't have dinner together that night, and he didn't come to her room. Kassiani was glad. Or so she told herself as she sat in a chair on her balcony, a soft throw from the foot of the bed wrapped around her for warmth. It wasn't a cold night but she felt chilled all the way through.

It was always this way with them. One step forward, a thousand steps back. She shouldn't be surprised. She should be reassured he was so predictable.

Except she wasn't.

The predictability hurt, just as his words earlier had hurt, badly. *"You will not get more from me. Not now, not ever."*

Kassiani pressed her chin to her knees, and hugged her legs tighter, determined to keep it together. She had to learn to keep herself strong. She wouldn't allow herself to be wrecked. She would try her best to be a good wife, but love shouldn't damage, and love shouldn't hurt this much.

What had changed him? What had made him despise love?

Something had happened to him. She needed to know so that she could understand and help him. And if he wouldn't talk to her, she'd find someone who would.

Damen couldn't find Kassiani the next day, and none of his staff could locate her, either. They all could remember seeing her that morning, or at lunch, and each one suggested a place to find her, mentioning the spot they'd seen her last—the dining room where she had breakfast, the sunroom where she'd been reading, the garden with the fountain, the patio where she'd had lunch. Multiple sightings, with the last about two hours ago, so she was around. So where was she now?

He was searching the lower pool and the terraced garden when he crossed paths with one of his gardeners. He asked the gardener what he'd been asking everyone. "Have you seen my wife?"

The old gardener nodded. "She'd borrowed a bike and she asked me how to get to town."

Damen suppressed a sigh of frustration. But of course she'd go to town, and of course she hadn't waited for him, or his permission.

He also had a sneaking suspicion he knew whom she'd gone to see in town. Because why would she listen? Why should she do anything he wanted?

Damen headed quickly to the garage and climbed into the nearest Jeep, before driving toward town, chest tight, temper humming.

He didn't want to be this angry, but if Kassiani tracked down his mom without his permission, she was in serious trouble.

It turned out to be a longer bike ride than Kassiani had anticipated, but once she reached the village, it wasn't very difficult finding Mrs. Alexopoulos.

Kass did have to stop and ask for people to repeat the directions more than once, but everyone she talked to seemed happy to point her in the right direction. People also seemed to know who she was, and greeted her politely, respectfully.

She rode down the narrow lane toward the simple two-story house with butterflies in her middle. Kassiani was nervous but determined. She needed to be a good daughter-in-law. She needed to be respectful and start things on the right foot with her new mother-in-law.

Mrs. Alexopoulos emerged from within, just as Kassiani showed up on her doorstep.

"Mrs. Alexopoulos?" Kassiani asked.

The woman inclined her head. She was surprisingly small, with a slim, wiry build. Her gray hair was twisted and pinned up and she wore an apron over her blouse and skirt. Damen must have inherited his height from his father but the light gray eyes seemed to have come from his mother, along with the high pronounced cheekbones.

"I'm Kassiani," she introduced herself in Greek, handing Mrs. Alexopoulos the bundle of flowers she'd gathered from one of the villa gardens. "Damen's wife. I wanted to come meet you right away."

Mrs. Alexopoulos took the flowers without much enthusiasm and carried them into the house, where she placed the bouquet in a jug she took from a sideboard. Kassiani had followed her into the house, hoping she was meant to follow, as so far Mrs. Alexopoulos hadn't spoken.

The house was just as simple on the inside as the outside. It was the house of a laborer with just one room downstairs with a small galley kitchen on one side, chairs near the hearth on the other, with the round farm-style table in the middle. A ladder in the corner provided access to the second floor.

"Damen didn't come with you?" his mother asked, finally speaking.

Kassiani felt fresh butterflies. "He was working this morning and I had nothing to do and wanted to meet you."

The older woman gave her a long, unsmiling look that did nothing to put Kassiani at ease. Maybe she had made a mistake coming here uninvited.

"How is my son?" Mrs. Alexopoulos asked.

"Well. He works a lot."

"Hmph." The woman studied Kassiani. "You are the other sister, yes?"

"I'm not Elexis, no." Kassiani suddenly felt like throwing up. This was most definitely a bad idea but it was too late to run away now. She'd wanted to come, and now that she was here she had to make this work. "I'm sorry you couldn't make it to the wedding. It was quite nice—"

"Was it? I heard you didn't go to the dinner."

"I got nervous. I'm not comfortable with crowds."

"I don't like crowds, either. Or people who pretend they are something they're not."

Kassiani didn't know what to say to that, uncertain if Damen's mother was implying that Kassiani was pretending to be someone she wasn't.

"How is he as a husband?" Mrs. Alexopoulos asked abruptly.

Kassiani's mouth opened and then closed. Again she didn't know how to answer. "He will be a good provider," she said at length.

"He wasn't cold as a boy. He was a good boy, with a good heart. Very loving."

Kassiani didn't want to betray Damen, and yet she desperately wanted to understand him so she could help him, as well as help herself. "He doesn't like feelings now," she said carefully. "He doesn't want love, but everyone needs love."

His mother's head tipped, her expression thoughtful. "He doesn't know you're here, does he?"

"No."

"Hmm. So you disrespect him?"

"*No.* I want to make him happy. I care very much for him." She struggled to find the words. "I had hoped maybe you could tell me how to…talk…to him. He is very…reserved."

"He doesn't talk."

"Did he ever?"

"As a boy, yes. He was—" she broke off, eyes darkening "—perfect."

Perfect.

Kassiani's heart seemed to fill her throat. She couldn't speak for a moment and she couldn't swallow. She looked away, blinking, fighting tears. She was tired and overwhelmed and it struck her quite forcibly that this visit wasn't a good idea. It would be what Damen called "pushing." It was the very thing he told her he didn't want her to do.

"I love him," she said softly, shoulders rising and falling as she glanced back at Mrs. Alexopoulos. "He doesn't want me to, of course, but it happened anyway. Life's funny that way, isn't it?"

The older woman studied her for a moment. "Ask him about Aida. Maybe he will tell you."

Kassiani was riding her bike back to the villa, silently repeating the name *Aida* to herself, when she spotted a dark green Jeep heading toward her.

It was the same kind of Jeep that she'd traveled in from the yacht to the villa and she had a sinking suspicion that it was Damen heading toward her now.

The weight in her gut turned to lead when the vehicle slowed and pulled alongside her. "Hello," she said to her husband as he shifted into Park.

"Nice ride?" he asked, his bronze arm resting on the steering wheel.

He was so unbelievably beautiful, and his mother's words came to her. *He was perfect.*

Kass's chest squeezed. He still was, at least physically. "It's a lovely day," she answered.

"Where did you go?"

"Into town. Heading back to the villa now."

"I'll give you a ride home."

"It's—" She broke off as he climbed out of the Jeep. She swallowed the rest of her protest and stepped away so he could place the bike in the backseat of the Jeep. "Great."

They drove in silence for several minutes and then Damen pulled off the road onto the shoulder next to a grove of olive trees thick with gnarled branches.

"I don't feel like playing games," he said tightly. "So let's not, okay?"

"Okay."

"Who did you see in town?"

"I don't know all their names—"

"Kassiani."

"And your mother."

He closed his eyes, rubbed at his temple. "Why?"

"Because she's my mother-in-law and it's respectful to take her flowers and pay her a call."

He held her gaze, as if daring her to say more but Kassiani's courage failed her. She did want to ask about Aida but now wasn't the time. Now was most definitely not the time.

Back at the villa, Damen handed the blue bike to one of the gardeners and then walked away from Kassiani as if he couldn't bear looking at her another moment.

Kassiani stood rooted to the spot, feeling sick and sad and dangerously close to shouting something at his retreating back, something that would bring him back but only create more tension. But at least he'd come back to her.

She wanted him with her.

She wanted him.

She loved him.

Kassiani pursued him, catching up with him as he was entering a handsome sophisticated office at the end of the corridor. His windows overlooked the water and a pristine garden dominated by a fountain.

He glanced at her as she closed the door behind him, one black eyebrow lifting. "Yes?"

"I think we should have your mother join us for dinner tonight, and if not tonight, then tomorrow. I know she'd like it—"

"You don't know her."

"But I should, shouldn't I?" She saw his expression tighten and she hurriedly added, "I don't have a mother anymore. I haven't had a mother since I was fifteen. I'd like to have your mother part of our lives—"

"She wouldn't understand our lives. She wouldn't appreciate the…extravagance."

"Maybe not, but shouldn't we at least give her the option? Why decide for her?"

He crossed the pale marble floor. "Obviously you don't trust me because you question every decision I make."

"I just want to be part of the decision making—"

"That's not going to happen."

"But if we're friends—"

"Maybe we're not friends."

"Damen!"

His powerful shoulder rolled. "Or maybe we are, as I'm going to give you the truth. I broke my mother's heart many years ago, and I hurt others many years ago, and I'm not going to let that happen again. End of story."

Kassiani held her breath, wishing his words didn't bruise her. Maybe they wouldn't bruise if she didn't care so much about him. For the first time in forever, Kassiani wished she was Elexis, because Elexis wouldn't care about Damen's past or any hurt he'd suffered. No, she'd simply be grateful for his wealth. She'd love the freedom Damen gave her. She would be able to party and shop and travel, perfectly content with an absentee husband, a man who came to her only when he had a physical need. An itch to scratch.

Kassiani's lips pursed in distaste. She didn't love Damen because he was rich. She loved him because he'd become hers. He, even with his hard edges, was her person. Her man. Her husband. And she wanted her husband to want her, and love her, the way she loved him.

"I respect that," she said carefully, "and since we are friends, I'm going to ask that you at least take time to consider my request. Maybe you don't need a relationship with your mother anymore, but maybe I do." And then she left the room before the conversation took a turn for the worse.

Damen exhaled as the door closed behind Kassiani.

He couldn't do this. He shouldn't have brought her here. Why he'd given in to her requests he didn't know, because it was a mistake having her here on Adras.

A mistake meeting his mother.

There was too much water under the bridge. Too much had happened, things that couldn't be undone.

Even if he could forgive himself, he couldn't forget. He shouldn't forget. And so he wouldn't forgive himself, either.

Kassiani paced her room hot and agitated. It wasn't until she caught a glimmer of the sparkling pool from her bedroom window that she realized an afternoon swim might help clear her head and calm her agitation.

The pool did feel wonderful, too. It was heated, but still refreshing, and it soothed her just floating on her back, soaking in the sun, letting her worries go.

Everything would be fine.

She needed to be patient.

She needed to keep fighting for Damen and their relationship. He was worth it. They were worth it.

A shadow stretched over the pool, blocking her sunlight. Opening her eyes, she saw Damen standing at the side of the pool. He'd changed from earlier, and was now wearing a dark suit with a white dress shirt.

She swam to the side of the pool and lifted a hand to shield her eyes. "Where are you going?"

"Back to Athens."

Her heart lurched. "Now?"

"Soon. I'm having your things packed. They've left dry clothes for you on your bed."

Her pulse drummed. Her stomach turned inside out. "Why are we leaving now? We only just got here."

"It was a mistake to bring you here."

"No—"

"You know I am not a fan of the past. I have done everything in my power to close the door on the past. I only brought you to Adras so you can see where I was born and raised, and you have seen where I was born, you have seen my childhood home, microscopic as it is. You have met my mother. And now we return to Athens so I can get back to work."

"And our honeymoon?" she asked.

"I can't do this anymore. It's not useful. It's counter-productive—"

"I thought we would have fourteen days together." She swam to the steps and rose from the pool, crossing the deck to retrieve her towel and wrap it around her. "You had promised Elexis fourteen days."

"That was Elexis, not you. I promised you nothing. You are not even supposed to be my wife."

She flinched. "Why do you have to fight dirty? It's ugly, and so unfair."

"Why do you have to probe and dig? Why can't you be happy with what I tell you? I have given you more of me than I have given any other woman—"

"Except Aida."

He stiffened, and paled, his gray eyes glittering against his sudden pallor. "What did you say?"

She swallowed hard. "Aida," she said more softly.

"What do you know of her? Who told you her name?"

"Your mother."

His lips compressed. Lines etched whitely at the corner of his mouth. "I should have never brought you here. I shouldn't have trusted either of you."

"She is your mother."

"Yes, and I am her son and I have paid all the debts I owe her. I have given everything to provide for her. She owns my first fourteen years. She cannot have my future."

"She said you weren't always like this. She said something has made you cold."

"You're making this up."

"I'm not. She said I should ask you about Aida—"

"Stop saying her name."

"Was she your girlfriend? Your lover?"

He made a hoarse sound and took a step away, turning his back on her. "You know nothing about anything—"

"Then tell me so I know something!" She went to him and put her hand on his back. "Damen, please talk to me."

"I cannot speak of it. I won't."

"But maybe if you spoke of it, I could help."

"No one can help. It is in the past. I won't go there. I won't open that door."

"And yet, my love, the door is wide open. The past is ruining your present. The past still holds you in its grip."

His back tensed, muscles rigid. "What happened is sordid. It was ugly. When I speak of it, I feel all that ugliness again and not just the ugliness, but the destructiveness. I want to destroy things... I want to destroy people."

"Who hurt you?"

He pulled away from her. *"What?"*

"Who hurt you? Or have I got it wrong? Damen, let me in. Let me help, please."

"What are you now? A psychiatrist? A psychologist? A therapist who is going to sort out all my problems?"

"So you know you have problems."

He swung around to face her. "Is this fun for you? Are

you enjoying yourself?" The savagery in his voice made her flinch. "Do you feel better about yourself now? No longer the pathetic daughter of Kristopher Dukas—"

"Why are you turning on me? There is no reason to make it personal!"

"Because you have made this personal. You insist on talking, and talking and talking even when I'm feeling sick and my skin is crawling with self-loathing, but this is what you want. You want to see me brought down, reduced to your level—"

"No. You're wrong."

"Am I?" He drew a deep, ragged breath. "You want to know who Aida is? I'll tell you. She was the wife of the man who owned this island. She was pretty and spoiled, and her husband was old and she didn't enjoy sex with him. She wanted a beautiful young virile man in her bed, and she picked me. I was fourteen. I didn't want to be her lover. I had a girlfriend. I'd been in love with Iris since we were five years old, and she was the girl I was going to marry. But Aida didn't care about what I wanted. She liked that I was big for my age, and muscular and had a handsome face. And so her husband forced me to go to her, and plea-sure her, over and over, because if I didn't, he'd kick my parents out of their house and take away their work and we'd be homeless. We'd be paupers. We'd have nothing. All I had to do was sleep with Aida and make her happy and life would be fine for all of us."

Kassiani had asked him to share the past, and now that he was, she wanted him to stop. She'd tried to imagine what would make him so hard, and what would make him so detached, but none of her imaginings had prepared her for this.

"For one year of my life I belonged to them. I was Aida's pet. The sex was both exhilarating and awful. She taught me how to make a woman feel good. But she also made me hate myself, and others. Part of our deal was that no one could know. No one could know the terms of this arrangement. I thought it was a secret. I was grateful my mother and father didn't know. It allowed me to at least keep my head up because as long as no one else knew, I could pretend it wasn't happening, that I wasn't this boy toy. But I was wrong, people knew. In fact everyone on Adras knew, everyone except my parents. And then they finally found out, just before my fifteenth birthday, and it was Iris who told them."

Silence stretched. Kassiani curled her fingers into fists and pressed them to her rib cage. Her heart was beating so fast. "Did Iris end things with you?" she whispered.

"No. She pitied me. She said she forgave me because she knew it wasn't my fault. But it *was* my fault. If I had been a real man I wouldn't have been manipulated the way I was."

"You were young—"

"Not just young, but poor and uneducated," he interrupted harshly. "I had no power. No control. That was my ultimate crime."

No power, no control. And suddenly so many of the jarring pieces came together in a wild tumult of words and recriminations.

His inability to feel. His inability to be physically intimate without erotic power games. His refusal to discuss the past. His desire for a wife who would be hard like him...

"Do you still love Iris?" Kassiani whispered.

"And there you go, stirring up the past. It has no bearing on the present. It is gone. Dead—"

"Not dead. It's very much alive, and it continues to haunt you even now, coloring every single thing you do today."

He made a dismissive sound and turned away but she followed him.

"Elexis," she said, chasing after him out of the pool area and up the garden path. "You wanted to marry Elexis because she was polished, and hard. You thought she'd be a good wife because neither of you would expect love, and therefore, you wouldn't hurt her, or disappoint her. Not the way you hurt, and disappointed, Iris."

"You don't know what you're talking about. Iris is nothing like your sister. She is nothing like you. She was just a girl, innocent and lovely—" He broke off, jaw tight, expression grim. "Enough. No more. *Please.*"

It was the first time she had heard him say *please* quite that way. He wasn't commanding her, he was begging her. *Begging.*

Kassiani felt a stab of pain. Not just because of his tone, but because of the way he'd spoken of Iris. With reverence. With love. Iris had been his first love and apparently his last love. "You should have married her," she said softly. "You might have had a chance at happiness—"

"Happiness doesn't exist."

"It does. Only you don't want to be happy. You'd rather keep torturing yourself over the past. But you could move forward if you wanted. You could have moved forward with Iris—"

"Iris is dead," he ground out, turning to grab her by the arms. He gave her a slight shake, silencing her. "Iris took her life after I left Adras."

Her lips parted but she made no sound.

"So no," he added, giving her another slight shake. "I don't feel and I don't care and it's better this way. I am happier this way."

Kassiani understood so very much more now, but understanding his secrets wouldn't make them closer, nor would it change the distance between them because Damen was determined to hang on to the pain. His pain was his motivation. His pain fueled his decisions, driving him forward.

His pain allowed him to be ruthless and hard.

She swallowed around the lump in her throat. "If you hated this place so much, why did you buy the island? Why make it yours?"

"It was my revenge on Spiro and Aida. They had over-extended themselves financially and were looking for an investor to help them save their business. Instead I forced them out. I took everything from them—their home, their livelihood, their reputation. The family had been here for generations and I wiped every trace of them out." He paused, and his upper lip curled. "It felt good. It felt great. It was maybe the happiest moment of my life," he concluded, dropping his hands.

Kassiani felt numb and nauseous. She reached for her damp towel, tightening it around her chest, unable to think of a single appropriate response.

"You might have excelled in school," Damen added mockingly, "but you know nothing about real life, and you know nothing about me. I am not a wounded man in need of saving. I don't wish to be saved. You see, the only time I feel, and feel good, is when I hurt others."

"No. That's the pain in you, that's not you. You are a good person, and you are worthy of love—"

"Stop it."

"I love you, Damen, but I need you to get help. I'll help you get help—"

"We're done here." He paused and then added even more flatly, "We're done."

They returned to Athens by helicopter. He had a driver chauffeur her to the villa in Sounio while he remained at his penthouse in Athens.

It was strange being back at the villa where it had all started. She was in the room she'd slept in as a guest of Damen's. This was the room he'd come to after they'd married and she'd failed to show up for the reception.

The room was familiar and unfamiliar at the same time. She had changed so much since she'd first arrived in Greece.

Kassiani couldn't sleep, though. Her brain felt as if it was on fire, her thoughts swirling, her pulse pounding. She couldn't catch her breath, not when everything seemed to be closing in on her.

Everything he'd told her explained his behavior, but it also made her grieve for him, and them. He'd been treated terribly—abused repeatedly for over a year—which explained why home was still so difficult for him. She hated what had happened to him, but he wasn't going to let her in, and he wasn't going to include her in his world. He needed his boundaries and rules to cope with emotions... which meant he was determined to shut her out. Keep her at arm's length.

She couldn't handle being at arm's length. She needed to love, and be loved.

Kassiani hadn't married Damen to leave him. She really hadn't.

Her vows had been sincere. She'd wanted to be a wife, a *good* wife, and she had just gotten to the point where she could picture their children—gorgeous children with dark hair, and bright eyes.

And maybe this could have worked, if she hadn't fallen in love with him. Loving him made his cynicism so much worse. Loving him turned the lovemaking into something heartbreaking. To be so close to him, to be possessed by him so thoroughly, while he felt absolutely nothing for her... It made her heartsick.

She'd known going into this that he didn't love her and would never love her, but she hadn't imagined falling for him. She hadn't imagined the sizzling sexual chemistry.

She thought she could handle his moods. She thought that she could remain emotionally detached—and maybe she could have, if the lovemaking hadn't been so fierce, so intense, so consuming.

When they were together, when he was with her, in her, his arms wrapped around her, the world shrank to just him and her.

When they were together she lost track of herself, and her focus became him. He felt like an obsession.

It wasn't good for her head, and it wasn't good for her soul. She felt damaged…hopelessly damaged, damaged to the point where she worried about her ability to survive this life.

And hadn't Damen warned her of this?

Hadn't he said that he'd chosen Elexis because she was hard, and she wouldn't care, and he needed a wife who was as hard as he was?

Kassiani hadn't understood what he meant. She hadn't understood his past, and the abuse he'd suffered—abuse she couldn't bear to think about because it was beyond horrible—but that abuse shaped him, and his past haunted him, and she hadn't been prepared to fall in love only to be pushed away because she loved him. Unrequited love was one thing if the significant other was distant and far removed, but Damen was close, always so close, and his appetite for her only seemed to grow. In his bed, she felt stripped bare—mentally, emotionally, psychologically.

Now tonight, she couldn't breathe. In her room, on her bed, she lay on top of her covers, fighting for air. It had been years since she'd had a panic attack. Was that what this was? Kassiani felt as if there wasn't enough oxygen left. She lay on her bed, gasping for breath, feeling as if she was suffocating, and it terrified her.

This was no way to live. This was not a healthy marriage. Damen was destroying her but Kassiani had been through too much to just wither away and die. Her survival instinct was too strong. She had too much of the fighting Greek spirit to just self-destruct without trying to save herself.

On Adras she'd told Damen that he needed help, but maybe she was the one who needed help. Maybe she was the one who needed a therapist to help her come to terms with her past, so that she could have a future. Right now there was no future.

If she wanted a future, she had to go. She had to leave him. It was the only way. They weren't good together. They just inflicted pain.

Tears stung her eyes but she drew a slightly deeper breath and felt some of the terrible pressure in her chest ease.

Leaving was the right answer. She needed to go. She needed to return home.

Kassiani sat up and stared out the window to the sea. Clouds obscured the moon but she could see a gleam of light from Adras's lighthouse on the water and it calmed her.

She wouldn't go back to her father's house. She'd find a place of her own. She had money of her own now and she'd use the money to start over in San Francisco and from now on, she would be smarter and braver and more self-aware.

It had been a brutal week, but she would feel better once she was back in California. Damen could initiate the divorce proceedings, citing her for desertion. As long as she was the reason for the marriage failing, the marriage contracts would hold. Damen would retain control over

Dukas Shipping. She didn't feel guilty. Dukas Shipping needed proper management. Dukas Shipping was in shambles, and it'd be far better to have Damen step in and save what he could than allow the family business to end up in bankruptcy.

She didn't feel sorry for her father, either. He had pursued this relationship with Damen, offering up his daughters as if they were bargaining chips. He'd wanted the merger and the marriage for purely selfish reasons—he didn't want to be poor. He didn't want to be a failure. Damen Alexopoulos would save him, and his company, and so he brokered a deal that was a travesty in hindsight.

Elexis hadn't wanted to marry Damen.

Kassiani had married Damen to earn her father's approval.

But how could her self-esteem have been so bad that she thought marrying a stranger, much less marrying a man with a reputation like Damen's, would be a good thing?

She felt stupid and pathetic. But now she'd be wise. She was returning to California smarter and stronger, and more self-aware. She didn't care what others would say, or think. She didn't care that people would talk about her, or gossip that she'd gotten divorced just weeks after the wedding. She had tried. She'd truly tried. But she was no match for Damen. She never had been.

CHAPTER ELEVEN

IT WAS STRANGE being back in California.

She'd been gone only a couple of weeks and yet once back in San Francisco, it felt like months since she'd flown to Athens for Elexis's May wedding.

Kassiani didn't even feel like the same person. Maybe because she had married and lost her innocence. Maybe because she'd fallen in love and had her heart broken. Maybe because she missed Damen even though he was not the right man for her.

She knew when Damen was in San Francisco because her father told her. The first time he was in the city, she prepared herself for his visit, getting a blowout to make her hair silky and gleaming, and having another one of those excruciating waxes that left her completely bare down there. She paced her house, anticipating his arrival, hoping he'd come to say he missed her, anticipating his words, wanting desperately to hear him say he'd made a mistake…that he'd made many mistakes…and he was sorry and wanted to try again. He wanted a fresh start.

But Damen never came to her house.

Damen never tried to see her. He didn't even attempt to contact her.

He did whatever business he needed to do and returned to Athens.

Kassiani was crushed when she discovered Damen had gone, and she hardened her heart so that the next time, four weeks later, when he was back, she didn't have such high hopes. She still had her hair done, but that was all, and she didn't walk around in a state of anxious anticipation. But she did hope because she wanted him to miss her because she did miss him.

All she wanted was to hear him say that he'd realized he'd made mistakes and he wanted to try again with her, and then they could discuss the marriage each of them wanted, and how they could meet in the middle.

Or something like that.

But he didn't see her on his second visit, either.

She wasn't in town for his third visit or any others. It was deliberate. As August drew to an end, she told herself she no longer wanted to see him. She wanted nothing to do with him. Kassiani prayed the divorce papers would come soon.

The divorce papers weren't the only thing she was waiting for.

Her period hadn't come. In *months*.

At first, she'd thought she was merely late—it happened a lot with her—and then she thought maybe it was stress that was playing havoc with her system since she'd lost a lot of weight since the wedding, but when the weeks became months and she was fully settled into her lovely house in the Presidio, she couldn't ignore facts any longer.

Something was wrong. And she suspected she knew what was wrong, and once she took a test and discovered, yes, she was pregnant, her dread turned to horror. Kassiani was so horrified she took the test three times at home before going to a doctor.

She didn't want to be pregnant. It felt like such a betrayal to even admit such a thing, but being pregnant would change everything. Pregnant, she would be forever tied to Damen.

Pregnant, she'd given him what he wanted, an heir.

He would be happy. It was what dynasties required... children. Another generation to carry on the family name, to continue the legacy.

Even as September drew to a close, she found it hard to wrap her head around the pregnancy. She'd always wanted to be a mother but this wasn't how she wanted to be a mother.

Single, alone.

Unless she reunited with Damen, but everything in her recoiled at the thought because if they reunited now, it would be only for the child's sake. Damen had made it clear he didn't want her, and while being together might be good for the baby, it would destroy her. Her soul would shrivel up into nothing.

During the long nights when Kassiani couldn't sleep, she didn't doubt that Damen would be a good father, at least, he'd be a good father until the child was a teenager and began to defy his father. Damen didn't like being challenged. Damen didn't like anything that made him feel. Children would make him feel. But there was nothing she could do about that. The baby had been conceived.

Kassiani spent many long, sleepless nights trying to figure out when and how to tell Damen about the pregnancy. Obviously, she would have to tell him. Eventually, he'd need to know and she'd never keep something like this from him, but she had months to go before the baby was born. She was only just entering her second trimester. In clothes you couldn't even tell she was pregnant, her ripe curves overshadowing everything else.

Still no divorce papers arrived.

Why?

What was he thinking? No contact, no communication, no nothing. What did he want from her? Was he trying to intimidate her, or force her hand? Was this just another power play at his end?

And then suddenly, on the last day of September, he was there, on her doorstep, in a dark suit, looking gorgeous and polished and hard, because Damen Alexopoulos was nothing if not hard.

She was shocked to see him and her legs wobbled but she was never going to let him know he still could rock her world simply by standing in front of her, being himself. It was worse feeling her heart race. How could she still love him so much?

"Are you going to invite me in?" he said quietly.

Her anger returned, fueled by love and pain. Who did he think he was, just showing up four months later and demanding privileges? He should have been here weeks—months—ago. "I don't know yet."

One of his black eyebrows lifted. "Whatever makes you the happiest—"

Outrage rushed through her. "You are so wrong, and so unfair, on so many levels," she choked, spotting the large leather folder in his hand. The divorce papers. He'd brought them to her himself. Her heart tumbled to her feet. Hot tears prickled her eyes. "Just give me what you have come to give me, and go."

"No. Not until we talk."

"But I don't want to talk anymore. You've made me wait for months—"

"I was still…working…on things." His lips twisted. "Working on…me."

She stilled, caught off guard by the very American-sounding expression. Greeks didn't work on themselves. "What do you mean?"

"Could we please do this inside? Somewhere more private than Vallejo Street?"

She turned away and walked to the living room, where she took a seat, determined to be calm, and cool, and as unemotional as possible, which wouldn't be easy because everything inside her was going haywire. She'd missed the arrogant bastard so very much, and she was only now realizing just how much she wanted him to still want her. How much she wanted him to fight for her. And how devastated she'd be when he gave her the divorce papers. "What have you brought with you?" she asked tightly, when he joined her in the living room.

"These are for later. I'll leave them with you when I leave."

"You don't want to discuss them now?"

"No." He took a breath. "I want to discuss us, and our marriage."

"Which means, you've come with another lecture on how I disappointed you, and how I wasn't a proper Greek wife."

The corner of his mouth curved, and yet there was no hint of a smile in his cool gray eyes. "No lecture today, sorry."

"You're not sorry."

"But I am. I'm here to apologize. I'm here to ask for a second chance. I'm here to fight for us—"

"Why? When all I've done is disappoint you? I can't count the number of times you told me you didn't even want me…that I'd forced myself on you." Tears filled her eyes and she swiped them away furiously. Pregnancy hormones weren't helping her resolve to be calm and collected. "You were constantly lecturing me and trying to change me—"

"I was wrong. Forgive me. Who am I to teach you anything? How could I possibly teach you about being a proper wife, when I haven't been a proper husband?"

The air caught in her throat. She blinked hard, scrubbing away the remaining tears, even as hope warred against hope. Did he know what he was saying? Did he mean what he was saying? "Then what are those papers?"

"Ignore the papers, please. The papers don't matter right now. The only thing that matters is you understanding that I was an ass, and wrong, and hurtful because I was scared. You were making me feel and feelings confuse me. I didn't want feelings, but I did want you."

"No, you wanted the best daughter, the one my father promised you."

He reached out and lightly touched her knee. "I was promised the best daughter and I was given the best daughter."

"But you said—"

"I know what I said, and it wasn't true. I was hurt and angry and lashing out at you. I'm sorry about that and ashamed. I've spent months—" he broke off, drew a short, sharp breath "—talking, trying to work through my anger and I've come to you, finally, to say that I have never, ever been disappointed by the Dukas I married. Any disappointment I have felt, and continue to feel, is disappointment in myself. I loathe myself for the pain I have caused you, and I am deeply sorry for behavior, and the choices I have made."

She'd found it hard to focus on anything after he'd said that he'd spent months *talking*. Her forehead furrowed as she looked at him. "*Who* have you been talking to?"

"A therapist. You said I needed help, and so I got help."

"You did?"

He nodded, expression somber.

"Why?" she breathed.

"I hoped that if I changed, you'd come home. I'd like you to come back. It's not home without you."

She held her breath as he spoke, afraid that if she made a sound, he'd disappear, and this would all be just a dream because Damen was saying everything she'd wanted to hear. He was saying exactly the words she needed. Was this a trick? Was this real? "You never came to see me on your other trips to San Francisco."

"I was trying to let you be in charge. I was trying to let you control the relationship, but as weeks turned to months, I became increasingly fearful that you truly wanted out of our marriage, and the thought was unbearable."

"I was waiting for the divorce papers."

"You would have been waiting forever. I had no intention to ever file for divorce. You are the only wife I will ever have because you are the only woman I love. I couldn't imagine ever being with anyone else. You are mine. You are absolutely who I want and need at my side, for the rest of my life."

She felt a tremor course through her. His words were powerful and overwhelming. "I don't know what to say. You are so different. It's almost as if you are a different man."

"Words are still not easy for me, but trying to live without you was far more difficult than learning how to be a better husband and a better communicator." He hesitated. "But I'm not here today to try to force you into making a decision that you might regret later. I'd rather we take this slow so that you can be confident and comfortable that I really am the husband you want. I have had months to think about what I need, but it's important we make sure you have what *you* need. With that in mind, I prepared papers that I will leave with you to read after I go, as you don't need me to read anything to you—" He broke off, and a flicker of a smile warmed his eyes. "Because you're quite a good reader. Just know that there are a number of different documents and agreements in the envelope, and each of them have been created with you in mind, so that no matter what you eventually choose—to come home with me, or to remain here, independent of me—you are secure, and protected, and taken care of."

She rose, and he did, too. "I don't want your money, Damen. I only ever wanted you."

The smile faded from his eyes and a shadow crossed his features. "I realize that now. And it might be too late for us. I hope it's not too late for us. I have no intention of letting you go, but at the same time, I won't force you to stay married to me if it's not the right thing for you. And saying that, I also recognize that you deserve more than what you've ever been given and while I can't right all the wrongs, I can make an attempt to correct the balance of power, so the future is nothing like the past."

He closed the distance between them and pressed a kiss to her temple and then another to her cheek. "I love you, my heart," he murmured, his fingers brushing lightly across her jaw, "but I want you happy. You deserve to be happy. You deserve all the joy and the love in the world."

And then he walked out, leaving the leather folder on the chair where he'd been sitting.

Kassiani sank back down and stared at the folder. She'd waited four months for this conversation, and it had been even more wonderful than she could have imagined, except—was it too good to be true?

She hated her doubts, but she was terrified to hope and open herself to love, only to be crushed when he reverted to the same cold, brusque behavior again.

Hands shaking, she reached for the folder and pulled out the various documents. There were three different sets of documents, each with an original cover letter.

As Kassiani read through each of the letters, she discovered Damen hadn't given her money. There was no allowance or settlement on her per se. Instead, he'd given her three different options—all included a hefty stake in his businesses, and none of the options was contingent on her remaining married to him. All three options were still hers, even if she chose to divorce him.

Option 1: Live independently in San Francisco and join Dukas Shipping's Board of Directors, taking an active leadership role in Dukas Shipping.

Kassiani paused, her gaze riveted to the words *Dukas Shipping*. Was he not going to change the company's name? Had he possibly changed his mind?

Option 2: Take a management position at Dukas Shipping, and provide management and leadership for the company, living in either San Francisco or Athens.

Option 3: Work at Alexopoulos's corporate office in Athens in a management capacity, providing leadership for both Dukas Shipping and Aegean Shipping.

Kassiani sat back in shock. He wasn't giving her money. He was inviting her to become part of the shipping industry. He was giving her an opportunity to do what she'd always dreamed of.

She skimmed one of the cover letters until she found what she was looking for. Damen's mobile number. She called him immediately. He picked up immediately.

"It's Kassiani," she said.

"I know," he answered.

"How?"

"I have you saved in my Favorites. You're number one."

"Stop."

"It's true. You are my favorite."

She went hot all over, and it was hard to focus when her heart was racing so. "Those options," she said breathlessly. "They're...amazing."

"If anyone should head up Dukas Shipping in the future, it's you."

"When you say Dukas Shipping, do you mean to leave the name in place?"

"It all depends."

"On what?"

"You. If you are at the helm, it should remain Dukas Shipping, shouldn't it?"

"At the helm? Damen, I don't know anything about the business yet."

"You can learn it. You're a fast study. You figured me out in less than a week."

She exhaled softly, her eyes stinging. "Do you mean this?"

"I do."

"What if it doesn't work out?"

"The business relationship, or the personal? Because they're separate, Kass. You can have one without the other. You can choose any option and not be with me."

A lump filled her throat. He was saying all the right things and giving her all the reassurance she needed, but it made her feel worse. It made her feel impossibly guilty. She had to tell him about the pregnancy. It was time, more than time, but it also might change everything because she was sure he'd be upset that she'd kept the secret so long. Telling him the truth might ruin everything now.

Blinking back tears, she blurted, "I'm pregnant, Damen. I'm twenty-two weeks along."

He didn't immediately reply. The silence was deafening. Her heart pounded so hard she thought she might get sick.

"Damen?" she whispered after a long minute. "Please say something."

"Open the door, kitten. I'm still here. Outside."

She raced to the door and flung it open, wiping away tears as he stepped into her foyer.

"Why are you crying?" he asked, drawing her into his arms.

"Please don't be mad—" she choked.

"Not mad." He kissed the top of her head. "Is the baby healthy? Are you okay?"

"We're both good. It's been an easy pregnancy. The only hard part is knowing you were so far away."

He released her, his hands on her shoulders. "I haven't been far away. I've been here in San Francisco the entire time."

"What?"

"I didn't want to be far in case you needed me."

"Damen."

"How could I be sure you were safe if I was on the other side of the world?"

"But you never came to see me! And my father let me think you were coming and going—"

"That was him being dramatic, that was not from me. I never went anywhere. I have a suite at the Palace Hotel and it's where I go every night after I leave Dukas Shipping."

"Did you ever come by the house? Did you ever try to see me?"

"I drove past every day. I sometimes parked across the street just to watch your lights come on and off."

She drew back, feeling worse, not better. "Did you know I was pregnant?"

"I suspected, but wasn't sure." He grimaced. "My mother thought you might be."

"What? How?"

He shrugged. "She's always had a sixth sense about things like this."

Kassiani blinked. "So why give me those options if you knew I was pregnant?"

"Because you have always wanted to be part of the business, and there is no reason this pregnancy or future pregnancies should keep you from being part of the business. The only reason you shouldn't work is because you don't want to."

"I thought traditional Greek wives stayed home."

"I don't want a traditional Greek wife. I want you."

"What if I choose Option 1, to remain in San Francisco and live independent of you?"

"Then I'd buy a house here so I could be part of our child's life."

"You love Greece."

"I love you and our child more."

"I don't know what to say."

"You don't have to say anything right now. Think about it. Take time. In fact, take a lot of time. Just allow me to woo you and court you, and spoil you. Let me show you that I can be a good husband. Let me prove to you that I can be trusted."

Her heart ached. "It's been a bumpy four months."

"Very bumpy. And it's my fault—"

"No. It's mine. You were promised the best daughter—"

"And I married the best daughter," he said fiercely. "You were the best and only option for me. You and your strength and your courage helped me confront a past that has kept me from living, and loving, and I wouldn't be here, who I am now, if it wasn't for you being you. I love you, Kassiani, and I will love you for as long as we both shall live."

* * *

He did woo her properly, too, taking her out to dinners and the theater, and even to an American football game, which neither of them enjoyed very much, but Damen had reserved a whole luxury box and they ended up sitting at the back, kissing and talking, and it was there that Kassiani asked him about Iris, and his parents.

"I don't understand why you blame your parents for what happened to you when you were a boy," she said softly, uncertainly, "unless it's because they couldn't protect you—"

"I don't blame them, at all."

"But you don't…like…your mother?"

"Dislike my mother? No! Whatever gave you that idea?"

"Because you don't see her and she said you've changed, and become hard—"

"Not toward her, kitten. But, yes, I changed. And it isn't easy seeing her, knowing that she refuses to let me buy her a nice house, or make her more comfortable, and a son is supposed to provide for his mother, but she's stubborn and insists on living as she always has."

"So you're not punishing her?"

"Is that what you thought?"

Her shoulders lifted and fell. "I thought because of Iris, you maybe…blamed them…"

"No. I don't blame them in any way for what happened. They were victims, too. And I would give anything to have my mother come to Athens, and be part of my life there. But so far, she's stubborn and has refused my invitations."

"And you struggle with going to Adras."

He nodded. "Our stalemate, yes."

She processed this for a moment. "And Iris? You've blamed yourself for her death, too, haven't you?"

He nodded again, his strong jaw flexing.

"Do you know why she took her life? Did you two have a fight?"

"No. But I've had plenty of time to think about that as well, and the only thing I can come up with is that she felt betrayed by me after I left Adras."

"Why? Was she pregnant?"

"No! But we'd always talked about our future and how we were going to marry and then I left, and I never looked back."

"A year after I left, she died."

Kassiani squeezed his hand. "You do know that you weren't responsible—"

"She'd reached out to me, a number of times, writing letters, long letters. I never answered them. I never—" He broke off. "I did fail her. I know I did. But I thought I was doing her a favor. I thought she'd be happier without me. I was so damaged at that point. I was not the boy she'd loved."

"And you blamed yourself all these years."

Kassiani reached up, her hand lightly cupping his jaw with just a hint of rasp from his beard. "No more guilt, no more blame," she whispered, kissing him. "No more looking back."

"I love you."

"And I love you, my husband."

After a month and a half of dating her husband, Kassiani chose Option 3, and they were now back in Greece, in time for her third trimester. And while Greece wasn't yet home, she felt comfortable there because Damen made everything feel right. Wherever he was, she wanted to be.

She went into the corporate office with him each day, and he kissed her goodbye at the elevator and she went to her office while he went to his. She worked closely with one of his managers, learning the ropes and everything she could about the shipping industry. Some of the men she worked with were crusty and unhelpful, while others were delighted that a member of the Dukas shipping family had joined Aegean's team.

The weeks leading up to the new year were passing so quickly now. In a little over a month the baby would be born.

After work one evening, Damen drove her to a north Athens suburb to show her a house that had recently been built.

"It literally just came on the market today," he said, as the huge gates swung open and he headed up the long private drive. "It was a custom build and the owner is deeply in debt and is desperate to offload it. I know you prefer older architecture, but the house is on three acres, in a great location and has fantastic views. The only thing we would need to do is buy furniture and prepare the nursery."

He rounded the corner and the coastline came into view, along with the dazzling blue sea.

"How many acres did you say?" she asked.

"Three."

"Perfect. Yes. Buy it."

"You haven't even seen the house yet. You might hate it."

"We can fix it."

He parked and turned to look at her. "I don't want you having to worry about anything. I just want you to relax."

"I'm relaxed."

"And happy."

It felt as if she'd swallowed the sun. Everything within her glowed warm and bright. "I'm unbearably happy, Damen."

He smiled and leaned toward her, kissing her. "Marry me, Kassiani."

She kissed him back. "We're already married, my love."

"But let's do it again. Because this time it's a love marriage. I need you to know—"

"I know."

"I need the world to know."

"Who cares what the world thinks?"

His smile was crooked. "Maybe I just want to show you off. Maybe I just feel like celebrating because I have the most beautiful, brilliant wife, and we're going to have a baby soon."

She couldn't help smiling back. How could she not when the ball of happiness inside her shone bigger and brighter? "You are sleeping with me every night."

"All night. Now that I have you back in my bed, I'm not going anywhere."

She laughed, because yes, that was true. He did stay all night with her now. He'd stopped leaving her room—their room—after lovemaking. Damen slept touching her, a hand always near the small of her back.

She liked it.

She loved him.

Desperately.

EPILOGUE

THE VOW RENEWAL took place on New Year's Eve.

She wore a Grecian-style wedding dress, a simple one-shoulder gown in a gorgeous creamy white. Her long dark hair was loosely pinned up with a delicate antique wreath of gold leaves on top of the gleaming dark curls.

Kassiani was just four weeks from giving birth and she felt huge, but also blissfully happy. Damen came to check on her just before the ceremony began. "How are you feeling?" he asked.

"I'm good."

"You look so beautiful."

She ran a hand over her huge belly bump. "There is so much of me."

"I have always loved every bit of you, even when I didn't know how to tell you."

"The past is the past, my love. It's time to let it go and focus on the future."

"Maybe I can, after tonight. I have made so many mistakes in my life."

"No one is keeping score."

"I have. You deserved a proper wedding and a proper wedding day. I just want the world to know how much I love you."

"I don't really care about the world, and what they know or think. I care about what you think."

"Which is why we're doing this tonight. We're going to have a party with a few close friends and family, and we'll dance and take pictures and put those pictures in an album, and other pictures in frames, so our children will know how much their father loved their mother, and we can be an example to them that true love is worth fighting for."

Her eyes burned and a lump filled her throat. "I had no idea I'd married such a romantic."

"I adore you, my wife, my heart, my life. I adore you and am grateful for every day with you."

The ceremony went off without a hitch, as did the elegant, intimate reception at the Dionysus Restaurant. The restaurant overlooked the sacred rock of the Acropolis and the Odeon of Herodes Atticus, and both were illuminated at night.

Kass thought there was something profoundly spiritual about dining and dancing with the Acropolis in the background, and the evening was made perfect by having a few of their respective families there. Her father had flown into Athens, and Mrs. Alexopoulos had traveled by ship. Mrs. Alexopoulos had made Kassiani's bouquet, adding bits of olive branches from the groves on Adras, the olive branches for peace. And love. It was perfect. Kassiani had found her home.

And when Kassiani went into labor two weeks later, Damen was there at her side. Her father sent flowers but Mrs. Alexopoulos returned, anxious to provide help.

Damen had been worried that Kassiani wouldn't want his mother in the house, but Mrs. Alexopoulos wasn't one of those critical, interfering mothers-in-law, but an unending source of wisdom and encouragement.

Kassiani felt grateful to have a husband who loved her so much that he was willing to fight for her, and them, and a doting grandmother for her baby boy. Their baby boy, their son Alesandro, a symbol of their love, and a commitment to the future.

As winter shifted to spring, Kassiani looked forward to

returning to the company office on a part-time basis. She enjoyed the work, but adored her son, and was thankful she didn't have to choose between them.

The past year hadn't been easy. Both she and Damen had fought hard for their marriage and fought hard for their love. But wasn't that the true definition of family?

Families fought for each other, not against each other.

Love healed, and love hoped, and love endured.

She hadn't always made the right choices, and yet she'd never given up on him. And just when she didn't think she could fight anymore for them, Damen had shocked her by coming through, by choosing to fight for her, for them, for the happiness they all desperately needed.

Dreams really did come true.

* * * * *

AN INNOCENT
TO TAME
THE ITALIAN

TARA PAMMI

For Jen—for talking me up when I'm down, for untangling complicated plots only we could come up with, and for always being there to discuss how much we can push these cranky, arrogant Modern heroes. This book wouldn't have been possible without you.

CHAPTER ONE

"Did you figure out why the security breaches keep happening? And how?"

Massimo Brunetti looked up from the three monitors on his desk in the lab that was the hub of his cyber security business. It was a high-security center with thumbprint access only.

A measure he'd taken at the age of sixteen when his father, Silvio, had still been living with them, a matter of self-preservation for Massimo to keep him out. Now, this was his tech center where his servers were stored and where he designed software worth billions.

Only his older half brother, Leonardo, who was currently scrutinizing everything, and their grandmother Greta's stepdaughter, Alessandra, had access. On the condition that they disturb him only at the threat of the building burning down or an equivalent emergency.

Greta wasn't allowed. Her emergency the last time had been an epic tantrum on his thirtieth birthday three months ago. The cause was that Leo and he were going to die childless, leaving the dynastic legacy of the Brunettis to perish with them.

She should know Massimo didn't give a damn about family legacies, especially theirs.

"We have a meeting scheduled for an ~~~ n a half hour, Leo," he said, without raising ~~~ You know do not like it when you bars~~~

"You've been locked up in here for the better part of a week." Leo's mouth pinched. "I can't hide it from the board any longer, Massimo. If it gets to the press that BCS had clients' financials open for any little Dark Net hacker to find... *Merda!*"

It would be a disaster of epic proportions.

"It's bad enough we lost that ten-billion-dollar contract," Leo finished.

Massimo rubbed his eyes with the heels of his hands, hoping to alleviate the pulsing prick of pain in his forehead. He *had been* cooped up in here for too long. "It's not my fault if people remember the trail of destruction Silvio left in his wake."

It had taken Leo and him close to fifteen years to restore their family company—a multi-billion-dollar finance giant, Brunetti Finances, Inc.—to its original glory. In fact, it was still a work in progress.

For Greta, it was the family legacy, the name Brunetti synonymous with its prestige. Even now, she could call out half the skyscrapers littered through Milan that had housed the main offices of Brunetti Finances through its two-hundred-year history.

For Leo and him, however, it was the satisfaction of building it up again, bigger and better, a force to be reckoned with, after their father had almost brought it to its knees.

But...for the last six months, more than one contract had fallen through at the last minute. In the first one, they had fou~~~~ accountant had leaked their bid details. In the ~~~~e subcontractor they'd hired had been bought ~~~~n unholy mess on Leo's hands.

~~~~ed a ~~~~ was this security breach Massimo
~~~~per Secur~~~~wn brainchild company,

Someone was clearly targeting their business. The security breach was far too much a direct attack to ignore. If Silvio wasn't being monitored 24/7 at a clinic with no resources at hand and no communications beyond Leo, they would know the culprit was him. Their father, once they had grown taller, bigger and stronger than him, despised being powerless.

"Are you sure Silvio's the only enemy we have?" Leo asked, cocking an eyebrow at his brother. "What about your recent fling? She's certainly making a lot of noise."

"Gisela and I are done. Four months ago now." Massimo let his displeasure show on his face. Leo had no business delving into his personal matters.

"*Sì*, you and I know that. Does the daughter of the most powerful banking tycoon in Italy know that? *Maledizione*, Massimo, the woman calls *me* now."

The pain behind his eye intensified. If everything hadn't been going so wrong, Massimo would have laughed at his brother's expression.

Leo didn't even give out his number to his own mistress. Who was, very conveniently, a supermodel who had a shot at the end of the world, with an expiry date of two more months, if Massimo's calculations were right. The last one had been a CEO who met his brother once every two weeks for six months. Before that, had been a photojournalist studying migration patterns of an exotic bird species in Antarctica who went into hibernation for about ten months out of a year.

Leo seemed to have the algorithm for the best kind of mistress all figured out—distance, just as ruthless as him and ambitious. All his relationships ended on amicable footings, too.

It wasn't that Massimo wanted a cold and clinical relationship like that. He just didn't have the time or the energy for a deeper one. And he wouldn't for the next twenty years at least. He doubted he knew what deep, meaningful relationships looked like, anyway. His mother and Silvio—it had been a war. Fought by her, for his sake.

"You need to do whatever is needed to make her understand," Leo added. "Do not antagonize her father in the process."

Massimo hated when Leonardo was right. "I'll take care of it."

It had been a stupid move tangling with the selfish, spoiled socialite Gisela Fiore. But after the months he'd spent designing his latest product—an e-commerce tool and its subsequent release hitting ten billion in revenue—he'd needed to play. Hard.

Which Gisela excelled at, according to her reputation. The *only* thing she excelled at. A torrid two-week affair had ensued. At the end of which, Massimo had been itching to get back to work. As was *his* reputation.

Except Gisela was still sending him alarmingly disturbing texts full of threats followed by sobbing messages. When she wasn't camping outside the Brunetti brothers' office building.

"Do you want to hear about the hacker or not?" he challenged Leo.

"Please."

"I found the trail last night. I also figured out how he gained access through the multiple firewalls I built. Both times."

"Two times?" Leo asked with cutting focus to the gist of the vast problem on their hands.

"Sì."

"Cristo, you're a freaking genius, Massimo. How is that even possible?"

It wasn't arrogance that made Massimo nod. Computers were his thing. The one thing he was the master of. "The hacker is obviously extremely talented. A true genius, no doubt."

Leo's curse exploded in the basement. A few minutes later, his brother was all business again. "But you have the proof tying it to this person, right?"

"*Sì*. I used the bots to piggyback onto the malware he—"

"Normal people words, Massimo, *per favore*," his brother said with a smile, for the millionth time in their lives. "Words a small brain like mine can understand."

As always, a spurt of warmth jolted through his veins at Leo's joke. His brother was no fool. But when Massimo had been at his lowest, Leo, with his words, full of concern and praise, had urged him toward realizing his full potential. "I have proof. I have even triangulated the hacker's physical location. New York."

"That's fantastic. I can arrange for a meeting with the commissioner in a half hour. He'll get the cybercrime division involved. We'll have the hacker behind bars by tonight and the identity of whoever orchestrated this—"

"*No*. I don't want the *polizia* involved. Not yet."

"What? Why the hell not?"

"I've already figured out a cyber club where this hacker plays. I've established contact."

"Contact with the hacker? Why?"

Massimo shrugged. He couldn't exactly put it into words—curiosity, thrill, even a certain amount of camaraderie. The hacker intrigued him. "I want to get to know him. Learn how he operates."

"*Dios mio*, Massimo, he breached our security. Twice."

"*Essattemente!* He could do it again and again. You have to admit that there's something…fishy about the whole thing. None of the clients' financials were leaked. I have bots working everywhere they could be sold, like black markets, on the Dark Net. They haven't surfaced anywhere.

"It's as if the hacker is taunting me, playing with me. He's hard to pin down."

"What are you suggesting?"

"Let me develop a relationship with him. Let me get into his head. When I know how he works, how he's doing it, I'll spring the trap."

"I want your word that he won't hit our servers again."

"You losing faith in me, Leo?" he taunted, that resentment in him finding voice. Reminding him that Massimo wasn't still the always sick runt their father went off on whenever he was on one of his frequent alcoholic tirades. That he wasn't the younger brother running to his older brother's arms to hide from his father. That he was the computer genius who'd designed products that generated billions in revenue.

Leo paused at the high-tech sliding doors, frowning.

"Give me a week and I'll give you the hacker, his life story and the proof of his illegal activities, all tied up with a bow like a Christmas present."

"A week. At the most," Leo pushed back. "I want him behind bars."

One week later

Massimo stood outside the cyber club exit—a metal door of undistinguishable color at the rear of a dilapidated building in one of the run-down neighborhoods of Brooklyn. A far cry from his penthouse that overlooked Central Park that he'd left behind an hour ago.

March snow carpeted the parking grounds in the dark alley, thankfully suppressing the odors emanating from the vast trash containers that stood two feet from him.

The hacker, he'd found, was very much a creature of habit. Unlike Massimo, and much against the popular culture's rendition of a chaotic, free-spirited genius. Two evenings a week, the hacker came to this club, at exactly eight minutes past nine p.m. and stayed for exactly forty-three minutes. Before going completely off-line.

Like a junkie allowing himself a very strictly mandated and measured fix.

Massimo hadn't found him anywhere else.

Which meant all Massimo had had were two sessions of forty-three minutes to get to know how the guy operated. And he had. Hackers were a mysterious and antisocial bunch, and yet boastful, too, especially someone at the level at which this particular one operated. All he'd needed to do was compliment him on his modification of a security challenge posed by the master of the club. He hadn't quite owned up to the breach but the connection had been made.

His heart fluttering against his rib cage like a caged bird, Massimo tucked his hands into the pockets of his trench coat. Adrenaline hadn't hit him this hard since the release of his latest software product. No, that wasn't true. The last time he'd been this excited had been when he'd shored up the tunnel this very same hacker had created into BCS.

The metallic whine of the heavy door made his spine lock. Buffeted by the collar of his coat against the harsh wind, Massimo watched a slight figure swathed in black from head to toe, a dark contrast against the snow clinging to every crevice and roof of the building, walk down the steps.

The howl of the frigid wind pushed the hood away from the figure's face, revealing a delicate jawline with a wide, plump mouth. A too-sharp nose and a high forehead. Broad but sharp cheekbones. A pointed chin. Slender shoulders held an almost boyish figure with long legs swathed in black denim and knee-high boots.

Jet-black hair, wild and curly, the only thing that betrayed the fact that she was a woman. No, the soft fragility, the sharply delicate bones, couldn't be mistaken for a man.

A painfully young, delicately beautiful woman.

It couldn't be her... This fragile young woman couldn't be the hacker that had taken down his firewall, could she? Couldn't be the diabolically intelligent computer genius that Massimo had been chatting up for the last week. The hacker that Leonardo wanted behind bars *pronto*. The one who'd kept him up for a fortnight now, given him sleepless nights...

Not a single one of his girlfriends had ever done it.

He laughed, a harsh bark that sounded loud in the silence.

Like a deer caught in the headlights, the hacker's feet frozen in the snow, her face turned toward him.

Brown eyes with long lashes alighted on his face and paused. He saw her swallow, felt that gaze dip to his mouth and trail back up to meet his eyes. A soft sound, almost like a kitten's sigh, filled the silence around them. Followed by the soft treads of her boots as she returned to the car.

No, he wasn't wrong.

He'd even had a quick chat with the hacker from his car before he'd stepped out. He...or *she* had been inside that building. On an impulse, Massimo grabbed his tablet from the car and sent a quick message through the chat boards.

It wasn't a sure thing since the hacker never used the chat boards outside of the cyber club. And yet, Massimo had teased him today with a glimpse of the new security software he was building for Gisela's father's company. He knew the hacker had been intrigued, had even stayed beyond the forty-three minutes he usually allowed himself.

Vitruvian Man: I can show you the double encryption layer for the new design.

His heart raced. *Dios mio*, he felt like a teenage boy waiting for his first kiss.

The woman paused, pulled her phone out from the coat jacket. Massimo realized what it meant to wait with bated breath.

His tablet sent out a soft chirp that sounded like a fire alarm in the dark silence.

Her reply shone up at him.

Gollum: Not tonight, thank you. My time's up. Maybe next time.

The message flashed on his screen and a smile curved his mouth, a flare of excitement running through his veins.

So polite, he'd thought during his chats with her. A certain softness buried even in the software jargon in contrast to the ruthlessness with which she'd attacked his firewalls.

It was her.

She was the hacker he'd been chasing, the hacker who it seemed was truly Massimo's match.

In the few seconds it took him to accept this new discovery, and course-correct his strategy for her, she'd reached her car.

His long legs ate up the distance. The tightening of her shoulders made him stay a few steps from her. He didn't want to scare her. Not yet.

"Why Gollum?" he said, keeping his tone soft, even as

anger and excitement roped through him. "Why not Aragorn, or Gandalf the Wizard?"

She turned. Her eyes ate him up, her breath coming in short, shallow spurts that had nothing to do with the cold. "I don't know what you're talking about."

When she made to pull the driver's door to her beaten down Beetle, he crowded her. Still not touching.

The subtle scent of lavender filled his breath, a jarring thread of softness that made him breathe hard. He lifted his phone, the screen showing the chat boards. "I know who you are. I have proof of what you did to Brunetti Cyber Securities. Every last bit."

The smile faded from his face just as the innocence dropped from hers.

The pointed chin lifted up, the expression in her eyes clear and sharp. "What do you want?"

He let the full power of his fury settle into his words. "Your purse, please."

She looked at the sea of white snow around them.

"There's nowhere to run. Nowhere to hide. I recommend doing as I ask."

Slowly, she pulled a wallet out of her back pocket and handed it over.

"Natalie Crosetto," he said loudly. The name reverberated in the silence, and he breathed a sigh. "You've led me on a merry chase all over the internet, Ms. Crosetto, and now, I will run this game. We will go back to my hotel and you'll explain to me why you've been attacking my systems."

"No!" She took a deep breath. "You're a stranger. You can't expect me to let you just…kidnap me!"

"What do you suggest, then?"

"My home. Please. Tomorrow morning."

"I didn't take a trip over the Atlantic to let you escape

me once I found you. We'll go to your home if that offers you a modicum of security. You're free to keep your cell phone and dial the police if you feel a threat to your person at any point, even.

"But you'll answer each and every one of my questions and you will do so tonight."

That stubborn chin raised even as her mouth quivered. Scared, and yet she challenged him. "Or else what?"

"Or else you'll be behind bars tonight. I will even let you call the cops yourself. And you'll stay there for the next decade, if I have anything to say about it."

CHAPTER TWO

NATALIE CROSETTO STARED at the man lounging on her couch—a soft but old piece she'd picked up at thrift store last month—as if he were a king sitting on his golden throne, surveying a subject brought up for judgment.

Her.

Sweat gathered on her upper lip and the nape of her neck. The tremors that had taken over her body wouldn't abate.

Jail. He could send her to jail…which meant any chance of her getting custody of Frankie would go up in flames. Christ, why the hell had she let Vincenzo talk her into this? What would happen to her brother if she ended up in jail? No, God, no…

"Head down between your knees. And deep breaths, Ms. Crosetto." He stood to give her room to sit.

She automatically followed the commanding voice and bent her torso down. The blackness taking over her vision faded, breath rushing into her lungs with the force of a storm. In, out. In, out.

Panic receded, bringing rational thought in its wake.

She couldn't count on Vincenzo coming to her rescue. Not when she didn't know how to contact him beyond a number she could text. Not when she didn't know what the stranger would do with that information.

She had no one to count on but herself. As always.

Still keeping her head down, she went over the jumble of thoughts in her head, unraveling each one.

She'd covered her tracks very well, the first time. This man…he'd have never tracked her by that. But then, she'd tunneled through the firewalls a second time. Albeit with utter reluctance at Vincenzo's behest. That had been her mistake.

Still, the man on the other end had to be a genius to have tracked her. With unlimited resources. And not just online but all the way here. To show up right outside the cyber club, to taunt her with that text, to trap her so neatly…

She looked up and panic threatened to overwhelm her again.

A stranger in her apartment.

Her sanctuary. Her only safe place from the cruel world outside. She had never even invited Vincenzo here.

God, what a mess.

She pushed a hand through her hair and tugged at it. Her scalp tingled, the pain dispersing the remnants of panic. She'd survived worse situations. She'd find a way out of this, too.

First, she needed to protect herself from him. Needed to get him out of her home.

From the trench coat he'd discarded to the crisp black suit, the cuff links at his wrists, which she'd guess to be platinum, all the way to the handmade black leather shoes he was tapping on her cheap linoleum floor—he was expensively dressed. She might not know all of Vincenzo's background but he had expensive tastes.

This man was no different.

Even his jet-black haircut, carefully piled artistically at the top of his head, looked expensive, catering to the high cheekbones and forehead, sharpening those features even more. He was no mere IT officer or a hound sent to track her down.

Even if she could get away from him, he or his higher-ups would come after her. Again. Neither could she be a fugitive for the rest of her life. And yet…the need to take control of the situation was overwhelming.

Keeping her eyes on his lean frame lounging against the opposite wall, Nat pushed herself to her feet. Shuffling her feet, she slowly reached for the baseball bat she kept next to the bookshelf. One of the numerous things she'd been collecting to make the tiny apartment a home for Frankie.

The wood felt solid in her hand as she lifted it.

"Drop it, Ms. Crosetto," he said in a mildly bored tone.

She couldn't. Not for the life of her.

For a man who topped a couple of inches over six feet, he moved with a grace and economy she couldn't believe. In two seconds, his lean frame was crowding her. A gasp fell from her mouth when his fingers wrapped around her wrist, forcing her to drop the bat. The *thunk* of it hitting the floor reverberated in the small space. With a firm grip, he pushed her arm behind her until her upper body arched toward him. Her skin tingled where he held her tightly, but not hurting her.

Head falling back against the wall of his chest, she looked up at him.

And the impact of the man beneath the expensive clothes hit her hard. Hit her in places she didn't want to think about in front of him.

Intelligence and something else glimmered in his gaze. Dark shadows hung under his penetrating gray eyes. His sharp nose had a small dent right in the middle. His mouth…wide, the bow of the upper lip carved, it was so… sexy.

Awareness rushed in through her blood, settling into a warm throb in her lower belly. A shocking heaviness in her breasts.

Her breaths became shallow. He stood so close that she

could see the slight flare of his pupils, the harsh breath he pulled in before his fingers tightened on her wrist.

She wouldn't be surprised to discover he was one of those male models that seemed to have been born with the perfect bone structure. To whom everything in life came easy. Women at their feet and millions in their bank account.

"Do not dig yourself a deeper hole, Ms. Crosetto."

The arrogance in his tone banished the airy lethargy in her limbs. "You're in my home. You cornered me and intruded into my apartment. You—"

He released her instantly. Stepped back, and Nat felt air rushing back into her lungs. "I mean you no harm. Not physically at least. Also, may I remind you that you invited me into your home. And I—" he cast a dismissive look around her living room, that upper lip turned up into a sneer "—expected to find you in something better than this hovel. Didn't you get paid enough for the hacking job to upgrade from…this?"

She rubbed the sensitive skin at her wrist, more to rid herself of the warmth he left behind than because of any hurt. And to stop herself from smacking the distaste off his curling mouth. "I've no idea what you're talking about."

He sat back onto the couch, leaning his arms onto his long legs, every movement utterly masculine. And yet graceful. "How much did you get paid for taking down the firewalls at BCS?"

"You're mistaking me for someone else. I'm nothing but a low-level clerk at a cheap easy-loan company in Brooklyn."

He rubbed a long finger over his left temple. "No more lies, *per favore*." His accent sent shivers down her spine that had nothing to do with fear.

When he looked up at her, impatience swirled in his

gaze. "Let's cut through the innocent act. Now that I have your actual identity, it will take me no time at all to find your financials, every personal record, from your date of birth to how often you visit your ATM."

In a bare, few words that sent all her assumptions of him grounding into dust, he rattled off, step by step, the date and time to the exact second when she had bypassed his security measures and brought down the firewalls at BCS. And not as if he had learned it by rote.

"So, you're not just a pretty, rich boy?"

He stilled, except for raising a brow on that gorgeous face. She could swear his eyes twinkled but then she didn't trust herself right now. "A pretty, rich boy, huh? Remind me to tell my older brother that, *sì*? He'll find it amusing."

Nat could only stare.

"I don't think you comprehend the trouble you're in."

"I'm terrified at the trouble I'm in. You've no idea what…" She took a deep breath and pushed her shaking hands behind her. "But attacking even when you're cornered is sometimes the only defense you've left in life."

Something like interest dawned in his eyes before he went on to outline how he'd tracked her signature to the cyber club, made contact with her. How he'd triangulated her physical location. How when he'd given her a small opening in the guise of his latest tech, she'd all but opened herself to him.

Her foul curse rang like a gunshot.

"It was clever. No, not clever. It was sheer genius. But you made a mistake. You—"

"I came back a second time without masking my trail," she finished, a knot of tension in her throat. He had her. Nicely trapped. Without doubt.

"Yes, that. But you also shouldn't have returned to the scene of your crime—that cyber club. Why did you?"

She shrugged, refusing to give any more information. Like how every inch of her had been fascinated by his diabolical talent after he'd patched the tunnel she'd created. How she didn't even really have the kind of technology on hand to pull off something like this, how even membership to the cyber club had been gained for her by Vincenzo.

"Why are you talking to me instead of turning me in, then?" she challenged boldly, even as fear coated her skin with cold sweat.

If only she could somehow contact Vincenzo...

"How and why."

"What do you mean?" she said sharply, feeling as if she was a prisoner whose execution had been stayed.

He looked at his fingers and then up. Uncrossed his legs and then crossed them again. Pulling the material of his tailored trousers upward. She'd never realized how distracting a man's powerful thighs could be. "I want to know how you did it. My firewalls, every bit of technology I design, is cutting edge, the best in the world. What you did should have been...impossible."

"You're dangling jail time over my neck as a sword because your ego got dented?" The words pushed out of her. "You and I both know I didn't touch a single client's financials. I...didn't *steal* anything. I'm not a thief. In any sense of the word."

"Which brings me to the second question. Why attack the security, bring down the firewalls...something that would have taken you days, if not to steal millions worth of financial info—"

"Five hours," she chimed in, and could have kicked herself. Damn it, where the hell was her sense of self-preservation? What was it about this man that pushed all the wrong buttons in her?

A stillness came over him. He rotated his neck on his

shoulders with that casual masculine elegance. But this time, Natalie saw through it. He was shocked. It was clear in the pinched look around his mouth when he cleared his throat and said, "You did it in five hours?"

"Yes."

If she could trust her judgment right then, Nat would have called the expression in his eyes excited. No…fascinated. He sounded fascinated and thrilled, his body containing a violent energy. More than angry that someone had attacked his design.

This was personal to him, too, this security breach she'd caused. She had to use that to her benefit, to persuade him to be lenient with her.

But she didn't trust herself right then, didn't know if she could pull it off. Not when he distracted the wits out of her. Jesus, the man held her future in his palm.

"How long did it take you the second time?"

"Fourteen hours. I… You made it much more complicated and I was under…duress."

Another smile, this one flashing his perfect white teeth, the warmth of it reaching his eyes. Nat blinked at the sheer beauty of the man. Dark skin at his throat contrasted against his white shirt. "Nice to know I'm not the only one who gives in to their ego. I had you penned right."

"You don't know anything about me," she whispered, a sane defense for once.

"I knew enough to put a tracker on the malware you introduced when you came back the second time. I have bots scouring through every black market, in case you stole the financials. I'll find out if you're part of a hacking syndicate. Any money you took for the job, I'll find the financial trail."

"There won't be any." Thank God she'd refused Vincenzo's financial offer. Thank God she'd retained some of her moral sensibilities. Her life had been too much of a bitch for her to afford them. But she'd refused. Because she hadn't wanted to benefit from illegal activity. "You'll see that I have two thousand and twenty-two dollars in my checking account and credit cards with over nine thousand dollars in debt. I live in this hovel, as you call it. I don't own a car. And most weeks, I live on ramen. I didn't make any money on this. It wasn't a job. I'm not... My services aren't for sale."

"So why do it? If it had been just the one time, I'd have assumed you had chickened out at the sheer scope of what you'd done and its consequences. But to come back..." He raised a hand when she opened her mouth. "Think carefully before you decide on an answer, Ms. Crosetto. And stick to the truth, if you can, *si*?

"I'm on a deadline to submit the security designs for a major project and I'm grouchy when I'm pulled away from my lab. Forget the fact that my older brother is breathing down my neck for not just having thrown you in jail when I first found you. One wrong word and I'll take his advice."

Sweat rolled down between her shoulder blades. A torrent of lies came and fell away from Nat's mouth. "I..." She swiped her tongue over her lips. Truth, as much as she could afford, was her only option. "I had no intention of stealing anything. I...have been stupid but I'm not greedy. I'm not a thief...by profession," she added at the last second.

His arrogant gaze bore through her. "I'm waiting, Ms. Crosetto."

"I did it on a challenge." It was the last answer he'd been expecting from his shocked expression. "I... Someone in the club issued a challenge."

"Who?" he demanded instantly, clearly not buying it.

"I don't know. All I gathered is that BCS's security was unbeatable. That your security guy's a genius. That he... no one could ever bring down his firewalls. I...

"I was foolish enough and egotistic enough to want to beat it. Not to prove anything to anyone. Just for myself."

"And the second time?"

"Hubris." This time, she was relieved to speak the truth. "You closed the tunnel minutes after I created it. It shouldn't have been possible. What you did the second time to put them up—to try to bring it down—it was a high." She'd constantly moaned about how wrong it was with Vincenzo, but it hadn't stopped her. He'd known how much she'd wanted to do it.

How exhilarating she found it to pit her mind against the security expert at BCS.

"Once I started, I… I lost the little sense I seem to have been born with. I… I swear, I'll never do it again. I… I've never done this before. Please, you've got to believe me."

"It's not that simple, Ms. Crosetto."

"Why not? You said—"

"I don't trust that brain of yours. I can't just…let you walk free."

She reached for the wall behind her, her knees giving out. Fear felt like shards of glass in her throat. "You'll send me to jail?"

He looked at her with a thoughtful expression, as if she were a bug under a microscope he was wondering whether to crush or not. He studied the beads of sweat over her upper lip. The shivers spewing over her entire body. "*No.* But I'm not letting you go, either."

"What does that mean?"

"You'll accompany me to Milan."

She shook her head, trying to swim through the emotions barreling through her. Fear and hope knotted painfully in her stomach. "I can't leave the country. I have… responsibilities."

"You should have thought of them before you decided

to embrace the criminal life. Until I get to the bottom of this, until I decide what to do with you, you'll be my... guest. If you give me your passport, I'll arrange for travel immediately. I can't let you out of my sight and I do not like the idea of—"

"That's kidnapping!" Nat broke through his casual planning. "You're kidnapping me."

He didn't even blink. "The alternative is jail, Ms. Crosetto. There's too much at stake to magnanimously forgive you." He turned to his tablet, as if the topic was done. "Pack your things. We leave as soon as possible."

"I can't just... I have to tell someone that I'm leaving the country."

"A boyfriend? Perhaps the man who put you up to this?"

"No one did," she repeated, biting away Vincenzo's name at the last second.

This man was dangerous, in more than one way.

More than panic shimmied through her veins as his gaze touched her face. "My job, my... I don't even know who you are. What if you were a serial killer? A human trafficker? A harvester of organs who's salivating at the thought of getting his hands on my body?"

His hands on her body... What was wrong with her?

This time, there was no doubting the twinkle in his eyes. Or the languid heat flaring beneath.

Nat stepped back at the mere thought of what that meant. The last thing she needed was an...attraction between them. She knew squat about men. And less than squat about ambitious, ruthless, gorgeous men like her accuser. "Criminals, Ms. Crosetto, dead or alive, however diabolically clever—" his gaze raked her from top to toe and dismissed her in the same breath "—are not my type." He couldn't sound more upper class, refined and sophisticated, if he tried.

Everything she wasn't.

"But since I do not want a hysterical female on my hands on a long transatlantic flight, I'll tell you." He looked around her tiny living room, frowned and then settled those broad shoulders onto the wall behind him. The action pushed his hips and thighs away from the wall, highlighting the lean masculinity of the man. Every gesture, every movement of his, called all her senses to attention.

"I'm Massimo Brunetti, the cyber security genius you took on with such ease. And since I won't let you near an electronic device in the near future, I'll also give you the Google version, *si*?

"I founded Brunetti Cyber Securities a decade ago when I was nineteen. I'm also the CTO for Brunetti Finances, an international finance giant. My brother, Leonardo, is the CEO. That's the one who wants you behind bars *pronto*.

"Our family, if you hadn't realized already, is old power and wealth, the kind of European dynasty others try to emulate unsuccessfully," he added, with nothing of the pride that was in his tone when he spoke of his security company. "So, yes, far more than your average pretty, rich boy who likes to have his way. Proceed with caution, *si*?

"Also, I'll allow you one single call and you'll make it in front of me."

CHAPTER THREE

LACK OF SLEEP made Nat grit her eyes as dawn painted the New York sky beautiful shades of pink and orange. Unlike the light pollution that dimmed its shine in the city, the sky here in the country that she'd been driven into at three a.m. in a tinted limo, her sad little bag in hand, was gorgeous. The private airstrip was a hubbub of activity.

Massimo Brunetti...that name and all the power, wealth and reach that came with it had kept Natalie up all night.

She had Googled him the moment Vincenzo had mentioned BCS to her. Him and his CEO brother, Leonardo Brunetti. If Massimo was the brains behind Brunetti Finances, Leonardo was the heart. Cut in the same cloth as Massimo, ruthless when wielding his power, but much more socially active among the glitterati of Milan. The face of their business, the man who flashed his teeth at his enemies, brought in investors, managed the funds, while Massimo built brilliant software that brought in billions of revenue.

"Powerful men make powerful friends or enemies," Vincenzo had said, when she'd asked if he knew them. "A small favor," he'd called it. *Easy for her incisive mind.*

"Can you bring down BCS's security, Natalie?"

When she had argued that she couldn't risk anything criminal, she could never go down that path again, he had clasped her hand.

"I'd let nothing happen to you, *cara mia.* Find a flaw, bring it down. Nothing more. I'll not ask you to retrieve anything you discover, if you do crack it. Nothing to steal. Just find a weakness in the system."

"Then why?"—the only question she'd even thought to ask.

"Let's just say I have my eyes on the man who built it. I need to know if he's as good as they say. Not a single hacker I've hired so far has been able to get through."

And that had been his lure and she'd more than happily taken the bait.

She could've refused. He hadn't insisted on it. He hadn't called it as a return on all the favors he'd done for her and Frankie. He hadn't once, in the ten years since they'd met, mentioned how he'd saved her from a bullying foster parent, or from a wretched future in the juvie system. He hadn't mentioned not turning in Nat herself when he'd caught her stealing his wallet the first time they had met.

And yet, she'd done it.

Now she wondered at the questions she should've asked then.

What did Vincenzo have against Massimo?

Why this particular man?

Why his company?

Why had Vincenzo targeted the brainchild of tech genius Massimo Brunetti?

Instead, she'd thrown caution to the wind, given in to her one weakness and risked everything.

She hadn't even been able to reach Frankie during the one call Massimo had allowed her. While he'd watched her like a hawk circling a carcass, Natalie had left a message that she was going out of the country for a friend's sudden wedding, freeloading on the chance. That she would be out of coverage for a while but would call when she could. Her brother knew what a cheapskate she was.

"You're quite the storyteller, Ms. Crosetto," Massimo

had said in his delicious Italian accent, all sleep mussed before he'd rushed her out of her apartment in the middle of the night, to collect their documents.

Nat pressed her fingers around the coffee cup in her hand—no rest-stop diesel-like coffee for Mr. Pretty Rich Boy. The dark roast felt like heaven on her tongue, anchoring her.

Her spine straightened against the limo as she heard Massimo step out on the other side. His security detail—one broad six-and-half-footer—and his two assistants: a thin man in his twenties with thick glasses and messed-up curly hair. What she'd expected the computer genius to look like—not the sleek, lean, sex-on-legs stud that was Massimo, shame on her prejudice... And the second one—a woman with a dark complexion, in her forties—followed him while he spoke into his cell phone.

Coffee forgotten, Nat watched him with wide eyes as he walked back and forth in front of her speaking in rapid Italian that she couldn't understand a word of. After every other sentence, he paused, looked at her, and then started again.

Suit jacket gone, three buttons of the white dress shirt undone, that stylishly cut hair all rumpled up from his stint on her couch, he should've looked disheveled. At least a little tired. After all, he'd traveled across the Atlantic the previous day.

Instead, the stubble that coated his jaw and his upper lip, the V of his shirt glinting olive against the white of it, the snug fit of his trousers against lean hips—he was an erotic fantasy given form. The assault on her senses that had begun when she'd found him on her couch, trousers pulled up tight against powerful thighs, shirt equally snug against his shoulders, long lashes fanning against his sharp cheekbones... Her heart hadn't still recovered from it.

And then while she'd stared at him like an enthralled

idiot, he'd opened those gray eyes. For just a second, there had been something in his eyes. Something that made liquid desire float through her veins. Before he sat up with his ubiquitous cell phone attached to his ear.

"The jet is ready. Let's go."

That was all he'd said to her, before bundling her into the limo. Coffee had been acquired on the way.

When she'd refused, he'd frowned. "Drink up, Ms. Crosetto. I need you awake and alert."

She'd tensed so hard her shoulders hurt. "Why?"

"Don't worry. I'm not going to ask you to breach the security of another company."

She'd immediately relaxed and then cursed herself when a shrewd light dawned in his eyes. Afraid he'd see even more, more than what she'd already betrayed, she'd looked away.

"I want to know exactly how you were able to create that tunnel through the firewall. Both the first and the second time. Each and every step. I want to also know of any other ways you can breach BCS's security. All the truth, Ms. Crosetto. Not just the convenient parts.

"If I even get a sniff of duplicity from you, you'll wish I had sent you to prison in your own country."

Even the wonderful aroma of coffee had felt like poison then.

The threat still ringing in her ears, she swallowed when he beckoned her from the foot of the air stairs. The arrogance of the man scraped her raw. She'd survived the cruelty and negligence of a foster care system that was supposed to protect her, the heartbreak of knowing that she wasn't good enough, just yet, to be her younger brother's family.

No way was she going to let Massimo Brunetti control her with the threat of incarceration. No man was going to make her live in fear every day, not after everything she'd been through. Not this easily.

And just like that, an idea began to percolate in her mind. Her shoulders straight, she tilted her chin and walked toward him with confidence.

The narrowing of his eyes made her smile.

Yep, she'd do what he asked of her, but she'd do it on her terms.

"Call the cops if you'd like. But I'm not getting on that plane. Not until you hear me out."

Massimo disconnected his call with Leo, Natalie's husky voice filled with determination sliding over his skin like a sensuous whisper. That same voice whispering at his ear, after a night spent in bed together, limbs heavy around each other, those dark brown eyes languid with sated desire... His imagination fired up the picture faster than he could breathe.

Dios mio, of all the women to spur this insta-lust in him...she was the worst choice.

He wanted to blame the last six months of his self-imposed celibacy for it. But then, after the fiasco with Gisela, he'd been a little bit disgusted with himself. He should've known better than to play with a spoiled princess.

He'd been more than a little tired of playing the same old game of chasing a woman just for sex. He had nothing more to give right now. Not at this point in his life.

And now Leonardo had informed him that Greta had been pulled into the whole mess with Gisela. His *nonni* had decided that Gisela would make a suitable bride for the scion of the Brunetti dynasty, that she was rich enough, sophisticated enough and blue-blooded enough to spawn the next generation of Brunettis.

Which was happening...*never*. But it did mean handling

Gisela and, now, his *nonni* without giving offense to the former and hurting the second.

Of all the messes…

"Mr. Brunetti? Did you hear me? I'm not—"

He turned slowly, bracing himself. Still, the up-tilted chin and the wide brown eyes packed a punch.

This morning, she'd dressed in a light green-and-black sweater dress that hugged her slender frame, pointing out curves he'd missed last night. The loose neckline kept sliding off her shoulder showing glimpses of silky skin that beckoned his touch.

The dress ended beneath her buttocks—he'd seen enough when she'd walked ahead of him toward the limo, the knee-high leather boots displaying long legs that went on for miles. The mass of her black curls was pulled away into a tight knot at the top of her head, but in no way contained. Thick stray curls kept framing her face and she blew at them. A nervous tell that had made him smile in the limo. High forehead and a sharp nose only emphasized her gaunt face.

He frowned at the increasing appeal she held for him.

She wasn't the lush, curvaceous beauty he usually went after. Neither was she, he was sure, the experienced type he preferred, the way she'd jumped every time he came near. Women who owned their sexual desires usually meant uncomplicated but pleasurable affairs.

Delicate collarbones jutting out, the only lush thing about her was that mouth. Collagen had nothing on those luscious lips.

She had that million-dollar look that runway models seemed to have. A fragility that, despite her very clever mind, roused a protectiveness in his chest. The last thing she deserved, given the daggers she shot at him. He'd expected her to try to change his mind this morning, *sì*, but not with that brash confidence she exuded just then.

"Come, Ms. Crosetto." He gestured her back toward the limo, taking her wrist in his hand. She was truly delicate in his fingers, and they tightened instinctively. He guided her into the waiting limo and shut the door behind him. Even with the luxurious space, their knees bumped before she tucked them away.

Good, at least one of them needed to be wary of this attraction between them. "You seem to think you have a choice in this situation. My patience runs thin especially as my *nonni* is cooking up a scheme I abhor on the other side of the ocean."

"Your *nonni*?"

"My grandmother."

"I'll make this quick." She swallowed and looked up. "I'm calling your bluff."

He smiled. "You don't have any cards."

She leaned back against the seat, and crossed her legs. Her dress pulled up toward her thighs and he peeked at long, taut muscles. Shamelessly. "I'll not surrender my freedom to a stranger, a stranger moreover with the power and reach that you have, not only in your country but here, to arrange my visa at such short notice, without some security in place. God knows what you'll do to me when—" whatever she saw in his eyes, color darkened her cheeks and she cleared her throat "—what you'll decide for my fate. Even in the worst situations, one always has a choice."

She roused his curiosity so easily and held it. Turned his expectations upside down. So frequently. Unlike any woman he'd ever known. "Why do you think I'll accept any condition of yours?"

"Because you and I are alike. Hungry for new challenges. So full of arrogant belief that we're the best there is. I knew what I was risking when I attacked your security the second time. I knew…and I still couldn't stop. And you…you want to know how I did it. More than you want me in jail. You want to know what other weaknesses there could be in your design. You hate knowing someone better than you exists."

"You're not better than me." He hated that he sounded like a juvenile teenager trying to get one over the smart girl.

She smiled and grooves dug into her cheeks. Her front two teeth were overlapped, a small imperfection that only made her face more distinct, more memorable. More lovely even. Challenge and knowledge simmered in that smile, tugging at his awareness. "Sending me to jail right now doesn't serve your purpose. I'd rot there for who knows how long while what I was capable of doing eats away at you. So I'll let you kidnap me, yes, but at a price."

Laughter punched out of his mouth. *Cristo*, she had guts. And smarts. And a tart mouth he desperately wanted to taste right then. Humor and arousal were an unusual combination but had a languorous effect on his limbs. He ran a hand over his bristly jaw, trying to find the rationality, the reason, beneath both.

If he had any sense, he'd dump her at the nearest police station and wash his hands off.

It was what Leonardo was expecting. What the sane part of him said to do.

But he hadn't arrived at his place in this world without taking risks. By denying his instincts. Forget also the fact that if she went to jail, all her secrets went with her.

He didn't believe for a second that she'd only done it for the challenge. Either it was an impersonal job she took on for money, or someone she knew was deliberately targeting them.

Leonardo and he had worked too hard, for too long, to let some unknown enemy destroy everything they'd built. For now, he'd play along. Plus he'd be no kind of businessman if he didn't use her talents to his benefit. At least in the short term. He'd just have to convince Leo of her usefulness to them.

"Bene," he said.

In the intimacy of the leather interior, her soft gasp pinged on his nerves. Her eyes wide, she stared at him, swallowed, looked away and then back at him again. Her knuckles white against the dark leather.

Cristo, the woman blushed even when she was cornered.

He couldn't help liking the little criminal. He knew what it was to be the weaker one against a stronger, terrifying opponent, to have no way out, the powerlessness that came with it. "State your condition."

"You'll pay me for any services I render, like an outside consultant."

He raised a brow. "You're not bargaining for me to destroy the proof of your crime?"

She shook her head. And he had a feeling it was to hide her expression. "You won't give that up. This way, if I end up in jail, I'll make money to show for it. During the stint, I'll work on proving to you that I have no agenda of my own."

"Making money for hacking my system and then more for fixing it? I was right about you."

"If you were the computer whiz kid the world calls you, you'd have my financials in hand by now."

"Believe me, I was tempted to find the salacious details of your criminal life last night. But my brother reminded me of the importance of doing this through official channels.

"So I ordered a background check on you. Your whole life will be in my hands in a matter of hours," he added, making sure she understood the consequences. "Just because I accept your condition doesn't mean I trust you. Or intend to let you get away with it forever."

Devoid of color, her skin looked alarmingly pale against the black leather. "Is a background check necessary? All you need is to confirm that I'm dirt poor."

He shrugged.

What else was she hiding? And how was he going to explain her presence near him, 24/7, to his family, to the world? The last time he'd been in an actual relationship had been…never. He worked hard, partied hard. For more than a decade, he'd worked sixteen-hour days, buried in his lab. Coming up only for refueling.

Brunetti Cyber Securities came first. Always would.

First because he'd needed to prove to his father that he wasn't the runt he'd been called all his childhood. And prove himself to Leo even, because he'd been the golden son, the adored Brunetti heir at first. Because Leonardo had been everything Massimo hadn't been able to be.

Later, when Leo had realized the extent of their father's bullying of Massimo, he'd hated Leo's pity, his concern for him. Resented him for thinking Massimo needed handouts, that Massimo was weak. But then success itself had become the motivator; the challenge of building better and better cyber systems had become its own drug.

The more he had, the more he'd wanted. The more he wanted his father and his family and his brother to be beholden to his company for fueling much needed funds into Brunetti Finances.

Suddenly, the answer came to him. Two problems and one solution. A tangible use of the attraction between them. An explanation for her presence with him, night and day.

He'd get her to trust him with the complete truth, then

he might even take her to bed. Scratch the itch out of his system. Her innocent act would have to drop when he had the background check in his hands.

He pulled up his phone and texted his assistant waiting outside to ready a contract with all the required confidentiality clauses. Another text to notify Leo about the slight modification to his plans. "You'll have the contract by the time we land. Under one—"

"I won't leave without it."

He shook his head. "Not even I can come up with a contract like that immediately. Not without having that background check in hand first."

"How do I know I can trust you?"

"You don't." He shrugged. The hiss of her breath, the filthy curse reverberating in the confined space, made his mouth twitch.

He was enjoying this—this pitting his will against hers, this anticipation in his gut as he waited to see what she'd do next. More than he enjoyed anything with a woman in a long time. Even more than sex. He frowned at the runaway thought. "I have a countercondition of my own."

"You're already blackmailing me, kidnapping me, threatening me with incarceration. What else is there?"

"You'll be my partner for the duration. I'll compensate you for that, too."

"Partner? What kind of a partner?" Color left her cheeks, her eyes searching his. "For the last time, Mr. Brunetti, I'm not for sale. I'm not what you think—"

"Calm down, Natalie," he interrupted her, trying her name on his tongue and liking it. Her eyes sought his in the relative dark, awareness shining through them. She hadn't missed the intimacy of it, either. "It's just another part of our deal, *si*?"

"Explain. Now, please."

"I have to explain your presence at my side, 24/7. I need a romantic partner for the foreseeable future. This way—"

"You've lost your mind. I'm not staying in Italy any longer than I have to. And I refuse to be your... Why the hell would a man like you need a pretend girlfriend?"

"A man like me?"

He grinned. She glared. "You're supersmart, obviously given you're one of the tech billionaires under thirty in the world. You're—" she licked her lips then and he waited with arrested breath "—a walking, talking stud muffin. Not counting all that dynasty crap you threw at me. Why—?"

"What does a woman do with a stud muffin?"

She rolled her eyes and he laughed. "Why do you need a pretend girlfriend?"

"I was thinking a pretend fiancée actually." Her eyes bugged and he grinned, explaining, "An ex-girlfriend that I can't shake off and my *nonni* have joined forces. Believe me, it's enough to scare a grown man."

"So you don't want to hurt their feelings?"

This time, when he laughed, it felt as if his chest would burst open. The minx was such a contrasting mix of street savvy and naïveté, of smarts and innocence. She'd make a hell of a distraction from the lethargy that had filled him of late when it came to women.

"Feelings, of any of the parties involved, are the least of my concern. Greta, my *nonni*, is extremely stubborn, and has antiquated views about the whole dynasty and its continuation and legacy and all that rot. For some unfathomable reason, apparently, she's decided that Gisela Fiore, who comes with a fortune of her own, would be a sweet, biddable wife for me. Gisela is a mistake I shouldn't have indulged in, and has been...problematic since I ended our purely physical relationship almost six months ago."

For all her sass, color skimmed up Natalie's cheeks. "Problematic how?"

"She knows my relationship patterns. She knew it was only an affair. When I retreated to my lab—refueled and ready—"

"What do you mean...refueled?"

"After every big project release, I need to fill the well, so to speak."

"And you do this...*refueling* by sleeping with a woman you don't care about?"

Her distaste made him frown. "I care about the woman's pleasure. And mine. But, *sì*. Gisela knew that. Knew my pattern. I made it clear. After it was over, she started texting me a hundred times a day. She'd cry, make a scene at the few social events I attended. She flew to San Francisco and accosted me at a cyber security conference.

"Showed up outside our estate in Lake Como. Cornered my brother, Leo, at one of the events where her father was present, too."

"And her father is someone whose feelings you do give a damn about?" she said tartly.

Massimo scowled. "Giuseppe Fiore is one of the most powerful banking tycoons in Milan, in all of Italy. BCS is in the running for a hundred-billion-euro security contract with his banks that spans a decade. Leo thinks it's going to make dealing with him awkward because of Gisela.

"Why should a fling she came into with her eyes open cause problems for me now?"

"Because people are not algorithms that give you the same, expected results every time?"

"Once Giuseppe sees me with you, he'll understand that Gisela and I are long over. And this is the best way for me to keep an eye on you."

"If this tycoon's so rich and powerful, and his daughter's

good enough to be your...*whatever*, why not just marry her? Or are you holding out for love?"

He stared at her, wondering if she was joking again. Steady brown eyes held his. "Tut, tut, Natalie...you disappoint me. The last thing I need in my life is a wife who wants love and all the rainbows it brings with it. I have nothing to give a wife at present. Or in the foreseeable future.

"Just do your part, *sì*? The compensation I provide should be big enough for you to get over your distaste for me," he mocked.

Her nostrils flared. "And if I say no? If I tell your ex and your grandmother that it's all a big pretense?"

"You won't do that."

"I just—"

"Be smart about this, Natalie." All humor fled his tone. "If I find you've told me the truth about your financials, about this not being a job, then what do you have to lose? For once in your life, maybe you could use your interesting capabilities to make a living. Spend a few months in the lap of luxury in Milan. Pretend to be the fiancée of the most—"

"Arrogant, high-handed man on the planet?"

"So?"

"Fine. I agree to your conditions."

"Bene."

He stepped out of the limo and helped her do the same, keeping his fingers around her wrist. He liked having the feel of her in his hands, this mystery hacker who'd haunted his days and nights for weeks.

"All that's left now is to swap our life histories and practice the intimacy we have to pretend in front of my family and the whole world."

A pithy curse fell from her mouth and Massimo looked down at her.

She was truly the most interesting woman he'd ever met. He wouldn't hesitate to send her to jail if he found her loyalties lay with their enemy, but he would regret it all the same.

And he didn't understand even that negligible emotion dogging his rationality, his judgment.

It had never done so before.

CHAPTER FOUR

AFTER A TRANSATLANTIC flight to Milan with a creative genius who peppered her with a million incisive questions meant to unsettle her lies. Throwing in a magnificent view of white-tipped Alps, which she'd probably never see again in her life—except maybe on the return flight on her way to jail in New York. Then a quick helicopter ride up to the shores of Lake Como—because, of course, the once-in-a-lifetime scenic drive from Milan to the lake would take forever and time was a precious commodity to a tech billionaire. Finally arriving at a destination where she was nothing but a prisoner, Natalie foolishly assumed she would become oblivious to her surroundings—not the man, of course—or at least be too exhausted mentally and physically to take much more in.

She was wrong.

The chopper landed on the side of a hill, in a sea of lush, perfectly manicured gardens with azaleas and gigantic rhododendrons and a long avenue of tall plane trees that created a walkway to the lakefront. A small boat floated at the end of the steps. Beyond, the calm waters of Lake Como glittered like a dark blanket creating a stunning sight littered with boats of various sizes floating lazily to the gorgeously lit-up houses and villages scattered about.

As Natalie followed Massimo, who seemed to have forgotten about her existence, amid carefully sculpted flower beds, she spotted a hidden cave enclosed by more azaleas and even an artificial Japanese-style pond.

"Your family owns this villa?" she said, her breath catching in her throat.

Massimo stopped, took a look around absentmindedly and then turned to her. "*Sì*. One of the Brunettis, a count or a duke, maybe, I think in the nineteenth century, took possession of a Benedictine monastery in these grounds and converted it into a sumptuous noble residence. It's been in the family's possession ever since. Greta will cram a history lesson down your throat if she catches you staring at it like that."

Even his mockery couldn't fracture the awe in her chest. Fountains with water glittering out like liquid gold because of strategically placed lights, a gazebo with creepers enveloping it, two statues of majestic lions at the sides of the carriage entrance... How could he sound so dismissive and unaffected by his family's legacy? "I've never seen such beautiful gardens."

"You'd love it in spring when they're a riot of color. They're Leonardo's pride. He personally tends to them along with a team of gardeners. He can make the most reluctant plant blossom. He...loves the land and the villa and the...legacy of it all."

She was out of breath as they walked up the small, steep path while he simply marched on. "You don't?" she asked, something in his tone snagging her attention.

"I like being the one who saved it, the one who held it for the Brunettis so that they could show it off for another century," he added mysteriously.

She frowned, wondering at the contradictions of the man.

Finally, they came around the bend to a square plot that

housed the villa itself. A grand entrance portico with wide stairs that sloped toward the lake straddled the villa, which would offer three-sixty-degree views of the lake and the mountains from the grand terrace even now overflowing with guests.

The white stucco facade gleamed under the light thrown from the lake. Nat sucked in a breath as the sounds of music and people chatting in Italian flowed over her skin. A line of luxury cars stood like gatekeepers, tasked with keeping riffraff, like her, out.

She shivered even though the wind coming off the lake was more balmy than cold. Cicadas whispered all around them, the scents from the orangery they'd walked by thick and pungent in the air.

It was a world away from Brooklyn and her cheap studio apartment, a world away from everything she'd ever known.

Through the high arched front entrance, she could see suave men dressed in black suits and refined women dressed in cocktail finery with diamonds glittering at their throats and wrists. Uniformed waiters passing around champagne flutes so fine that Nat wondered if they'd break at the slightest pressure.

She rubbed her sweating palms on her hips, which only brought her attention to her own outfit. A thread of shame filled her chest and she chased it away with much needed anger. God, she'd worked hard for every small thing she owned. To make an honest living for herself and for Frankie.

She felt the heat of Massimo's body next to her, before she heard the curse from his mouth. Frowning, she craned her neck to see him. Flashes of light revealed the tension in his brow, that perfectly carved jaw so tight that it almost seemed fragile. If she didn't know better, she'd have thought he was no more inclined to go in than she was.

The suavely sophisticated man who'd taunted her was

nowhere to be seen. In his place was a stranger with tension thrumming tightly through his lean frame.

"Massimo?" she whispered, unable to stem the concern she heard in her voice. "Is something wrong?"

"My father is here," he answered softly, before he blew out another soft curse and shook his head. "He is a bully of the worst kind."

"Must run in the family, then," she quipped.

"No." His soft denial was emphatic enough that her head jerked to him. Glittering gray eyes held hers. "I'm nothing like my father." He rubbed his jaw, a tell she was beginning to recognize he did when stressed. "*Dios mio*, I forgot it's his birthday week. That means Greta checks him out of the rehabilitation clinic and parades him in front of our family and friends in an annual tradition. That means—" his gaze swung to the luxury vehicles "—everyone is here."

"Your father lives at a clinic?" She'd gotten the sense from him that family was important to him. Yet, he stared at his family's villa like it was a nest of vipers.

"He's a recovering alcoholic. The recovery, if we can call it that, has been in progress for a decade now. Leonardo put him there years ago. My brother…he's the best at eliminating anything that could damage our name, our business. Our legacy."

The bitterness in his words was unmistakable. "What do you mean your grandmother parades him?"

"You didn't get the sordid Brunetti history online before you attacked BCS?"

The man changed skins as easily as a chameleon—one minute a charming rogue, the next a cunning businessman determined to make her spill her secrets against her own best interests. "I told you, I knew nothing about who and what you are."

Hesitation flickered in his eyes, before he cast another

glance toward the villa. "If you're to be exposed to them… My father, for most of my childhood, went on alcohol-fueled rampages. He embezzled funds from the company account for his personal use. Affairs with numerous women—both willing and unwilling—lavish parties at the villa… Think of it as a decades-long, out-of-control party that Greta turned away from.

"By the time his misuse of company funds and resources came to Leonardo's notice, Brunetti Finances, which had once been the leading finance giant in all of Italy, had been on the verge of bankruptcy. A dynasty reduced to nothing but a deck of cards standing on quicksand.

"Leo had to use every inch of his business acumen to stop it from crumbling around our ears. He slogged night and day to get us out from under debt, took control of the board. I designed an e-commerce tool at the same time. He brought in millions in investors, persuaded me to build and release it myself instead of selling the design like I had planned to. I created Brunetti Cyber Securities under the family company's umbrella and launched the tool. With the revenue from it, we stopped Brunetti Finances from going under.

"Silvio, kicking and screaming, was checked into rehab. My father's still a powerful man—so many of the investors Leo brought in are of his generation. So…lest the world think we're any less than the grand dynasty we're supposed to be, lest they wonder we're not all one big happy family, we parade him annually and pretend to be his adoring sons."

Natalie refused to let the stringent quality of his words, something that almost sounded like pain, touch her.

Massimo Brunetti had blackmailed her. He was a ruthless bastard who thought women were for refueling his… He was the scion of a powerful if *dysfunctional* dynasty;

he wouldn't have even noticed her if she'd fallen at his feet. There was no need to see him as anything but a two-dimensional enemy.

No need to feel this...answering emotion in her chest, this urge to touch him and smooth out his brow.

Nope, nope, nope. So not going there.

She tugged his wrist. "We don't have to go in, then. It's not as if you can't go against their wishes, is it? I mean, you're a grown man. You run your own company. Who cares if—"

His laughter cut through her persuasive tirade, sending shock waves through her body. The warm, masculine sounds reached through her skin, into her chest, enveloping her. Burrowing inside of her.

She turned to look at him and it got worse. Much worse.

Moonlight bathed his perfect bone structure, caressing the high planes of his forehead and cheekbones, lavishing that lush mouth with tender care. His nostrils flared, grooves digging around his mouth.

She tried to ignore the attention his laughter had drawn toward them. A shiver went through her as she felt more than one set of eyes watching her, watching them from the lounge and from the terrace above. "What?" she said, channeling sarcasm.

The flash of his white smile in the darkness sent awareness through her. It wasn't fair that one man could be that gorgeous.

"You sounded as though you were championing me. Is it possible I'm growing on you, *cara mia*?"

The endearment threw her even more off balance. "As much as a malware bot could grow on an encrypted system," she threw at him. "Seriously, Massimo, can we leave?" she implored.

This time, his smile reached his gray eyes, deepening

them into molten pools of warmth. "It would only be post-poning the drama. With Greta, it's better to get it done as soon as possible. All you have to do is bat your eyelashes, pretend to adore me and thank the guests when they tell you what a lucky woman you are."

"At what time during our short and forced acquaintance did I give the impression that I'm of the kind to bat my eye-lashes and adore a man for simply existing?"

He reached for her, his large hands encompassing her in warmth. "What worries you so much, anyway?"

"I'm not worried. I…"

His gaze held hers, searching, studying. "Natalie…"

"No one's going to believe you, Massimo."

"Believe what?"

"That I'm your fiancée. That you could fall for me. I don't—" she moved her arm to encompass the sheer el-egance of everything surrounding them "—belong in this world."

His gaze raked over her, from her wavy, curly hair—even more uncontrollable after the flight—to her off-shoul-der sweater, which instead of looking stylish, to her just felt tacky in this environment, to the scuff marks on her secondhand leather boots. "*No*, you don't."

No way was she going to let him see the ridiculous dis-may settling like a boulder in her throat. What the hell was wrong with her? "We finally agree on something."

"They'll believe exactly because of that," he said cryp-tically. "It's too late, anyway. Even she's here."

"She who?"

He turned completely toward her and ate up the little distance separating them. When he raised his hand to her face, every inch of her froze. Her mouth felt dry, her pulse racing through her.

"She who I need to send a message to in the most diplomatic way possible." Gray gaze holding hers, he paused an inch away from her face. "I'm going to touch you, *cara mia—sì*?"

"Not *sì*, Massimo," she said, panic brewing in her belly, and his mouth twitched. "Why do you want to touch me?"

"For the audience," he said, his eyes saying something else completely. "I'm going to touch you and kiss you, and maybe… All you have to do is close your eyes and think of your future, unmarred by visits to jail cells."

"You're a rogue and twisted to get your kicks from a woman you're blackmailing."

Instead of anger, his eyes glittered with warmth and desire. "Shall I tell you the bare truth, then, *bella mia*? The one small nugget that distracts me when I should be focused on a hundred other priorities?"

It took everything she had to not give in to the urge to lean into him. Already, the scent of him—cologne, sweat and the cigar she'd seen him smoking this morning—entrenched deep under her skin. "What?"

"It's for the audience, *sì*. But also, for me. For us. I should very much like to learn what you taste like, Natalie, and every time you lick your lower lip, which you do, any time I set my eyes on that mouth, it's like you're inviting me to do the same. Every time you devour me with those big eyes, my nose, my mouth, my hair…you're—"

Warmth unlike she'd ever experienced uncurled low in her belly, spreading its wicked fingers to each limb until she was made of honey. He'd barely even touched her and she was branded by the honesty in his words. Desire pervaded his every word, his accent deepening with each breath. "I'm not, I mean… I wasn't…"

Something almost like possessiveness flitted in his eyes. Because, really, what did she know of men. Especially of men like Massimo Brunetti. "One kiss, Natalie. Be honest. Tell me you haven't wondered, too. Tell me you haven't been thinking of the heat between us and I'll make do with a kiss on the cheek."

She simply nodded, no words coming to her aid. A light-headedness traversed through her entire body, stealing her good sense.

If he'd coerced her, if he'd grabbed her hands or pulled her to him roughly, the spell of the moment would have broken. If he had taken it as his due, instead of asking, the tentative connection between them would've fractured. She would've regained the little common sense she possessed.

But he didn't.

Massimo didn't do anything that she expected of him. And when he did the unexpected, he stole away the ground from under her.

As if she were the most precious possession to come into his hands, his fingers landed on her wrists softly. Turning one, he raised it to his mouth. The first press of his lips against the sensitive skin sent tremors of longing through her. He didn't let her look away, either. The flick of his tongue over the plump vein, the stubble surrounding his mouth scraping in contrast, the sight of his arrogant head bent to her wrist…everything conspired and coalesced into a temptation neither her body nor her mind could resist.

Knees trembling, she let out a soft gasp, an erotic sound that deepened the gray fire in his eyes. When he pulled her toward him, she went, desperately needing more. And he delivered, his fingers digging into her shoulders, moving lower, touching every inch of her. The first, barely there slide of her breasts against his chest was a sensation she'd remember forever. Breath punched out of her on a long hiss, the strength of his powerful thighs a teasing caress against her own.

He let his fingers splay on her back. The tips reached the

dip of her waist, spanned it and then moved back up. The rough hitch of his breath was music to her ears, bringing the knowledge to her ensnared senses that he wanted her just as much as she did him. When he moved his hands up from her waist, just a couple of tempting inches, the tips barely even grazing the sides of her breasts, she stiffened, tried to move away and stumbled until her hip bumped against his front and her thigh was caught between his.

Electricity zinged through her veins. He was so solidly masculine around her, both a haven of warmth and demanding need. Fingers on her shoulders held her rigid as he bent that mouth finally. A kiss from that mouth at her cheek, at her temple, the tip of her nose—like wings of a butterfly. And then he brushed his mouth against hers. "From the moment I realized you were the hacker who'd haunted my days and nights...all I could think of was doing this."

Nat jerked in his embrace, the sensations generated by the contact so delicious. So hot. If not for the heat in her veins, she'd have laughed for he did it with that scientific precision, as if an inch of her couldn't be left unexplored. Tired of waiting for him, she followed his lips with her own, seeking the heat and promise.

Sensations jerked through her at the hard contact. She licked his lower lip, pressed herself into his warmth.

She heard the soft curse he left on her lips, saw shock and something indefinable widen his eyes. As if he, too, had been unprepared for the spark to turn into a full-blown fire. And then he was repeating the torment all over again. For a hard, lean man, he had the most incredibly soft lips. And his beard, oh, it was such a contrasting scrape against the softness of his kisses, a pleading moan pushed out of her own mouth.

"You taste sweet and tart, *cara mia*," he said huskily, as lost as she was.

Kissing her all over, his long fingers climbing up her back, sliding around the nape of her neck, sneaking into her hair. And then, suddenly, his grip tightened there. When he pulled, her face tilted back, an offering she willingly gave.

Desire stamped out everything else from his arrogant features—the casual humor, the ambitious billionaire—leaving a starkness to him.

Gaze locked on her own, this time, when he bent that mouth to hers, there was no exploration. No entreating. He nipped at her lower lip, and blew warm breath over the hurt. Licked and plundered. A continuous assault that made tingles spread out. He took, and yet gave, such indescribable pleasure. The stroke of his tongue was a caress that had her gasping into his mouth. He licked into hers with an erotic hunger that had her rising up to her toes, burrowing into him to get even closer, clinging to his solid shoulders with shallow breaths. The scent of him, so familiarly male already, coated every inch of her.

Her own hands wandered restlessly, from the scrape of his beard to his neck and into his hair, pulling, tugging, wanting more of him. Desperate to keep the madness going. She moved them over his chest, loving the sinew, thanking the stars that he'd taken off the jacket. His shirt was no barrier against the heat he radiated. Air was something he granted her amid the hungry kisses.

"*Altro*, Natalie *mia*. I need more." His heated whisper inflamed her with its honesty. The differences between them melted away under the heat of their touch.

Tongues dueled, teeth banged, as the kiss lost its finesse and became nothing but hunger. A gateway to something much more.

Her back was bowed, his hands at her waist pulling her up, his fingers digging painfully into her hips. Her breasts crushed against his chest. Natalie could do nothing but drown in the avalanche of sensations. Revel in the pleasure coursing through her.

With a growly moan, Natalie pushed away at his hands, and thrust her hips into his. Driven by instinct, desperate for more. Not wanting the moment to end.

The slight graze of his erection against her soft belly before he pushed her firmly back jolted her out of the feral need pumping through her veins. His curse was loud and harsh in the slumbering silence of the night all around them.

She stared into the piercing gaze, stunned, mouth stinging. His breath was harsher than her own, his pupils dilated. The lean chest falling and rising in a rhythm her own matched. Her hands fell away from him, empty. Slowly, softly, their surroundings—the air redolent with the scent of flowers, their audience, more than one set of eyes devouring them—began to filter through her consciousness. Yet, nothing could penetrate fully the haze of pleasure the kiss had left in her mind. Her limbs, her belly, her breasts… she felt like she was swimming in honey. Naked.

"That went farther than I anticipated." He spoke slowly, as if each word had to be pulled out. Hoarse. His English thickly accented for the first time. "To go any further, *cara mia*, we'll have to revisit our—"

"I'm not sleeping with you," Nat somehow managed to whisper, her pulse still zigzagging all over the place. Desperate to cut off whatever asinine, calculating announcement he'd have made. It was bad enough she had crawled all over him, in front of his family and friends, no less. Had lost herself in that kiss, completely.

She couldn't let him insult her, too, by offering to pay for more services rendered or some such.

The kiss and the intensity of it had thrown him, too. As inexperienced as she was with arrogant, confounding men who kissed like fantasies given life, she could see the contradiction in his eyes, the tension in his brow. He'd expected it to be a pleasant diversion, for both himself and his bloody audience, a game of kissing the criminal, but it had slipped out of his control and morphed into something much more.

But for her, it had been her first kiss. A memory to be cherished.

For once in her life, she'd been allowed to be selfish. Given the sex-god incarnate staring at her, she was allowed to be foolish and flighty. Once. But no more.

"Why not?" he taunted back.

"Now you sound like that pretty, rich boy denied his new toy."

Color flooded his cheeks. "You can't deny the connection between us. From that first moment. It's already messing with my rationality."

She fisted her hands at her sides. Better than running them over her trembling lips. "Because we're not equals, Mr. Brunetti." He scowled at her use of his formal name. "How can I be sure what your motives are? How would I know if you're doing it because you want to try the novelty of having the hacker who bested you catering to your desires, under your control, in your bed—" she purposely made her words crude, for her own benefit "—or because you're arrogant enough to believe that you're such a good lay that I'll spill all my secrets to you in gratitude?"

He tilted her chin up, mouth tensed. "I know my own mind, *cara mia*. I want you, Natalie." His gaze touched her lips with such possessiveness that contradicted the logical, rational man she glimpsed in him. "I've never been attracted to a woman so much that I want to own both her body and mind."

His jaw tightened, the raw honesty of his words a revelation to both of them.

She wanted to believe him so desperately. Wished she had that innocence, those rose-tinted glasses she'd lost so long ago, to see all of this as some fantastic fairy tale. That all of it could have a happy ending.

Even for a short affair where she could live, be herself for a small capsule of time. But she wasn't built to have casual, torrid affairs with complex men.

"It doesn't have to complicate matters."

"Could you be so arrogant to think I'll fall at your feet?"

"Arrogance has nothing to do with it. That kiss speaks for itself."

"You've turned my world upside down in the matter of a few hours. You hold my fate in your hands.

"If I sleep with you, can you ever be sure if I was doing it because I wanted to persuade you to let me go or because I really wanted to have sex with you?" She wiped the taste of him from her mouth, feeling a sudden dejection. "All the power is in your hands, Massimo. Which means neither of us could ever be sure of our motives."

He didn't quite flinch. A vein jumped in his temple, and he sighed. "Even having been on the other side once, power and privilege are still hard to separate from yourself."

Just like that, he shredded all the defenses she'd propped up against him into mere dust. She'd have been less scared if he'd been less understanding, less kind, less... *Massimo*.

No man, she had a feeling, was close to the complexity of Massimo Brunetti.

And if he grew up amid this, how could he know what it meant to be powerless?

He took her hand in his and laced their fingers. When she shivered, he pulled her to his side with an arm around her shoulders. Even fighting it, Natalie couldn't help leaning on him, stealing his warmth for herself.

When he propelled her forward, she went, like a puppet whose strings he held with those elegant fingers.

The logic she'd sprouted sounded so right.

Now if only she could get her body to stop fixating on the taste and warmth of Massimo's kiss and treat this whole thing…as a job. A job on which her entire future depended.

CHAPTER FIVE

THE THEME OF elegant affluence continued indoors including the wide steps and the portico. More fool her if she expected anything less. Even the remnants of his kiss couldn't numb her to the decadent elegance of his home.

The large marble foyer had a wraparound marble staircase with beautifully dressed men and women drifting around it. A large Venetian chandelier hung from the high ceiling with hand-painted frescoes that she had to crane her neck to look at. Her entire apartment could fit into the front lounge. A dark red Persian rug covered a small area and beautiful, original works of art hung on the wall.

Natalie could feel so many sets of eyes on her and Massimo and soft whispers across the room as if the cicadas had drifted inside. She was suddenly glad Massimo had vetoed her request to leave. Prolonging this moment wouldn't change the reality of who she was.

A large, rectangular, gold-edged mirror hung on one cream wall. One passing glance at it as Massimo tugged her with him told Natalie she stood out like a sore thumb in this crowd. She grabbed a champagne flute from a uniformed waiter and threw it back as if it were cheap, boxed wine.

Massimo cast her a wry look. "You're not getting drunk on me, *cara mia*."

"Why not? It's not as if I can contribute anything important to the conversation around me."

He rubbed a finger over a drop lingering on her upper

lip. The heat from the pad of his thumb tingled her skin. "Maybe not to them, *si*? But to me, you're the most interesting person in this room." A lock of hair fell forward onto his forehead as he leaned down to whisper. His eyes shone with a roguish glint, his mouth tilting up on one side. "Take pity on me, *bella mia*. Only you here with me is making this evening bearable."

Her pulse raced. The villa, the grounds, nothing could equal the effortless magic he weaved with his words. "You're even more dangerous when you set out to be charming." She pushed the lock of hair away from his face, and then snatched her hand back when he leaned into her touch. How could his face, his body, his expressions, feel so familiar already to her? Granted, it was hard to maintain animosity toward a man who kissed like it was the single most fascinating experience of his life. "You want me to believe you're not part of this crowd?"

"I was the stereotypical geek growing up. Socially awkward, sick far too often, hiding behind the escape that computers provided. Trying to persuade myself that I didn't need my father's or this crowd's approval."

She could do nothing but stare.

My father is a bully. Suddenly, his words, the tension in him before coming in, made all the sense.

"Ah... I've rendered you mute with my sad story, *si*?"

She shook her head, something she'd long buried searching for voice now. Longing to be shared with a man who was from a different world and yet, somehow, she knew would understand. "The loneliness was the hardest for me. For all their rationality, computers don't offer warmth. Or a kind word, when needed."

His jaw tight, his eyes searched hers. "Now you pity me."

She grabbed his hand and pulled him to her. The stubble on his jaw pricked her palm, his sharp breaths stroked her skin, and still she couldn't pull away. Couldn't get her heart to disengage. "I'm just having difficulty imagining this...hot, sexy, gorgeous man in front of me as an awkward, pimply, pasty geek."

"I never said pimply or pasty," he said, before he took her mouth in a savage kiss that knocked the breath out of her very lungs. The searing press of their lips lasted maybe a few seconds and yet it was hot, all-consuming, a synergy of more than just their mouths.

Hands on her shoulders, he pushed her back too soon. His eyes mesmerized with the heat in them. "If I apologize for that, I will not mean it."

She licked her lip, wanting to savor the lingering taste of him. "I...just..."

He grinned and she grinned back like a fool.

If nothing else, the fast and hard kiss made Natalie numb to every other dynamic and drama that played out over the next few hours. Numbed her toward the glittering butterflies sipping champagne ever so delicately and the men fawning over them.

Only her *bitchery* felt more than justified as she met an awful number of perfectly horrid people who stared at her as if she were an exhibit.

"Ooh, look at the low-class, unrefined American in her thrift-store clothes and shoes, pretending to belong on one of Milan's most wanted bachelors' arm," she whispered, sick of that feeling in her belly.

"You didn't tell me you speak Italian so well," he said, confirming her understanding of the looks cast her way. A pinprick of hurt flashed and she shrugged it away.

"I don't have to speak Italian. Elitist snobbery, apparently, transcends the boundaries of language."

His laughter was raucous, booming, shaking his body, translating the motion to her own as she was neatly wedged against his side. He looked breathtakingly gorgeous. Conversations around them came to a stunning halt, the silence left behind so loud that Natalie gazed around with wide eyes.

"You know what I like about you the most, *cara mia*?"

The stupid organ that was her heart went pitter-patter. "That I'm far cleverer than you are?"

His teeth flashed at her and she had the overwhelming urge to taste that smile again. To take the warmth of it into her. "That tart mouth and what comes out of it…" His voice dipped, turned huskier, his gaze riveted to her mouth. "How is it possible that it also tastes so incredibly sweet?"

Her cheeks heated. "Massimo, please don't—"

"How much longer must I wait before you introduce your latest toy to us, Massimo?"

This had to be Greta. Natalie cringed at having been caught staring at Massimo like a lovesick fool.

The older woman, clad in a white-and-black cocktail dress that went superbly well with her gray hair, speared her with a frosty look that made her disapproval apparent without words.

Massimo dutifully bent his cheek for his grandmother's kiss.

"Nonni, this is my fiancée, Natalie Crosetto—" the lie flowed smoothly from his lips "—the most interesting woman I've met in…forever—" turned into a truth that knocked the breath out of her lungs in the next second. He lifted their laced fingers to his mouth and pressed a kiss to the back of her hand. "She let me…*persuade* her to marry me."

He winked at her as she shook Greta's hand, answering her invasive questions about her life. About her family. About her past. For a wicked moment, she played with telling the woman all the details of her colorful past. But she had no wish to embarrass Massimo or herself. She nodded like a dutiful child while Greta, with a voice that sounded like a boom box and with heavily accented English, told her what a privilege it was to land the scion of the Brunetti clan.

Natalie had had enough when Greta started rattling on and on about pedigree. "Is your grandson a fish to be caught, Mrs. Giovanni?" she said, tongue-in-cheek.

"You would offend your relationship with Giuseppe Fiore for this nobody, Massimo?" Greta said, loudly enough for everyone to hear her. "Reject an heiress like Gisela, who would make you the perfect bride?"

"I offer insult to no one, Nonni," Massimo replied in an equally steely tone, before he tucked Natalie into his side protectively. The smile bestowed on Natalie was warm, his embrace too honest and too possessive. So dangerous that even she wanted to buy in to their pretense.

He placed another kiss on the underside of her wrist.

Natalie shivered, struggling against falling into his spell again. Neither did she miss the presence of the petite woman, her voluptuous curves dressed in a green silk that was the height of sophistication, her pretty face artfully made up to accentuate the dark black eyes and the scarlet painted mouth, hanging a few steps back, listening to their conversation as if her life depended on it.

"I fell in love with a woman with whom I have a world of things in common," Massimo said in a husky voice, his eyes holding hers. "She's nothing like anyone I've ever met. Even I didn't expect it. Giuseppe or you or any other person has nothing to do with this."

With that he pivoted them away in another direction without waiting for Greta's reply.

Nat swallowed the thanks that rose to her lips. She was damned if she was going to thank him for rescuing her from a situation he'd put her in in the first place. She managed to flit through the guests at his side for the next two hours without running away screaming.

All through it, Nat was aware of the tall, dark, striking man who watched her every move like a hawk.

Leonardo Brunetti, the only other person there who knew what she was. The cold hauteur in his eyes, the distaste in his expression as he noted Massimo's arm around her waist, said more than enough.

Massimo seemed to be saving the best for last, *yippee*.

"Silence and the four walls of a jail cell don't sound like such a bad prospect right now," she said as he pulled her in yet another direction. "What do you think is the market rate for enduring emotional trauma these days?"

Massimo smiled down at her. She tried to ignore that it lit up his whole face. The reassurance in the way he squeezed her fingers. Devil or angel, she didn't know what to make of this man. "Ahh...but I would miss you, *cara mia*." She stiffened when he tugged her tight against him, his mouth buried at her temple. "Don't let Leonardo scare you, *sì*? My brother's bark is much worse than his bite."

Natalie nodded, not at all surprised that he'd noted her reaction to his older brother. He was far too perceptive. Barely two days since they'd met and he'd already tripped her up far too many times.

The only person who would actually meet her eyes, despite the confusion in her own when Massimo introduced her, was his grandmother's stepdaughter, Alessandra Giovanni. Who turned out to be *the famous supermodel* Alessandra Giovanni, naturally. Almost six feet tall, the woman had a stunning face that photographers over the world loved, with a bombshell body that would fire any red-blooded man's fantasy. *And* she'd grown up with Massimo and Leonardo after coming to live with Greta and her father when she'd been twelve.

Any twinge of jealousy Natalie was foolish enough to feel that this gorgeous creature knew Massimo intimately died at the genuine affection in her smile. "Love and you, Massimo? Has the world turned upside down?" she said in an American accent that warmed Nat.

"She's a hacker who can take down the best security systems in the world," Massimo whispered in outraged mockery that made Nat roll her eyes. "She took me down, Alex. Me!"

"Ah..." Alessandra said, her twinkling gaze studying them both. "Now that makes perfect sense." Then the woman colored. "Not that you're not lovely enough for Massimo to want beyond that. You're just...so not his type." She grimaced and covered her face with a groan. Natalie liked her a lot for that imperfection. "I'm making an utter ass of myself, aren't I? What I mean is you have to be extraordinarily special for Massimo to have not only fallen in love with you so quickly but to have even considered forever... Nothing, and I mean nothing, comes before his tech empire for Massimo."

"Let's just say Massimo couldn't bear it that I might be better than him," Nat replied. "And in a strategy of if you can't beat them join them, he locked me down in a contract I couldn't resist."

Alessandra laughed at that. A lovely, genuine smile that was like a beacon of light amid the artificial glitter around them. "Oh, I like you, Natalie. Please feel free to come to me if you need ammunition against him."

Her smile dimming, Natalie nodded. She would've loved to have a friend like Alessandra for real. But this wasn't her life. This incredibly sophisticated woman wouldn't say hello to Natalie if she knew all the things she'd done to survive.

None of these people would, even Massimo.

This was a virtual reality program she was projecting herself into.

By the time they reached the two gentlemen—she used that word for lack of a better term, for they both studied her from top to toe with an invasive and at the same time dismissive curiosity that raised all her hackles—Massimo had saved for the last, Nat couldn't give a damn.

Leonardo Brunetti, like Massimo, dominated the space he occupied. Like his brother, he was lean but broad-shouldered, his face more rugged and brutish than sharp like Massimo's, cynicism and disdain all but set into the planes. An aura of power clung to him like a second skin. Unlike Massimo, who she'd realized possessed a devilish sense of humor, there was nothing gentle or merciful about the curve of his mouth or the icy blue gaze he leveled at her.

Here was a man who was determined to be pleased by nothing and no one. At least, not just her.

The second man, Silvio, was as tall as his sons and a mixture of both. Hair gray at the temples, his face only retained a vestige of the handsome youth he must have been. His features seemed as if they'd been smudged and distorted by years of alcohol. Puffy bags sagged under his eyes while his mouth seemed to be curled into a permanent sneer.

Next to his powerful, dominating sons, he was a pale imitation, in both stature and presence. And yet, having been a recipient of it far too many times, Natalie could see the casual cruelty he was capable of in his rough features, in the sneer he directed at her, could imagine him as a rough brute bullying a young, innocent boy.

Massimo's arm around her waist tightened. Nat leaned into his weight, seeking and giving comfort automatically. As if they were together against the whole world. Not that he noticed. He was too caught up in whatever mind game ensued between his father and him.

"Massimo?" She nudged him, needing for the long day to be over.

"Natalie, this is my father, Silvio Brunetti, and my brother, Leonardo. This is Natalie Crosetto, my fiancée."

"What do you do, Ms. Crosetto?" Silvio shot at her without a preamble, his gaze utterly dismissive of her attire.

"I'm a clerk at a loan office, Mr. Brunetti," Natalie answered, refusing to let another snotty man make her feel ashamed.

"Your family—"

"My family is no one, since my father walked out one night and left me to fend for myself. If not for a conscientious social worker, I wouldn't have known he had fathered a son with a different woman who he also abandoned."

She felt Massimo's surprise at her side, his frown.

It wasn't as if he wasn't going to find out soon, anyway. And really, having met his snotty family, she felt as if she had nothing to be ashamed of. Even her deadbeat dad.

"Ah...at least you've saved us the bother of a background check," Silvio finished simply.

Natalie couldn't even muster outrage. Massimo could be called Prince Charming if this was the role model he'd grown up with.

His gaze swung to Massimo's. "You should be careful, Massimo, or you'll lose more than Giuseppe's contract. Empires are not built on weaknesses." Something oily smirked from his eyes. "You do not need to marry the girl to enjoy her."

"I don't need your advice," Massimo ground out through gritted teeth. Fury cast a dark shadow on his features. "On empires or weaknesses. Or how to treat women for that matter, *sì*?"

"You were always the weak link in our family," Silvio said, a cruel sneer to his mouth that disturbed her on so many levels.

Was this what Massimo had had to put up with, growing up?

Silvio bent toward Massimo. "Leo tells me the security system you've built has been breached. I knew you shouldn't be trusted, not in the long term. I warned your brother to not tie Brunetti Finances with you. Don't let the little success you've enjoyed thanks to your older brother's benevolence go to—"

"Basta!" With one arm casually extended, Leonardo stopped Massimo from launching at their father, while with his softly delivered command, he shut his father up. Thankfully, most of the guests had already ventured into the next room when dinner had been announced.

"It is not your company anymore, Silvio. Do not forget that you come out of the clinic for one week per year at my discretion. *Mine.*" Leonardo's warning packed no punches. "One word from Massimo and you'll not even see that little freedom."

Silvio left without another word, a little sliver of fear in his puffed-up eyes.

Natalie wondered at how the older man cowered in front of his eldest. Leonardo reminded her of a predator—one who would cock his head and look at you in one breath and then pounce in the next.

But it was the fury on Massimo's face as he turned toward Leonardo that had her chest tight with pressure.

"You told him about a small breach after everything I've done for that blasted company and this family?" he said, his jaw so tight that it seemed to be cast in stone. Pain and anger swirled like shadows in his eyes. "You enabled him for years, you let him abuse…" Massimo turned away, his lean frame vibrating with contained tension.

A whiteness emerged around Leonardo's mouth. Neither had Nat missed his flinch when Massimo had turned on him. "I had to tell him, Massimo. He's the biggest shareholder after you and me. I need…*we* need his help to manage the old cronies on the board if I have to tell them about the breach. You're supposed to be fixing it. Instead…" Leonardo's gaze swung to Natalie.

There was no overt hostility in his dark eyes but she felt like scum on the underside of a rock.

A challenge dawned in Massimo's eyes as he pushed himself into Leonardo's personal space, shuffling Natalie behind his broad shoulders. She fought against the warmth that curled in her chest. If she wasn't careful, Massimo was going to tie her up in knots, swinging from one emotion to the other.

"Would you like to finish that sentence, Leonardo?"

Her heart pumped so hard that Natalie felt it like an ache in her chest.

"Do you know what you're doing, Massimo?"

Massimo didn't back down. "Do you not trust me now?"

The space of a heartbeat, filled with so much tension, before Leonardo said, "Of course I do. I have never trusted anyone more than I do you."

Massimo walked away. Without another word.

If Massimo could be influenced by Leonardo, if things didn't get fixed soon… She shivered at the consequences. Would Massimo ever let it happen?

She turned to Leonardo, her throat strangely achy. "Aren't you going after him?"

Leonardo's head jerked toward her. He'd forgotten about her. And suddenly, she wished she'd just quietly disappeared. "Excuse me?"

She tried to spot Massimo through the crowd. "He's clearly…distressed. Shouldn't you see that he's okay?"

"Massimo is not a child."

"No, but it's clear that he still resents you for what you failed to do when *he was a* child, isn't it?"

The barb pricked the hard face. The all-powerful Leonardo Brunetti flinched again. "Stay out of our family's matters, Ms. Crosetto. If your fate were up to me—"

"But, notwithstanding your father's assumptions, it's not up to you, Leonardo." He raised a brow at her familiarity with his name. She found she didn't care. "It's up to Massimo.

"Save your threats for someone who hasn't seen the skeletons in your family's prestigious closet."

He studied her with such an intensity that her cheeks burned. "Ah… I see it now."

Nat folded her hands, feeling as small as a bug under a microscope. Her cheap clothes, her untamed hair, even her shoes—nothing was missed by his gaze. "See what?"

"The draw you hold for him. You're obviously talented since you bypassed his design. You're bold, even when cornered, and from that conveniently sad backstory, you're quite the damsel in distress, *si*?

"My brother—" again that flash of concern sat oddly on that ruthless face "—has a weakness for the unfortunate. You're a novelty, Ms. Crosetto. Once that wears off, once he realizes what a liability you are against his ambition, he'll send you where you belong.

"Massimo has an unending thirst, a relentless ambition, to be the master of the world."

"You get your kicks by scaring people who can't defend themselves?"

"I saw that kiss. I saw the way you look at him already, the flash of concern in your eyes when my father spewed his usual poison. This will not end well for you, even if not in jail.

"Tell him the truth and get out of our lives while you still can."

He bowed his head and walked away, leaving Natalie reeling. She'd have ignored his threats if not for the ring of truth in his words. That was two people who were close to him that had warned her about Massimo's ambition.

Suddenly, she felt as lost as she'd felt the morning she'd woken up to discover her father had walked out on her. Wanting to trust and hope that things would right themselves and then being crushed by that hope. Learning to lean on no one but herself. Learning to look out for herself in the big, bad world.

Leonardo Brunetti was right.

Getting out of here without sinking farther into the pit she'd dug herself was the most important thing. She couldn't afford to risk getting closer to Massimo, not even to save herself. She'd no idea how long his leniency toward her would last.

She had to forget that kiss, had to forget Massimo's laughter, the way his eyes glowed when they shared a joke, the sense of challenge he issued to her. She needed to forget the shadows of pain in his eyes when he'd spoken to his father.

She needed to remember that gorgeous, complex man had only looked at her because she had thrown herself into his path by recklessly posing a threat to the most important thing to him—his company.

CHAPTER SIX

IT TOOK A few hours before Massimo emerged from the dark mood a confrontation with his father always left him in. From the quick but ugly jaunt into childhood memories.

He navigated the unlit corridors from his wing to the new guest suites with his rescue dogs, Lila and Hero, limping along by his side, without encountering any more of his family members or their unending drama. On a given day, he could only stomach so much of Greta's relentless carping about the Brunetti dynasty, the increasingly frequent glimpses of loneliness in Alessandra's eyes, Silvio's penchant for spewing poison—a whole year's worth, in a week—and Leonardo's cynicism.

Dios mio, he should be immune to his father's taunts by now.

Instead, he reverted to that emotional, always sick *runt* Silvio used to call him, would still call him if he weren't so terrified of Leonardo.

The boy who'd been heartbroken and unable to protect her when his mother had put up with Silvio's emotional taunts for so long just to be near him, the teenager who'd had to contend with the four walls of his home instead of the outside world and friends, the young adult who'd been terrified that each vicious asthma attack would be the last one.

Only thanks to a miracle drug in his teens had he started getting better, started seeing that he had a future.

The tech world lauded his genius, praised his innovative

capabilities that had designed an e-commerce tool worth billions by his nineteenth birthday...and yet, the shadows of that boy still echoed within him.

Computers and the rationality they brought to his tumultuous life, the control and power they'd brought to his hands in a powerless situation, had been his lifeline. An escape from his father's constant verbal abuse away from the eyes of Greta or Leonardo.

That he'd left Natalie to the pack of wolves that was his family had fractured his mood. For all of Silvio's crude remarks, it was Leonardo who was the most dangerous of them.

He grinned, remembering Natalie had no problem standing up to him. No doubt the little minx could hold her own against them. This protectiveness he felt for her...was ridiculous. Unnecessary.

But he couldn't arrest the pulse of excitement as he knocked on the door to her suite. Twice. He was about to knock for the third time when a muffled curse made him grin.

The door opened wide with her leaning against it, eyes mussed with sleep and dark shadows under. Her hair was in such a wild disarray that it was a cloud around her delicate face. The overhead lights she'd switched on outlined her body in caressing lines. A loose T-shirt fell inches above her knees, the neckline baring the delicate crook of her neck.

Innocence and wildness combined together, she made him want to pick her up and crawl into the bed behind her, to drown himself in all that rumpled warmth, to bury his mouth at that pulse at her neck, to discover every rise and dip...

"All the power is in your hands, Massimo."

An uncomfortable sensation skittered in his chest.

She was right. They were not equals.

He wasn't the kind of man who preyed on the weak. He'd never be another Silvio, not even in thought. He couldn't kiss that luscious mouth of hers until he didn't hold her freedom in his hands.

It was imperative that he get to the bottom of the truth. And not just so they could explore this…thing between them. At leisure. No, he needed this threat to dissolve before they could continue talks with Giuseppe Fiore.

But it didn't mean he couldn't enjoy the delectable sight she made. Or rile her up. Or pit his smarts against hers. Or needle her. To give him the truth and more. Natalie was the first woman who challenged him on every level.

He leaned against the archway and smiled at the confusion in her eyes. *"Buongiorno, cara mia."*

"Massimo?" She thrust her fingers through her messy hair, which thrust her breasts up and revealed a little more of her toned thighs. Devoid of makeup or that intractable expression she wore like an armor, he was reminded of how painfully young she really was.

Twenty-two, the report had said. *Cristo*, he'd hate sending her to jail.

"What time is it?"

He grinned. "Four-ten."

"Four-ten when?" she said, grumpy and cute and sexy.

"In the morning."

She looked behind her, peeked into the corridor, then back up at him. Her hand went to the neckline of her T-shirt and tugged it up. Her knees bumped, color climbing up her cheek. "What do you want? I went to bed barely a few hours ago."

"We need to get to work."

"Now?"

"Sì."

"Are you mad? You flew to New York, you barely slept at my apartment, didn't even nod off on the flight and now... Massimo, don't you need sleep?"

He shrugged.

"Well, normal mortals like me do. And that bed is... heaven."

He kept his gaze on hers. "I'll allow you an early night so that you can enjoy the bed some more."

She shook her head. "I'm messed up thanks to jet lag. I barely survived that vicious attack by your family. I don't have enough brain cells to rub together much less—"

"*Sì*, you will, *cara mia*. Keeping you out of a jail cell depends on your performance in my lab, every day. Your freedom needs to be earned. Starting now. I'll give you thumbprint access to my lab and—"

"Your lab?" Her eyes widened. "You're letting me near a computer?"

"I got your financials back."

She folded her arms and leaned against the door. "And?"

"You have a lot of debt."

White teeth dug into her bottom lip. "Do you believe me now?"

"That you didn't do it for personal gain? *Sì*." He ran a hand over his neck. "I paid it off."

"What?"

"I paid off your debts."

She moved closer to him, unaware of her movements, the heat from her body licking against his. The skin of her cheeks looked so soft he had to fist his hands. "You paid them off...nine thousand dollars...you paid it off..." She swayed against the door and righted herself. "Why?"

"It was no more than a little change for me. And if it keeps your loyalties directed away from—"

"You think you can buy my loyalty?"

"I'm taking away reasons for you to do something so stupid again. To decouple yourself from a person who led you into jeopardizing your future."

"You didn't pay it off because you felt sorry for me?"

"I'm a businessman first and foremost, Natalie. I'll do anything to protect an asset."

"Not even a little bit relieved that your instincts were right about me?"

He frowned. "I took a calculated risk by bringing you here, whether you took money for the job or not. But trusting some vague instinct, no."

"Does a cold report with numbers make so much of a difference?"

"Of course it does. Numbers don't lie, numbers don't make you lose objectivity. And those numbers will shut up Leonardo's questions about whether I'm sane to be bringing you into the biggest contract we've ever courted.

"Numbers over everything else, *bella mia*, over emotions, over instinct, over weaknesses. Always."

Her face fell. And the question hurtled out of his mouth. "Why does it matter to you that I trust instincts and feelings?"

"What if I can't always provide concrete proof for my innocence?"

Her question came at him like an invisible punch. Reminding him that she stayed a step ahead of him. That for all that innocence in her kiss, she was always thinking of her own survival. That she was just as ruthless about protecting herself and her lies as he was with his company.

"Then I suggest that you don't get involved in anything that might require you to prove your innocence, *cara mia*." He pushed her into the room, before he was tempted to grill her about the truth, and kiss her when she lied. "Change and meet me outside. I'll show you my bat cave."

* * *

She was debt free—like, completely debt free. For the first time in her life.

Unless Massimo was playing games with her...

Wrapping her arms around herself, Natalie stared at the man walking in front of her, taking in the wet gleam of his jet-black hair, the thick cable sweater lovingly caressing his shoulders and the light blue denim doing wonders to his behind and... God, where was she?

No, Massimo had no reason to trick her. And, she knew, there was no point in arguing with him about paying him back.

Dawn swept into the long corridor through the exquisitely designed arches in ever increasing curtains across the cream marble floor, creeping up and up, slowly illuminating the even more exquisitely detailed murals on the other wall that reached up toward the colorful frescoes upon the domed ceilings.

Every arch and crevice spoke of elegant wealth, of subtle power.

Like he'd said, it was mere change for him.

But for her, suddenly, the world felt like it had opened up into infinite possibilities.

She reached for him as they turned the corner into another hallway. "Thanks, Massimo. I just... You've no idea what it means to me to be debt free."

He tightened his fingers over hers, pulling her to his side. "Tell me."

Surprised, she searched his eyes. "Digging for information?"

"You never stop looking for hidden meanings and agendas, do you?" Exasperation coated his words.

"I'm sorry. It comes with never having had anyone to rely on for so long."

His gaze held hers, understanding and curiosity and so much more in it. "Forgetting your crime and my blackmailing you and all these lies…you're a mystery to me, Natalie. I never could resist one."

She looked away at the beautiful gardens awash in soft pink light. "It means I can start saving instead of just paying interest on my loans. It means I can get out of that dingy studio and maybe find a two-bedroom apartment in a much nicer neighborhood so that Frankie can go to a good public school. It means that I can adopt him much sooner than I had planned. Much, much sooner."

"So you didn't make him up?" he said, a tenderness in his eyes.

She laughed and punched his bicep. "Of course I didn't. When you return my cell to me, I'll show you a pic of him."

"When did you learn about him?"

"About…three years ago." Just the memory of the day put a lump in her throat. "I grew up thinking I was all alone in the world. Apparently, my father, after walking out on me, went and did the same to another woman and her child. This social worker who'd known me when I was in the system…she contacted me when he entered the system.

"I went to see him and Frankie—he was six and so scared. When I held him, I felt as if the universe had done something right in my life for the first time. He…is this adorable, funny, cute little guy. I told him right there that one day he'd come live with me.

"Until then, I'd just drifted from minimum wage job to job. I took out a loan the next day, enrolled in a couple of classes at the community college and…realized it wasn't going to be as easy as I'd thought it would be."

"You had no one to help you?"

She hesitated. The tightening of his jaw told her she'd betrayed herself. The last thing she'd needed after Vincenzo had already loaned her money to get her off the streets when she'd turned eighteen was to beg him for another loan so that she could get a degree.

"No. I didn't. But now…when I get out of this mess, I… So, yeah, thank you." She looked away from him at the wall in front of her.

The wall stretched out far in both directions, reaching up into the domed ceiling. There were murals detailed on the wall, tall, aristocratic figures looking down their long noses—shared by both Massimo and Leonardo—brows drawn together, almost as if sneering at a mere mortal like her walking their hallowed hallways.

Her frown deepened as she spied someone who resembled Leonardo, then Silvio and then Leonardo himself. But no Massimo.

"You're not here," she mumbled, searching for his familiar face among the stern, boorish ones.

"I hadn't earned my place with them when Leonardo invited the artist."

"And now?"

He didn't turn but she saw the tightening of his shoulders just as they reached a building separated from the main villa.

She kept thinking he was part of all this…this dynastic family of his, this alien world that dined on caviar and champagne. But the tension between him and Leonardo, Silvio's thoughtless comments… What if his childhood had been just as awful as hers had been, even in this magnificent home? Even surrounded by family?

The odds he must have had to overcome to build something like BCS when he'd been so sick, when he'd been constantly told he wouldn't amount to much…

She rubbed her face—all traces of sleep gone, confusion roiling through her. Even knowing that Vincenzo hadn't really asked her to steal anything, she didn't want to give up his name. Not after he'd helped her get out of a destructive spiral that would've ruined her life.

Not when he'd never asked for anything in return. Not when he'd been keeping an eye on Frankie's foster situation in the past two years.

Her loyalties, as they were, did belong to Vincenzo.

The very thought while she stood here thanking Massimo for his generosity made her faintly nauseous.

A huge metal door with an electronic thumbprint-access console guarded a huge stone structure that seemed to be built with pure mountain rock. Natalie watched with wide eyes as Massimo pressed her thumb against the console and pushed the door open.

They stood on a ledge with stairs leading down. A thick scent of…grapes lingered in the air as Natalie followed him down. "It smells like…oak and grapes and—"

"It used to be a wine cellar," Massimo said, before he pushed open another glass door. "Leonardo had it designed for my exact specifications. We took out the old stone fireplace, added temperature control and left the original stone structure intact."

Her mouth fell open as Natalie took in the glory of Massimo Brunetti's tech lab. The rock structure provided a magnificent contrast to the high-tech servers stored to the left, while more than three stations on her right housed state-of-the-art supercomputers and glossy monitors she'd only dreamed about. Because of the dark background provided by the rocks, the light from the overhead fixtures gave the whole lab a golden glow.

On the other wall stood a gigantic whiteboard with a leather couch, a snowy white cashmere throw hanging on it and a stand with tech magazines thrown haphazardly.

Through the narrow corridor, she saw a small kitchenette with a refrigerator and a small wine rack.

"Wow, this really is your...bat cave. Like the hub of your tech genius."

Teeth digging into his lip, hands tucked into his pockets, he somehow managed to look painfully gorgeous and adorable like a little boy showing off his biggest toys. "You could say that."

"I did wonder at the strangeness of you living at the villa, with your family," she said, laughing. "Doesn't it put a damper on your...extracurricular activities?"

He burst out laughing. "How is that you can strip a layer off even Leonardo but can't speak plainly about sex?"

She hoped the soft light hid her blush. "I'm a complex modern woman."

"That you are.

"I have a flat in Navigli that I use for my...extracurricular activities. Bringing a woman to the villa would only confuse matters."

"Ah...what with the expiry dates and all?"

He shrugged. "I did consider moving out almost a decade ago. When my tech was released and turned into a billion-dollar revenue generator, I had been on a high, raw, so full of myself. I partied so hard," he said with a smile, and she couldn't help but get swept away by his energy. "Very keen to cut my association with my father and Leo and just...the whole lot. But Leo convinced me otherwise. Also, since he was the one who brought in the capital to scale it up in the first place, he had ownership of the IP, too.

"Keeping BCS under the umbrella of Brunetti Finances, Inc. was imperative for Leonardo."

She heard that faint whisper of resentment in his words, the whisper of a boy who'd been measured and found wanting against his older brother. Was he even aware of it?

"Is that when you transformed from gawky geek to sexy stud?" she said, wanting to make him smile.

"Probably, *sì*." Color scored his sharp cheekbones. "I don't think I've ever been complimented in such a... straightforward way." His gaze warmed and he pushed away from the wall. "It provokes me into wanting to return the compliment in the way I know best."

She took a step back, her pulse racing so fast that she felt dizzy. "You could just say I look good, too," she somehow whispered.

"Only you can make an oversize sweater look so sexy. There. But I also believe in giving one thousand percent ROI, *cara mia*."

She looked away from that irresistibly wicked light in his eyes, the grooves digging in his cheeks. "I'm going to need to carry an oxygen tank with me soon if you continue to look at me like that." She stopped his stride with her palm. A huge mistake. His abdomen was like a slab of rock that surrounded them, and yet somehow warm. "You'll fry my circuits if you kiss me again and I'll be of no use to you."

He laughed and she shivered at the joy and warmth of that sound.

"So this lab...it's a fantasy or what? Those servers, Massimo, I'm salivating at the thought of getting my hands on it."

He switched one on, and yet, his gaze never left hers. "Hard for a man's ego when he has to compete with a machine, *cara mia*. I'd give anything to star in your fantasy. Why is it such a big deal that we both want each other?"

All that rough masculinity leveled at her...her skin prickled with heat. With need.

Still smiling, he leaned against the wall, ankles crossed. Hips slightly thrust up. Denim pulling tight against those rock-hard thighs. His eyes looked blue in this light. Twinkling. Full of naughtiness.

Hair-dusted arms folded at his belly beckoned her. Wet, blue-back hair piled high, gleamed. She had the most overwhelming urge to walk up to him, and kiss that curling mouth. To lean her breasts against those corded arms. To press her hips against his. To tunnel her fingers through his thick hair and pull his head down to her until she could kiss that smiling mouth. To make those laughing eyes turn dark with slumbering desire.

To meet him as his equal, to trust him so fully that she could give herself to him beyond any misgiving or doubt. To live like a normal twenty-two-year-old for once.

She shook her head to rid herself of the stupid longing. They were going to be working here for who knew how long.

"You're a fantasy all right," she said, her words coming out soft and husky. His nostrils flared. "When you look at me like that, when you laugh at things I say, when you touch me, when you…kiss me, it feels as if I was the center of your world. As if you couldn't get enough."

"I can't. Even knowing that you'll run at the first chance, that you'll betray me for some twisted notion of loyalty, that this will only get complicated even more if I do touch you… I still can't stop." He ran a hand over his nape, his voice husky.

Take a step toward me, then, his eyes seemed to say without saying.

She cleared her throat. "But fantasies don't become reality. That's their very nature. Even if you and I had met without my little attack onto your system…we're too different, Massimo. For you that kiss was a pretense. A challenge. A pleasant diversion. A case of kissing the criminal. For me…" She bit her lip, wondering at how easy he made it to be vulnerable with him when all she'd been her whole life was tough.

He had this…insidious way of getting past her defenses.

She couldn't leave her fate to him, yes. But in this, in this, the only way to protect herself was by showing him her weakness. Trust him to do the right thing. Because all she wanted to do was ask him to make those erotic words into vivid reality. "It was my first kiss."

He came away from the door. "You've never had…" He considered his words, as if this moment was important to him, as if she were important. "You've never been with a man?"

She shook her head, heat crawling up her neck at his prolonged silence.

"Why?"

Again, that feeling of warmth filled her. He never assumed. Massimo always asked.

"It's hard for me trust anyone. Hard for me to let people close. I… I grew up in foster care, got shuffled from home to home. At a young age, I realized that I couldn't count on anyone, that people can bully, berate, be unkind for no reason other than that they have the power to do so." A note of defensiveness crept into her tone, daring him to mock her background, like his family had done.

But all Massimo did was watch her with that intensity. "To give over my security, my feelings, into someone else's power is hard for me. I have friends, of course, but none too close.

"I don't trust easily," she said, wondering if he understood what she wasn't saying.

He did. "And when you give it, it's been earned. Neither will you betray it so easily."

He'd already earned her trust that he'd never harm her

physically, but... She nodded, bracing herself for his anger, for his temper.

"Then it is up to me to make sure you trust me and do what is right for both you and me, *si*? You better believe it, *bella*, I can be very persuasive."

With a wink, he pulled out one of the chairs for her and helped her get settled. Joined her at the next station. Natalie smiled.

"Now, let's forget the outside world, *si*? Show me what you're really made of, Natalie. You have free rein."

She logged into the system, and looked at his network infrastructure. Anticipation built like an inflating balloon in her chest, electrifying her very limbs. "What...what do you want me to do?"

"I want you to mount an attack and show me any more security holes you can find. In BCS and BFI."

"You're not joking."

"No."

"I need a lot of tools and I use open source tech. And get this...some twisted, creative genius named it after a Hindu demon hunter. I need Wi-Fi adaptors that can go into monitor mode and inject packets for penetration testing, a Bluetooth device to monitor traffic, a separate device to install—"

"I have everything you need. If you dare, take me on, Natalie?"

On a wild impulse, Natalie threw her arms around him and took his mouth in a rough kiss. God, he tasted like sunshine and warmth and rationality and wildness, and in two seconds, he turned her awkward fumbling into a knee-bending kiss that stole the very breath from her lungs. His tongue danced sinuously in her mouth, chasing and rolling around hers, his deep groan sending reverberations to the wet place between her thighs.

And it was he that broke it off and settled her back into her seat. "Thank God you did that," he said, rubbing his lower lip with his tongue.

She smiled. "What do you mean?"

"I'm an Italian man in his prime, *bella*," he drawled, thickening his accent. "I cannot have the woman I want panting over some technology more than she does over me. I would have kissed you if you hadn't." He took a deep breath until his chest expanded and his brows were drawn into a leer. "How else would I validate my masculinity?"

Laughter rushed out of her like a firestorm, burning her stomach, bursting through her chest. His gaze filled with laughter, he was the most beautiful man she'd ever seen.

Blushing, Natalie kept her gaze on the screen while the rogue whistled a merry tune as if he'd already won the battle between them.

CHAPTER SEVEN

MASSIMO CAME TO a standstill as he located Natalie in the oval pool, a nightly routine she religiously followed for the last ten days once he called a halt to their workday.

Soft lights illuminated the entire area, including the figure swimming laps in the pool in a blur of yellow. Giant trees artistically grown around the pool gave it privacy and made a paradise that he'd never appreciated fully, before tonight.

Moonlight followed her in splashes of silver on her bare skin, sometimes the dip of shoulder or a toned calf, sometimes that dainty curve of that waist that fascinated him.

All the steam that had built up while Leo had told him of the latest problem he'd come upon with the Brunetti Finances board hissed out of him, all thoughts of business and schemes of revenge and throttling little hackers who lied through their teeth, evaporating like mist.

He'd been so angry with Leo for extending Silvio's stay. But the master strategist that Leo was, he'd expected this situation. Whatever their internal quarrels, it had been essential to present a united front of their family—with Massimo and Leonardo's stalwart presence behind their father's back. The trio of them a force to be reckoned with for any board members with delusions of grandeur.

But that it had come to that...this was on Massimo.

This was on his obsession with the little hacker.

Every day he spent with her, he was beginning to lose

his mind. Was losing his path a little. And they hadn't even kissed again, not since the last time.

There was such strength, such force, to her personality that he found the fragility of her physical form an endlessly alluring contrast. Ordering Lila and Hero to heel, he settled onto the closest lounger to her, his legs stretched in front of him.

The *swish-swish* of the water and the occasional whisper of a cicada were the only sounds surrounding them. He noticed her focus falter for a few seconds as she noted his presence and his silent scrutiny. Her head went under the water, her arms flailing ungracefully. He pounced to his feet, ready to jump into the pool when she surfaced, spluttering and choking, followed by a litany of inventive curses that chased away the tightness in his throat.

He grabbed a towel and waited while she swam to the edge of the pool. Pushing her hair out of her face, she pulled herself up above the water supported by her forearms over the ledge. Brown eyes shot daggers at him. Kissed by the water, her skin looked so silky smooth that he wanted to run his fingers all over. "You almost made me drown."

"You shouldn't be in the pool if you don't know how to swim, *cara mia*."

"Of course I know how to swim," she said, a note of defensiveness creeping into her tone. "You're watching me without a word and…" He raised a brow and she sighed. "I only learned how to swim recently and haven't perfected my strokes. I was doing perfectly fine until you showed up. You're not good for my focus, Massimo."

That irreverence, that honest but baffled admission…she disarmed him so effortlessly. "You didn't learn as a child?"

"Swimming lessons weren't really a priority for a foster kid." She blew at a wayward curl that was already dry and framed her face. Hair plastered to her scalp, there was a stark simplicity to her face, a soft beauty that was utterly without artifice. "Not when you're shuffled from home to home. I started taking classes at the local Y. When I get out of here, I want to bring Frankie to a beach."

She'd hate it if he felt sorry for her, he knew that instinctively. "The local Y?"

"Y is the YMCA. The lessons are free, for the most part."

A tremble in the slender line of her shoulders made him say, "Get out of the pool."

"Help me up."

He put his hands under her shoulders and pulled her out of the water. The T-shirt and jeans he'd changed into splashed with water but he couldn't give a damn.

Desire fisted low in his belly, rising through him as quickly as the rivulets of water running down her silky bare skin. The yellow two-piece bikini clung to curves he'd dismissed as meager, only held together by a flimsy string at the nape of her neck. The two triangles of the top held her high breasts like a lover's hands. He could imagine his own hands there, holding them, pushing them up to be savored by his mouth. Could imagine her throwing her neck back, her body arching as he ran his tongue over that rigid nipple pushing against the flimsy fabric. Her thighs were corded with lean muscle, yet somehow so sexy.

Cristo, how could he be so fascinated by her?

He released her hands suddenly. She squealed, her upper body bowing back, her feet slipping on the smooth tiles.

With a curse, he grabbed her. The motion brought her into his body, plastering her to him, from breast to thigh… Time seemed to thunder down to a halt. As if to better equip him to process the amazing sensation of her warm, soft body clinging to his.

"Where did you get the bikini?" he asked hoarsely.

Wide brown eyes gazed at him with liquid longing as he lifted his hands to her shoulders. Rubbed at a drop of water lingering teasingly at the juncture to her neck.

"Alessandra. I didn't pack for a vacation."

"Oversight on my part, *sì*. I'll arrange for a wardrobe for you." Polite words to drown the sounds of their harsh breaths.

Her own hands stayed on his chest, his heart thundering like a wild horse under her palm. "No. This pretense that I'm your fiancée...works if they believe I'm different. From my background to my cheap clothes." She swallowed. "That I'm a novelty to you."

Water drops shimmered on her hair like silver lights, spraying him on his face. She was silk under his hands, warmth and feminine hunger.

"And yet... I've never wanted to do all the things I want to do to you, right now. Even knowing that you're probably colluding with an enemy, that you're as complicated as they come." His gaze, with a mind of its own, followed other drops of water running down the valley between those breasts, down the dip and rise of belly and into the bikini bottom. "All I want is to sink to my knees, follow that drop of water across your silky skin. Trail it all the way to the seam of your bikini. To dip my tongue into—"

Her palm on his mouth cut his words off.

He took a long breath, cursing himself for having so little control around her. Tried to push her away from him. But she didn't let go, her arms going tighter around his waist. "Massimo, we agreed we wouldn't do this."

He sighed, the feel of her body molded to his, conversely taking the edge off. Fingers under her chin, he tilted her face up to his. "No, we shouldn't. You're right. Not when you'll hate me when you hear what I have to say."

She stepped back from his hold, fear swirling in the brown depths. "What? What's happened?"

Right and wrong had never been so blurry. Desire and ambition had never been so muddied together. This needed to be resolved before he did anything he would regret later. In his business life and his personal life.

Natalie shivered even though the glass-enclosed pool was balmy. A luxuriously soft towel instantly covered her shoulders.

He took her willing hands in his. The rough pads of his fingers—another riddle for her to solve—traced the plump veins on the back of her hands. Mesmerizing. Soothing. Arousing. She tugged her hands away. "Massimo, you're scaring me. Just tell me what it is."

"I've given you time. Let you understand that I pose no threat. But I don't have the choice anymore."

"I told you. No one put me—"

"Stop, Natalie!" He stared at her for so long with such intensity that Natalie felt stripped to the bone. After what felt like eternity, he sighed. Resolve tightened the soft curve of his lips. He let go of her hands and she felt the loss so acutely that she had to hide them behind her.

"Would your answer change if I told you the security breach is not an isolated incident?"

Shock made her reaction come in slow, horrifying sweeps. Her stomach plummeted. "What? There were other attacks into BCS's security design?"

"No, that was all you. Only you," he said with a grim smile. Even then, easily acknowledging her brilliance when more than one man scoffed at it. Interestingly, Vincenzo and he had that much in common—an easy acceptance of her talents. "But there have been other things happening at both BCS and its parent company, our finance giant Brunetti Finances, Inc."

She could almost hear the rapid tattoo of her heart. "Like what?"

"Three deals that we had in our pocket fell through. Silvio's colorful, abusive past keeps being recycled by the media and the press. Dragging all of us into the news cycles. Alessandra's personal life, her past, her family in the US, keep getting news time, which, in turn, makes Greta crabbier than usual."

"Your grandmother and Alessandra are close?" she asked, surprised that the crotchety old woman liked and approved of anyone.

"She's not a complete dragon. Nonni was devoted to her second husband. Alessandra's father. Carlo was a good man—he tried to be a good role model to me and Leonardo."

"Didn't quite take?" she said, being drawn into his life. Despite the feeling of a sword hanging over her head. How much had Vincenzo orchestrated? What did he want of the Brunetti family?

Instead of being offended, Massimo regarded it seriously. "He made a world of difference to me. Made Greta and Leo realize what a toxic man my father is. I think...all our lives changed for the better thanks to Carlo. Alessandra shuttled back and forth between her mother in the US and here, and Greta made a lot of effort to make her feel welcome when she finally moved here. For a long time, she even hoped, I think, that either Leo or I would..."

Natalie's heart kicked against her rib cage. "Would what?"

He shrugged. "Would maybe welcome her into the family officially."

"And?" Natalie said, aware of the demand in her tone

and unable to quell it. She could even see it from Greta's view. Alessandra would be the perfect bride for one of her grandsons—sophisticated and beautiful and intelligent.

Massimo smiled, his teeth gleaming in the near darkness. Whether at her or the idea of Alessandra with him, she had no clue. "Leo and I like Alex too much to saddle her with us romantically, I think."

Because Alessandra was too good to be played with. Because Alessandra was the kind of woman he respected. The kind of woman to not trifle with.

Whereas Natalie was perfect for an affair.

She felt as if he'd kicked her in the chest. That he was unaware of how awful he sounded didn't help.

Damn it, why did she keep hoping that he'd see her as something more than novelty? Men like Vincenzo and Massimo only had certain uses for women like her, was that it? Another commonality he shared with the man he was hunting.

"So, yes," he went on, unaware of her confusion. "Alex getting dragged into this mess riled Greta, interestingly, even more than the Brunetti name being muddied.

"Anyway, resources for planned projects have been falling through at the last minute.

"And the day before yesterday, there's been a new development. It's why Leonardo kept Silvio here for this long when he knows I loathe it. He had a feeling this was coming."

Natalie had come to hate Silvio's presence, too. The very look in his eyes made her remember all the stuff she was hiding from Massimo. "What new development?"

More than fear gnawing at her insides, Nat hated the doubt in his eyes.

"Massimo, you have to tell me."

"Should I, *cara mia*?"

"You can't think I've got anything to do with it. You've got me locked up here, cut off from the rest of the world."

"Someone leaked about the breach to one of the board members. Forcing our hand to come clean to the entire board. You can imagine how that went down. That our clients' information wasn't stolen becomes irrelevant, do you see?"

"It can't be anyone else?"

"The board member who accused Leonardo of hiding this from them, this is not the first time he's tried to cause trouble for Leo, not the first time he's strategized to oust him from the board. He's not going to give up his source, either. But don't you think it's a little too convenient that of all the board members, Mario Fenelli was the one who's been told about the breach? The only people who knew were me, Leo, Silvio, you and the person who leaked it."

Dread so complete enveloped Nat's limbs that she felt frozen. "Wait, you think someone is sitting there strategizing all this?"

"Yes."

Jesus, what was Vincenzo doing? It wasn't bad enough that he'd dragged her into the middle of this, now he'd gone ahead and leaked the news about the…breach?

Massimo's gray gaze stayed far too calm. Far too intense on hers. "It's too much of a coincidence to think otherwise. So far, nothing has been so bad as to bring us down. Not too much of a financial hit for BCS or Brunetti Finances. Until now, with the breach so cleverly exposed where it could do maximum damage to Leo. It feels almost as if—" he frowned, clearly struggling with something "—someone is trying to figure out—" his intense gray gaze pinned her, leaving her no way to escape "—what would hurt us the most."

The truth of his statement hit her like a lash. He ran a

thumb up and down her cheek. She sank into the feath-erlight touch, desperate for the warmth of it, despite the tension surrounding them. Despite the lines she'd drawn between them. "Maybe you didn't know what you were getting into. I will allow for that. Maybe you were never meant to know more about this. But now it's up to you to make the right choice."

He was not quite the stranger from the first night again—cold, powerful and a little bit frightening. But neither was he the man who had laughed with her, the man who had kissed her as if she were the only anchor in his storm.

Was Vincenzo behind the other attacks, too? Why? Why was he targeting Massimo and Leo? How could he involve Nat in something so underhanded knowing how precious Frankie was to her? How could she give him up to Mas-simo when she owed him so much over the years?

"You have a week, Natalie. I need a name. I need this to end."

"Or else what, Massimo?" she demanded, a shiver in her very words.

"Or else I will let Leo handle the situation. I would let him do the dirty work of sending you to prison, let him be the villain. See, I'm no one's hero, *bella mia*. In fact, I'm even worse than Leo. Because Leo accepts the reality of what he is.

"I…on the other hand, like to pretend, as long as it's convenient and easy to do, that I'm better than him. That I'm better than my father."

CHAPTER EIGHT

HEART THUMPING AGAINST her chest like a bird trapped in a cage, Natalie pressed her thumb against the electronic access panel. The soft *ping-ping* of the panel as it turned green had the same effect on her as a meteor hitting the earth might have. Her belly swooped and her sweaty palms slipped as she pulled the door to the lab open.

Just thinking about the gray gaze looking at her as if she were an unknown criminal, someone not deserving of even the little consideration he'd shown her, she shivered, even in the thick woolen sweater she had borrowed from him on that first day. Walking to the terminal he'd set up for her, she pulled the loose neckline by stretching it and buried her nose in the soft wool.

The scent of Massimo seeped into her breath, into her blood, calming the panic in her muscles. An almost hysterical laugh bounded out of her mouth, echoing in the huge space. How strange that here she was planning to betray his trust again and it was the scent of him that calmed her.

She watched her reflection in the huge monitor as the system booted. Two days and countless conversations in her head hadn't made this decision easier or given her a different solution.

Yes, Vincenzo was a sneak and a master strategist and he was completely in the wrong for doing what he was against the Brunettis and for putting her in the middle of it. And no, she still couldn't betray him. Which meant she had to look out for herself.

Thoughts jumbled, tangled, piled and raced through her head while her fingers raced over the keyboard, creating the bot program that would search all of Massimo's cyber infrastructure for the proof against her. For the record he'd diligently put together to track her and nail her.

When her program found it, it would destroy the proof that he could use to send her to jail. Come tomorrow morning, Massimo would have nothing on her.

Except pure hatred.

Sweat gathered on the nape of her neck, the lab suddenly feeling like a jail itself, taunting her for what she intended to do.

God, she couldn't bear to see the disgust and the shock of betrayal in his eyes, couldn't bear for him to see the reality of what she was.

If she did this, there was no going back. He wouldn't trust her ever again; he wouldn't smile at her, wouldn't laugh with her, wouldn't kiss her ever again.

She buried her face in her hands and groaned.

And yet, to leave her security to the whims of a man, even if the man had shown her kindness and generosity, a man who prized his ambition over everything else…it went against every grain of instinct that had helped her survive for so long.

God, she was tired of fighting, so tired of being tough.

All she wanted, desperately needed, was to leave this lab, this place, this man who threatened her security on so many levels.

She had to.

The soft chirrup from his wristwatch grabbed Massimo's attention as he waited in the foyer for everyone to arrive.

An alert from the access log for his lab.

He frowned, but pushed the notification away with a swipe of his finger. Right now, he had more important things on his mind. Already, he was far too distracted and excited about the prospect of seeing Natalie. Eerily, it was the sensation he remembered from being a skinny geek, hoping the girl he liked would notice him at university.

Wait till you see her tonight.

The pithy text from Alex almost two hours ago while he'd been finishing his workout had filled him with all kinds of anticipation. He had trouble enough to focus when Natalie was close even when she wore her usual skinny jeans and any old T-shirt. Even now, he could recall the sight of her pulling on his thick sweater, flashing him her belly, by simply closing his eyes. Oversized, hanging off-shoulder, it should have looked anything but sexy on her. And yet, when he'd spied her burying her nose in the fabric, a smile playing around her lips, he had gone hard as stone.

Cristo, she revved him up so quick just by being present. Who knew what she would do to him if she actually dressed up for him.

Tonight was the night of the annual charity gala that the Brunettis hosted at the Galleria Vittorio Emanuele II. The one evening that Leo and Greta insisted they present a united front to Milan and the world at large. Much as Massimo preferred to toil in his lab over playing political games with the most powerful families of Milan, tonight was one night even he didn't dare buck tradition.

Giuseppe Fiore would be there, and Massimo wanted to see him in a setting away from the usual meetings. Without being surrounded by all his yes-men with their own agendas to push.

The man was an incisively clever businessman, noncommittal to the last moment, and Massimo needed to see if the news of the security breach had reached Giuseppe's ears. If it had, he would have to do damage control. Both on the business front and the personal. And having Natalie on his arm, he hoped, would smooth over any drama with Gisela.

No one who could see them together could doubt he had only eyes for her. The decision of what to do with her—on so many levels—had begun to give him sleepless nights.

"Keeping an eye on her is one thing, Massimo," Leo said. "Scratching an itch is one more indulgence. But letting her access your security designs for the Fiore contract... isn't that a bit much?"

Massimo had expected this confrontation the same evening that he'd introduced Natalie to his family. That Leo had waited a whole two weeks when his ruthless brother never hesitated to cut anyone, whether personal or business.

He frowned. Was Natalie right?

Had Leo kept away because of Massimo's harsh words? Was it possible that his accusations had hurt his brother?

"Stay out of this, Leo."

"I stayed out of your lab, literally, for ten days, Massimo. Left you to indulge in whatever you...want with her. Hasn't that been enough?"

"Do not speak of her that way," Massimo gritted through his teeth, the very idea of Natalie as some kind of toy to be used disturbing him on multiple levels. Even though that's what he'd always used women for. Meaningless, casual affairs so that nothing could distract him, nothing could become an obstacle to his ambition. "She's been working around the clock with me to fortify the security of BCS. She's brilliant. If I can get her to commit to us, she'll be an asset to us on the Fiore banking project."

"Despite the fact that what she did might jeopardize our

chance to get the contract? Before we clear up the problem she created, Massimo?" Leo set his perceptive gaze on Massimo. "She committed a crime. She refuses to tell you why or the name of the man responsible. You conveniently set all that aside because you want her.

"It's a little too close to Silvio's behavior—"

"Natalie isn't like any other woman you or I know."

Leo's eyes widened. "You like her."

The words washed over Massimo.

He did like her. For the first time in his life, it went beyond physical attraction. He'd threatened her that he would turn her over into Leo's hands, but could he, really?

Protecting a woman who was determined to keep her secrets over sound business decisions... For the first time in his life, Massimo wondered at the weakness that Silvio had always said resided in him. Was this it? Was this... unwillingness to threaten everything she held precious a weakness in him?

No! It couldn't be.

Leo pushed his fingers through his hair as if he'd discovered a bigger problem to solve. "I never thought you would be a fool for a woman."

"I'm not marrying her, Leonardo. I just refuse to take advantage of her."

"You really can't believe that act of innocence."

No, he didn't think Natalie was unaware of her own culpability. Or that she would ever stop looking after her own interests first.

But her shock when he'd told her about the other attacks had been genuine.

They'd spent days fortifying BCS's security design, patching up flaws that Natalie found with an incisively brilliant mind. He'd seen her brilliance with security design, her sheer joy in playing with it. He'd also seen her struggle with what he'd told her. She'd asked him questions again and again, sifting through detail, trying to connect the dots. He could almost see the picture emerge in her head last evening. See the conflict in her brown eyes, eyes that had never been able to hide anything.

Leo turned his gaze to Massimo. There was still that wariness in his eyes. As if Massimo were a stranger. As if Massimo could attack again and possibly hurt him.

His brother—the powerful, cynical, ruthless Leonardo Brunetti—hurt by Massimo's words? If not for Natalie, he'd have never seen it.

"If she's poor, buy the truth from her," Leo said into the awkward silence. "We need to know who's behind all this. She's our only lead. Nothing else is panning out."

"Natalie is not the type to be bought." She was brilliant, and funny and naive and more than a little defensive about her background and a whole lot loyal. Discovering the complex depths to her only made her even more interesting to him. Made him to want to protect her. Made him wonder what a man had to do to earn that loyalty.

"How do you not see that's worse? It means her loyalty has already been given to another man."

"She'll tell me the truth."

"Why?"

"I don't know, okay? I'm putting all the pressure I can on her," Massimo said, hating that he had no better answer or way of getting it. Hating that he was acting weak. Was he being foolish enough to hope that she'd open up to him eventually? When did being fair turn into weakness? Why the hell didn't the woman just save her skin? "Leave it, Leonardo, *per favore*."

The words he really wanted to say to Leo lingered on his lips. He cleared his throat. "Have you considered it might be someone Silvio cheated or abused or plain pissed off? Both you and I know his sins are numerous. Against many."

"That's the first thing I thought of." His brother rubbed his face. "I'm looking into it."

"*Bene.* I thought you might have forgotten what kind of a man our father is."

"I tolerate him better than you do, *sì.* Does not mean I forget what he is capable of."

Massimo nodded. *Cristo*, emotions were hard to put into words. But he had never shied away from the truth, either. "I owe you an apology."

Leo jerked his head up.

"For blaming you for Silvio's actions. All these years."

Whiteness emerged around Leo's mouth. As if his biggest fear about their relationship had come true. "Massimo, you didn't… I have never held that against you."

"No?" He smiled at his brother's uncharacteristic lenience. "Then you should. You were just as much a child as I was. Just as much brainwashed as I was. When I see him, I only see the bully. The insecure, pathetic narcissist who made Mama's life hell.

"The face he showed you…it's much more dangerous— it's charming and loving and you had to see beyond and beneath all that. Until Natalie pointed it out to me, I… I didn't realize how much that resentment still festered. How easily I could believe that you would choose him over me."

Leo's eyes held a wealth of regret before he looked away. "I… I wish I had realized sooner. Massimo. I wish…"

Massimo rubbed his brother's shoulder. "It's in the past. And even knowing it, Mama had never been able to stop it. But that's the kind of woman Natalie is, do you see?

"I'm not saying she's not culpable. Even as you advise me to incarcerate her, knowing your opinion, she made me see how much resentment I still harbored toward you.

How much I pitted myself against you. How much it hurt you. Even knowing the both of us for so many years, can you see Greta doing anything like that? Calling me on it.

"As if I had to prove I was better than you. As if I were still in competition with you for his affections," he finished, disgusted with himself.

"You're a much better man than me, Massimo."

"I think I forgot that."

Leonardo raised a brow in mock arrogance, his mouth split into a smile. "Good to see you back on form."

Massimo laughed at this dry wit. How had he not seen that his brother showed this side of himself only to Massimo?

"No, that's not right. It's not a competition between you and me," Massimo corrected himself. "I'm my own man. There are, of course, shadows of Silvio in me, but Mama and Carlo tried their best to cancel that out, I think." He looked at Leonardo and realized how lucky he had been, in a way, that Silvio had shown his true colors from the beginning.

"Now I can sleep better, knowing that whoever is causing this at least won't come between you and me." Leo gestured between them.

Massimo nodded, ashamed that he had caused Leonardo that fear. "We'll find a way, Leo. Even if—"

His brother's gaze turned away from Massimo, a pithy curse flowing from his mouth. Massimo frowned and turned.

His own intake of breath sounded like a shout in the quiet lounge.

Dressed in a gold evening dress that left her slender shoulders bare, Natalie walked down the steps. The bodice of the dress was two wide strips of silky gold fabric that roped up from her midriff, crisscrossing, to cover her breasts, like a lover's demanding hands, before the ends tied behind her graceful neck. Under the bright lights of the crystal chandelier overhead, the valley between her breasts shimmered, drawing his gaze.

Desire made his muscles tight. He had the most overwhelming urge to run the tip of his tongue there, before uncovering the plumpness of her flesh. The dress, designed to make men salivate, left the sides of her midriff bare, showcasing more bare silky skin, the sexy dip of her waist flaring into her hip.

Her glorious hair was tied into a knot at the back of her head, unruly, wavy tendrils falling forward to frame her jawline. Her eyes shimmered with a false brightness while her mouth, painted a wild red, curved into a tremulous smile. The pulse at her neck fluttered rapidly.

The slinky fabric fell to her ankles, shimmering with every step, the thigh-high slit in it revealing glimpses of a toned thigh. Three-inch heels finished her outfit. One hand anchored on the banister while she pressed the other palm into her belly.

She'd never be sensationally beautiful like Gisela or Alessandra. But her beauty was more than skin-deep. It lured with those intelligent eyes, made him laugh with that beguiling mouth, stripped him to the core by peeling off her own layers. But in that dress that highlighted the innate sensuality of her slim figure, delicate cheekbones carefully highlighted by clever makeup, she looked incredibly fragile, wild. As if one touch from him would mar her innocence.

She came to a halt at the last step, her gaze holding his, inviting and teasing and alluring. Lust spread through his limbs like drugged honey.

She had chosen the dress with him in mind. Her expressive eyes said as much without coyness, without artifice. She let him see the desire in her eyes, demanded he do the same. Never had a woman continually stunned and stripped Massimo to his core like Natalie did.

"Do you still believe her innocent?" Leo's voice at his back sounded eerily like his own beneath the desire drumming through his veins. "She stands there like a Christmas present waiting to be unwrapped by you. She's incredibly bold, such a tempting challenge, *sì*. What man can resist such open invitation? If this is not an attempt to seduce you into granting her freedom just when you tell me you're tightening the screws on her…then I will never speak against her again."

Massimo tightened his jaw, fighting the atavistic urge to punch his older brother, to hide Natalie away from his gaze.

She was dressed to draw a man's gaze and keep it.

Why was she into him now when nothing had changed, if not to seduce him into granting her freedom? Was he a fool to have trusted her this far?

CHAPTER NINE

NATALIE STARED AROUND her openmouthed, even after two hours, at the opulent grandeur that was Galleria Vittorio Emanuele II. The two iron-and-glass-covered walkways met at a central piazza below the grand, wide glass dome. The mosaic on the floor, depicting so many patriotic symbols of Italy, glittered under the bright lights.

Large circular tables covered with snowy white linen and adorned with beautiful floral arrangements that combined white orchids with bamboo were placed along the four branches of the gallery, welcoming eight guests on each. Each table, she'd been informed by Greta, cost five thousand euros, which would then be donated to a charity project offering meals to people in need throughout Milan.

There were designers from world-famous fashions labels, tech business leaders and even the mayor of Milan in attendance.

Massimo's subdued mood, something she couldn't get a handle on since she'd arrived at the lounge where he'd been waiting with his family, couldn't take away her attention for too long. The glorious setting and the dazzling gala felt like a stay on an execution that would come tonight.

But even the fear of where this night would end couldn't rob her appreciation of the setting. It was as if she had entered a different era—a different world. As the formal seated dinner finished, Massimo silently studying her responses all through it, the guests started wandering. Scents of the bitter coffee and decadent chocolate lingered in the air. A pianist sat in a corner, his fingers flying over the ivory keys, Beethoven's Sonata filling the air.

The Galleria, she'd been educated by a smiling Gisela in halting English, was the very heart of the city that married an intricate and complex historical period of Milan with technical, engineering and industrial accelerations. She wished she had her cell phone so that she could capture the glittering night and share it with Frankie later. To look secretly at night when she wished she was part of this world again.

Only families like the Brunettis—power and connections built into their very blood—could indulge the idea of using the Galleria, a cornerstone of Milan's history, for a private charity dinner.

During the day it was the site of the much-lauded Milanese luxury shopping, with many prestigious labels and brand shops. Even without any money to spare, Natalie wished she'd seen the place during the day. Wished she'd begged Massimo to bring her out for a trip to see the city.

They both needed a break, anyway—from being cooped up in the lab for seventeen-hour days and from the tension that seemed to corkscrew around them every time they looked at each other. Damn Vincenzo, the man was like an apparition between them, choking the air around them.

Natalie stole the chance to wander away from the Brunettis. She could already more than tolerate or ignore Greta's snide commentary, which almost seemed to be by rote. She laughed, surprised at the thought that Alessandra might have had a word with the old woman before she had left this morning after she'd seen Natalie crawl out of the lab like a thief, tense and shaking. Tongue-in-cheek, Natalie had attributed it toward nervousness for this party.

She was about to make her escape when Massimo

clasped her arm, and coiled it through his own. The tight cast of his jaw silenced her protest. "I want you to meet Giuseppe Fiore and his CTO."

She nodded, her heart beating rapidly at the frost in his eyes. Had he already discovered what she'd done this morning? How? She hadn't triggered the program to start until this evening. Even before she'd tweaked it again.

She let out a soft gasp when his thigh pressed against hers, the heat from his body a warm caress. His chest pressed into the side of hers, grazing her breast, setting nerve endings on fire. His fingers landed on her bare skin at her waist to steady her, searing her skin. Neither did he stop. He spread his palm out, maximizing the contact, his fingertips digging into her skin, the gesture utterly possessive. Breath coming out shallow, she raised her eyes to his. "Massimo?"

"You're playing with fire, *bella*. Are you prepared to burn?"

She could do nothing but stare into the desire he didn't hide.

Even seeing the beautiful Gisela on her father's arm, in a striking emerald creation, completely in her element as they joined them, commenting about casual acquaintances that Natalie would never know, sharing inside jokes, falling into rapid Italian that Nat had no way in hell of following—even that went over her head in contrast to the all-consuming possessiveness of Massimo's hold.

After all, her job tonight had been to hang on to Massimo with a doe-eyed adoring look that telegraphed to everyone that he was taken. For his part, Massimo was perfect in playing the adoring fiancé role.

Neither did she miss the way Gisela sidled to his side every chance she got, the way she put her hand over Massimo's chest, the way she leaned into him. While he didn't encourage Gisela, neither did Massimo look troubled by the way Gisela touched him without his consent. As if he were Gisela's property just because he was doing business with her father.

Natalie stayed by his side as more guests joined them and with effortless charm he soothed ruffled feathers about the continuing threats to Brunetti Finances. For a technical genius, he didn't talk down to any of them or dismiss the questions that Giuseppe's CTO raised as inconsequential. She couldn't help but admire the clear, concise way he explained the security breach—her hacking attack.

Natalie stiffened when he introduced her to them, expounding on her brilliance with cyber security design to the older man, surprising both him and Natalie.

When Giuseppe had asked for Natalie's experience and qualifications, Massimo smoothly slipped it in that it was Natalie that had launched the attack on BCS but very cleverly left it in the air for Giuseppe to think that she had done so at Massimo's behest and somehow the news had leaked of his own measures to tighten the security.

It was a brilliant business move—using mostly the truth, he calmed Giuseppe's fears about the security attack and yet proved that he had everything under control with Natalie at his side. Massimo might detest the business side of things, but it didn't mean he was any less of an astute businessman than Leonardo. She saw the flash of shock and admiration in Leo's eyes as Giuseppe bought it all.

The older businessman was much more gracious than his daughter for he wished Natalie well, congratulating her on landing "a most brilliant young man."

Once Giuseppe seemed to be satisfied, Natalie pushed away from Massimo and he let her go. She drifted from group to group, slowly making her way toward the bank of elevators a uniformed waiter directed her to.

She had held up her end of the pretense for tonight. Now, she waited for the ax to drop.

Voices thinned and drifted into soft whispers as Natalie made her way toward a smaller corridor that held the elevators to the HighLine. She'd heard walking on the HighLine over the Galleria would be like touching the sky. And right now, she couldn't bear to be around a man whose opinion was coming to matter too much to her.

The elevator car opened and Natalie stepped in. Before the doors closed, a handmade Italian leather shoe stopped them. His broad shoulders pushing the doors open, Massimo stepped into the car. Natalie pressed her hands against the cool metal, to puncture the tension filling the enclosed space instantaneously. Her belly swooped, more to do with him than the car rushing up.

"Running away, *cara mia*?"

"I just wanted to look around," she whispered. And then hating the quaver in her voice, she straightened her shoulders. "To get away from the woman fawning over you. That's allowed, isn't it?"

When he punched the button to stop it, she swallowed. "Then it's also allowed that I follow my errant fiancée, *sì*? At least to make sure she's not meeting another man in secret?"

Natalie paled. "You can't seriously think I've arranged to meet someone when you've cut me off from everyone. You...don't think like that. Did Leonardo plant that in your head?"

His jaw tightened. "Leave my brother out of this."

"Massimo, why are you so angry? You've been in a foul mood all night."

"Why did you dress up tonight—" his gaze roamed over her chest, and then pulled up, a banked fire in it "—when it took me three days to convince you that I need you here at the gala at all?"

That's what this was about?

"I didn't want to embarrass you or you to be ashamed of me. Even if it's all a sham, I didn't want you to realize I was beneath all those women. I wanted…"

To appear to be worthy of you. The words stuck in her throat.

How had he become so important to her that looking out for herself felt like a betrayal to him?

"You wanted what?"

God, she was sick and tired of being twisted by her own feelings.

She clasped his jaw, tugging his head down to meet her eyes. Never in her life had she felt so vulnerable, so willingly weak. Only this man did that to her. He made her wish for things that would always be out of her reach. He made her wish she was…different. And that was the worst sort of thing to do to herself. "I wanted to look like I belonged on your arm."

The rough stubble in his skin sent longing unfurling through her stomach. She dipped her face, burying it in the crook of his neck. The scent of his skin seeped into her very breath. Her hands crawled up from his waist, to his chest, touching him, exploring him.

His heart thudded under her palms, his harsh breaths feathering through her hair. Need and fear drove her to do things she wouldn't have dreamed of. Instinct spurred her on. Pressing her chest to his, she vined her arms around his lean waist. Inched her legs to be cradled between his.

Gray eyes darkened into the color of the sky during a storm. His breath came slow and shallow. Burrowing herself into him, she felt the stirrings of his erection against her belly. Hardness and heat.

She met his gaze, then stroked the tip of her tongue at the seam of his lips. "Kiss me. Please, Massimo."

"Why?"

She laughed. The soft sound filled the small space. "After all the teasing and taunting of the last two weeks, now, when I ask you…"

A vein in his temple throbbed. "Why the sudden change in mind, then?"

"Because when you kiss me, I forget everything else. I forget the whole damned world and what is right and what is wrong. When you kiss me, I'm not so tightly wound anymore. I'm not scared." She sent her hands seeking into his hair, and tugged his head down. Pressing her mouth to the sides of his, she drowned herself in him. With the tip of her tongue, she licked at the soft lower lip, stroked it along the carved line, from this end to the other until the taste of him was embedded in her blood. "Don't ask questions, Massimo. Please. Just for now. Just for a few moments.

"Imagine that the outside world—your company, your family, your ambition—none of those exist. Imagine you met me that first night in the cyber club and we connected. Imagine that I came to you willingly, desperate for the pleasure you could give.

"What would you do with me if I were all yours?"

What would you do with me if I were all yours?

Natalie's question unlocked all the desires Massimo had been struggling to bury since he'd set eyes on her. The press of her mouth against his, hungry and soft, seeking and searching, innocent and mind-numbingly addictive, destroyed the anger that had been brewing at her conniving intentions tonight. Right and wrong had never been so blurry.

Cristo, he was such a cliché of a man.

The slide of her body against his, his chest crushing her breasts, her long legs tangling with his, the way her soft belly grazed his thickening erection—it was heaven and hell. His hands crawled into her hair, tugging and pulling.

Yes, she thought to seduce him with a motive, with a goal.

Who said she would attain her goal?

Who said she would win in this game she'd started between them?

Who said he was going to grant her her freedom?

And not just because keeping Natalie around was good for BCS, even for the hundred-billion Fiore contract. Not because she still was the only lead they had in discovering the mastermind that was strategizing all this.

He wasn't going to let Natalie go, not for a long while yet. Because he wanted her brilliant mind around. Because he wanted to explore this thing between them, see this through to the end.

Acknowledging that freed him from his own guilt. From his own restrictions.

He pressed his mouth to her shoulder, dragged it to the tender nook of her neck, licked the pulse hammering away madly. Desire was a deafening drumbeat pulsing through his body. He opened his mouth, planting a wet kiss before sinking his teeth into the supple flesh, tugging it and releasing it until she was squirming against him. Burrowing into him as if she meant to reside under his skin. She tasted sweet and salty and soft and silky. Curling his fingers at her neck, he jerked her head back, until her spine curved, until he was all she could see.

Brown eyes muddied with desire stared up at him. Her glorious hair was coming away, rumpling all that innocence. Her chest rose and fell shakily, her nipples tight points poking against the slinky fabric. "Are you sure you want this, *bella mia*?" he said, desire deepening his tone, struggling to hold on to the last thread of sanity.

"Of all the rights and wrongs between us, this is the only thing I'm sure of, Massimo."

Pulling her up, Massimo took her mouth like a drowning man. Dove into the soft cavern of her mouth like a starving man. With rough movements, he turned them around, until her back was against the wall and her front was plastered to him.

She came into the kiss with a groan that pulled at his control, that reverberated inside him like a bloody gong going off. As if schemes and seductions were nothing compared to her hunger for him. Her voracious mouth. Her kisses tasted like honesty and passion and innocence and everything that aroused him, that tied him up in knots, about his little hacker.

"Anything, Massimo. Tonight, anything for you," she whispered in a litany, sinking into his kiss, sinking those misaligned teeth into his lower lip. Hard. Pain flashed at the edges of his consciousness, crystallizing the pleasure she drew from him even more. A feral groan ripped from his mouth as she swiped that tart tongue over the hurt she gave him.

He licked and nipped at her bottom lip, before thrusting his tongue inside. She was sweet, and hot, and *Cristo*, she was a quick learner the way she pressed her tongue against his when he went seeking. His hands continued their own foray, cupping her buttocks, squeezing her hips, learning every dip and swell, tracing the contours of her back before returning to her bottom again.

With his mouth, he trailed the silky softness of her cheek, her neck, licked at the pulse again before sucking it into his mouth. He was being rough, rougher than he'd ever been with a woman on their first time, rougher with a woman who'd so bravely admitted that his kiss had been her first.

Her little pants and mewls were like beacons guiding him, giving him a map to her body, a key to driving her as mindless as him. When he snuck his hand under the slit and cupped her bare buttock, she moaned.

When he buried his mouth in her neck and sucked at her skin, she pushed herself into his touch.

When he shifted the flimsy fabric of her dress away to reveal the globe of her breast that had been playing peeka-boo with him all evening, she shuddered in his hold.

When he rubbed the pad of his thumb over the plump pink tip he discovered, she sank her fingers into his hair and tugged.

When he licked the knotted tip begging for his caress, she ground her belly against his erection. When he swirled his tongue over and over around the pink peak, she let loose a string of curses that were music to his ears.

When he took her nipple into his mouth and caressed it with press of his tongue, when he closed his mouth around the peak and pulled, she came away from the wall, a litany of cries falling from her lips.

For every small action of his, she reacted like the sky lighting up, like thunder that shook the ground. With explosive passion. With unbound enthusiasm. When he moved his hand from her rounded bottom that filled his hand oh-so-perfectly to the line of her hip and tugged at the string of her thong, she stilled.

"Massimo?" she whispered, a wealth of desire and a flicker of doubt in it.

He covered the mound of her sex with his palm, the raspy brush of hair, the warmth of her stinging him like electric current. *Dios mio*, he didn't remember a time when he'd been more turned on. He lifted his head and kissed her. Softly, this time, slowly, letting their mouths dance to the tune their bodies demanded, willing her to trust him. In and out, he plunged his tongue, in a rhythm his erection desperately needed. "You're so responsive, *cara mia*. I want to kiss, lick and touch you everywhere."

Eyes so wide that he could drown in them filled with sudden shyness. "Here? Shouldn't we go home?"

He smiled, the sight of her swollen lips, lipstick all smudged, the dilated pupils, her hair in a wild disarray, her pulse fluttering—a visual feast he'd never be able to forget.

A sight that made every possessive instinct in him flare into life. The thought of any other man seeing her like this, knowing this intimacy with Natalie, being the recipient of her smiles and her joy and her brilliant mind... *Cristo*, where was this possessive instinct coming from? Why was he muddying sex with emotion?

"Massimo?" she said, prodding him softly. Kissing him, dueling her tongue with his, just as he'd taught her mere minutes ago.

"Here, Natalie," he said, resolve filling his very blood. She would be his, only his. Somehow, he'd make it happen. "I can't f—" He tempered his words, now, today.

Another day, another night, when he showed her how it could be between them, when she reveled in this heat between them, when she realized she couldn't live without him inside her, again and again, when she understood the power she could have over him and he over her, then he wouldn't curb his language. Then he would use the filthiest words he wanted and take her every which way.

But for now, this trust she gave him that was so hard for her to do was a gift. A gift he intended to prize above all else.

"I can't be inside you here. Not without protection." She

colored so innocently that he took her bruised mouth again in a rough kiss. "But I'm desperate to see you come, to hear the sounds you make when you do. When we walk out of here, and the boring monotony of that party makes me want to pluck my eyes out, the sounds and scent of your orgasm will be my strength to get to the other side."

She smiled, desire lighting up her eyes into a thousand colorful beams. A little naughty. A lot willing. Her hands trembled as she straightened his jacket. "Beneath all that ambition, you're a wicked man."

She was laughing when he took her mouth again in a kiss—a sound that seemed to burrow into his veins, and it was the most joyous, arousing thing Massimo had ever heard in his life.

Her mouth matched his this time, hungrily licking and nipping, teeth banging, tongues tangling. As if he and his kisses and caresses weren't just to meet the needs of her body but to fill her soul, as well. As if it were a challenge she was laying down at him, to meet her fully.

He ravaged her mouth roughly all the while pulling her up, until his hand lodged under her thigh, tugging her leg up, opening her center up for him, until his cock was pressed into the hot V between her thighs.

Goaded by instinct, he rocked his hips into the welcoming groove. Pleasure burst over his skin like a million little charges had burst into life. Their mingled groans filled the air with an erotic thrum.

Cristo, he wanted to be inside her now. Without protection. Without caution. Need was like a thousand needles under his skin, stealing away rationality, urging him toward making promises to her. Promises that would chain her to him.

Promises that would have given him nightmares a mere month ago.

Promises of a future he'd never once in his life even considered as an option.

Instead, he sent his fingers seeking her wet heat. Anticipation had nothing on reality when he pushed her thong to the side and found her sex. *Cristo*, she was willing and wanton. For him. Only for him.

Moaning, she threw her head back when he found her clit. Jerked as if a lightning storm had hit her when he rubbed her moisture at her entrance, when he slowly penetrated her with one finger.

She was a wet, hot sheath, and every inch of him tightened, imagining how she good she would be around his cock. Sweat beaded on his forehead, restless heat clamping every muscle. "*Merda*, you're tight, so ready, *cara mia*. Look at me, Natalie. Tell me how it feels."

Eyes glazed, she looked down, her two front teeth buried in her lower lip. Her hands descended to his shoulders, her forehead pressed into his shoulder. "It feels…new, strange. Achy, Massimo. Like there's a fever inside me. Please… don't stop."

"That's my brave little hacker," Massimo whispered against her mouth while he pushed another finger into her and stretched her slowly. Every inch of his body corkscrewed with tension, crying for release. He kept his thumb pressed against her clit while working a slow rhythm with his fingers. "Move over my fingers, *cara mia*. Tell me what feels good, learn what sets your body on fire."

She came up and away from him, her body tense and shaking, soundless cries falling from her lips. He used his other hand to cup her breast, loving the stiff poke of her nipple at his palm. Color filling her cheeks, hands clinging to his shoulders, she caught on to the rhythm of his fingers. He plumped and petted one breast after the other, rubbing and rolling her nipples, watching her—fascinated, hungry, obsessed with how sinuously she moved, how quickly she learned what made it good for her, how greedily she demanded he move the heel of his palm to exert counterpoint pressure to the slick movements of his fingers.

Panting and moaning, writhing against his fingers, release came upon her, sending her slender body into spasms. Her skin shimmered with a damp sheen, her eyes heavy-lidded. She opened her eyes and held his gaze with such crystal clarity, such a possessive light, tossing them both up into the intensity of the moment.

Dios mio, would he ever have enough of this?

He helped her ride out her climax, her pleasure feeding his, until she arrested his wrist, and flopped onto him like a spent storm. Arms cradling her, he held her while she clung, whispering inanities, telling her what a beautifully wild creature she was.

He leaned his forehead into her shoulder, the musky scent of her arousal filling his very breath. This was not him. This man blinded by lust, egged on by the need for possession.

BCS was his life, his goal, his everything. He never had, *didn't* have, time for relationships. He definitely didn't have what it took to keep a woman like her. Innocent and fragile, complex and defensive. He couldn't let her mess him up like this, couldn't let her—

The stinging peal of his watch fractured the moment with the same effect of a hammer swinging at the closed walls. He pulled himself away from the welcoming warmth of her body, frowning.

Natalie stiffened just as he clicked on the warning trigger he'd programmed into his cyber infrastructure.

The alert he'd put in himself took a few seconds to sink in.

A rogue bot program was loose in his network. Scouring every nook and cranny. Searching for something.

He looked up.

Guilt screamed from Natalie's stiff posture. She looked sexy and wrung out, mouth swollen, a pink mark on her neck courtesy of his teeth, dress rumpled.

"A rogue bot program is scouring through my personal security network, destroying each level of encryption like a deck of cards. I'm assuming that is you?"

That was why she'd been so restless and nervous all evening? Why she had...

He cursed so filthily that the air should have turned blue. "Was that—" he pointed to her disheveled dress, his mouth twisting "—to pacify me when I discovered what you'd been up to?"

Whatever color had filled her cheeks mere minutes ago fled, leaving her pale and shivering under the glare of the lights. But she bucked up, tilting her chin up, gathering that toughness she wore like an armor all around her again. Shutting him out. "Don't be nasty, Massimo. It doesn't come naturally to you."

He flinched. "Then what the hell am I supposed to think?"

Her arms went around her midriff. She looked lost, defensive, utterly enchanting. "I... I didn't exactly plan for... to throw myself at you tonight. I've been wound up all day, wondering where it would end. After that evening of—" her arm trembled as she pointed to the outside world "—pretending to be everything I'm not, of being near you and wanting you and not knowing what the hell is right and wrong—" she bit her lip and groaned "—something snapped inside me. I wanted to be reckless, and daring and just take what I wanted. You... God—" she pushed her hands through her hair "—only you do this to me.

"Really, if you use that incisive mind of yours, you'll

realize that I don't have either the experience or the confidence to turn…this thing between us to my advantage. A pity that, because then I could've gotten myself out of this mess the moment you caught me."

His watch emitted another beep, jerking his attention back to the pressing matter. This time, it was an alert he'd programmed to go off when anything accessed a particular directory. The one that had files pinning Natalie to the security breach. This time, he wasn't surprised. He knew where her bot program was going.

"When did you go into the lab?" he asked, trying to sift through the anger and outrage and so many other emotions.

"This morning, when you were meeting with Leonardo. And just before we left, again." Sweat beaded over her upper lip, a faint tension vibrating through her body. "That second alert means my program found those files, doesn't it? I saw the layers of encryption around that directory."

"You planned to destroy the proof?"

"Yes. Then I'd have my freedom."

"Brilliant as always."

She laughed, the sound edging into hysteria. Her fingers crept into her hair, tugged, and then she dropped them with a soft gasp. "All day, all night… I've been going crazy. When you said you'd let Leonardo handle the situation, I wondered…"

"What?"

"I wondered how long it'd be before you decided you'd been lenient enough with me. I was just waiting for him to turn me in." She swallowed and looked away. "I was terrified. I felt as if I'd lost everything all over again," she said, fear turning those beautiful eyes into wide pools. "I was determined to destroy all the files you have on me."

"What did you intend to do once you destroyed the files?" he said, something building in his chest.

"I was going to beg Greta's help and run far away from here. From you. She'd have helped me. She hates me."

"You had everything planned, didn't you?" He'd been expecting something like this from her. "The sheer nerve of you to hack into my network and let something like that loose...while you kiss me at the same time..."

"Sheer nerve? How about desperation? I'm sinking, Massimo. I don't know which man to trust and protect and which man to betray...terrified that I'll make the wrong decision."

"It's not hard to stay away from the man who's doing illegal things. Not hard to stay on the right side."

"Only a man born to privilege can be so absolute about right and wrong. A man who's never known hunger. A man who's never had to worry where he would sleep that night. I don't know why he's doing this, but he's not a monster.

"He saved me from a bully, from a bastard of a foster brother. He saved me from going to juvenile detention. He...he...for years, he looked out for me. He...caught me trying to steal his wallet and fed me a meal when I was starving.

"He found me a place to live, gave me money to get my own place. All these years, he never asked me for anything. He only gave, Massimo. He...said he saw something of himself in me. Years and years of favors.

"And when he asked me to do this one small thing of taking down BCS, wrapped it in lies I could swallow, I bought it willingly. I did him the favor. I... The second time, when he asked again, I could have said no. He wouldn't have pushed me. But I'd been caught in my own hubris, lured by the challenge of taking you on.

"So, no, I can't betray him. Even if I hate that he threw me into the middle of some awful vengeance scheme he's been cooking for who knows how long. Even if I hate that he's causing you…this much trouble. And I don't even hate him fully for involving me in this, because how could I?

"If not for him, I wouldn't have met you. If not for him, I wouldn't have known what it was to want a man so much that I can't breathe. Can you imagine how twisted up I am in all of it?" She wiped the lone tear off her cheek, her chin setting into that stubborn tilt. "So the only rational thing I knew to do was to try to steal that proof before you sent me to jail.

"But… I couldn't. I just couldn't. All evening, I've been wondering if I've gone insane. Wondering if I'm really losing it."

Massimo felt as if she'd hit him in the solar plexus. Punch after punch solidly connecting, knocking the breath out of him. "What do you mean you couldn't?" Another damned peal from his watch.

"That bot program is only meant to locate my files. I… I couldn't bear it if you hated me. I couldn't bear to break your trust.

"But I had to break this impasse. So I went back and I tweaked the program to just locate the files. I meant to show you that I'm capable of saving myself, of betraying you, again, but I choose to not do it. To show you that I… I would never break your trust again, Massimo. Just please don't ask me anything more. Don't ask me for what I can't give."

So much she held on to, so fully, so completely she gave of her loyalty even under the harshest conditions. It wouldn't have cost her anything to give this man up. To look out for herself. And yet, she wouldn't… He didn't know whether to kiss her for her guts or to banish her out of his life for making everything so complicated.

He thought he knew her.

Dios mio, she'd told him enough about her background. He knew enough to understand that to survive in a harsh world, she'd become tough, and that she hated to be vulnerable in any way, that she was a wild thing that wrapped herself in layers of armor to protect herself...but this, for her to be willingly vulnerable to him, for her to give over her freedom, her security, into his hands, trusting that he'd do the right thing—the devastating result of that was in her eyes wild with fear, in her mouth that didn't stop trembling, in her body vibrating with tension.

This was ravaging her.

And yet, she'd done it.

To gain his trust.

The weight of her admission humbled Massimo, the emotional expectation beneath that decision...did he even deserve it? Did he want it?

She rubbed her eyes, smudging the mascara, ruining the makeup that he hadn't, leaving her still breathtakingly lovely, starkly beautiful. Eyes that had glazed over during her release filled with alarming tears. "I hate that you make me so weak. But I'm done fighting it."

The *swish-swish* of the elevator doors behind him revealed the stunned faces of Leonardo, and Greta. With Gisela and her father behind them. They'd been gone too long. *Maledizione*, the last thing he needed was the whole world to hear that his fake fiancée had been ready to leave him.

And still, Massimo couldn't find a mask to pull. Couldn't dig deep enough to care.

Let them think it was a lovers' quarrel. Let them see how crazy Natalie could drive him.

He pushed his hands through his hair and went to her, not wanting the world to see her like that. Not wanting anyone to see the vulnerability in her posture. Clasping her jaw, he tilted her face up to him. "What shall I do with you, *cara mia*?" Laughter burst through him and she stared at him, as if he'd lost his mind.

Had he? Would she leave with him with not even a semblance of control? It felt as if he had crossed some hitherto invisible line, had left safety and sanity behind. She'd dragged him into a new place, a place where he didn't know who he was anymore. Where emotions barreled through him.

He struggled under the weight of tenderness, of possessiveness, of deflated outrage. God, this woman...she stole the very breath from him. "You'll drive me insane before you're through with me," he said, before he kissed her hurt mouth. His lungs seemed to fill with air, his limbs infused with energy again, as she sank into the contact. He tasted her tears, her soft admission, her vulnerability. He held her tight, wanting to capture the essence of her.

"I... I'm tired, Massimo." She clung to him like a rag doll. All the fight and fury had deserted her. Her breath whispered over his jaw, her hands roving over his chest. "I'm tired of being tough. I'm tired of being pulled apart. I'm tired of worrying about my brother, about you, about the man who started all this. About everyone else when all I want is to..."

"You...you're shredding me into so many pieces." Her fingers traced the bridge of his nose, his mouth, his chin, even the small scar on his temple.

The look in her eyes, longing and something more, arrested him. "With your kindness, and your charm, your laughter and your warnings. Your second chances. Your innate goodness. Your kisses. Your..." She looked down, dashing her gaze away. "But remember this, Massimo. When I could've freed myself from this dangerous game, when I could've protected myself—the only thing I know how to do—I chose instead to keep your trust.

"When I could've, *should've*, escaped, I chose to stay. With you."

CHAPTER TEN

MASSIMO STOOD IN the study that he and Leo used some-times, a drink in his hand, his mind drifting from thought to thought, landing on the woman in the guest suite upstairs.

What would you do with me if I were all yours?

Maledizione, he couldn't forget that line or the vulner-ability in her face when she'd said it. Still couldn't wrap his mind around what she'd done tonight.

He verbalized his frustrations into a pithy curse as he heard the door open and close behind him, knowing who it was.

Leo's laughter had such a shocking mirth to it that he turned. "I'm glad you think this is funny."

"I was just remembering Giuseppe's and Gisela's ex-pressions earlier. I think you erased any doubt as to where your…interests lie, back in that elevator."

"And you've come to congratulate me about it?"

"Are congratulations in order? That didn't look like a fake engagement."

He scowled. "Cut to the chase, Leonardo."

"The way you spun it with Giuseppe—that the hack-ing attack and the security breach was something you had planned to find flaws in the system, that you brought her on for that express purpose—Silvio and I can use that same logic successfully to calm the board's considerable doubts and questions at the gala. Thanks to your quick thinking, we're in a good place.

"But it is imperative that we do something aggressive about stopping this...man, Massimo. Before we sign on with Giuseppe Fiore. Even a whiff of scandal like this again—"

"Could ruin that project before it even begins," Massimo finished, giving voice to his greatest fear.

Relief filled Leo's eyes and Massimo laughed. "You think I do not see the risks? You think I'm that far gone?"

Leo shrugged. "Women, and relationships for that matter, this family, this legacy, have never been an important part of your life before, Massimo. Even with your mama, you hardened yourself, letting her go so completely. You... simply decided Silvio had tortured her enough, decided that you were a weakness dragging her down. I'm not quite sure I'd have been able to do that. You decided you'd focus on your career, your ambition, you decided you would conquer whatever demons you had, and you did it. For a decade, I've watched you work crazy hours, go from strength to strength."

Massimo frowned. He had never looked at it quite that way.

"But with Natalie, you went rogue, completely off script, from the minute you met her.

"Honestly, I don't know what to think. I can't help but think maybe you've lost your edge for...this."

His brother's perceptiveness rendered Massimo so shocked that he could barely muster a response. "I haven't."

"And maybe you need to be told that it's not a—"

"Leonardo! All I will say is that yes, Natalie disarms me like no one else."

"I have to admit that to prove to you that she could steal it but not actually do it... I still don't feel comfortable that she could so easily ruin everything you're working toward, but I have to admire her guts. I can admit to seeing the lure she holds for you."

Massimo's problem was that he was beginning to admire a lot more than just her guts. Was beginning to lose his control, his path. "The Fiore contract is still my first priority, Leo."

"Bene." Leo nodded. And his vote of confidence meant something to Massimo. "I will not waste time and energy worrying over you, then. Greta and Silvio are far too much already. What did you find out from her?"

Massimo looked away. He'd never been so conflicted in his life. And he didn't like it one bit that she did this to him.

He walked across the study, taking in the expansive room that had been the seat of his father's power when he had ruled most of Milan as the CEO of Brunetti Finances.

Usually, he preferred to not step foot inside here, since all the memories he had of this room were of being summoned by Silvio at all hours while he was recovering from another asthma attack or a fright induced by an approaching one or when he had failed to exhibit great athleticism or when he saved a kitten. There had been countless things, and then being shouted at that he needed to let go of his mama and grow up and be a man.

That she was coddling him too much. That she was making him soft and spoiled.

That he would never be man enough or strong enough or ruthless enough like Leonardo. Never good enough to be a Brunetti.

Today it seemed like the two parts of him—one with an unending thirst to prove himself to Silvio and Leo, the entire world and to himself, and the second, the weak boy whose mother had tried so hard to teach him right from wrong, who had told him to define himself in a different way, his own way, who tried to negate the harmful narra-

tive his father had perpetuated in the house for so long—
clashed violently.

Dios mio, his mother had put up with Silvio for so long
for Massimo's sake. She had tried so hard to stop Massimo from thinking that he had to be cruel and ruthless to
be powerful and successful. In the end, she'd found love
with another man, forced to choose between a new life
and Massimo.

Massimo had bid her goodbye happily at the age of fifteen, desperate for her to find a little happiness, desperate
for her to stop sacrificing herself for him. But there had
been selfishness on his part, too. He'd been determined
to prove that he could survive without her shielding him
from reality.

And he had succeeded beyond his wildest dreams.

He had carved his own path, found his own empire. His
cyber security business had infused much needed capital
into other branches of Brunetti Finances, a dynastic mul-
tigenerational financial institution, when it had been limping along on its last leg. His brainchild, BCS, was the only
reason they stood irresolute and unshakable today when
most of Europe—and Italy, in particular—were flounder-
ing and falling into financial crises.

And when they signed this hundred-billion-euro contract with Giuseppe Fiore…there would be no looking
back.

Yes, Leonardo was right that they still needed to find
the man who was targeting them. But no, he didn't need to
hold Natalie's freedom over her head to achieve it.

It was not a weakness to grant her her freedom. Not a
weakness to achieve his goal, realize his ambition without
crushing the one powerless person in all this. Not a weakness to grant her that desperate sense of control she needed
over her life.

I chose you, Massimo.

That constant knot in his gut slowly relented, a sense of rightness settling his breath.

He saw the study with new eyes. Leonardo had decided to redecorate the space. The transformation had been fantastic—it had gone from a cloying, ghastly room with so-called precious antiques to an open space with contemporary art and clean lines.

Greta had put up a dirty, vicious fight carping on about legacies and dynasties but Leo had shut her up. But it had been a new direction for Brunetti Finances, and even better, it had been a new direction for the Brunetti brothers to take the company, their legacy.

"She told me enough about this man to give us a trail to follow. A money trail. He transferred her money when she turned eighteen so that she could get off the streets. I'll dig down to the exact dates once I get out of here. All we need is to trace her bank account to see where the deposits came from."

"And his name?" Leo prompted, clearly not satisfied with what Massimo gave him.

"There isn't one."

"Massimo, you have to make her tell you—"

"*Nessuno!* I will not," he said softly, "coerce her or threaten her with imprisonment. That's my final decision. She has too much stake in this now, Leo. I need her by my side to keep Gisela in line, with Giuseppe so close to signing. I need her to work by my side on the security designs. You saw how impressed Giuseppe's CTO was with her tonight."

"You're basing a lot of important things—things we've worked years for—on the fact that you trust her. Her loyalty—"

"Is not something that can be bought or forced. The way

Silvio got things done, we swore we would be different. We swore we'd build our fortunes the right way.

"Natalie will be an incredible asset to not just BCS but Brunetti Finances in the long run.

"It's plain, pure business sense."

Leo finally nodded. "*Bene.* As long as you're sure that's your guiding principle, I will follow your lead."

"It is. It has to be," Massimo reiterated to an empty room long after Leonardo left.

Natalie let the stylist use her like a fashion doll. She let the makeup artist pull and prick her scalp, straighten her hair to an inch of its life, probably burning away most of it, in the process of making her good enough to be the fake fiancée of the Brunetti scion.

A week since the disastrous and most spectacular night of her life, Massimo hadn't decided her fate. Still. Despite her throwing herself at his mercy. Despite puking her guts about how much he was coming to mean to her. Worse, her emotional outburst seemed to have only pushed him away. Filled the space between them with an awkward kind of tension she couldn't disrupt.

Excusing themselves to a curious audience, he had dragged her home that night. Warning her to do nothing for once, if she knew what was good for her. Closeted himself in the lab. The next morning, he'd shown up at her door again at the crack of dawn, like clockwork. For a whole foolish minute, she'd hoped he'd come for…personal reasons.

Nope, the workaholic that he was, it had been back to business. At least he hadn't revoked her electronic access to his lab. He had made her sign what felt like a hundred contracts, officially bringing her on the payroll for the Fiore contract, including confidentiality agreements and waivers and whatnot.

Making it clear that she wasn't going anywhere, anytime soon.

Once she'd started thinking straight again and not out of a desperation born of lust and longing, she realized Massimo couldn't simply tell the world that his fiancée was a criminal or send her to jail.

There was the little matter of their fake engagement. She couldn't contest the fact that he needed her—at least as his fiancée—to keep Gisela in line. Especially since it looked like Giuseppe had been more than impressed with Massimo's initial design and, with his reassurance about bringing Natalie on, more than ready to sign off the contract to BCS.

Now, he had officially tied her to that contract, too, by bringing her on as a consultant. Her future was secure. Not just secure. Better than ever before. Because Massimo Brunetti was a generous employer. She could put away so much for Frankie's college. She could save for a future.

He'd even let her Skype with Frankie. More than once. Forced her to introduce him, too, since he kept hanging around during the call.

He hadn't asked her a single question again about Vincenzo.

All this generosity was beginning to choke her since he didn't even…really look at her anymore. She much preferred his accusation that she'd been trying to distract him while she deceived him rather than this polite distance, this courteous withdrawal. He didn't laugh with her, he shared no horrible hacker jokes that he found on the internet, he didn't tease her into kissing him.

A week since that night—the night her body had come alive in his hands so violently that when she went to bed every night, she closed her eyes and touched herself, trying to recall his warmth and scent and his desire. But her fingers were poor substitutes to his wickedly clever ones. So she tossed and turned, feeling a restless hunger after being cooped up with him in the lab for the whole day. Being near him, touching him accidentally, breathing the scent of him until he was a part of her.

And now this engagement party... It wasn't too much of a reach to think Greta was doing this to punish her.

She sighed when the stylist finally finished with her hair and the two too-cheerful assistants plonked a full-length mirror in front of her.

Despite her glum mood, Natalie's attention stirred.

Her hair straightened into a silky curtain fell past her shoulder, giving her the sleek sophistication she'd always wished she possessed. The white strapless gown that had been chosen for her fell a few inches past her knees, its beauty lying in the clean, classic A-line cut. It hugged her small breasts, clinging to the dip and rise of her waist and hips, ending in a big ruffle at the end, a beautiful feminine touch to contrast the severe cut of the bodice.

Pale gold powder accentuated her cheekbones and brow, and a glossy pink lipstick subtly enhanced her lush mouth. This look was night and day different from the one last week. Of course, that afternoon, she'd explicitly asked Alessandra for the kind of look that arrested Massimo's gaze, in her desperation to be worthy of him.

Tonight, about to be presented to Milan's Who's Who on the Lake Como estate, which was the home turf for the Brunettis, the stylists seemed to have been instructed that she needed to look classy, elegant. Instead of resenting the high-handed approach, Natalie decided to embrace it. Really, she had disadvantages enough when it came to Massimo without falling into a pit of insecurities about how she looked.

She'd just pushed her feet into bright pink pumps the stylist said would add a pop of color to her outfit when Massimo walked in.

His gaze swept over her, a soft smile playing around his mouth. The first one in a week. "You look...beautiful, *bella*."

In a black tux that highlighted his wide shoulders and lean waist, he looked absolutely gorgeous. Divine. "You look good enough to eat," she retorted, and he laughed.

"Well, it's the truth."

"I'm glad the true you hasn't been buried beneath all the primping, *cara mia*."

And just like that, her heart fell right into his clutches. God, she was really tired of the impasse between them. "Massimo, can we please not..."

She closed her mouth when he pulled out a small velvet box. Without asking her, he reached for her hand and pushed the princess-cut diamond ring in white gold onto her ring finger. "I... I have been remiss about that. Appearances must be maintained, *sì*?"

Natalie folded her lips inward, stalling the pinch of hurt. "Of course," she added, pasting on a fake smile. This was getting harder day by day. "Appearances are the most important. Even for fake Brunettis," she couldn't help adding.

He smiled, as if he were delighted by her snark. "Your bot program was brilliant. I didn't think you could take down the encryption around that directory, truly."

"Your ego is not dented?"

His mouth twitched. "You know me better than that, Natalie. I've never asked you to hide what you are capable of, from me. I never would."

Feeling like a fake of the worst kind, she nodded. What

would he do, however, if he knew the extent to which she'd used those capabilities to survive her life, she wanted to say. She swallowed the question, struggled to push away the niggle of shame. Her past was just that. The past.

And then he was pulling out something else from his pocket, and Natalie's breath stuttered in her chest. Palm up with it in the center, he looked at her. "I went the old-school route. I saved it on a flash drive. And the directory you found... I've scrubbed it permanently."

Her knees threatened to buckle from under her. "What?"

"The files are gone. The trail is scrubbed. This is the only remaining copy of everything I put together to find you."

"You're giving it to me," she finished lamely, her throat aching, tears gathering like a storm.

Only a nod.

"With no conditions?"

"*Sì.* You'll never have to worry about ending up in jail. As long as you don't do anything criminal again, that is," he said, the corner of his mouth tilted up, a glimmer of that teasing Massimo in his eyes.

She swallowed, but the boulder-size lump in her throat wouldn't budge. She wanted to grab the flash drive and run away. Far from this man she couldn't seem to dislodge from under her skin. Far, far away from her own heart's stupid longings.

"Why are you doing this?"

"I'm trusting you. Isn't that what that stunt was about?"

"It is. And I'm glad. But...where do you and I stand, Massimo?"

The warmth disappeared from his eyes. "We still have an agreement. You're clever enough to understand that you can't just up and leave. Not now when you're an official employee of BCS. Not when Giuseppe is ready to sign on the dotted line. Having heard of her unstable reputation, I shouldn't have messed with Gisela. Even if she knew the rules of the game. I'm afraid she's fixated on me."

She nodded, agreeing completely. "I won't let you down. I promise. I'll play the part of your perfect fiancée as if I was born for this role. I'll be nice and sweet to your family and in public—"

He laughed so loudly that his brother and Greta looked up from the foyer where the first guests were beginning to arrive. "Do you know the meaning of the words *nice* and *sweet*, Natalie?"

"I do," she replied, basking in the warmth of his laughter. She loved it when he was like this—smiles and teasing—and...she loved that he understood her so well, and that he...

A wave of shock rolled over her.

No, she didn't.

She couldn't love him.

How could she, when she didn't even know what it meant? When all she'd ever known was survival?

No.

She was mistaking gratitude for a deeper emotion. It couldn't be love—could it?—when the very prospect of it terrified her to her soul. When the very idea of giving him so much power over her threatened to break her out in hives. She trusted him more than she did anyone in the world and she wanted him. That was it.

"Leonardo thinks I'm foolish to take such a gamble on you again. Don't make me lose face with him, *sì*?"

"Sì." When he turned to leave, she grabbed his arm. "Wait, Massimo."

He folded his hands. *"Sì?"*

She turned the engagement ring over and over, feeling its weight on her soul. "What about you and me?"

"There is no you and me. There should never have been, you were right.

"I'm still recovering from a stupid mistake I made by tangling with Gisela. Even knowing that I was going to do business with her father, even knowing that she...had the reputation of being wild and unstable.

"And you—" his gaze drank her face in "—you've never even been with a man before. The last thing I need is to make another misstep like that, with you of all people. You're far too—"

"If you say I'm innocent, I'll hate you. Don't take away the power of my choice from me."

"We belong in different worlds. Want different things in life. I will not do anything that will rock the boat now, now that BCS is going to handle a hundred-billion-euro contract any day. Now that you're an important, moving part of the company.

"I can't afford to blur the lines in this relationship."

If he had thrown her into jail, Natalie would have been less shocked. A sense of falling, with no safety net, claimed her chest.

"Shall we go?" he said, offering his hand, and she nodded. Her other hand closed over the flash drive.

She was free, finally. For once in her life, she was getting a break. More than she deserved. And yet, freedom had never felt so costly to her emotions.

Tears stung at the back of her eyes but she held them back. Just. A cold that was absolute took hold over her.

He'd given her everything she'd asked for and more.

Gave her back her freedom.

Given her a secure future.

And yet, this...this distance he imposed, this calculation in his eyes that she was a weakness he couldn't afford, this was a rejection. Like he'd given her everything and yet taken away the most important thing from her.

Him.

He'd taken himself away. From her.

For a woman who'd built her whole life being self-sufficient, trusting no one, why did it feel like such an aching loss? Why did it hurt so much?

And was she prepared to let him do it? She'd always had to fight for what she had, worked hard just to keep her head above water. Now when she was faced with losing something truly important, was she prepared to let it go so easily? Was she really going to let Massimo push her away?

No. No she wasn't.

She wanted Massimo. And she was going to fight for him.

CHAPTER ELEVEN

PREDAWN PITCH-BLACKNESS WAS a thick blanket Natalie had to wade through as she made her way to Massimo's room.

She was done living in caution, done safeguarding her heart. She wanted, craved, that excitement. She wanted whatever pleasure Massimo could give her. She wanted, even if only for a few days, a few months, whatever time, to be the woman who brought out the wicked, wild side of the tech billionaire.

Except from the moment he had put the ring on her finger and dealt her that rejection several days ago, he hadn't looked at her once with that desire in his eyes. Not once had he been tempted among all the evenings they'd spent in each other's company. Not once had his polite mask slipped.

Enough was enough!

The marble was smooth and cold under her bare feet. Having learned his punishing schedule by rote—billionaires really worked the longest hours—she'd decided to just…show up at his door. She heard a sound from within just as she raised her hand to knock and decided against it.

Why give him a chance to reject her again?

Slowly, she turned the knob and stepped into the lounge. A small lamp at his desk illuminated the sprawling sofas and the contemporary art on the walls. She rubbed her feet on a thick rug, relishing the warmth of it. The sound came again—a cross between a moan and a growl, sending shivers down her spine. A thousand thoughts flashed through her mind—did he have a woman in there? Had he already moved on? God, was he *refueling*? If he was, she'd…throttle him, the unfeeling brute!

She didn't even have to barge into his bedroom for he had left the door open. Tugging the cashmere shawl she'd wrapped around her shoulders tighter, she stepped in.

The massive golden shaded lamps on both sides of the even more massive bed emitted a soft yellow light. Papers and electronic devices lay scattered on the nightstand. A gray suede headboard framed most of the wall. Dark gray bedcovers were rolled away. A white towel dangled off the end of the bed. And at the foot of the bed, leaning against it, stood Massimo.

Stark naked.

Head thrown back.

Breath coming out in harsh inhales and exhales.

Neck muscles corded tight.

Defined chest muscles gleaming with dampness. Falling and rising.

Abdomen so tightly packed that she wanted to run her tongue along it and see if he was really that tight.

Thighs rock hard and clenched, dotted with hair.

And his hand wrapped around his…erection. Even from the distance she could see the corded tightness of his wrist, fingers wrapped tight, and the head of his erection visible above his fist every time he moved his grip up and down with a grunt that seemed to claw up from his chest.

Heat licked up every inch of her stinging skin instantly. Every inch of her body reacted to the gloriously aroused naked man in front of her, reveling in sexual abandon. Her breasts turned achy and heavy, nipples knotted points rubbing against her T-shirt. And there was that wetness at her sex, readying her for him. Her skin felt as if it were two sizes too small for her feverish muscles.

Her breath left her lungs in an audible gush like a balloon deflating. And then she struggled to get more air in because there was none left in the room. She gasped under the overload of sensation.

Massimo's head jerked down, breath shallow. His gray gaze pinned hers to the spot, pupils dilated. He frowned, his hand coming away from his erection, which bobbed up against his taut belly. With shaking fingers, he rubbed his face with his other hand. And then looked at her again with an intensity that seared her. Twin slashes of color climbed up under his olive skin.

Had he realized she was there, not in his imagination? Oh, God, please let it be her that he'd been imagining…

"You shouldn't be here, *cara mia*," he said, husky desire making his voice low and raspy. Even his words seemed to ping on her skin, overheating her.

"Did I ever give you the impression that I'd abide by your rules?"

"No," he said, leaning that tight butt against the bed, jutting those lean hips up, so confident and comfortable in his nudity. So utterly, irresistibly male. "If you did, it would solve a lot of problems for me."

"I want to be here. All week, I've been trying to muster the courage to walk in here. All evening, I readied myself for you. I've plucked and waxed and bleached and shaved and peeled and massaged…"

He cursed. Then laughed. Then shoved his fingers through his hair. "You don't have to change yourself, in any way. I want you just the way you are, with an insanity that for the first time in my life even work won't do it for me. I think of you all the time…which is hard enough because you're there by my side 24/7."

Simple truth. No games. "Then why pull away from me?"

His gaze swept over her face, her neck, her sleeveless

tee and her shorts, her thighs, her legs. "I swore to myself a long time ago, even if I forget it from time to time, that I would never be the kind of man who hurts…fragile things. You're…breakable, Natalie. I'll use you, and then break you, before I discard you. I couldn't face myself then."

She'd never seen him like this—so desperately hungry, such stark need in his eyes. So much desire that her first instinct was that he would drown her in it, make her lose herself, and running away was probably the best thing. But she refused to listen to that flight instinct. No, she would stay. She wanted to stay. She wanted to drown in him. "I don't need you to save me from you or from myself, Massimo. I don't want a hero. I've never asked for one. I've always saved myself. Found another way, another path.

"I want a man to show me all the stuff I've missed out on because I was so afraid for so long. I want a man who will help me live, experience, feel. For however long we want it to be.

"I want you, flesh and blood, like this, desperate for me. Out of control. Stripped to the core. Because that's how I stand before you."

Each second of the silence that ensued let panic loose in her head. He was too honorable, too much of a protector, to take her. Not unless she drove him to it. She needed to be the aggressor, at least until he got his hands on her. Then all bets were off. She knew. She knew how desperately he wanted her.

She took a few steps toward him, not quite touching distance. The jut of his shoulders, those rock-hard thighs—every muscle in him clenched tight.

"Were you thinking of me?" she asked, licking her tongue, wondering why her mouth felt so dry. "Please tell me you were thinking of me and not another woman. Because I'd have to hunt her down and kill her."

A dark smile split his mouth, a beacon of light in the darkness. A flash of that wicked, wild Massimo that she adored. A glimpse of the man she was falling for, fast. But there was only exhilaration right now in her veins. Only anticipation, excitement.

"Morning, noon and night, I think of you. I go to bed thinking of you. I wake up hard thinking of you. You in that gold dress, a goddess teasing and taunting me. You in that yellow bikini, like a sunflower in a field of frost. You in that white cocktail gown looking so demure and classy and calm and nice and sweet."

"Are you insinuating I'm not classy?" She pouted, taking another step. She was walking into a lion's den, she had no doubt. A willing sacrifice. And yet, she'd never felt so alive. So present. So in touch with herself. All of her.

His gaze swept over her with a warmth that was just as arousing as the desire. That made her feel safe. Secure. That made her want to throw herself headlong into this. "You're tart, and down to earth and loud and snarky and wild and...you're a summer storm, *mia Natalie*."

Happiness was a fountain spurting in her chest, overflowing to every empty space within her, filling her with a warmth she always felt when she thought of him. She touched him with her gaze—that high forehead, sharp cheekbones, aristocratic nose, carved mouth, the tendons in her neck, the sparse sprinkling of hair on his pectorals, the defined lines of his abdomen, and his...his erection thickened and lengthened under her gaze, and her panties were soaked. A growl fell from his mouth, filling her veins.

She rubbed a hand over her nape and then over her breasts, aching all over. "Did it work?"

"What, *cara mia*?"

"Thinking of me, and doing that...did it relieve your...ache?"

Thick lashes flickered down and then up again. His shrug brought her gaze back to the jut of his shoulders. Tense. Taut. Really, his body was like a treasure, and she didn't know where to look or what to touch. "*Sì*. For short periods of time."

"It didn't for me."

A rough thrust of his fingers through his hair. An infinitesimal tremble of his chest. Her words were getting to him. A jolt of power filled her. "What?" he breathed.

"I...tried it, too. Touching myself, trying to find relief.

"After that night when you made me..." She swallowed at the devilish cast to his features. The need he couldn't hide. "Every night, when I go to bed after spending all day with you, I feel so restless. As if I were a prisoner in my own skin. I'd shower, remembering your smiles and your teasing and your hunger that night, and the strokes of your fingers... By the time I got out of the shower, I'd be thrumming with need. I'd get into bed and touch myself.

"One hand cupping my breast and one hand, delving into my... On and on... I'd be wet and I tried to... But I... just ended up making it worse." She swept a hand over her breasts and belly and his gaze followed her movements, like a hungry hawk circling. "I... If you're not going to take me to bed, at least maybe you can give me some pointers?" She bit her lower lip and took another step. Another soft growl from his chest.

He didn't look like the suave, charming tech billionaire that had people eating out of his hands. No, he looked savage and rough, like the lowest denominator of himself.

"You want me to show you how to get yourself off?" Disbelief couldn't puncture the desperation.

She shrugged.

He cursed and laughed and cursed again. His powerful

body rumbled with the force of it. "*Cristo*, you were sent to torture me."

"You look like you've had a lot of practice. I could just—" she turned around and saw the chaise longue "—sit there, y'know, and you could stand there, and we could—"

"Only since you came into my life, I've felt this madness, this constant fever. I'm like…a goddamned teenager, needing to jerk off every few hours."

"I've never been so jealous of a damn hand. That hand."

She pressed her palm onto his abdomen and he growled, arresting her wrist in his hand. He was like a slab of damp heat and delicious hardness under her fingers and all she wanted to do was roll around in his heat, in his scent, until he was imprinted on her very skin.

"*Dio en cielo*, Natalie. If I do this, one night won't be enough."

Lifting her gaze, she held his. Saw the last thin thread of control separating them. "Who said anything about one night?" One more push and he would be hers. She pulled her hand away from his grip, and ran a finger over his length and moaned softly. How could he get even harder and bigger? "Shall I go down on my knees?"

His eyes gleamed. With need. Danced at her offer. He was tempted. *Hallelujah!* "You've got guts, bluffing your way through this, daring me with your tempting offers. How do you know you'll like it?"

"Will *you* like it?"

"*Sì*. It's all I can think of when I want to shut you up. When you argue with me. When you use your damned loyalty against me."

"Then I'm sure I'll like it, too."

When he simply gazed at her, she gave voice to her innermost desire. Pressing her forehead to his chest, she licked his skin. Tasted the essence of the man. Salt and musk and pure Massimo. "Please, Massimo.

"I… I want to be here, Massimo. Only here. With you, in that bed. Under you. Over you. Any which way you want. I can't sleep, I can't think straight…even my dreams are restless and leave me aching and wanting. You're the only man that has ever made me want to live. Live for myself. Experience everything life has to give. Risk myself. To laugh, cry, howl, plead."

To love with such abandon that would have terrified her before… She didn't say it.

It was the simple, incredible truth. Like the sky was blue and the earth was green and the world was a harsh and lonely place but also joyful and full of wonders if only one had the courage to step out and reach for them.

Love and its demands and its constrictions and its expectations had no place here tonight. Or maybe ever, with Massimo. And that was a price she was more than willing to pay to own a part of this incredible man, even if for a little time.

His fingers sank into her hair, and he tugged so hard that her scalp prickled. That, too, added to the surfeit of sensations beating her down. She felt his mouth at her temple, his other hand running in mesmerizing circles over her back and buttocks and hips, and he was tugging her T-shirt up, up and away, over her head, and pulling her into him, and suddenly, her bare breasts were pressed against his damp chest, her nipples dragging against the wall of his muscles, and they were both sinking and drowning and gasping at how good it felt.

Her hand slid back to his solid erection.

"No," he said abruptly, practically screaming the word into the darkness that enveloped them. As if he needed to control and corral this boundless want between them. "No, you can't touch me, not yet, *cara mia*. Not tonight. If you do, it will be over before we even begin and there's so many things I want to do with you before I'm pounding into you. So, no, no touching me. Get it?"

Natalie could barely form coherent thought, her brain too busy processing the deluge of novel sensations pouring into her. All she could do was press her mouth into his shoulder and dig her teeth in. Holding on to him.

Rough hands on her buttocks picked her up, pushing her thighs shamelessly wide, her feet on top of his buttocks, his hip bones digging into her fleshy thighs, until her sex was notched oh-so-snugly against his shaft.

"*Merda*, you're dripping wet. Is this for me, *cara mia*?"

"All for you. All I…feel is for you, Massimo," she whispered, and then she took his mouth the way she wanted to. Thrusting her tongue into the warm cavern of his mouth. Pressing it against his, retreating when he tried to catch her, sucking on his tip, tugging at his lip with her teeth, drawing blood, licking at that spot, until he was shuddering and shaking and pulling her down, down, down into a vortex of sensation that swallowed her up.

And then he was turning them and rocking her into that massive bed, giving her the friction she needed exactly where she needed it. His shaft pressed and slid and glided and rubbed against her clit and she caught on to his rhythm and was pushing herself into him just as he rocked his hips… Her swollen nipples scraped against the rough hair on his chest, his mouth buried in her neck told her in explicit terms how he was going to take her bold offer one day and put his shaft in the warmth of her mouth, and Natalie was drowning as pinpricks of sensation poured out from her neck, her mouth, her breasts, her belly, pulling and tightening and building into concentric circles in her lower belly, and she was sobbing, clawing her nails into his damp back, demanding he give her more…

Instead, he pulled away. Brought her down shaking from the cusp of pleasure and Natalie railed at him with her fists. Afraid that he'd leave her unfulfilled. Afraid that this was another dream she was going to wake up from. Afraid that she'd go through her entire life and not know his touch.

"Shh…*tesoro*," he whispered at her temple. "Look at me, Natalie. I'm going nowhere. I couldn't even if a thousand hands tried to rip me away. I couldn't leave if my breath depended on it."

Her bottom met a cloud of soft sheets, and when she opened her eyes, he was looming over her, sweat coating his skin, smelling like man and heat and sex and belonging. He kissed her bruised lips, so softly, so sweetly, so tenderly. "You trust me, *sì*?"

"I do. Like I never have another man. I…" She rubbed her fingers over his swollen lip, the tiny cut she'd given him. She searched for something light to puncture the dam of emotion building up in her chest. "I took a risk on you, Massimo. Pay it up, *per favore*, *caro mio*."

He nodded, a wicked light in his gray eyes. "Put your hands above your head. Clutch the sheets if you need to. But don't touch me, *sì*?"

She nodded, biting her lower lip. And watched him. Anticipation built up slowly this time. His mouth drew down on the pulse at her neck, while his hands plumped her breasts, readying her. She arched like a bow when he tugged a nipple into his mouth and suckled, a little roughly, building that fever in her veins. That tension in her pelvis again. "*Cristo*, you will come like this if I continue, won't you?"

She nodded, and of course he released her breast. "And you're going to be thorough and detail-oriented, aren't you?"

With a roguish smile, he continued the foray of his mouth down her body. Licked maddening circles around her belly button. Natalie was panting again, gasping for breath as he separated the folds of her sex with his fingers.

She felt him pulling in a deep breath, pulling the scent of her arousal into him. Heard his pithy, foul curse breathe into her skin. Felt the tremble in his shoulders. And then his fingers were at her clit again. Stroking, swiping.

"Is this what you did?" he whispered against the crease of her thigh. "Is this how you pleasured yourself?"

She opened her mouth and swallowed air. Somehow she managed to say, "But it's nothing like when you touch me." God, nothing and no one in the entire world was going to feel like Massimo ever again.

Then his mouth replaced his fingers and his fingers were inside her and all her fears vanished under the onslaught of the sharp sensations. "Like this?" he whispered, weaving some new magic.

"Or like this," while he explored her, learning, and gave her the key to her own body.

And he was licking at her tight bundle and hooking his finger until he touched some magical spot that sparked fierce pleasure in her pelvis. On and on, again and again, until she was nothing but pure sensation. And when he pulled his mouth and fingers up and away from her, Natalie followed him with her hips, sobbing and begging. And then he tugged at her clit with his teeth.

Pleasure threw her apart into so many pieces, fracturing her, tossing her, and he continued crooning against her sex and she kept coming, tears flowing out of her eyes, and she dug her fingers into his hair, because she was afraid he had broken her apart and she would fly away. She writhed on the sheets as the waves slowed and ebbed, whispering his name over and over again.

She was lost in a sea of pleasure. She was lost to this man, forever.

When he climbed onto the bed and he pulled her into his arms, his thighs cradling her hips, she folded like a deck of cards, shivering and shaking. He was a fortress of warmth and safety at her back. She rubbed her nose in his bicep, loving the smell of him. When he stretched his arm to reach into the nightstand, she stopped him. Looked at him over her shoulder.

"I'm on the pill. Alessandra took me to a pharmacy."

He raised a brow, the ghost of a smile shimmering around his mouth, and she blushed. How could she blush when he'd put her body and her emotions through a ringer?

"I wanted to be prepared." She kissed his chin. Nipped it with her teeth. Felt his erection like a hot brand against her. She wriggled in his lap and his fingers dug into her hips with a curse, hard enough to leave bruises. So she did it more. And he groaned. "I was going to have you, come what may. If you didn't know already, I'm a determined woman."

"That you are," he said, turning her to face him. "I'm clean." A flash of white teeth. "You can tunnel into my network and see the medical certificate."

She shook her head, smiling. If only she could somehow tunnel her way into his heart, too… She pushed damp tendrils of hair away from his face, burying fear deep inside. "I don't have to."

"It will hurt," he said, his features severe. His strokes on her face gentle. "I… I've never made love to a virgin so you need to tell me if it's too much. If it hurts too much. If you just want a breather or want to stop completely. I'll stop, *cara mia*. Anytime."

"I want this, with you. Only you."

He touched his forehead to hers, and gave her the softest, sweetest kiss. Even inexperienced about men, Natalie had a feeling he was bracing himself for it. Gathering his control. Because she knew him. She knew he'd never forgive himself if he hurt her.

Muscles that seemed to have turned into so much blubber firmed up as he pulled her up into his lap, pushing her thighs indecently wider. His kisses shut rational thought away, going from soft and tender to hungry and urgent in a matter of seconds.

She felt his erection hard and demanding against her belly. Threw her head back as his hands plumped her breasts, rolled her nipples. He whispered endearments into her skin, tasted every dip and rise. Told her how much he'd dreamed of her like this—completely his.

Slowly, with infinite patience, with skillful touches, he aroused her spent body until she was shivering again, and there was wetness at her sex. His clever, wicked fingers played with her, working her over, building her to a fine fever, cranking her on and on. Already he knew her body so well. Better than she did. And she wanted to chase that mindless high again. Fall down hard from it into his solid arms. Again and again, until she didn't know where she began and he ended.

And then he lifted her, murmuring soothing, soft words, and she looked down, refusing to miss anything, and he took his shaft in hand and drenched himself in her wetness and then he was there at the entrance to her body and his hands on her shoulders were pushing her down, and with one smooth, hard thrust, he was inside her.

She cried at the sharp, unending pinch of pain, tugging at his hair while he buried his face in her neck. His breathing was loud and hot and his big body was so tight as if he were spending an enormous amount of control to stay still.

"*Merda*, you're like a glove. So good, so..." He looked at her and cursed. "I'm hurting you, *sì*?"

She nodded. And he kissed her softly. Butterfly kisses at her cheekbone. The tip of her nose. The corner of her mouth. Beneath her ear. At the juncture where her neck met her shoulders. "It's okay, *cara mia*. Just...just hold on. We'll stay like this. As long as you need. Or I'll pull out and we'll try again some—"

"No." He was like a hot, hard poker inside her and she never wanted to move or let go. And he was frozen like one of those marble statues littered all over his damned estate, so rigid and hard and taut and tense around her. Inside her.

Natalie pushed back with her fingers on the jut of his shoulders and gasped when even the small movement sent a sharp pinch through her pelvis again but she desperately wanted to look into his eyes, at this man who had stolen her heart. The invasion of his shaft and the pain of their joining, and the comedown from her orgasm—everything was conspiring, pushing her toward tears, pushing her toward hiding away from this moment, toward an emotional climax just as powerful and even more dangerous.

For the one thing she couldn't do was throw herself open even more. Not when she wanted a lot more of this intimacy with him.

So, she kissed his temple, tasted the sweat of his skin. She wrapped her arms around his shoulders, needing the glide of his bare skin against hers, needing the closeness. Needing the scent of him deep inside her. "Tell me, please, tell me what to do. I want this to be good for you. I want..."

He caught the tear falling down her cheek, and kissed her temple as if she were the most precious thing he'd ever held. "Good, *cara mia*? If it got any better, I'd die from the overload."

He rotated his hips slightly, softly, and Natalie gasped. Laughing. "That wasn't so bad."

When he laughed, she bit his lip.

"No, that was fantastic. Great. Do it again. Please, Massimo."

Massimo thought he'd die if he didn't start moving soon. Pressure knotted up in his balls, tingled in his lower spine. And yet, he'd rather die than hurt her. "Are you sure?"

"Yes. Hundred percent. Move. Now."

And she demanded that he move inside her like she demanded everything else of him. Boldly. Honestly. Courageously.

Holding her hips, Massimo pulled her up a little. And brought her down just as he thrust his hips. The friction was amazing. The pleasure she gave him indescribable. Another thrust. Another stroke. He stilled to delay his climax rushing at him. "Listen to our bodies, *cara mia*," he whispered, laughing, when she bumped into him on a downward stroke. "Listen to your instincts. Try swiveling your hips, moving this way and that. Just…find your rhythm with me."

"So less bumping and grinding, and color by numbers and more instinct, Massimo?"

"Yes, more instinct. Less numbers. Especially when it is this good," he said, giving her a wink.

She laughed, pushing her hair away from her face, thrusting her breasts in his face. This time, she met him thrust to thrust, in perfect synchronicity, creating magic.

Cheeks pink, brow dampened, hair a wild cloud around her face, eyes glazed with passion, mouth swollen, she was the most breathtakingly beautiful thing he'd ever seen. She was passion and enthusiasm and joy and he felt as if he was drowning in her.

He pushed her onto the bed and covered her, increasing

the tempo of his thrusts, all but mindless in the pursuit of his own climax. Picking her up by the hips, he angled her so that his abdomen rubbed over the top of her sex every time he retreated and she was sobbing again, writhing and digging her teeth into his bicep as she splintered, and Massimo followed her.

Two hard, swift thrusts and he came in a rush of heat and lightning. Afterward, laughter followed, for only his brave little hacker could make him laugh in such a moment by shouting, "Hell, yeah, that was awesome, Massimo. How soon can you go again?"

He let his hard body cover hers completely for a few seconds, needing this closeness with his lover for the first time in his life. Needing to steal away something from her, for himself.

Maybe he wouldn't ever be able to offer her what she deserved from a man. But he was determined to never hurt her, to never dull the spark that fired up his brave, little hacker.

CHAPTER TWELVE

"HOW MUCH LONGER are you going to avoid me?"

"What?" Massimo said, loosening the knot of his tie. He shrugged off his suit jacket and leaned against his bed, just…drinking in the sight of her.

A weak spring sun dappled her in golden light as Natalie stood in front of the French windows that framed his bedroom. She'd given up fighting to subdue her hair today apparently because it was loosely tied in a ponytail at her nape.

Today, she wore a pristine white sleeveless shirt that showcased her toned arms and flowy pants that sat low on her waist, leaving a slash of that taut abdomen he had licked just last night, on his way to other important things, bare for his gaze. The diamond pendant on a delicate gold chain he'd bought for her gleamed on her skin.

It had taken him three arguments, two days and one… session of persuading her with his fingers and mouth and tongue before she'd accepted the gift. Before confiding that it was the only piece of jewelry she'd ever owned.

And then, of course, being the extremely competitive woman that she was, she had proceeded to pay him back in return for his wicked persuasion. Her hair tickling his thighs, her mouth laughing and licking and wrapped around his arousal, she'd driven him to the most powerful climax of his life. Leaving him stripped to the soul.

Just thinking of it, of her, of her unflinching, unending desire to know all of him, to learn all of him—he was turned on simply by looking at her, his arousal a throbbing need in his trousers.

"Something's wrong, Massimo. You and I both know it."

He willed his body to focus on her words. His mind to maneuver the minefield of confrontation that they'd both been pushing away, desperate to not test this…thing between them just yet. Or was he the only one who thought like that? "I'm not used to sharing every small thing that occupies my mind," he bluffed.

Something was wrong with him, *sì*. But he didn't know what or how to fix it.

Her chin fell and she nodded. "But this is important enough that you distanced yourself from me. You do that when you have a design problem, did you know that?

"You swim endlessly…you box in the gym…you avoid looking at the problem until it works itself out in your head. I know you, Massimo. Better than you think."

Three and a half weeks since the night she'd snuck into his room and proceeded to blow his mind. His hunger for her only seemed to increase the more he touched her, the more he kissed her, the more he basked in her laughter and her quick wit and her affection.

She brought out the best in him, and yet, she brought out the worst in him, too.

He wouldn't have realized how seamlessly she seemed to work herself into his life until that meeting that had wrecked the bliss of long, drawn-out nights amid silky sheets and the exhilarating rush of pitting his mind against hers during the day.

Natalie was a woman unlike any he'd ever known, for he had a feeling he would never know all of her. Possess all of her. Just when he thought he did…another facet of her was revealed.

Even at a recent meeting with Giuseppe Fiore's CTO, his first instinct had been to defend her, to protect her from even a whiff of accusation, to storm out of that meeting until he could process it on his own.

"Your fiancée is a common thief."

"That association could cost you, Massimo, your reputation at least, if not this contract, if it gets out."

Since Giuseppe's CTO was a friend of his, Massimo had convinced him to put it aside. Massimo had used an invaluable business connection to vouch for Natalie. Created a debt for himself in a cutthroat business world.

A small thing but an unprecedented thing. A fissure in the line he drew between his ambitions and his feelings. Blurring the lines between what he wanted to be and what he was.

Dios mio, she complicated everything with her truths, and her lies and her dares and her kisses, and he needed to get a handle on this and her. Fast.

He'd screwed the chance of keeping things between them separate—professional and personal. He'd blurred all the lines between them from the moment he'd seen her walk out of that club.

When he'd decided she would be the perfect foil to discourage Gisela Fiore.

When he'd decided she would be an asset to BCS. When he'd brought her on board to work on the Fiore project. He'd lost his mind from moment one. Lost all caution and discretion and common sense that had made him such a world-renowned success before thirty.

She'd fought him from the beginning, on every arrogant assumption of his, at every decree he had laid down, even his short-lived honor. She'd told him clearly, point-blank, that she didn't give her trust easily. She'd told him, again and again, that her loyalty had to be earned and couldn't be bought. That her heart, she'd lived with it under lock and key for so long.

So, this was on him. And yet, he also wanted to blame her. To use this as a reason to push her away. To…stop this madness before it deepened and someone really got hurt.

Her—she would be the one who was hurt in the end.

"I've been busy," he fibbed. "This project is taking everything I have."

"I know you're busy. I'm in there with you most of the time. But this is not just work stress. This is not you tuning everything else out to untangle an analytical problem.

"You've been freezing me out for a week. I don't know why or what I did. You won't…look at me. You won't smile. You…don't talk to me in the lab. You…come to me in the middle of the night and make love to me, but by morning… you're back to behaving the same way again.

"It's almost as if you're…ashamed to converse with me outside of bed."

"You're being ridiculous," he said, an inane response to her perceptive gauntlet.

"No, I'm not. You didn't even tell me how exceptionally clever my design was for the bank's interactive portals. If nothing else, I count on you to tell me how brilliant I am on a regular basis, Massimo."

That irreverence, that honest but baffled admission—it was a balm to his masculine ego. Which the woman had the disconcerting knack of knocking off balance with a regularity. At least she was in this madness as much as he was.

"Are you done with me, with us, Massimo? Is that it? Do you want to move on?" Vulnerability in her voice even as she stubbornly tilted her chin up. "Because if you are, just…tell me."

"Nessuno," Massimo answered automatically, speaking his instinct before even processing that question.

"I can take it. I told you I don't need—"

"Fiore's CTO, Franco, summoned me last week to tell me he'd discovered that you had a juvenile record. As part of the routine background checks they do on every member of this team.

"For a *financial crime*, Natalie!

"Do you realize what that does to BCS's image? After everything we've had to put up with over the last few months? After all the fires I've been putting out? Now, when we're so close to that contract?

"*Cristo*, Natalie, is it true?"

All color fled her cheeks. She looked down at her hands and then up at him, her heart in her eyes.

Something in his chest deflated, as if he'd been expecting her to deny it. Call it just an accusation. Demand that he listen to the truth. What a coward he was that he couldn't face her truth. Couldn't face the power she already had over him.

"Yes, it was when I was fourteen."

His curse rang in the room.

But she didn't flinch. "I transferred some money from my foster father's bank account to his daughter's. He was a bully and she offered me two hundred dollars for it…" She shrugged, as if it didn't matter. "I had already learned how to break most security designs. I… The cyber investigator—it took him forever to pin me down for it. The judge sentenced me to community service, and a warning, and sealed those records. Those should have been sealed records. It was a juvenile offense. Before I met *him*. Before he persuaded me that I couldn't continue like that… I didn't know right from wrong, Massimo. All I knew was survival."

Tears filled her eyes and she looked away from him. Her body bowed as she stared out the window, and all he wanted was to pull her into his arms and hold her tight. To tell her that no one would ever push her to that ever again. That she'd never be so alone in the world.

Instead, he stayed where he was, watching her, willing this desperate need inside him to calm, willing rationality to take over again.

How had he picked the one woman who with every breath, every word, jeopardized his goals? Why didn't he just push her away, now that he knew the truth? Why couldn't he say yes, this association was too costly for him?

Why didn't he just draw the line here, now?

Every rational instinct he possessed urged him to do it. Better late than never. They could just be colleagues and still live under the same roof. He'd done it so many times before.

And yet, he stood, every muscle frozen.

Slowly, her shoulders straightened. He saw her dash away the tears with a rough gesture.

"You should have told me."

She turned back to him, her eyes shining with pride. "I didn't realize I was supposed to tell you every part of my unsavory life."

He rubbed a hand over his forehead, hating that he made her so defensive. "This is a hundred-billion-euro security project for a finance empire. All of us will come under the microscope. I can't keep covering for you. You should—"

She pushed away from the wall. "Did it ever occur to you that I was too ashamed to tell you? Or that it's not a part of my life I want to advertise to you when I'm begging you to not send me to jail? Or should I tell you when you already think I'm deceitful and low class and—"

He pulled her into his arms, incapable of not touching her.

She didn't come easily. Her fists came at his chest, her

body shuddered; she jerked in his embrace, but he held fast. Willing her to trust him. Consigning the war between his mind and his heart to hell.

"Let me go, Massimo."

"Calm down, *cara mia*. I just…"

"You what?" She pushed her hair away from her face, brown eyes shooting daggers at him. "You are ashamed of associating with me. You're already calculating damage control. You're…"

He flicked his lashes down, afraid of what else she'd discover that he didn't even know himself. Those eyes taunted him before she laughed. A sad sound filled with bitterness and pain. Pain he was causing her. Doing the one thing he swore he wouldn't do.

"Wow, you're no better than one of those supercomputers of yours, calculating gains and losses per transaction, per every interaction you have with me, huh?"

"Stop, Natalie. I told you to give me space. I was going to work it out. You're the one who pushed me into this… discussion.

"I've already asked the project manager to take you off the team for now. You just need to lay low until Fiore signs, that's all. It won't go any higher up than this. His CTO will arrest it there. Especially since those are sealed records.

"But we can't risk you being on the project. We can't… If there's anything else I should know…"

"How about I sleep separately for a while, too? How about you come back to me when this is done?

"Is that what you've been finding so hard to say? Too bad you tied yourself to me in front of your whole bloody world, *sì*? Too bad you can't just throw me out of your life as easily as you can cut me out of the project?"

"Natalie, you know what this project means to me."

"You… My past, who I've been, who I am, is a liability

to you. You…you weigh everything in life to see whether it serves your ambition or not. You weigh people around you in terms of assets and liabilities.

"I'm a liability. I'll always be a liability to you.

"But I refuse to be ashamed of who I am and what I've done in the past to survive."

Natalie let the hot water pound at her, washing away the sweat and grime of her workout. Wash away the tears that should have dried up a long time ago.

With a groan, she pressed her head into the cold tile. The worst part was that, despite her defiant words to him, she did feel ashamed. Wished she could change things she couldn't undo now.

And even worse was the feeling that she wasn't good for him. Good for his image. Good for the Massimo Brunetti who was going to take not only Milan but Italy by a storm with his innovative cyber security design for Fiore Worldwide Banks.

That she would never be good enough.

She rinsed off the soap, lethargy and tiredness crawling into her muscles. And she felt him standing outside the shower before she heard him, the scent of him calling her.

"Can I come in?" he asked softly, though he was already partly inside the open gap in the marble-tiled shower, his hair catching on water drops, the front of his unbuttoned shirt more than half-damp.

She turned, angling her body away from his gaze. She wasn't really a shy person but she couldn't brazen it out, either. Neither did it stop her skin from tingling in a million places. Waiting for his touch. For her body to tighten and clench and loosen in anticipation of the drugging pleasure he could give. And gave frequently and generously and at every chance they got.

God, he'd even persuaded her onto the table in his lab while they'd been working late one night. Dropped to his knees and tucked his head between her thighs and now she couldn't walk into that lab without blushing and heating up.

And here she was again, after that argument, standing there naked, letting him look her over, going weak at her knees wondering where he would take this... If she wasn't a pushover, she didn't know one. "I'm almost done."

A small smile played around his lips. "I don't really want to be in there if you get out." He leaned against the wall, pulled up his knee and watched her. As if his goal in life was to watch her bathe. "You have a little soap you need to wash off. There. Under your right breast. Where you have that mole. Where you..."

Her breasts were heavier, her nipples tight buds begging for his attention, her sex wet and willing by the time Natalie mustered enough senses to understand his game. "It's not fair. We had a fight and sex doesn't fix it. Even the fantastic sex you give."

His smile vanished, though the warmth of his gaze didn't. "*Sì.* We did have a fight. And maybe you could've been more honest—" he raised his hands in surrender when she opened her mouth "—if I had been more thorough about the scope and reach of this project. If I hadn't backed you into a corner.

"I brought you on, so the mistake is mine.

"But it doesn't mean, never did it mean, that I don't want you here. In my room. In my lab. In my life.

"I'm trying to make this work, *cara mia.* And no, I've not been and never will be ashamed of what you had to do to survive. You're right. I can't imagine what it must have been like to be that girl who had no one, the girl who had to make herself so tough." He cupped her cheek, his thumb pushing away the tears that trailed down them, his voice so infinitely tender. His lips were warm and familiar against hers. "Meet me halfway, *tesoro*. Just…let me get through this milestone. I need you here. I want you here."

And just like that, with easy charm and sincere words, he made mincemeat of her anger and her hurt and her defenses. He hadn't apologized, really, for putting that contract above her. He didn't even think of it that way.

He was far from admitting, even to himself, how much he cared about her, much less to her.

But he made accommodations for her in his life. And he let her know how much he wanted her. It was more than Natalie had expected of him, entering into this relationship. God, he'd never lied to her where his priorities lay.

She pushed her wet hair away from her face and nodded.

He inclined his head.

The antagonism in the air shimmered away, instantly replaced by hunger and heat.

"I missed you," he said, his head completely in the water now. "Yesterday. In my bed. I didn't sleep well."

She was tempted to say she had slept soundly. But they didn't play games with each other. Not when it came to this. Here, there was only truth. Utter truth. "I didn't, either."

"Say no if you don't want to do it in the shower, *cara mia*."

"Can I say yes?" she said, reaching for his shirt and pulling it out, seeking the hard, warm male skin.

He smiled and pulled her to him. And took her with a devouring hunger that filled all the empty places inside of her. He told her with his kiss, his touch, his hard, hungry caresses what he would never say in words. His arms caged her, as if he meant to never let her go, his belt buckle digging into her belly. "I want to be inside you, now. Please, Natalie."

"Now is good. Now is always good with you. Take what you need, Massimo," she said, and somehow, they managed to undo his trousers, push the wet fabric past his lean hips, and she wrapped her legs around him, and he rubbed at her clit to check she was ready and then he was inside her.

Natalie threw her head back, feeling him all over inside her, in this position. He was in her breath and in her blood and in her heart. And any fear that she was heading for a heartbreak of epic proportions melted away under the on-slaught of sensation when he flicked his tongue over her nipple.

She rocked into his thrust when he turned her to the wall and swirled his hips. Her breasts bounced and scraped against his chest, and she felt the tension coiling in her belly and when he pressed her against the cold tile and brought her hand to her clit and smiled wickedly, she massaged the swollen bundle.

And when he took her mouth, hard and fast, all the while rocking into her with short, swift thrusts, Natalie let go of all the fears and doubts and let herself be washed in him, in the pleasure he wrought in her, in the magic they cre-ated together.

A week later, Natalie clicked on the encrypted email that was sitting at the top of her in-box on the tablet Massimo let her use, her heart racing, threatening to rip out of her chest. She'd instinctively reached for her tablet, wanting to see if Frankie had replied to the stupid meme she'd sent him about cats.

Massimo lay on his chest with his arm over her mid-riff, still asleep.

Meet me tomorrow. One p.m. at Piazza del Duomo. V.

Her heart thumped, her pulse racing with fear. She exited out of the program quickly, spending two more minutes to clear out the history, erasing every inch of her account from the hard drive itself.

Vincenzo was here? In Milan? What did he want with her?

She wanted to throw up at the very idea of lying to Massimo again. At the very thought of deceiving him.

If she told him, he would forbid her to go. He would… tell Leonardo, and God knows what Leo would do.

But how could she just…not go?

What if this was her chance to convince Vincenzo to stop this crazy agenda? To find out why he was doing this in the first place? What if she could solve this problem, once and for all, for Massimo and effect some kind of peace between him, Leonardo and Vincenzo?

Then she would be more than a liability. Then she'd be worthy of his respect; she'd maybe even be worthy of him.

CHAPTER THIRTEEN

PIAZZA DEL DUOMO, Milan's main, spacious city square, was bursting to the brim with tourists and locals as Natalie walked in on Tuesday afternoon. Pausing, she looked up at the massive facade of the Cathedral of Milan. The architecture was magnificent and she desperately wished she could have a carefree day with Massimo.

On the other side was the world famous La Scala Theater he'd promised to take her to soon.

The cobblestones clicked beneath her black pumps, the air filled with the decadent scents of chocolate and coffee, friends and lovers calling out to each other, buzzing with energy. The constant knot in her belly she'd been walking around with since yesterday tightened when she spotted the dark head, sitting at a table outside a café.

Palm flat on her belly, she walked toward the table just as Vincenzo looked up. Almost severe in their sharpness, his features lent him an austere beauty that arrested more than one woman walking by. Dressed in a blue dress shirt and black tailored trousers, he was the epitome of masculine appeal.

"Come, Natalie," he said in that deep, bass voice she had known for so long. When she didn't move, except to stare at his outstretched hand, a dark smile played around his lips. "Come, little cat," he said again cajolingly, using that little moniker he'd always used. "I won't bite, *cara mia*. You know that."

Natalie shook her head and took his hand. He clutched her shoulders and studied her face. Bent his head and kissed her cheek. And slowly, his arm wrapped around her shoulders, pulling her to him. He was the same man who had done her a thousand favors, the same man who had kept her safe, helped her make a life for herself.

Natalie went into his arms, even though she felt as if she was betraying the man who'd again and again given her his trust, his loyalty, and earned hers in return.

There was something so familiar about Vincenzo—the scent of the cigar and his aqua cologne—that she calmed. "You're well?" he breathed the question over her head. "You weren't mistreated?"

She felt the tension in him dissolve when she nodded. He wasn't a monster. Not the man who worried about an orphan he'd saved years ago. "You know I can watch out for myself."

"I had to remind myself of your strength every day. There was no way to get in touch with you. I went to see Frankie and he said you'd called him and told him you were leaving the country for a friend's wedding. He was super excited for you."

Natalie's heart crawled up to her chest. "You saw him? He's good?"

"He's doing great."

"Thank you," she whispered.

"How are you doing?"

"I'm fine, Vincenzo. I've been...good, too."

He stared at her questioningly, but nodded.

He pulled a chair for her and then settled into the next one. When the waiter inquired, he ordered two coffees for them, telling the waiter to make hers extra sweet and extra milky, with a distasteful scrunch of his nose. Natalie laughed, and tucked an errant curl away.

His gaze arrested on the diamond on her finger, and she hastily dropped her hand.

"What I heard through the grapevine is true?" The warmth didn't quite leave his eyes but there was something else.

Natalie opened her mouth and then closed it. She wanted to ask him so many questions: how long had he been in Milan, in Italy, what was he planning and why. But she curbed her curiosity. She didn't want to get in the middle of this. Not after today. Also from everything she'd learned in the last two months, he was a master chess player, moving pieces back and forth, ten moves ahead of everyone else. "It's a fake engagement. Too convoluted to explain."

"Massimo shouldn't be trusted. None of them should be. Using people is in their blood—"

"You're the last man who should lecture about using others. You—"

"I never forced you. You could have said no at any time."

"You knew I wouldn't. You manipulated me... I could've gone to jail."

"I trusted you to look after yourself. I would have been there, within the hour. You know that."

Natalie wanted to say no, she didn't. But seeing him again like this, she couldn't. How could she convey all the complex emotion twisted around this man to Massimo? How could she convince him that Massimo didn't deserve what he was doing? "This is such a...mess. Please, tell me you're done."

He shook his head and her heart dropped. "Stay out of it, *cara mia*."

"You dropped me in the middle of it."

"You shouldn't have gotten caught. You're supposed to be brilliant."

"I got caught because Massimo's just as brilliant as I

am. But he's also kind, and funny and charming and… He could have sent me to jail and he didn't, even when I refused to give him your name."

"I wouldn't have held it against you. You're a survivor, Natalie, just like I am."

"Loyalty means something to me. Massimo's a good man, Vincenzo." She reached for his hands, as he'd done to her long ago. Hoping to get through. Hoping to stop this before more people got hurt. "Whatever you're doing, he doesn't deserve your hatred."

He studied her slender hands in his, squeezed them and then slowly released each finger. Slowly but surely shutting the door in her face. When he looked up at her, there was such dark emotion swirling in the depths of his gray eyes. "This started long before Massimo became the financial force behind Brunetti Finances, Inc. But he's a part of it. They all are. For years, they perpetuated what…" He looked away, as if to control himself. "This won't stop because you like him. This won't stop until…"

He stood up, and Natalie's hopes dashed into dust.

She looked up at him in his black suit jacket and tailored trousers and expensive haircut, and the way he stood…her heart ached for whatever drove him to this. "Until what, Vincenzo? How much more hurt will you cause before you stop?"

He offered her his hand and Natalie stood up, their coffees untouched.

Suddenly, he felt like a stranger. Like he'd never shown her his true self. She wanted to run back to Massimo, and beg him to fix the whole sorry mess. And he would, she knew it.

He would at least listen.

Vincenzo took her elbow as they stepped away from the table. "Return with me. My jet's waiting."

Natalie stared back, stunned. "With you? What? Where?"

"I don't want to leave you here, with them. Not after today, and not after… I want you far from here. Back in the States. Safe."

His words pelted Natalie's skin like small cold stones. She pushed away from his touch. "Vincenzo, please, put an end to this."

"This doesn't involve you. I'd hate to hurt you any more."

"It involves the man I trust and if you do this… I can't keep you a secret anymore. I won't. He's earned my loyalty. I work for BCS now. On a dollar-huge project for Fiore Worldwide Banks. I—"

"He won't win that contract."

Natalie felt as if he had punched her in the gut, as easily as he smiled at her. "Yes, he will. I designed it with him. I won't let you steal this away from him. I won't let you hurt him."

And it would, she knew for sure.

Massimo prized that contract above his relationships. Above everything else.

"Massimo Brunetti is a genius who treats women no better than his father did. In the end, he is his father's son. Prestige, family name, power, that's all that matters to them. He will delete you as he does yesterday's technology as soon as you become irrelevant. Come away, Natalie. I don't want this on my soul."

"Do you have a soul?" she whispered at him, and he flinched. "You can't escape the consequences." Tears filled her eyes. "I thought I could fix this, appeal to you. But I don't know who you are.

"Don't contact me. Don't try to save me. Just…stay away, Vincenzo."

The *tap-tap* of her pumps on the marble floor cranked up the panic running through her as Natalie walked into the sitting lounge. She came to a stumbling halt as four sets of gazes swiveled to her with a wide range of expressions.

The Brunettis were out in force.

She took a few more steps into the lounge, her heart beating so fast that she was afraid it would rip out of her chest. Massimo stood all the way at the back of the vast room, his back to her, the tension in his shoulders making her own tighter.

Her belly somersaulted with fear.

Did he know she'd gone to meet Vincenzo? How?

Leonardo seemed the most relaxed, sitting in an armchair, Italian-loafered ankle crossed over the other knee, swiping something on his cell phone. There wasn't the usual cynical amusement or contempt in his dark gaze. Just plain curiosity. As if he were a predator deciding whether he wanted to rip her apart now or later.

She walked past him to where Massimo stood with his back to her.

"Massimo? What happened?"

He turned, and the fury in those eyes stopped Natalie in her tracks. The dark emotion touched all of him—those perceptive eyes, the bridge of his nose, that mouth that could curve with such wicked laughter—making him look so severe, so much like one of those portraits she'd seen in that long hall, contemptuous and arrogant.

The Brunetti aristocracy of so many generations that he thought he didn't belong with. Men steeped in power and prestige and cruelty.

Dread knotted in her chest that she had to force herself to breathe first, but it was centered on what Vincenzo had let loose this time. "Massimo, why are you guys still here? I thought you were meeting the Fiore team for the official signing—"

"I canceled the meeting."

"You canceled the meeting? Why?"

"Our security design for FWB was stolen from the network server and published on the Dark Net. A half hour before our meeting." His body bristled with unspent fury. "A year's worth of work out there for any hacker to go through, to target the banks. Thousands of customers' financial information would have been in jeopardy. I had to disclose the hacking attack to them.

"The intricately detailed triggers you executed... I knew the plans were being stolen the minute someone tunneled in."

"Wait? I don't understand. That design was brilliant. The security layers literally incorruptible. You saw what I built...you went over that design with me with a fine-tooth comb. It can't just—"

"I thought so, too. But then it's not so hard if you handed over the blueprints to all the layers, is it? Or, say, if you logged into the server and created a tunnel for them to access it?"

Natalie stared at him, her mouth opening with an inaudible gasp, her brain processing his accusation over and over again. Because he couldn't be saying what he was saying, could he? "You're blaming this on me?" Her throat was achy and full of tears and she looked around as if she could gather strength from something or someone, but instead only saw the accusation now in their eyes.

"You think I... I gave them access to the server? I let them in? I helped steal plans I toiled over with you for the last few weeks?"

"It happened when you returned from your secret meeting and accessed the server for the plans."

Vincenzo had played her so well. "You can't... I did log on to it. I accessed the plans, yes, but only to make sure the security layer was tight. Something he said made me realize they might not be as safe as we thought. You can't think—"

"Something he said? Or something he asked you to do? Is it that much of a stretch for me to believe that you followed the instructions the man gave you when you met him this afternoon?"

Accusation after accusation and Natalie had nothing to fight them with. She'd been so foolish. God, if only she hadn't gone to meet Vincenzo this afternoon, if only she…

"Massimo, I didn't. I didn't betray you. I know how this looks, okay? But I—"

"Who did you meet this afternoon?" he finally said. As if she were a stranger. As if he hadn't made love to her this morning.

"Vincenzo. His name is Vincenzo Cavalli." His name dropped into the silence with the same effect as if a meteor had crashed through the roof, into the room. Natalie saw Leo coming alert, clicking away on his phone, but nothing could tear her gaze away from the cynicism in Massimo's own gaze.

"There, I said his name."

Massimo smirked, and she hated everything about it. "Did he give you permission now that he has done irrevocable damage to us?"

"He sent me an encrypted email, asking me to meet him, and I—"

"Then why didn't you tell me? *Cristo*, you were in bed with me when you got that email, weren't you? You smiled at me, you kissed me, and you lied to my face. You promised your loyalty was mine. You promised…" He thrust his fingers through his hair roughly, shaking. "You could have told me he contacted you. You could have told me where to find him. You could have solved this problem for us. But no…instead, you decided to protect him. Instead, you chose him.

"I trusted you. I let myself feel…but in the end you picked him. You jeopardized everything I've worked for, all these years. Leave, Natalie."

"Don't say that. Please, Massimo, I want to help you fix this. I can help—"

"Get out. Get out before I—"

"Before what, Massimo?" she shouted back, tired of his accusations, tired of being afraid. Tired of…the emptiness that waited if he kicked her out. "What would you do to me?"

"Call the *polizia* on you. Have you arrested for corporate espionage, for breaking a hundred confidentiality agreements, for selling your loyalty. I don't think you stopped being a thief."

If he had slapped her, Natalie would've been less shocked. Less hurt. Pain came at her in huge, rollicking waves, twisting her belly, knocking her out at her knees. "How… That's so unfair. You can't… I can't believe you would throw that at me? Knowing why I did it. Knowing… I trusted you to understand. To…"

He searched her face, studied the tears running down her cheeks. Maybe, for a second, he even softened. Natalie saw the familiar Massimo, the Massimo she loved with her whole heart, in his eyes before he shut it down. Before he shut that part down. Or maybe it was all her foolish hope. Her blinders still on when it came to him. "You didn't trust me with it, either, *cara mia*. You hid it. And you defended yourself, as you always do, when it came to my notice."

"Massimo, think it through before—" Leo chimed in.

"Now you support her, Leo?" Massimo's voice was cutting, so full of bitterness. "When all along you've been asking me to throw her out? When she's proved you and Silvio right? When my allowing her into all this, when my trusting her, trusting my emotions, is what brought us to this?"

With one last look at her, Leonardo walked out.

Massimo tucked his hands into his pockets, every inch that ruthless, powerful stranger who had cornered her that first night. "This is my fault. All mine.

"From the moment you came into my life, you never told me the truth.

"Why should I not believe that you engineered this? Why should I not believe that when I realized you were a liability…you jumped back to his side, you looked out for yourself once again?"

It was over, Natalie knew then. He wouldn't believe her. He had decided to not believe her. He had decided to finish this.

He had decided, maybe even before this, that she wasn't good for him, that he was done. And nothing she said would change his mind.

Her tears, her begging, nothing would dent that resolve she saw in his eyes.

Nothing… She wiped away her tears, anger rescuing her from the pit of self-pity and pain. Anger made her straighten her shoulders. Anger made her aggressive, see clearly. Anger made her realize how worthless she'd thought of herself when it came to him.

Anger made her realize how she'd strived to become worthy of him, how she'd foolishly assumed that he'd love her if she wasn't a liability anymore. She was done. God, she was so done with him, with thinking that she was less than him. "This is so convenient for you, isn't it?"

"Convenient?" he said, sneering. "You ruined a project that I've been working toward for a decade. You ruined my chance to—"

"To what? To prove to your father that you're not the

sick runt he calls you still? To prove that you're better than Leonardo? To join those heartless, arrogant, bloated with power ancestors that are hanging on that damned wall?

"Your chance to prove to yourself that you're a Brunetti through and through—cruel and power-hungry and looking for any excuse to push away anyone who cares about you?"

"You've no idea."

"Of course I do. This project means everything to you. *I was there.* But…it is also such a good reason to push me away, too.

"Look in your heart and tell me you truly believe that I sold you out to him? This is not about me. This is about you.

"Because you feel something for me, too. A weakness that could weigh you down. Because I was becoming a liability to your goddamned reputation, your pursuit of billions, your ambition with my petty theft record. A liability to what you think Massimo Brunetti should be.

"Anything's better than examining what you feel for me. Anything's better than letting yourself love me. Anything's better than becoming what your father thinks you are.

"Because Brunetti men don't have weaknesses. Because Brunetti men are monsters.

"You act like you're better than them all but…you're the worst of them. You know better and you still cling to it. There's a little good in you and you kill it every chance you get.

"I fell in love with you. I was twisting myself up in knots that I wasn't good enough for you…but you're the one who doesn't deserve me. You're not the man I thought you were.

"Congratulations, Massimo. At least there will never be a doubt in your mind that you're a Brunetti, after all."

CHAPTER FOURTEEN

MASSIMO STARED OUT the window of his office at Brunetti Towers in the financial district of Milan, not really seeing the noisy crowds of tourists and locals.

The city's financial pulse—something he had always felt so strongly, something he'd strived to be part of for so many years, left him feeling nothing but emptiness. The villa, his flat in Navigli, even his lab—his lab, which had always been his sanctuary... Guilt haunted him, consumed him, ate through him.

Leo had probed and pushed and, in the end, given up. It wasn't as if BCS would die without him at the helm for a week. Vincenzo Cavalli could raze BCS to the ground for all Massimo cared.

He hadn't eaten or worked or slept in so many days. In the two weeks since he had thrown his dirty accusations at Natalie.

She'd been right.

He'd behaved worse than his father or Leonardo. He had always thought himself as better, prided himself that his mother raised him with different values, had assumed that when the right woman came along—someone with class, and sophistication, and someone who understood that her place would always be second to his ambition—he would treat her well.

For all his arrogance and ambition, instead he'd found a

woman who was fire and passion and love. When push had come to shove, he had proven himself to be worse.

The first day when he'd discovered that Vincenzo had hired a consortium of hackers to leak the security designs, using Natalie's past hacker activity as the key, he'd made a hundred excuses for his behavior.

She had been the gateway for them to steal the plans. He had never been taught how to process his feelings for a woman, especially such a complex one. She had come into his life at the wrong time. Part of it was her fault because she had gone to see Vincenzo behind his back…on and on and on.

He had prioritized the wrong thing in life. Looking for ways to end the one thing that made him look deep into himself, to reach for something he might not be capable of.

He was a Brunetti man who courted power, prestige and billions because he'd been terrified that if he wasn't the most powerful of them all, then he was nothing.

And yet, she had found something in him to like. To love, even.

"I fell in love with you," she had thrown at him, so full of pain, her eyes big and bright, bowed by his cruel words. But not broken.

Because she was right. He was the worst of the Brunettis, after all. He was the one not worthy of her.

She had survived with her heart whole, and courageous.

And if it took him the rest of his life, he'd spend it making himself worthy of her.

After numerous calls from his secretary and Leonardo poking his head into his office all of four times for an urgent meeting, Massimo forced himself to move.

He owed Giuseppe the courtesy of showing his face,

even if the association they had both sought was a pile of ash. Pushing his gray suit jacket on, he ran a hand over his jaw.

Cristo, he must look like he'd been living under the green moss under the crappiest rock after his trip to New York and back to Milan in the space of thirty-six hours. Exhausted, he couldn't sleep because he hadn't found her. He'd even made a trip to see her little brother but Frankie hadn't heard from her except the usual, weekly check-in call.

Where the hell was she? Had she gone back to Vincenzo, knowing now that Massimo didn't deserve her?

Nauseated by his thoughts, he walked into the conference room and grabbed a bottle of water.

Giuseppe and Leo sat on the opposite sides of the long conference table with Franco next to Giuseppe and... *Natalie next to Leo.*

His heart thumped so hard against his rib cage that Massimo dropped the bottle of water. It hit the carpeted floor with a soft thump, rolling away with a swish. And he had the most ridiculous notion that it was his heart and he wanted to groan and laugh and share it with her, but he had hurt her with his cruel words.

Perversely, he'd never been so cruel to anyone else in his life, only the woman he loved. If that didn't tell him everything that was wrong with him...

He wanted to tell her he had all the time in the world to listen to her now but only silence was left. She'd taken joy and light with her.

Dressed in a white dress shirt that hugged her slender frame and black trousers, and hair—*Dios mio*, that wavy, thick hair, bunched into a sophisticated knot at the top of her head—she looked like composure, and sophistication, and brilliance and beauty and heart, all combined into a complex woman.

The woman he adored with every breath in him. The woman he'd go down on his knees for. The woman who could strip him to his soul with one look, one word, one kiss.

The woman who refused to shift her gaze from the laptop screen in front of her and spare him a look. The woman who was even now digging those misaligned front teeth into her lower lip.

"Massimo, take your seat," Leo said. Massimo covered the distance to Natalie, his chest such a tight knot that it was a miracle he could breathe. The scent of her, so familiar, made him shake.

Somehow, he kept his head as Leo began the meeting and Franco asked questions about the recent leak of the security designs while he made copious notes, and in between, there was Natalie, pulling up schematics for a new multilayer security design on the projector, addressing Giuseppe's and Franco's questions, and Massimo went from dumb disbelief to utter amazement.

She had come up with a new set of security designs? She'd been working with Leonardo? Giuseppe—who apparently appreciated Massimo's proactive backing out of the contract because of the security leak, whose CTO had been smart enough to recognize Natalie's unusual talent—had persuaded his board to give BCS another chance.

Natalie's frantic, almost feverish movements in collecting her laptop, her handbag.

He moved his body into her space and she stilled. "I've been to New York to see you. I've seen Frankie." When she turned her stunned gaze at him, he nodded. "He's good. He's excited to see you soon."

"Thanks, but I'll see him in a day. I've tried to repay any damage I've done to the project. You have it, Massimo, everything you ever wanted."

She hitched her bag over her shoulder, calmly dismissed Massimo and moved to Leonardo. There was no spark in her, no fight, no laughter, no joy. Just a…pale imitation.

"Thank you for letting me fix this. I'd prefer to work from home if you still want me on it. If you arrange for a ride to the airport—"

"You're not going anywhere," Massimo bit out.

"Massimo—"

Fury burned through him as he met Leo's gaze. "You know I've been going mad trying to find her."

Leo shrugged. "That day, you weren't in a place where you'd hear a word I said. No chance for rational talk. You persuaded me that she was brilliant. I saw no reason to not use her. Later, after I convinced her to fix it, her condition was that I not tell you."

Had she written him off completely? Had he lost her before he had realized what he'd had?

Leo closed the door behind him. When Natalie moved to follow his brother, Massimo waylaid her, trapping her between the table and his body.

"Let me go."

"*No!* Tell me why you helped." He wanted to touch her so desperately, more than he needed his next breath.

"Because that project meant something to me. Being on a team that created cutting-edge technology, being on a team with you and Leonardo and all those men and women, discussing strategies with you, building something real out of all those years of dreams…it meant something to me.

"More than money. More than the power or prestige of it. More than…" She looked away. "All my life, I've never been a part of a community like that. I wanted to finish what I'd started."

"Then stay. See it through."

"I can't stay near you."

He placed his hands over her shoulders, bracing himself against the waves of pain crashing through him. "Natalie *mia*, will you please look at me?"

He fell for her all over again when she leveled those beautiful eyes at him and gazed steadily.

"Where do I start, *cara mia*?"

"There's nothing to start, Massimo. Nothing to say…"

He clasped her jaw with his hand, his heart bursting with all the things he wanted to say. "First, I beg for your forgiveness, *tesoro*. Please, Natalie, if you ever thought that there was something worth knowing in me, loving in me, please, *cara mia*, you will stay a minute and you will listen, *sì*?"

She looked up at him then, meeting him square in the eye. Gaze filled with tears. "You shamed me. You… You gave me everything…everything I never asked for, everything I never expected to have in life. Everything I had never even dreamed of…and in one moment, one moment, you took it all away, Massimo.

"I've never felt so alone. More alone than that night when my dad didn't return. To not have known you would have been okay.

"But to know you and love you and love the best of you and then…" She looked down, and her tears poured onto her chest, dampening her white shirt. Massimo pulled her into his arms, unable to bear her pain, hating that he'd done this to her. "You made me doubt myself. As if I was less. As if I didn't deserve you. I only went to him to talk about—"

"No, look at me, Natalie! I don't care why you went. I don't give a goddamn about him. *Cara mia*, all I care about is you. About you and nothing else in the world." He tilted her chin up to look at him and the pain there skewered him. "*Cristo*, you're the most wonderful thing that has ever come into my life. The most joyful thing. The thing that Mama hoped I would find and nurture."

He kissed her soft cheek slowly, softly, breathing in the scent of her. Looking for courage in the tension that swept through her body. "Forgive me for all the dirty accusations." A kiss at her temple. "Forgive me for not listening." A kiss on the tip of her nose. "Forgive me for putting the bloody contract before you." A kiss on her forehead. "Forgive me for not trusting you."

He dropped to his knees, anchoring his hands around her hips, burying his face in her belly. Pressed countless kisses to every inch of her he could touch and feel. He was shaking and he couldn't stop himself because he was still afraid he would never hold her like this.

He let the fear and the joy and the warmth gush through him, let himself breathe it in. Because this was what loving Natalie meant.

Embracing this…emotional storm. Embracing the fear. Embracing the fact that she'd make him weak and strong but better for it. And he let her see all the things he couldn't put into words in his eyes. "Forgive me, the most, for not trusting myself. Forgive me for not listening to the part of me that is worthy of you.

"Forgive me, *cara mia*, for not saying that I love you. Forgive me for being an arrogant bastard who couldn't see love when it kissed him on the mouth and held him in the night and told him there was a hero inside waiting to get out. *Ti amo*, Natalie. You make me a better man, *cara mia*. If you were with me I'd be the best of them all. The best Brunetti of all. And I'd maybe start a new trend of what it means to be a Brunetti, *sì*?"

Natalie fell into Massimo's waiting arms, the sob she'd been trying to bury bursting out of her chest. "I love you, too, Massimo, so much that it terrifies me. I… I've never loved anyone like that. I…want to trust this but—"

"Shh…*cara mia*. No, there's no place for fear or doubts

between us. There's no place for anything but love." And then he was kissing her mouth, so softly, so tenderly, and Natalie fell into the kiss. His desperation, his relief, his warmth, his love—his kiss spoke of a thousand things and she took it all in. "Say you'll believe me, Natalie."

He had believed her when he had no reason to. Given her a chance to prove herself. She would give him a million chances, she realized, shaking with alarm, but whatever fear and doubts came at them, Natalie wanted to face it with him. Together. "I do believe you. I'm all in, Massimo."

"We'll bring Frankie here immediately. We'll build a home for ourselves. We'll start fresh, *cara mia*, with no shadows. And when you marry me—"

And just like that, Natalie fell in love a little more. "What?" Her heart thudded in her chest.

His eyes shining, Massimo slid his lips over hers in a silky caress. "When you marry me, we'll start our own brood of Brunettis and the first thing and the only thing we will teach them is—"

"How to be courageous in love," she finished, her eyes full of tears.

His teeth dug into his lower lip and he nodded. "So you will, *sì*?"

"*Sì*. You're my hero." He was so solid and warm and hard around her. "And you're all mine," she said, and he nodded, and when he pulled her into his lap and buried his hands under her shirt, looking for warm skin, she gave herself over to it.

He was her hero. Her man. Her entire life.

EPILOGUE

IF SOMEONE HAD told Natalie a few months ago, or even a
few weeks ago, that she'd be walking down a beautifully
manicured path with elegant trees and boxwood and wis-
teria on either side, while her little brother walked in front
of her, toward a stunning vista of lakefronts and mountains in an ivory designer gown that supermodel Alessandra
Giovanni had requested personally of a designer friend who
never did private commissions, toward the tech billionaire
Massimo Brunetti to make her wedding vows, she'd have
laughed hysterically.

She'd have rolled on the floor, laughing her ass off.

No woman was so lucky to have a wedding at such a
stunning location with the elements behaving perfectly as
if they'd conspired to give her their best on her most important day.

No woman could be so selfish as to demand a designer
gown that was yards and yards of lace and tulle that made
even skinny little hackers look like a princess.

No woman would hope to have a kind, sexy, absolutely
wonderful man waiting for her at the end, his heart in his
eyes, looking knee-meltingly gorgeous in a black tuxedo.

No one in their right mind would at least guess that all of
the above could happen to an orphan who'd never thought
she was worthy of anything so wonderful.

But it was happening. Alessandra and Greta looked stunning on one side and Silvio and Leonardo on the other side,

the latter with a warm smile for her that still stunned Natalie even after a month since she'd saved the Fiore project.

And then she was there, close to the man she adored with all her heart.

As she reached Massimo and he took his hands in hers and tugged her closer with a little too much enthusiasm that had the small, intimate crowd laughing, Natalie was trembling, sheer terror that it was all a dream that would disappear taking hold of her.

His fingers tight around hers, his breath whispering against her temple, Massimo said, "I have you, *cara mia*. You're the most beautiful woman I've ever seen and I love you so much, and whatever comes our way, we'll face it together, *si*?"

"I'm scared, Massimo. I love you so much and it robs the very breath from me when I think of our future and with—"

His finger covered her lips, the warmth of his body a comforting cocoon. "But I shall never, ever let you go. If you fall, I will always catch you. We will build our empire or take down someone else's if that's what you prefer, *si*?" he whispered, and Natalie laughed because this man knew her so well and each day he showed her what she meant to him.

She licked her lips, knowing that everyone was waiting. But God, she didn't want to start their life together with lies and shadows. "I wanted to tell you but I was afraid. Afraid that it would hurt you," she added quickly when she saw the light dim in his eyes. "This…this tiara—" she touched the exquisitely delicate diamond tiara wrought in the finest white gold that had been delivered three days ago sitting on top of the elaborate coif that her hair had been beaten into "—I… I didn't borrow it from Alessandra. I lied. Because I was worried you wouldn't understand.

"He…he sent it to me."

"I knew it, *bella*."

"What?"

"From the moment you opened the package and tried to hide the packing material and then burst into tears when you saw the card."

"Please don't be mad, Massimo. I've cut my association with him but he was still a big part of my life. He'll always be a big part of my past and I can't change it and I hate that I hid this from you—"

"I have long decided to forgive him, *cara mia*," he said, stealing the ground from under her. "I will help Leo find him, and stop him from causing further havoc in our lives, but how do I stay angry with a man who protected you when you were alone in the world? How long do I hate a man who gave me the most wondrous, beautiful gift of you? *Ti amo*, Natalie. Your past and your present, your stubborn but loyal heart, your fire and your flaws, I adore everything about you, *cara mia*."

Her tears plopped down her cheeks and Natalie didn't give a damn if her makeup was ruined. "I love you, too, Massimo. Now, hurry up," she whispered against his mouth, "so that we can start building that empire and a brood of Brunettis."

His eyes glittered with wicked warmth and then the priest was admonishing them and Alessandra sighed and Frankie asked Leo in a loud whisper if they were going to kiss so frequently and then in the midst of the chaos and the love and the laughter, suddenly, she was now Natalie Brunetti.

And when Massimo took her mouth in a soft, tender kiss she lost her heart all over again.

* * * * *

COMING SOON!

MILLS & BOON

Coming next month

AN HEIR FOR THE WORLD'S RICHEST MAN
Maya Blake

Dr Chang returned just before midday.

Saffie, having managed to keep down a piece of dry toast and two cups of tea, stood in the middle of the living room. Aware of Joao's imposing presence beside her, she linked her fingers in front of her as Dr Chang entered. The two technicians who followed, wheeling in a large ultrasound machine, couldn't have spelled out her condition louder if it'd been written in fifty-foot letters in the sky.

The room spun around her but Saffie wasn't aware she'd moved until Joao's arm wrapped firmly around her waist.

'This is our new reality, Saffie,' he rasped softly, almost soothingly, in her ear. His voice was gruff, but there was a layer of intent as he watched her that drew goosebumps across her flesh.

Dr Chang approached, leaving the butler and technicians at a discreet distance as he gave a shallow bow. 'Miss Everhart, I have the results of your blood test.' He cast a quick look behind him. 'You can probably guess what it is. Congratulations.'

Her nod was shaky, her heart hammering against her ribs so hard she feared she would pass out. 'Thank you,' she murmured.

'Would you still like me to perform the ultrasound?'

Beside her Joao stiffened, a coiled tension seizing his frame.

'Yes, thanks.'

Joao relaxed a touch, his arm temporarily drifting over her hip before claiming her waist once more.

Within minutes, she was lying on her bed, Joao's over-whelming presence beside her as Dr Chang rolled the wand over the cold gel on her abdomen.

When the coloured 3D image appeared on the screen, Saffie's heart leapt into her throat. A moment later, a rapid heartbeat joined the picture. A breath of wonder shuddered out of her, her eyes prickling as she watched the wriggling bean on the screen.

Her baby. Her family. Every hope and aspiration within reach. But as she watched the dancing blob, Saffie's breath caught for another reason. For as long as she'd yearned for this dream, she'd pictured just herself and her baby. Two against the world.

In all the years of hoping and dreaming, all she'd wanted was a mother. Someone to hold her close, tell her she mattered. Perhaps because she knew it was her mother who'd left her behind, she'd been the parental figure Saffie had wanted the most. A father had been an even more impossible dream. One totally out of her reach.

But now she was faced with an even more impossible scenario.

The shadowy shape of the stranger who would one day father her child had taken the form of the most formidable man she'd ever met. The richest man in the world, with endless power and influence, who would remain way out of her league for ever. A man who intended to claim her baby, but not her.

Continue reading
AN HEIR FOR THE WORLD'S RICHEST MAN
Maya Blake

Available next month
www.millsandboon.co.uk

LET'S TALK
Romance

For exclusive extracts, competitions
and special offers, find us online:

 facebook.com/millsandboon

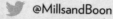 @MillsandBoon

@MillsandBoonUK

Get in touch on 01413 063232

MILLS & BOON
MODERN
Power and Passion

Prepare to be swept off your feet by sophisticated, sexy and seductive heroes, in some of the world's most glamourous and romantic locations, where power and passion collide.

...at Modern stories published every month, find them all at:

millsandboon.co.uk/Modern